I0593432

the
ROSETOWN MAN
BRENDAN WRIGHT

THE ROSETOWN MAN

Copyright © Brendan Wright 2022

Cover designed by Damien Wright
Cover image purchased from depositphotos.com and used with permission

ISBN: 978-0-6484294-3-2

Brendan is not currently represented by any publishers or literary agents.
He can be contacted at: enquiries@brendanwrightauthor.com

Connect with Brendan:
Instagram: @brendanwrightauthor
Facebook: /brendanwrightauthor
Website: brendanwrightauthor.com

This book, as grim and dark as it may be, is dedicated to my grandmother, Kathleen Wright. You were the kindest and most loving person I've ever met. Though by the end you couldn't remember us, I promise you'll never be forgotten.

Foreword

Rosetown is a fictional story, based in a fictional suburb of Sydney. Before you read this novel, however, it's important that you know there is a real-life cold case that inspired a big part of this story. The case of the Somerton Man, also known as the *Tamam Shud* case, is an unsolved mystery that occurred in South Australia in December 1948. There was very little evidence, and what evidence exists baffles police and the public to this day. The case involved an unidentified corpse with no discernible cause of death, with a hidden note in a secret pocket that led to an unbreakable code handwritten in the back of a Persian book of poetry called 'The Rubaiyat of Omar Khayyam'.

In late 2019, the South Australian Attorney General granted conditional approval to exhume the body, with the caveat that the Government would not use taxpayer's money for the exhumation. The exhumation officially began on June 1, 2021. At the time of writing this book, no more information has been discovered and the case is still a mystery. There are many theories about the identity of the Somerton Man and what may have happened, but to this day there are no answers.

What follows is fiction, and though the Tamam Shud case isn't the focus of the story, where possible all details related to the Somerton Man have been written based on publicly available evidence obtained by the South Australian Police in 1948 and 1949.

<u>Prologue</u>

27 November 2019 3:14pm (Wednesday)

"I still think killing him was a dumb choice," Jack said.

Amanda smirked.

"It made sense to me," she said, "honestly, he kind of deserved it."

"Seriously? Why the hell would you think that?"

She shrugged, her smirk growing into a broad grin.

"I was getting sick of him. I mean, he never shut up. Always had to be the centre of attention, you know?"

"Well, he is the one who started it all. Didn't he deserve the attention?"

"Some of it. Maybe. I'm still happy he died though."

"You're pretty messed up Amanda, you know that?"

Amanda laughed, shaking her head.

"Hey, he had a bunch of movies under his belt before he went. I'm not saying I don't love Iron Man, but as far as character deaths go, it was totally justified."

It was a hot day, school was just finished, and Jack was already sweating as they walked through Alpha Park to the shopping mall. They always ended up talking about superhero movies when they went shopping together. Jack wouldn't complain; he was the one who usually started it. But they disagreed on a few big things, and it seemed to only be those things that came up. Amanda loved arguing, simply for the sake of arguing, and Jack loved her company too much to put a stop to it.

"Well, at least we can agree that Tom Holland makes the best Spider-Man," Jack said, and Amanda laughed.

Ahead of them, the park's entrance appeared. On the corner of the street opposite the shopping mall, Alpha Park opened onto one of the car park entrances. They usually went shopping for Amanda's benefit; Jack hated shopping except for book stores. Amanda and Jack weren't exactly dating, but according to their friends, they may as well have been. The truth was, if Amanda showed any interest, Jack would have been thrilled to date her. But friendship was better than nothing, and Jack wouldn't have ruined their friendship for anything.

"I mean," she said, smirking again, "it also helps that he's hot, and British."

Jack rolled his eyes, smiling through a pang of jealousy. Amanda had a way of pointing out every single guy she found attractive. He was getting used to it, but it still hurt a little; even if it was a celebrity. They walked in silence for a brief moment before Amanda frowned and nodded towards the street corner.

"You see that guy?" she said.

A drunk man stood at the entrance to the park. At least a dozen other people strolled around the area, but he stood out. He wore a jacket despite the heat, and swayed as he stared at something they couldn't see.

"Ew, don't tell me you think he's hot too," Jack said.

"Shut up Jack, seriously. He's creeping me out, can we go around?"

Jack nodded.

"Sure," he said, "but just for that I'm not sitting around for ages while you try on a hundred outfits."

As they watched him sway on his feet, a school kid came into view. The man stared at the kid as he approached. A sick feeling spread through Jack's stomach, and Amanda cleared her throat with a strangled sound.

"Is he going for that kid?" she asked.

"I don't know... yeah, fuck, I think so."

"Wait," she said, "I know that kid. He goes to our school."

They were still too far away to do anything but watch. The drunk man walked towards the boy, and Amanda grabbed Jack's arm.

"Jack, should we do something?"

"Maybe he knows him," Jack said.

"It doesn't look like-"

The man raised his hand, a flash of metal glinting from his closed fingers, and two loud bangs shattered the noise of the street. Jack watched the kid crumple, and Amanda screamed. More screams reached them from closer to the man, and the people he could see sprinted from the shooter. As he watched, unable to look away, the man stepped up to the kid. Four more bangs echoed through the park.

"Shit," Jack said, "fuck."

Amanda pulled her phone out and called triple zero.

"Hello? Some guy just shot a kid. A school kid. I think he's—I'm pretty sure he's already dead."

Amanda's voice broke, and she sobbed out the last few words. The streets in front of them were empty; everyone had already run. She started breathing heavy; Jack recognised the beginnings of a panic attack. He put his arm around her shoulder, and they started backing away from the park's entrance.

"Alpha Park," she said, "he's still here."

She glanced at Jack; he'd never seen so much fear in her eyes before. Cold numbness filled his body, and an unreal quality settled over the park. He felt like he was dreaming. He'd had a nightmare once before where a child died in front of him; this had to be another dream like that. Amanda held the phone to her chest and looked at him.

"The police station is down the street," she said, "they're already on their way."

Her voice shook, and instead of looking at Jack, she stared at the man. Jack stared as well, and as they watched, the man threw up. A few seconds later, he crumpled to the ground, like a strange echo of the kid a moment before. Jack stared, holding Amanda close until the police showed up. They didn't approach the scene; Jack saw a thin splash of red even from a distance, and he didn't want to see any more.

"Should we go?" he said, "I kinda really want to get out of here."

Amanda nodded, and they went to the closest roadside that left the park. As soon as a gap in traffic opened, he guided Amanda across the road. He looked back as they reached the opposite side; police had already appeared.

They walked in the opposite direction of the shops for a while, circling around the entire block to avoid the park entrance. Amanda was still breathing heavy when the shopping centre finally came into view again. Her hands shook, and her face had gone pale and clammy.

"Let's get some juice or something," Jack said, as they entered the centre, "you look like you're gonna faint."

"I can't believe it," she said, "I can't believe we saw that. Jack, what the hell? That really happened, right?"

"Yeah," he said, fighting the urge to throw up, "that was real. But you called the police, which is more than I could've handled. You're brave as hell. I couldn't even talk."

A tiny, shy smile played briefly over her face, barely showing under the shock. Jack squeezed her shoulder, smiling back.

"I hope I don't have nightmares about this," Amanda said, "oh God, I'm not going to sleep tonight."

"Me neither," Jack said.

How about we hang out, he thought instead, *and get no sleep together?* He wouldn't have dared said it out loud. *Especially right now.*

"Do you think that kid survived?" she asked, her face growing even more pale.

"I don't know. The police got there really fast though, I'm sure they know what they're doing."

"I can't remember his name. I feel so terrible, but I swear I know him."

"I guess we'll hear his name soon enough," Jack said, "either at school or on the news. Do you think we'll get a day off school if he dies?"

4

"Jack!" Amanda smacked his shoulder, outrage flushing her skin with colour, "I can't believe you just said that. You're horrible."

He tried to laugh it off, but he knew she was right. *Shit,* he thought, his heart dropping under the weight of Amanda's expression, *I really hope that kid's okay.*

27 November 2019 6:01pm (Wednesday)

"... And in local news, a man in Sydney was arrested today for the murder of eleven-year-old Jacob Turner. The young boy was on his way home from school when the man, who is so far unidentified, allegedly shot and killed him at the entrance to Alpha Park in Rosetown. Witnesses to the crime were reported as saying the killer walked up to the child's body after shooting twice, and kept shooting until his gun ran out of ammunition. He was arrested shortly after at the scene of the shooting, with witnesses saying he had vomited before collapsing. He was remanded in custody pending a court appearance tomorrow..."

Chapter One:
The Shooting

27 November 2019 3:26pm (Wednesday)

Detective Sergeant Phoebe Wilson sighed, squinting through the low angle of the sunlight to the other side of the street. She didn't put a hand up to her eyes for shade, nor did she look at the pavement on the side of the street where she stood. Even as she saw it for the first time, she knew she would never forget seeing Jacob Turner's body. It was small, fragile, and broken. His eyes and mouth were open, the colour drained from his skin. He lay on his side, one of his arms splayed at an inhuman angle against the pavement. Short dark hair and delicate features that almost mirrored her own pushed her mind towards a memory that threatened to overtake her. *No, don't think about that. Focus. There's work to do.* She looked into the park, trying to push the past away.

The park itself was vibrant, different greens layering together into beautiful scenery that would have been at home in a gorgeous painting. The kind of scene that most people might have conjured in their minds when they thought of a nice picnic. Phoebe herself had walked through the park countless times, when she needed to think or if she wanted a quiet place to drink coffee, a few precious minutes out of the office on a nice afternoon.

A child, she thought. *God damn it, a child.* She'd never seen anything like it. Jacob Turner, only eleven years old according to her Senior Constable, had been shot six times in a public street. Broad daylight. *Eleven.* The number echoed in her mind like broken wind chimes. *It's the same age* he *would have been...* But she stopped the thought before it

7

drowned her. Jacob had been short for his age, and somehow, he looked even younger than eleven.

Bright red blood pooled on the pavement at the entrance to Alpha Park, next to Jacob's body. Close to him, a thin puddle of vomit sat congealing, twisted chunks of unidentifiable food scattered through it. Right next to the vomit lay a scruffy middle-aged man. More than scruffy, actually; he was *filthy*. His smell, worse than the acidic smell of vomit, assaulted her nostrils; it was only made worse in the heat of the afternoon.

He wore a heavy jacket despite the heat, and though his stillness mimicked Jacob Turner's lifeless body, the man was alive. According to the triple zero call they'd received just over ten minutes ago, the middle-aged man was the shooter. The vomit was his, and from the smell of it—and him—he was severely intoxicated.

Footsteps tapped through the quiet noise of the street and Phoebe glanced up. Constable Justin Wilks ducked under the yellow crime scene tape, smiling briefly at her—a look that said *we'll get through this*—and settled next to her in the park's entrance. Though he wasn't second in charge strictly speaking, he was often Phoebe's go-to guy. With the crime scene barely metres away from her feet, Phoebe's eyes locked onto Wilks. He had a friendly face, like a young and enthusiastic primary school teacher, average height and build, and plain features. Wilks noticed her looking, and motioned at the other members of her team.

"Matt, Andy and Aaron are questioning the witnesses who stayed behind," he said, "I got to a couple earlier, but they gave me nothing. And Mike is directing the evidence guys. Anything else you want us to do, Sarge?"

The unmistakable sound of a camera went off, and a bright flash despite the sun. Phoebe looked at Mike—Senior Constable Michael Timms, her second in charge—as he glared at the two constables taking photos of the body and the alleged shooter lying next to each other. Mike was tall, broad, and imposing; especially when his expression fell on the harsher side, as it did now. He took his work seriously, and Phoebe respected him for it.

Evidence tags lay all over the scene, yellow plastic with bold black numbers. Another camera flash went off, reflecting in the pool of Jacob Turner's blood and sending the beginnings of a headache lancing into Phoebe's brain.

"Check CCTV footage if there's any cameras around. Locate cameras pointed this way, contact whoever you need to get the footage. How many people have we spoken to so far?"

"I've got a handful, not sure about the others. If they've had the same luck as me, we don't have anything useful."

"None of them actually saw him shoot Turner?"

"One or two saw him shooting the kid on the ground after the first two shots, but it was from a distance. I doubt they'd be able to ID him from a photo, or in a line up."

"He passed out immediately after the shooting, right?" Phoebe asked, "so the person we arrest—" Phoebe gestured at the unconscious man "—has to be the shooter they saw. As long as we have some corroborating evidence to link him, he's ours."

Mike cleared his throat right next to Phoebe; he had somehow approached without her hearing anything.

"Evidence team is done," he said, "ambulances are ready to take the kid and suspect."

"Thanks, Mike," she said, "once they're gone, I want you to run a quick search through the park itself, just in case there's anything the evidence team might have missed. I didn't see them look through the park, just the entrance."

He gave a curt nod. His eyebrows went up, and he pointed a finger up as though he'd just had an idea.

"Oh," he said, "and the evidence team thought you might want the information on this."

He held out a card; Jacob's student ID. Phoebe pulled in a breath as a short, sharp hiss without meaning to. She took the ID card off him almost gingerly, slid her small notepad from her pocket, and copied what she needed; his parents' phone number and address. It would be up to her to contact them.

Mike took the card back to give to the evidence team, nodded once again, and strolled towards the ambulances. Though the crime scene itself still ate at her nerves, watching Turner's body and the suspect being put on to stretchers and loaded gently into the ambulance helped a little. Somehow, a strange pressure had built in her chest every moment the child's body remained sprawled on the pavement, as though the longer he stayed there, the more he would haunt her mind.

Justin walked away, casting his eyes over the nearby buildings, searching for CCTV cameras. Phoebe gave a heavy sigh, the sound ragged and fraught even to her own ears. She watched her team as they worked, consciously keeping her gaze away from the still-bright pool of blood nearby. Though she didn't look at it, the vivid red pulled at her attention, dragging her eyes towards it.

Jacob Turner's dead body did not leave her mind, even after it was taken away from the scene. It felt to her then that the image of his pale face with the open mouth and eyes might never leave her. The school uniform riddled with jagged entry wounds, the way one of his arms had twisted as he fell so that it lay at a stomach-churning angle.

A sudden, horribly loud hiss cut through Phoebe's thoughts and she gasped. Almost immediately next to her, a hose fired high-pressure water onto the pavement, manned by a cleaner Phoebe hadn't seen approach. Nearby, Mike stood watching, once again glaring as he oversaw the clean-up.

Phoebe took a deep breath, the cool smell of water and some kind of detergent finally overcoming the horrid smells of blood and vomit. She closed her eyes, briefly, and then looked directly at the pavement for the first time since she'd arrived. There was still blood, a lot of it; but it was slowly being diluted and flushed away by the powerful hose.

The sound of rushing water pulsing as the hose moved back and forth might have been comforting, like waves lapping at the beach, if not for the situation. Phoebe stayed until the pavement was clean. *Almost like it didn't happen,* she thought, *if only*.

05 March 2008 9:56pm (Wednesday)

A comfortable warmth lingered in the night air, and Phoebe breathed it in as they left the restaurant. Ben took her hand, and they stumbled down the stairs to the road. He'd ordered a taxi not long before; they were both drunk.

"I can't believe how amazing that dessert was!" Phoebe said, laughing as Ben's eyes widened in response.

"Best dessert ever."

She kissed him, pulling him close and almost dragging them both to the concrete.

"Thank you for tonight," she said, "I love you."

"I love you too," he said, "and you deserve it. Five years together is a big deal, you deserved a treat tonight."

"Well, how about we go home," she said, "and I give you *your* treat?"

He grinned like a kid on Christmas morning, and she laughed. The taxi was already waiting for them, and Phoebe pushed him towards the car.

"Let's go, let's go!" she said.

The whole trip home, they tried to pretend they weren't drunk. They weren't convincing at all, but it only made them laugh more. *Five years,* she thought, *he still makes me laugh so much*. She knew the alcohol was making her emotions more powerful, but the swell of pure love she felt for him in that moment was indescribable.

Pulling him close to her again, she kissed him hard on the mouth. He laughed, the sound muffled by her kiss, and she laughed as well. Feeling bold and too excited to wait, she put her hand on his upper thigh, squeezed, and then slid it up to his bulge. He groaned, as quietly as he could, and Phoebe giggled again. She squeezed gently, and watched as his eyes fluttered closed and open again.

"Babe," he breathed.

She squeezed again, rubbing just a little, and grinned at his reaction.

"Babe," he said again, "we're almost home."

"So?"

"So, let's wait until we get there."

She left her hand where it was for a moment longer, gave him one last loving squeeze, then pulled away.

"Fine," she said, "but you better be ready as soon as we get home, mister."

He was. They thanked the driver, not noticing his chuckle, and scrambled out of the car, laughing and joking all the way to the front door. As soon as it closed behind them, Phoebe grabbed him again, rubbing and squeezing a little more vigorously.

"Oh my god," he said, running his hands over her back and hips.

"Let's go to the bedroom," she said.

His shirt was off before she'd taken more than a couple of steps into the room. Staring at his body, she bit her lip and smiled. He wasn't in the best shape, but he had broad, strong shoulders, and his torso tapered in the most appealing way. Watching her watch him, he smiled and unbuttoned his jeans.

Without a word, she stepped close and dropped to her knees.

"Holy shit, babe," he moaned, staring as she yanked the front of his pants down and took him into her mouth.

After a few minutes, he pulled her back up to her feet and kissed her. He tugged the zipper of her dress down, and helped her step out of it when it slipped to the ground. His eyes grew wide the second her dress fell away; he hadn't seen her getting dressed for their date, and didn't know she wore nothing underneath.

Kissing her neck, the way he knew she loved, he guided her backwards to the bed. When they reached it, he picked her up and fell with her onto the mattress. She squealed and then giggled, and his lips moved down her body until they reached hers. Her giggles turned to moans as he licked and kissed her passionately.

"I thought this was supposed to be *your* treat?" she said.

"It is," he said, grinning up at her, "but I can always stop, if that's what you want."

"No! No, you do whatever you want to do."

He stayed where he was, and kept pleasing her for what felt like a long time and no time at all. When the tension peaked and fell from her body for the third time, he crawled onto the bed with her. He smiled, and she fell in love again. Brushing her hair back from her face, he kissed her, and then the real pleasure began.

27 November 2019 4:40pm (Wednesday)

Her notepad was small, with thin blue lines spaced over the white paper. It had become such a common tool that most of the time she didn't even really see it; just the notes she made. But now, it sat heavy in her hand, giving off a malicious energy that shook her to the core. It felt like holding a venomous snake.

Jacob Turner's mother's phone number burned from the otherwise blank page, the strokes of her black pen vibrant and deadly. She was frozen; never in her career had she needed to tell a parent that their child was dead. There were no words she could say that would make it any easier to hear. *This really should be a face-to-face talk,* she thought, *but the media already know about it, and it'll be on the news within the next hour or two. His parents need to hear it from us, not from the TV.*

A flash of white and a burst of bustling noise erupted in her mind; she remembered the fear and heartbreak, rage and denial. Every emotion a person could feel, smashed together and rushing through her mind like a waterfall. *Everything was white,* she thought, *I remember that. And cold. Why do I have to do this to someone else?* Pushing the memory down would only work for so long, she knew it. But for now, all she could do was try to ignore the guilt she felt, and get the job done.

She wanted to call them, if for no other reason than to have it over and done with; but at the same time, she desperately wanted to bury the notepad in her desk drawer and never look at it again. Jacob's parents were, right now, blissfully unaware of his death. If she dialed the number in her notepad, she would be destroying them. Utterly breaking their hearts.

"Fuck," she whispered. *Just have to do it.*

Forcing her hands to move, she copied the written number onto the number pad of her desk phone. *It'll be okay,* she thought, *you'll survive. It'll be a few minutes of unpleasant conversation, and then you'll focus on the case again.*

Before she hit the final number, she froze again. Her hand simply wouldn't move. *Couldn't* move. Without warning, stinging tears bled from her eyes. *This is not going to go well.* The urge to make one of her Constables call Jacob's parents was almost overwhelming in that moment; but it was her responsibility.

Her finger hovered just above the last button, trembling and numb. *What do I even say?* She thought, scrambling for any words and coming up with nothing. *Your son is dead. I'm sorry, but your son was killed.* Nothing sounded right; the words were ugly and wrong. Phoebe kept grasping at words, as though if she thought about it hard enough, she would come up with the perfect phrase. As though if she said it perfectly, they wouldn't be heartbroken.

She played it through in her mind, a wishful delirium turning the scene into a pleasant, peaceful chat.

"Hi, this is Detective Sergeant Phoebe Wilson. I'm really sorry, but your son was killed this afternoon in Alpha Park."

"Oh, I see. Well, that's awful news, but thanks for letting us know."

"No worries. We'll do everything we can to bring the killer to justice, rest assured."

"We couldn't ask for more than that, thank you Sergeant!"

Before the stupidly pleasant vision faded, Phoebe jammed her finger into the final number and picked up the headset. She heard her heart thudding in her ears, felt a cold emptiness in her stomach. Sweat began beading on her face, and for a moment she couldn't differentiate between sweat and tears.

The phone rang, long and shrill, and each ring echoed into the pit in her stomach. She tried to control her breathing, but her lungs wouldn't cooperate. *Any second now, one of his parents will answer.*

A click ended the ringing abruptly, and Phoebe's heart stopped.

"Hello?"

Here we go. Shit.

"Hello, is this Jacob Turner's mother?"

"Yes, that's me. Who's this?"

"This is..." she didn't want to lead with her title; Jacob's mother would panic the moment she realised a detective was calling about her son. But she didn't know what else to say. Clearing her throat, she tried again.

"This is Detective Sergeant Phoebe Wilson."

Dead air filled the phone line, and Phoebe's panic grew with each moment. *What now?* She had to say it; the conversation had already started, there was nowhere to go but forward.

"What's happened? What's Jacob done now?"

What's he done now? It wasn't the type of fear Phoebe expected.

"He's..." Phoebe trailed off again, pure panic wiping her mind blank.

"He's what? What's going on?"

This is it. Phoebe had gone skydiving when she was younger, and trying to tell this woman her son was dead felt exactly the same as standing thousands of feet above the ground and preparing to jump. Tears fell from her, her breath hitching as she tried to force the words out.

"Mrs. Turner, I'm so sorry," she finally said, "but Jacob was killed this afternoon."

Phoebe listened to the silence, her panic growing even more as she waited for some kind of reaction. Would it be fury? Grief? Disbelief? Would she just hang up? Finally, Mrs. Turner's voice broke the silence, tense and sharp.

"What do you mean? What happened?"

"He was shot, at the entrance to Alpha Park. We've caught the shooter, and we're doing everything we can to make sure justice is served."

"*Shot?*" Mrs. Turner's voice cracked, and Phoebe had no idea if it was grief or fury. "He... someone *shot* him?"

Phoebe breathed as best she could; her lungs felt unable to draw in breath. She nodded, realised Mrs. Turner wouldn't see it, then tried to breathe again.

"Yes, I'm so sorry."

More silence sat between them. Phoebe's vision blurred as her heart beat sped up. The faint sound of breath catching in Mrs. Turner's throat crackled into the headset.

"He does love that park," she said, "or... he *did*, I suppose. Oh, God."

Sobbing echoed faintly through the phone line, distant, as though Mrs. Turner held the phone away from her face. Phoebe waited, uncertainty growing with the cold panic in her stomach. *How do you end a conversation like this?* She thought, *"okay, bye"?* At any rate, she wouldn't be able to speak again until Mrs. Turner brought the phone back to her ear. When she heard a ragged sigh, she forced herself to speak again.

"The next step is to come in to identify Jacob," Phoebe said, "I know it's hard, but we need a family member to be certain it's him."

"Oh. I... I see. Well, I'll tell my husband and he can do that."

"That would be best, yes. A social worker from the hospital will be in touch with you today to guide you through it. In the meantime, I'll give you my contact details in case you need anything."

She repeated her details twice, and listened to Mrs. Turner's faint mumbling as she copied the number and email onto paper. When it was done, she tried once more to express her sympathy.

"I'm so sorry. Please take care of yourself."

The line clicked before she'd finished the sentence, and Jacob's mother was gone. She sighed, sitting back in her chair and staring at nothing for a moment. Now that it was over, the panic seemed almost ridiculous; *she took it okay, after all.*

"Okay. That's it. I need a drink tonight."

With the more daunting phone call handled, Phoebe called the kid who'd made the original triple-zero call; the number had been identified in the call logs, and Phoebe looked forward to getting anything out of them that she could.

"Hello?" a small voice answered.

What was her name? Phoebe thought, rifling through her notepad, *Amanda, there it is*. She'd written the number down underneath Jacob's parent's number, but her nerves had gotten to her, and she hadn't written the name. Luckily, Phoebe wrote all the relevant names on an older page of her notepad. No one else could have deciphered the way she wrote notes down, but it worked for Phoebe.

"Hello, Amanda," Phoebe said, "my name is Phoebe. I'm a Detective Sergeant with the Rosetown Police. You called us earlier today, and I just wanted to talk with you in person about the incident you witnessed."

There was a slight pause. Phoebe felt Amanda's fear through the gently crackling phone line.

"Um, okay," she said, "when do we have to come in?"

Phoebe checked her calendar, then frowned.

"Wait," she said, "*we?*"

"Jack was with me," Amanda said," he's my... we're... friends. He saw it too."

"I see. How about tomorrow," she said, "around midday?"

"I can do that," the girl said, "but, um... can I get a lift or something?"

"Sure thing."

Phoebe got Amanda's address off her, writing it next to her name in the notepad, and ended the call.

It's done, she thought, *now to focus on the case.*

27 November 2019 4:52pm (Wednesday)

Rosetown police station was a glorified shoe box attached to the community corrections office, which was larger and far nicer looking. Where the police station was a simple square with plain white walls and glass, the corrections office was red brick with a large arched window on the face of the building.

The station was on the back end of a shopping centre, right across from a loading dock. Phoebe hated walking out the front doors and coming face to face with nothing but blank wall, and a giant ugly hole where loud trucks came and went all day.

With the crime scene recorded and cleaned up and Phoebe's shift still not over, she was back at her desk. The suspect was in the nearest hospital, passed out cold and with a police guard on him. She'd seen a lot of assaults, robbery, car related crimes, and drugs; but although she had seen a lot of death in her career, she'd never dealt with cold-blooded murder. And never a child.

What kind of monster shoots an innocent child? In the middle of the street, for no reason... She found herself oddly looking forward to the suspect finally regaining consciousness; the police would interview him, and she needed to hear what he had to say for himself. Not that anything could justify his actions.

"Sergeant Wilson."

Phoebe glanced up, though she immediately recognised the voice.

"Inspector Rogers, how are you?"

"You're on the Alpha Street murder case?"

She nodded, and he grunted in approval.

"Seems open and shut, but I want you to make sure it gets shut. We'll get a lot of attention for this, good and bad."

Inspector Rogers was on the way back to his office before Phoebe could even respond, but she did anyway.

"Yes sir."

Her team still wasn't back from their extended search of the scene, but she knew the record team was. They had their own office, for cataloging and temporarily storing all evidence from active cases. She'd met one of them before; Les Hopkins. They barely knew each other, but Phoebe knew her well enough to say hello.

"Hi, Sergeant Wilson," Les said, "you're working the Turner case?"

Phoebe nodded, and Les kept working.

"How much solid evidence do you have?"

"Almost nothing."

Phoebe's chest buzzed, the ball of electric panic growing again. *How is that possible?* The man hadn't exactly been careful about it. They'd found more evidence in cases far less straight forward than this one. But somehow, despite the shockingly public nature of the shooting, it felt as though the suspect was already slipping away from her grasp. *It's early,* she reminded herself, *there's still a lot of evidence to find yet.* Panicking now would help no one; *it's still only the first day of the investigation.*

"Well, what do you have?" she asked, her voice sharper than she intended.

"Swabs, fingerprints, every non-invasive test we could run." Les said, oblivious to Phoebe's tone. "It's all been processed on our side and it's on its way to the lab."

"What about his belongings? ID?"

"Nothing."

"The crime scene photos are solid though, right? I mean, they're incriminating enough on their own, surely?"

Les shook her head absently as she worked. It seemed almost casual, and Phoebe had to fight against a wave of anxious fury that rose from her stomach to her throat, as though she was about to throw up.

"The photos just show the victim and a random man passed out and covered in vomit. Far too circumstantial. Without further proof, he may as well be a witness who went into shock after seeing a child murdered."

"The witnesses can describe him well enough," Phoebe said, "so the photos combined with their statements... But there has to be *something* more that was left at the scene."

Les shrugged. Phoebe thought about the evidence on its way to the lab. Swabs and fingerprints could go a long way. DNA, though not the fix-all most people thought it was, could mean the difference between a conviction and the suspect walking free. As long as his DNA was on the murder weapon, and no one else's was, they could have him.

"All we'd need is a trace of residue on his hand from the gun firing," Phoebe said, "that and the gun would convince any jury, along with the photos and witness testimony."

They wouldn't need much evidence. Just enough to cover the gap of vague witness reports and potential lack of security camera footage. *My team will hopefully find enough footage to cover things anyway*, she thought.

"We won't know if there's any trace on him until the results come back," Les said, "but I wouldn't get my hopes up."

She fell silent as she kept working, and Phoebe tried to breathe through the tightness constricting her chest.

"Why wouldn't there be any residue? Any time someone fires a gun, there's always a trace."

"I'm just saying, this case is a weird one. We've got almost nothing, don't get your hopes up. You know there weren't even spent casings, right?"

The tightness spreading through her chest grew to a strangling, cold panic. Of all the cases she'd had, this was the one that should've been the simplest to close. It was also the one she *needed* to close more than anything she'd ever worked on; the kind of monster who would murder a child deserved to be locked away for life.

"What are you talking about? The gun, the photos, results from the lab... Why don't we have enough evidence?"

21

"I already told you the photos don't prove anything. I don't bank on anything helpful coming back from the lab at the best of times, let alone with a case like this."

Calm down, Phoebe thought, *she's just managing expectations. It doesn't mean we won't close this case.* But something nagged at her mind, and as she watched Les work, avoiding Phoebe's gaze, she realised what it was.

"Wait, you haven't mentioned the gun. Wouldn't that have his prints on it? His DNA?"

"Well," Les said, sighing and finally pausing her work, "that's the thing."

For just a moment, the room faded underneath a cloud of hazy grey. Somehow, she knew exactly what Les was going to say. *No,* she thought, *don't say it. It can't be true.*

"We looked over the entire crime scene, from every angle. We never found a gun."

04 April 2008 11:09am (Friday)

It was at once the most terrifying and exhilarating thought that Phoebe had ever experienced; *I'm pregnant. I'm going to have a baby.* She wanted a child. They both did, and they'd both talked about it for a while now. But wanting it was very different to knowing it was going to happen. Talking about it, even planning for it, were very different things.

They sat in the waiting room, and Phoebe couldn't stop a frantic wave of energy that forced her feet to tap rapidly on the sterile linoleum floor. Ben noticed, and smiled. His smile helped, but not enough to calm her panicked feet.

"We're just here to confirm the date, babe," he said, a note of almost exasperated humour in his voice, "there's nothing to be nervous about."

Easy for you to say, she thought, *the baby's not growing inside you.*

"I know," she said instead, "I know."

The fear was only part of it. Phoebe had never looked forward to anything more in her life; except becoming a detective in the New South Wales police. She didn't consider herself to be a stereotypical woman in most regards, but having a child was certainly something she craved.

Ben was just as excited as she was, though he handled it much better. He was always calm somehow. Always steady. *How does he do that?* Even when they first met, he'd been calm and self-assured. *But not in a cocky way.* Phoebe hated arrogance. Ben seemed to perfectly straddle the line between confident and cocky, and it was what drew her to him in the first place.

"Phoebe," her doctor said, his head poking out his office door, "come in."

23

It was an office she'd been in many times; so many that she barely noticed the details any more. Her family had been with the same doctor since before she could remember.

"So, this is exciting, isn't it?" Doctor Hatzis said.

"Yeah, we've been wanting this for a while."

"Of course, and I'm sure you'll be great parents. Now let's get a test done, and then we can find your due date."

"Okay…" Phoebe said, refusing to ask what type of test, though she already knew.

"It's just a blood test to confirm," Doctor Hatzis said, "and check your general health."

The doctor called a nurse in. She held a sterile sealed packet; Phoebe saw the needle inside. *Oh shit,* she thought; Phoebe didn't do well with needles.

"Yep," Phoebe said through gritted teeth, "okay."

Ben's hand came to rest on hers. He looked at her with his gentle smile, and there was no trace of worry in his eyes. Somehow, the ball of anxiety in her chest half melted away, and she breathed again. The nurse gripped her elbow, firm but still gentle, swabbed at the vein, and Phoebe turned back to Ben.

Gritting her teeth, Phoebe stared hard into Ben's eyes, trying to focus on anything but where the needle was about to go. She tried not to tense, but she couldn't stop herself.

"It's all right, babe," Ben said.

A slight sting slid into the crook of her elbow, the cold of the needle harsh in her skin. The strange feeling of blood being drawn out washed over her, turning the room pale and foggy. Barely a moment later, she felt the needle slip out of her again, just as uncomfortable on the way out as it was being inserted.

"There we go," Doctor Hatzis said, "all done."

The room swam in front of her, Ben's face comforting despite moving with the room itself. Phoebe felt the blood drain from her face, a slight chill spreading over her skin.

"Drink some water," Ben said, his warm hand still resting on hers.

She took a few small sips from his water bottle, and his face came slightly more into focus. *His smile is so beautiful,* she thought, *I hope our baby has his smile.* He smiled wider, as though he heard her think it.

"Now," Doctor Hatzis said, "when was your last period?"

Glancing briefly at Ben, she frowned and tried to think back. *He should have asked before taking my blood,* she thought, *I can't think straight.*

"Umm," she said instead, "six weeks maybe? I can't remember, I'm sorry."

"Yeah," Ben said, "about six weeks."

"Alrighty," the doctor said, picking up a colourful cardboard wheel and fiddling with it as he mumbled.

"Uh huh. I'd say the twenty-sixth of November. For the due date, I mean. We'll re-estimate after a proper scan, but we're usually quite close the first time."

Ben nodded, and smiled at Phoebe again.

"Close to Christmas," he said, "that'll be fun."

"Shut up, Ben," she said, laughing, "thanks, Doctor Hatzis."

"We'll get the results back in a few days, and we'll give you a call."

27 November 2019 8:29pm (Wednesday)

Phoebe's couch was old, but comfortable. Although the sun had set, a lingering warmth still hung in the air outside. She had the air conditioning on, but in the moments when the fan pointed away, a tiny bit of heat crept in. Lately the smoke in Sydney's sky left its people feeling stuffy and suffocated. It bothered her, but not as much as the case. Her career as a detective had so far spanned almost ten years. In that time, she'd never seen anything that disturbed her as much as this.

She'd never met Jacob, but the shooting still left an ache in her chest. Somehow, it felt as though Jacob Turner had been a member of her own family. *Like the son I never had,* she thought, and choked back a sob. A burning, heavy rage boiled in her chest when she thought about the man who shot Jacob.

He was arrested while still unconscious, and had no identification on him at the time. His identity and motives were still a mystery, but she was at least relieved they'd caught the killer immediately. The case would be hard enough to work without having to chase down a child killer.

"Fucking monster," she said.

What could have prompted such a vicious attack? Drugs or alcohol were a likely candidate. Or potentially a serious mental illness. Or even a combination of all of those. Drugs or alcohol certainly would have explained the vomiting and passing out. She had to make sure the shooter ended up behind bars, but more than that; she needed to understand *why* he did what he did. It was just too senseless otherwise.

A TV show played on Netflix, bursts of laughter ringing out every half a minute or so. She barely heard it. The wine in her hand had warmed to room temperature without her noticing. She'd eaten dinner not long ago, but never tasted it.

She realised there were tears slipping down her cheeks, and wiped her face with the palm of her hand as another peal of laughter hissed from the TV. Watching the characters argue about something without actually hearing the words, she drank half her glass of wine in one gulp.

"Where is the fucking gun?"

Phoebe always swore when she was stressed. And she wasn't just stressed; she was furious. The case made no sense. It should have been so straight forward. The series of events made sense, it could be followed easily. There were witnesses, the suspect had been caught, it all added up. She would make sense of it eventually, she knew that; but for now, the mystery clawed at her mind relentlessly.

"Where is the fucking *gun*?" she said again.

He shot the child. He was seen shooting the child. Gunshots were heard. Everything added up, except for the actual evidence. Waiting for the lab results would be the hardest thing; she needed an answer more than anything else in the world, and that was the most likely way to get one. If something as horrible as a child's death happened, it had to at least have an explanation. She would accept nothing less.

There was also the interview. She wasn't looking forward to that either. When the suspect—who so far had remained unconscious—finally woke up, it would be Phoebe's job to question him. *I need answers,* she thought, *but how likely is it that he'll just confess?* Even if he was guilty, he gained nothing by giving the police everything. *Except a faster trial and sentencing.* She'd interviewed enough criminals to know they rarely made it easy.

They'd had to turn him in to the hospital until he woke up; he'd clearly been dangerously intoxicated on some substance. The possibility that he might not even survive occurred to her. *It's not normal to remain unconscious for that long,* she thought, *the hospital will do what they can, but if he's overdosed on something there's a chance he won't even live long enough to wake up.* As much as she wasn't overly keen to interview him, having him die before she could speak to him was a far worse option.

She took another long sip of wine, trying not to think about talking to him. He could wake up at any time. As much as she wanted to, she wouldn't be able to drink more than the huge glass she'd already poured for herself.

There was no evidence to bring to the suspect, nothing she could fall back on to strengthen the case against him. *Yet*. If he denied everything, if he had even the semblance of an alibi, it would extend the case and put more pressure on Phoebe. At least until she did find evidence.

"There's got to be *something*," she said, "there will be something. He won't just get away with it."

It would take a week for anything to come back from the lab in Lidcombe. Her team had found two cameras pointing at Alpha Park; but the record team would have to scan through the footage for anything helpful before she could rely on it. Even that was being overly optimistic; there were no cameras in the park itself, so anything captured on the cameras they found would be from across the street at best.

Their best chance was to find the gun. Her team had searched through the park itself, and the record team took photos of every inch of the crime scene. No gun was found, but it had to be somewhere.

Calm down, Phoebe, she thought, *it's early. There's evidence to be found, we just haven't found it yet.* Muttering to herself, Phoebe grabbed her notepad and pen. Whenever she was on a case, she made notes on things that didn't make sense; or possible theories. Still muttering, she wrote her thoughts down:

Theories:
1: Killer had help (two killers? Second took the gun?)
2: Suspect is innocent (killer ran with gun, still on the loose)
3: Someone else found/grabbed the gun (witness? Criminal?)

She didn't like any of the options, but they at least explained the missing gun. Even distant security footage would show if there was another person involved, so her theories would be tested soon.

It was quite common for a murder weapon to be thrown out somehow, or at least an attempt was usually made to dispose of it. But it wasn't possible for the suspect to have hidden the gun anywhere; he'd reportedly thrown up and passed out immediately after the shooting. Unless one of her theories were correct, the missing gun was a total mystery. Although Phoebe was a detective, she hated mysteries. Any unresolved questions or riddles plagued her endlessly until she found out the answer.

When she was young, she'd read the Hobbit, and the famous riddle scene in the cave had given her nightmares. Not because the Gollum was scary, or because caves were full of creeping horrors; but because the idea of having to answer riddles she'd never heard in such a horrible place was worse than anything else she could think of. Except for not being able to answer the riddles, and never finding out what the answer was; that was worst of all.

That was her nightmare as a child. As an adult, her nightmare now was whoever killed Jacob Turner walking free. The idea of never finding out what happened to the missing gun was a close second.

27 November 2019 11:54pm (Wednesday)

The call came in just before midnight. Phoebe was still awake, and answered after the first ring. Inspector Rogers' voice crackled through the phone.

"Sergeant Wilson. Alpha Street's woken up. He's been transferred to the interview room. Get over here ASAP."

She dressed as quickly as she could and locked her door on the way out. Gentle rain still pattered the concrete walkway outside her apartment, only just loud enough to hear over the sound of her footsteps.

Her car park was in a secure garage underneath the apartment building, but the door leading down to it was outside, and her front door opened directly to outside as well. Stepping out of the light rain, she walked the familiar steps down to her car. The echo of her steps in the stairwell put her on edge; they always did. Garages always made her feel exposed and vulnerable, even as a Detective Sergeant.

For a brief moment, Phoebe wished she had her gun. It only lasted a few seconds, and then she shook her head. *Having my weapon wouldn't fix anything right now.* No one said it in movies or TV shows, but having a gun didn't actually make you feel safe; it just made you scared of a different outcome.

She didn't want to shoot anyone. Ever. She wasn't even sure she could if she had to. If she had her gun, walking alone through an underground car park at midnight would have just made her terrified that someone would attack her, forcing her to draw her weapon and fire. Most people wouldn't attack a detective out of nowhere, at least not in Australia; then again, detectives didn't wear a uniform, so a potential attacker wouldn't have been aware. Her echoing footsteps and the open darkness of the garage frayed at her nerves as she walked.

When she reached her car, she glanced around the garage before opening her door and getting in. Maybe it was the case, or maybe she was just tired, but something felt off.

Phoebe lived fifteen minutes' drive from the station, very close by Sydney standards. This time of night, the traffic wasn't too bad. She'd parked and walked into the main office by twenty past twelve, dreading the interview but as ready as she could be. Taking a deep breath, she entered the interview room where the murderer had been moved.

Everything was set up. A camera on a tripod sat in the corner, its steady red light punctuating the dull grey room. A table stood in the centre of the room, with two chairs on one side and a single chair on the other.

The suspect sat on the single chair. He was openly crying, his eyes staring at nothing, pulsing with shock yet still sickeningly empty. Phoebe had seen the same expression many times; trauma. It was not an expression she expected to see on this man's face.

For a moment after the door closed behind her, she simply stood and stared at him. He didn't react. The camera's red light pierced her concentration from the edge of her peripheral vision. Words eluded her, and she felt her heartbeat speed up and her stomach clench painfully.

When Phoebe was young, she'd wanted to be an actor. Like a lot of other kids, she supposed. She was in a school play at the age of ten, and she still remembered the dread building in her stomach as her single line of dialogue drew closer. The crowd of parents, siblings and teachers stared at the stage without seeing her, until it was her turn to speak. Never had a group of people been so utterly alien and terrifying to her.

She couldn't remember the words she'd said, but she remembered her voice hitching and catching in her throat as she tried to speak, choked, and then tried to shout so everyone would hear.

She didn't know if people had laughed, or stayed silent, or if she'd even said her line correctly. In that moment, nothing existed but her and her terror, and the only way to make it end had been to shout as loudly as she could whatever words she'd been taught to say.

The memory was so vivid, and yet so empty; the details were gone, wiped out by sheer terror, but the experience still felt so solid in her mind.

Facing the man who'd shot a young boy six times in cold blood felt the same way. Even though he wasn't looking at her, hadn't even acknowledged her existence, she felt the same paralysing fear. Jacob Turner had been only a little older yesterday than she'd been on the stage at her school play.

She checked the red light on the camera one more time, and faced him directly. Her voice hitched, caught, and then she finally made herself speak.

"I am Detective Sergeant Wilson. Please state your full name clearly to the camera."

Her voice was sharp, far sharper than she'd meant it to be, and it yanked him out of whatever daze he'd fallen into. He blinked, confusion flooding his face as though he'd woken from a twenty-year coma. An agonised moan strangled him for a moment, his wide eyes darting like a terrified animal's.

"I'm sorry! I'm sorry, I—had to! You don't understand but I didn't have a choice, you don't know what he did!"

He kept shouting, and Phoebe was paralysed again. His eyes were bloodshot, his hair a mess, and his breath stank. The smell of whiskey and beer and vomit assaulted her nostrils, and for the second time in a handful of hours she had to fight to stop herself from throwing up.

"Stop shouting," she said over him, "I need your name for our records. State it clearly for the camera."

He finally calmed down a little, his focus drawn to her voice. His eyes never stopped roaming, wide and unreasoning. They reminded her of a panicked horse, all fear and madness with no understanding. She felt sick looking at him, and not just because of the smell. He moaned again, the noise grating her nerves like the squealing of rusty door hinges.

"Michael Lee Taylor, why not? Something simple, right? Plain, boring. That's me. Three names. Sounds a bit like a killer... a lot of them have three names like that. Not *him* though, he had just the two."

"Michael Lee Taylor, you were seen shooting an innocent child by no less than seven witnesses and at least one security camera."

"No! Not innocent—No! You don't understand. You don't—three hundred and fifty-eight! You have no idea! So many, so many!"

This time he fell silent on his own, shaking and looking at everything. Something happened then, in the silence that followed his ranting. She felt in control. Maybe it was the fact that he wasn't a cold, calculating psychopath like the serial killers she'd studied at university. Maybe she'd just gotten over the fear of speaking with him now that the conversation had started. Either way, she embraced the confidence. Her one burning question escaped before she could stop it.

"Michael," she said, quietly this time, "where did the gun go?"

"They couldn't leave it lying around, had to get rid of it. Drinking helps, drugs are better!"

He cackled, his voice breaking unevenly as the laugh turned to a sob. She knew she'd have to re-watch the recording of this conversation over and over, and she already felt exhausted by it.

"No one saw the gun after you shot Jacob Turner," she said, seeing him squirm at the boy's name, "but it's gone. Where did the gun go?"

"So many, so many. I told you, I don't know! I had to practice for so long. I didn't want to."

She squeezed her eyes shut and pinched the bridge of her nose. Normally she wouldn't show vulnerability like that, but he hadn't so much as glanced at her the entire time she'd been in the room. She'd never spoken to an insane person before.

People with learning disabilities, sure. Drunks, junkies, and abusive spouses, absolutely.

Her grandfather was in the latter stages of dementia; speaking with him sometimes was heartbreaking. But she'd never had a conversation with anyone who was as obviously insane as this man. She had to fight to stop herself from pitying him; regardless of any mental health problems he might be suffering from, he'd murdered a child.

"You must know where the gun is. You're the only one who touched it. It can't have just disappeared."

"Poof! Vanished! Just like the others. Things appear and disappear, you know? That's what this is all about!"

He cackled again. A thin line of drool slipped out the side of his mouth and down his filthy, stubble-covered chin.

"Twenty twenty-four, yep, keep an eye out! You'll see. May, or April, or one of those. Who knows? I lose track of the days now, alcohol helps. They told me not to bring it with me, but I had to! You'll see. Things happen in the future. Not him, though. I changed him."

Trying to ignore his gibberish, she took some time to look at him, really look at him; beyond the filth, the stink. Beyond the insanity. He wore an oversized coat despite the heat. She was sure that if she took it off him, he'd be sweating underneath, even in the cool of the station. He'd been fully searched when taken into custody; the murder weapon wasn't on his person, nor did he have any other weapons. Just the too-big coat. His clothing, including the coat, was old and filthy. Frayed threads and old stains covered him from neckline to ankle. Even the shoes were falling apart.

Phoebe had never felt comfortable judging a person on their appearance, but the man clearly wasn't looking after himself. She dreaded searching his residence, if they ever found it. If he was as lazy with it as he was with himself, it would be a garbage dump.

Forcing herself to move to the table and sit across from him, she leaned back in the chair. He breathed through his mouth, ragged and volatile. The smell hit her, washed over her like a sudden wave at the beach.

She just needed a clear confession. But even after being in the room with him for a few minutes, it was obvious a confession from the man in his current state would be worthless. The filmed interview would show his mental state, and even if it weren't for that, his blood-alcohol level had to be off the charts. It would be easy for him to claim intimidation or forced confession. They'd have to hold him in custody, wait him out until he was sober, and hope his mental state improved.

"I'm really trying to help you, Michael. You're in a lot of trouble right now."

"Oh yes, yep, this way it comes! But worth it, right? I mean, that's what they said, anyway. I'm not... don't think so. No. No!"

He slammed his hands down on the table, and then he was crying and moaning as though he was a witness instead of the murderer.

"I didn't want to! You have no idea, three hundred and fifty-eight! No, no. No. I'm so, so sorry. I'm *sorry*, okay?"

He broke down, smashing his head on the table and screaming. His shoulders jagged up and down as he sobbed into the cold, smooth table surface. Phoebe was mesmerised, staring with her mouth open and her breath caught in her throat.

"Why... Why is everything so fucked up?" He said without raising his head, "I didn't ask for this. It's not my fault."

"Did you shoot Jacob Turner?"

She knew a confession wouldn't mean anything at this point, but she couldn't help asking. Her mind had turned from revulsion to pity, and now to a deep, morbid fascination. The same fascination that had propelled her through university, pouring through serial killer profiles and cold cases like they were Grisham novels.

The man's sobs picked up, racking his body, making him sound like he was being strangled. He brought a fist down on the table again, shaking his head savagely.

"He had to die, you don't understand. You have no idea. I didn't want to, it's not my fault!"

"Did you shoot Jacob Turner?"

This time she emphasised each word like a school principal berating a naughty child. Forceful, authoritative. Wiping the pity from her own thoughts and focusing on the fascination she felt, the drive to know everything that had happened.

He brought his head up from the table, a bright red mark covering most of his forehead. His eyes somehow looked even more bloodshot. For the first time, he stared directly into her eyes, his gaze perfectly still and even.

She saw a depth of horror and sadness in his eyes which slid straight into her heart like a knife, cold and deadly. In that moment, he seemed completely sober. Completely sane.

"Yes," he said, his voice as cold as it was quiet, "I shot him, you fucking bitch. You would have done the same thing."

28 November 2019 1:08am (Thursday)

You would have done the same thing.

Taylor's words echoed in her head the rest of that night. By the time she was half way home, the light rain had petered out and the air was finally cooling. She opened the car window as she drove, trying to clear her head.

Why would he say that? In what world would she ever shoot a child?

"He couldn't be claiming self defence, could he?" She asked the night air whistling through the car window.

"Even someone as crazy as him couldn't think he was being threatened by a child."

She never listened to the radio. When she was in a good mood, she played her own music through her phone, but on nights like these she simply let the sounds coming through the car window wash over her. The slick sound of tyres running over wet road, a light breeze, and distant traffic. Driving at night was soothing.

When she got home, she was too tired to do anything, and too uneasy to sleep. The interview with Taylor left her feeling like she was one of the cops in the cases she'd studied. Chasing a deranged killer around in circles and not finding evidence until years later, when a busted headlight or some other chance encounter brought the killer into focus again.

God, please don't let this case take years. It wasn't a genuine prayer; Phoebe didn't believe all that. But still, she found herself begging the universe to let her solve it soon. *The sooner that man is locked away,* she thought, *the better.*

Her glass still sat on the coffee table. Snatching it off, she poured the rest of the bottle of wine into it and took a long drink. Rubbing her left hand over her face, she tried to let the image of Jacob Turner fade. *And Michael Lee Taylor,* she thought. His face still leered at her from some dark place in her mind. He disturbed her in a way that she'd never experienced before. Even after watching countless documentaries and interview footage of real-life psychopaths, Taylor stuck out in her head as an unsettling monster.

His words echoed in her ears, most of them utter gibberish. *I've never seen alcohol turn someone that unintelligible,* she thought, *there had to have been drugs in his system too.* She found herself replaying the things he'd said, focusing on the way he spoke and the words he'd chosen. It really had sounded as though he was trying to tell her something. *Something really important; to him at least.* As uncomfortable as the interview was, she'd have to go back and watch the footage several times.

There was no chance she would ever consider him innocent unless they found incontrovertible proof. *But still, his apologies actually sounded genuine.* Most violent criminals denied everything, as aggressive in self-preservation as in the crimes they committed. But Taylor was horrified by what he'd done. *Or he's an incredible actor.* Somehow, neither idea was comforting.

She had to sleep. A while ago, she'd begun to have problems sleeping. Her doctor had prescribed her some sleeping pills, and though they worked like a charm, she'd only used them once or twice. Most of the pills were still sitting in the package, ready to knock her out in one hit.

Snapping one out of its plastic and aluminium parcel, she dropped it into her mouth and swallowed a sip of water. Stripping, she took a quick shower, dried off and slid into bed. As she drifted into a sterile, dreamless sleep, the last image her mind conjured was the wide, bloodshot eyes of a child murderer. His broken cackle followed her into oblivion.

17 April 2008 7:35pm (Thursday)

They sat together on Claire's couch, a mostly empty glass of wine next to her and one of water next to Phoebe. She wasn't a very social person, but the few friends she had were everything to her. Claire was the closest friend she had; and was the first person Phoebe told.

"Holy shit, Phoebe!" Claire laughed, wrapping Phoebe in a tight hug, "congratulations!"

"Thanks," Phoebe said, "I can't believe it's really happening."

"Yeah, you're telling me. Do you know if it's a boy or a girl?"

"Claire, I'm still barely pregnant. I won't find that out for a while."

"You know I never wanted kids, Pheebs," Claire said, "I don't know about that stuff."

"My first ultrasound is in a week, but even then, I don't think I'll find the sex out until later."

Claire nodded, a subtle eye roll almost escaping Phoebe's notice. Claire and Phoebe went to school together, and had been best friends for most of their lives. Even if she hadn't seen it, Phoebe would have known that Claire was rolling her eyes.

"What about names?"

Phoebe shook her head, shrugging a shoulder as she did.

"Haven't decided on any yet."

"There are none you like?"

"Not yet."

Claire put her hand on her chin in a mock gesture of thought.

"How about Claire? If it's a girl?"

"You're an idiot," Phoebe laughed.

"That's not a no."

Claire smirked, then doubled down on her pretend thoughtfulness. She gave Phoebe an expectant look. Phoebe laughed again, and then managed to wrestle her expression back to serious.

"No. Not Claire."

They sat together in silence for a few minutes, Claire sipping at her wine, and Phoebe shook her head.

"I honestly just can't think of any names," she said, "nothing sounds right."

Claire said nothing. *She's not going to have much to say when it comes to the baby,* Phoebe thought, *she's pretty much the opposite of a typical mother.* Even when they were young, Claire had always known she didn't want kids.

"It's just a name, Pheebs," Claire said, getting up to refill her glass, "I'm sure it'll be fine, whatever you pick."

It was Phoebe's turn to roll her eyes. *Of course she doesn't care.*

"Haha sure. Anyway, what's new with you?"

Claire filled her glass, returned the bottle to her fridge, and sat back down.

"The usual," she said with a smirk, "working hard and playing hard, you know me."

Ever since high school, Claire had been intent on avoiding long term relationships; *they're doomed anyway,* she used to say, *may as well just have fun instead.* Phoebe assumed she would eventually grow out of it and settle down, but she still hadn't.

"How many boyfriends are you up to now?"

"Oh please, they wish they were boyfriends."

Phoebe raised her eyebrows, forcing herself not to laugh. She tried not to judge Claire's lifestyle. *I just could never do what she does,* she thought, *I'm not even sure how many men she's been with.*

"Have any of them had a second date?"

Claire laughed, hysterically, almost choking on her wine.

"They never even had a first date, Pheebs," she said, "that's kinda the point. I don't do dates."

Phoebe rolled her eyes again.

"I don't get it, Claire. Why wouldn't you want a relationship? You've seen what Ben is like, you know there are good guys out there."

"Sure there are," Claire said, "but I have a roster of hot guys I can have whenever I want." Claire laughed and took a long sip of wine. "My question is, why don't *you* want *that*?"

It took Phoebe long enough to feel comfortable being intimate with Ben after they started dating. Sex had always been a big deal to her. Ben helped her open up. He'd turned physical intimacy from a scary mystery into something beautiful they shared and indulged in together.

"Strangers?" Phoebe shook her head, "no thanks."

"Well, you're missing out, Pheebs."

Phoebe scoffed, took a sip of water, and stared at Claire with her eyebrows raised again. She thought of Ben, and a slow smile spread across her lips without her realising.

"So are you, Claire," she said, "so are you."

28 November 2019 6:00am (Thursday)

Staccato beeps and buzzes shot through her head before she realised she was awake. She knew the sound, but it still took a moment to hit home; *my alarm*, she thought. It came slow, like the tide on a beach rising at the start of the day.

The sound kept playing, and finally she pushed herself into movement, sitting up and swiping her finger over her phone's screen to cancel the alarm. Sitting on the edge of the bed, she rubbed her eyes and blinked as her room came into focus. A comfortable emptiness still filled her mind. Sunlight speared through the gap in her bedroom curtains; she never could quite close them properly.

Up, she thought to herself, and stood on shaky legs, walking carefully to the kitchen. A glass of water cleared her head a little, and a cold handful splashed on her face finished the job. Her kitchen and living room were part of the same space, just inside the front door. It was darker than her bedroom, the curtains far thicker and without a perpetual gap in the middle.

Halfway through the room to open the curtains—Phoebe preferred natural light—she remembered she hadn't put any clothes on after getting out of bed. She stopped next to the couch, shaking her head. She lived in a block of apartment buildings that nestled against each other; her windows faced the front doors of the building next door.

"Close one," she said.

Her voice was a little slurred; the sleeping pill had really done its job. Remembering the pill made her remember why she'd taken it, and Taylor's deranged face swam into her mind again.

"Fuck. What a nightmare."

His smell was still in her nostrils; or maybe that was just her imagination. She wasn't looking forward to seeing him again, but she knew she would have to conduct another interview when he'd sobered up.

At least they had his name now; they could search for history, friends, family. They could find his residence, if he even had one. She wouldn't have been surprised if he was homeless; though that would beg the question of how and where he obtained a gun. If he had a home, she certainly wasn't looking forward to seeing it. She was certain it would be as filthy as he was.

"You can take the pig out of the sty, but it'll still smell like shit," she said.

She laughed a little, though she had no idea where the thought came from. Even to herself, the laugh sounded uneasy. But then she was laughing properly, standing naked in the middle of her dark living room. The momentum built, and soon she was doubled over, tears squeezing out of her eyes.

She supposed it was fear, or anxiety, or maybe even the sleeping pill; but whatever caused it was quickly becoming irrelevant. Soon enough the joke itself was irrelevant too, the words forgotten as a desperate kind of mania settled in.

Her laughter built until it hurt, and when his face swam in her mind again it disappeared as quickly as it started. Rubbing her hands over her face, she stepped into the shower. The hot water helped, but she still spent the entire shower trying desperately not to think about Michael Lee Taylor.

After her shower, she made a coffee and some toast. *I should have moved my alarm until later,* she thought, *even with the sleeping pill I slept less than five hours*. Her head swam a little, even as she sipped her coffee. It would take a while to wake up fully. *I just hope Taylor doesn't sober up too soon, otherwise I won't be thinking clearly during the next interview.*

Pulling on clean work clothes, she finally left the apartment. Today was not only potentially the day she would have to interview Taylor again; Jacob Turner's parents were coming in to the station for an interview too. His mother would have been fine without coming in, Phoebe suspected, but his father apparently insisted on knowing where the police were up to. *Hopefully they can answer some questions about him,* she thought, *that might help clear up some of what happened.*

She was still a little hazy during the drive to work; clear enough to drive safely, but not enough to think much. The station looked the same as it always did, but a cold emanated from it that made her shiver. *A child murderer is in there right now,* she thought, *waiting to talk to me.* Going into the first interview was scary enough; knowing he would be sober the next time forced every worst-case outcome into her mind.

"You're early, Sarge," Senior Constable Timms said as she got to her desk.

"So are you."

"I'm always early. No offence, but you don't look so great. You okay?"

She realised she'd forgot to put make-up on. Though it was true that she felt terrible, being told she looked ill or tired without make-up never failed to annoy her.

"Gee, thanks, Timms. How about you handle the next interview of Taylor for me, if I don't look well enough?"

"Actually, don't mind me," he said, "you're looking better already."

Shaking her head, Phoebe sat down and logged in to her computer. The Jacob Turner case was already open in her case log, and she clicked into it without bothering to check her emails. She knew she wouldn't be able to focus on anything else any way.

"The parents will be here in a few hours, Sarge," Timms said, his voice gentle and full of caution, "seriously, do you want me to interview them?"

"No," she said without looking away from her computer, "I'd like to see them myself."

28 November 2019 11:14am (Thursday)

Jacob Turner's father was a strange man. The day after his son's violent death, he displayed no signs of grief or sadness. Instead, a coiled rage sat behind his eyes, burning everything his gaze touched. *I'd be angry too,* Phoebe thought. He was tall, and though quite slim, a palpable strength emanated from him. *He's older than I expected,* she thought, *his hair is already grey.*

"Thank you for coming in, Mr. Turner," she said, sitting across from him at the interview table, "I'm sorry for your loss. I'll make this as quick as I can."

"Has he accused my son of anything?"

You would have done the same thing.

"No," she said, "he was just a child in the wrong place at the wrong time, as far as we can tell."

"Then why is the investigation still going?"

"It's standard procedure, Mr. Turner. We need to complete all our investigations, and that can take a little time."

He stared, unmoving. She couldn't even tell if he breathed. Finally, his head tipped in the barest nod.

"Ask your questions, then."

"Do you know if Jacob was hanging around any suspicious people recently?"

"No."

"Have you noticed any strangers around your house, or anywhere near your family?"

"No."

"Do you know any people who may wish yourself any harm?"

"Not enough to murder a child."

His tone never changed. He barely even blinked; his dangerous eyes burned into her own, quietly raging. *There's something wrong with this guy*. She understood his anger, but she'd never met anyone who exuded the sheer, controlled rage that Peter Turner did.

Michael Lee Taylor was asleep in the holding cells, almost directly below them. Looking at Turner's face, she was glad he didn't know that fact. *We'd have another murder on our hands if Jacob's dad got his hands on Taylor*.

"Jacob was shot at the entrance to Alpha Park," Phoebe said, "was that somewhere he went often?"

"Yes. He spent time in the park after school most days. He spoke about it to me every now and then."

"What did he say?"

Mr. Turner's eyes narrowed a fraction.

"He just enjoyed being there. That's not a crime, is it?"

"No, it's not a crime. I need to be clear, Mr. Turner, Jacob isn't in any trouble. I'm just trying to gather as much information as I can."

"You've caught the killer, haven't you?"

"We've apprehended a suspect."

"Did he do it?"

This man is infuriating.

"I can't answer that, Mr. Turner. The investigation is still going."

"He better be going to prison."

"Is there anything more you can think of that might be relevant, Mr. Turner?"

"He's a child, detective. He was shot randomly on his way home from school. Other than that, he was a smart and capable child, just like many others at his school. What information could I possibly have that would help you?"

"You could answer my questions, for one thing."

His jaw clenched tight, his eyes hard as steel. Phoebe stared him down.

"Did he say anything specific to you about Alpha Park?" she finally said.

"No."

"You asked earlier if the suspect accused your son of anything," she said, watching his eyes closely, "what exactly do you think he would accuse your son of doing?"

"He's presumably insane," Mr. Turner said, "how would I know what he said?"

"It's not a normal assumption to make," Phoebe said, "so why would you think he accused Jacob of anything in the first place?"

"You said my son isn't in trouble. If that man didn't accuse him of anything, I don't need to speculate on what it might have been."

She almost sighed out loud. *This man is impossible.*

"Okay, Mr. Turner," she said, standing and opening the door for them, "I think we've got all we need. Thank you for coming in."

20 April 2008 3:12pm (Sunday)

Her grandfather's house felt old to her even when she'd been young; now it had the air of a museum. But despite looking frail, Charles Wilson was as lively and intelligent as when Phoebe had been a child. His eyes sparkled, his smile glowing with genuine warmth. Phoebe sat facing him, with Ben sitting next to her.

She hadn't shared the good news yet. Although she knew he would be happy for her, and for them, she felt a faint throb of anxiety. *I told Claire already,* she thought, *why is it more difficult telling grandpa?* He'd been more of a parent to her than her actual parents; maybe it was just the fear of somehow letting him down. They shared so much with each other, and she was certainly far more comfortable with him than with her mother. *Not that mum's a terrible person,* she thought, *she's just... a little difficult sometimes.*

They'd been at her grandfather's place for close to an hour already, talking about other things and laughing. Ben promised to let her break the news; she could feel his anxiety as strongly as she felt her own. A lull in the conversation brought some silence, and Phoebe's anxiety filled it with frantic energy.

"So," Charles said, "what's the big news you're here to tell me?"

Phoebe's jaw dropped. *How does he always know?* She thought. No one could get anything past her grandfather. When she was younger, she remembered thinking Sherlock Holmes might've been based on him; he used to read the books to her whenever her mother took her to his house. He wasn't a detective, or a consultant; his job had nothing to do with crime in any capacity. But he was so smart, and he seemed to see everything. It wasn't until she was older that she realised how long ago the Sherlock books had been written, and felt incredibly stupid. She'd never told anyone that, even as a child, but for that brief period of time she looked at him with the same wonder as she regarded Sherlock Holmes himself.

Ben stared at her, then at Charles, and back at her again. Phoebe forced her mouth closed, blushed, and laughed, shaking her head at her grandfather's superhuman perception.

"I wanted to tell you... *we* wanted to tell you that, well... Grandpa, I'm pregnant."

His eyes went wide, his smile broadening into a huge grin. He rose from the comfortable lounge he'd sat in and opened his arms.

"Phoebe, that's wonderful!" he said, tears glistening in his eyes, "I'm so happy to hear that."

She jumped to her feet and into his embrace. Ben joined them, and for a moment Phoebe was overwhelmed with love and warmth from both of them. If no one else found out about her baby, she would still feel complete. Her three favourite people in the world now knew, and that was all she cared about.

They sat down again, and Phoebe basked in the comfortable silence that followed. Her grandfather beamed like a child, looking from her to Ben as though they'd just given him a million dollars. She didn't expect so much support and love so quickly, though she wasn't sure why; Charles Wilson had always been her most supportive family member.

"Well now," he said, dabbing his tears away with the handkerchief he always stored in his pocket, "it's just the waiting game. I can't wait to see the beautiful child you two make."

"If we're lucky," Ben said, "it'll take after Phoebe more than me."

"Oh please," Phoebe said, laughing, "you're the handsome one."

"I think we can all agree that the child will be very good looking, regardless of who it takes after more," her grandfather said.

Ben nodded, and Phoebe saw him struggling not to press the point more; he'd mentioned several times he wanted the baby to look more like her. *I'm beginning to think it's not a joke any more,* she thought, *even though he's so hot.* She was always telling him how gorgeous he was, but it never seemed to get through to him.

They sat together for the rest of the afternoon, talking about everything and nothing. Her grandfather was one of those people who could make any conversation fun, regardless of the topic. Ben got along well with him too, which just made Phoebe love him even more.

"How's work going?" her grandfather said, glancing at both of them.

"Great," Ben said, "really great."

"I can imagine it's great for you, being a writer and all. I read *The Halloween Hitchhiker*, by the way. Lots of fun."

Ben inclined his head in a sort of modest half bow, smiling his *thanks but I'm not that great* smile. Phoebe found it both charming and infuriating. He *was* great.

"I told you it was good, babe," Phoebe said, shaking his arm gently, "Grandpa doesn't give out compliments unless he means it."

Ben did have a regular job on top of writing; but he only worked a few days a week, and whenever anyone asked him what he did for a living he ignored the part time job. He'd always wanted to be able to say "I'm an author", and it wasn't until two years ago that he actually could say it and mean it. Now he'd published two novels and a handful of short stories, and wrote articles for several different magazines.

His second novel, *the Halloween Hitchhiker*, was in negotiations to be picked up for a movie by a major studio. It was far too early to tell anyone, even her grandfather, but he'd told Phoebe about it. All he could say to anyone else was things were going well.

"What about you, Phoebe?"

She thought about it, frowning a little. She was a police Constable, which was the first step towards the career of her dreams. *Which is great,* she thought, *except there's still a way to go before I'm a real detective.* She enjoyed the job, but not as much as she hoped she would. There was no actual investigating, for one thing. For another, she mostly just dealt with drunks and shitty drivers.

"It's good," she finally said, "I'll be a detective eventually. Not sure when, but I'll get there."

"I always told you that you would, didn't I?" her grandfather said, his eyes shining.

She'd always loved puzzles, mysteries, and research. But she never would have tried to make a career out of it if not for her grandfather. From as far back as her memory could stretch, he'd always told her she would be great at it. If not for him, she wouldn't have discovered Sherlock Holmes at such a young age. She wouldn't have fallen in love with the idea of detection and investigation.

"Yeah, you did."

"I promise," he said, "you'll be a detective before you know it. A great one, too."

28 November 2019 2:17pm (Thursday)

Michael Lee Taylor had been sleeping off whatever was in his system from the night before again when Phoebe arrived at the station that morning. He stayed that way almost the entire day, well past even her interview with Jacob's father; a Constable remained with him to make sure he wasn't at risk, but they kept him at the station instead of sending him back to the hospital again.

After Jacob's parents, Phoebe interviewed the two kids who'd originally called triple-zero. They were both pale and scared, and told her nothing she didn't already know. She thanked them, gave them contact details for a counselor, and escorted them out of the station.

With almost nothing else to do, she tried to focus on the case itself. They still had almost nothing, but the witness statements had been transcribed and recorded, and she read through them.

Almost nothing useful. Taylor's personal effects were either with the record team or at the lab. *This is the worst time,* she thought, *waiting for evidence.* She could think, come up with more theories, obsess over the details she already knew; but at the end of the day, she couldn't do anything real until she had something concrete in front of her.

She was also tired. *So, so tired.* Her fifth coffee of the day sat on the desk, steam curling from the cup and disappearing almost immediately. The day had passed in a blur; she could barely focus. *I'll have to speak to Taylor again soon,* she thought, *as soon as he wakes up. Whenever that will be.*

Her phone buzzed in the desk drawer where she kept it during office hours. She checked the name, then answered.

"Hi, mum."

"Your grandfather's gone."

At first, the words fell flat in her mind, their meaning lost on her. The last word grew, echoing, until the full sentence finally hit her.

"He's... he's *gone?*"

"The home just called me," her mother said, "he got out somehow and no one knows where he is."

Phoebe sighed, the breath leaving her in a ragged, shaky rush.

"God, mum. I thought you meant he died!"

"Who knows what could happen to him if they don't find him."

"They'll find him, mum. Residents walk out of those places all the time."

"Aren't you worried, Phoebe?"

She took a breath, shaking her head a little and screwing her eyes shut.

"Of course I'm worried. What am I supposed to do about it? He'll be found by the people whose job it is to find him. I have a lot going on at work, mum."

"Oh darling, yes I heard about that poor child. What a tragedy. But that man was caught, wasn't he? So that's all done, why don't you come and help find your grandfather?"

There it is, she thought. Her mother had a habit of making the hardest parts of her life sound trivial.

"You have no idea what's happening here, Mum. I can't go anywhere. They'll find Grandpa, let me know when they do."

Phoebe hung up before her mother could respond. She would catch an earful for it later, but she couldn't handle that conversation for a second longer. Her grandfather was one of the most important people in her life, and if she could be there to help him, she would. But for now, the only difference it made to her life was adding another layer of stress to her already anxiety-riddled and sleep-deprived mind.

How long has it been, she thought, *since I visited him at the home?* Too long. Gathering the courage to visit him, talk to him, when she knew he wouldn't remember her, was getting more difficult with each day that passed. He was the source of most of her happiest childhood memories. Him and her grandmother, who had died when she was still young.

Phoebe's mother knew she hadn't visited in a while, and the pressure was always on her to do so. She found herself angry for not visiting when she had time; with the Jacob Turner case, she would be too busy until they had the actual evidence to put Michael Lee Taylor away. *Excuses,* she thought, *I could visit him if I really tried.*

He was thin now, gaunt and weak. Her mother posted photos on Facebook every week, and Phoebe watched him wasting away from a distance, too terrified to see it happen in person. *He doesn't even know me anymore.*

Facing Michael Lee Taylor and the mess of a case she was working on was far easier than watching her grandfather slowly die. And far easier than being a stranger to her own family.

"I'll visit him soon," she said, "I will."

She shook her head as though it would clear all her doubts and fears. Sipping some more coffee, she tried to focus on the case again.

28 November 2019 3:37pm (Thursday)

A fairly short walk away from the park where Jacob Turner had been killed was a local pub. On a hunch, Phoebe visited the pub a little while after the call from her mother. Heat pulsed down from the sky and up from the pavement as she stepped into the cool pub.

Stale beer and the smell of old damp carpet crept into her nose the moment she entered. A few people sat alone, one at the bar and a couple at different tables. All of them hunched over their drinks, not bothering to raise their heads when someone new walked in.

She could picture Taylor fitting in perfectly here. If he'd been quiet, he might have even gone unnoticed. But Phoebe didn't think he was quiet. She saw the man behind the bar's eyes widen momentarily when he spotted her.

"Good afternoon," she said, "I'm Detective Sergeant Wilson. I'd like to ask you a few questions about an incident that occurred nearby."

"Yeah, I heard about that. What kinda questions you got for me though?"

Phoebe had a printed mugshot of Taylor, and handed it to the bartender. She didn't say anything at first. He looked at her as he took the photo, not looking at it until he'd held it for a moment. The second he glanced at it, his eyes briefly widened in recognition, then immediately narrowed again. *I knew it.*

"When was he last in here?" She asked.

"Dunno who he is."

"That's not what I asked you."

He looked at the photo again, scratching his head.

"Look, I'm not responsible for what people do after they leave here drunk, right?"

Her heart skipped a beat, then made up for it with a sickening thump in her chest. *He drank here just before shooting Jacob.*

"Not necessarily, though he was particularly drunk. You're not under investigation, mate, we're just looking for information on him. His movements before the incident."

The bartender took a last look at the mugshot and handed it back to Phoebe.

"Alright, alright. He came in yesterday, late morning, I think. Around eleven?"

Clenching her teeth, she tried to think about what she knew of that day already. Even through her excitement at finding a lead, she couldn't stand people ending statements with a question.

"Okay, around eleven. Was anyone with him?"

"Wait, eleven thirty actually. Nah, he was alone."

"What was his behaviour like?"

The bartender stared at the pub's front door, squinting as though he was looking directly into the sun.

"Well, I mean, he was really weird."

"We're investigating the murder of a child, sir; you're going to have to do better than 'really weird'."

"Yeah, alright, I know. He was wearing sunnies and a big coat, he sort of looked like he thought someone was after him, y'know?"

"Did he speak to anyone?"

"He ordered drinks, but he was quiet for ages. Then after a couple hours he started talking like crazy. I thought he was having a stroke."

"Was he drinking the entire time?"

"More or less, yeah. He seemed in control for most of it. He drank a lot, but he didn't *seem* drunk, y'know? Not until he started talking, anyway."

"What kinds of things did he say?"

"Oh man, I mean... a lot of gibberish, really. I don't remember any of it. It was hard to keep track of, y'know?"

"Did he say anything that made you think he might do something bad?"

"Well like I said, it was pretty hard keeping track of what he was saying. I tuned most of it out, to be honest... I get a lot of messy drunks. You kinda learn to just smile and nod, y'know?"

"Did he threaten anyone?"

"Nah, but he mentioned Hitler killing all the Jews actually. That was pretty weird. Came out of nowhere."

Phoebe shook her head, glancing around the pub. The few people in the room had the air of comfort she'd seen in many other pubs and bars in her career.

"These your regulars?"

"Yeah. Well, Danny and Rick are, I don't know this idiot," he said as he gestured to the man sitting at the bar.

"Oi fuck off mate, you're the idiot," the man replied.

"Careful Matt, or I'll ban you again."

Matt scoffed and downed the rest of his drink. Without asking, the bartender poured him another. Matt tapped his card and took the drink with a muttered thanks and a chuckle.

"You'd never ban me, Rob. I give you way too much of my hard-earned money."

The bartender, named Rob apparently, stared hard at the little card reader until it beeped and said *transaction approved*. He did it without thinking, and without worrying about offending Matt. A well-established habit then; he must have had payments declined without realising. Something occurred to her.

"Did he pay with a card?"

"What—oh you mean the guy?" He gestured to Phoebe's pocket, where she'd put the mugshot away.

"Yes, the guy."

"Uh... Hmm. No. Nah, he paid with cash actually, every time. I remember thinking it was weird for someone so shabby looking to have so much cash."

Taylor had almost no cash in his wallet when he was found; he'd obviously spent all of it on alcohol before the shooting. *Was this just an act of random violence because he was so drunk,* she thought, *or was he drinking because he was nervous about killing Jacob?*

28 November 2019 4:50pm (Thursday)

Michael Lee Taylor woke up again in the late afternoon, mostly sober and far more calm. Phoebe was back at the station when he woke up, adding the bartender's statement to the case record. She would need to call the man into the station to give an official statement, but for now the interview was enough to fill in some blanks.

"Sergeant," Constable Brouwer said, "We got CCTV footage from both cameras processed. One is useless, but the other looks like it might come through okay. It'll be ready later this afternoon, we're having screen shots printed for you."

The stress that had been building lessened just a little, and Phoebe breathed a sigh of relief. *There we go,* she thought, *finally we start getting evidence. I knew it was just a matter of time.* She smiled her thanks to Brouwer, and he cleared his throat.

"Also, Taylor is awake."

She leapt from her chair; she wasn't particularly looking forward to another conversation with him, but she'd finished another coffee and she needed to get further in the case. The bar gave her some information, but she needed to find out as much as she could from Michael Lee Taylor himself.

He was in the same interview room, sitting quietly with the same haunted look in his eyes. She knew he was guilty; knew it without a doubt. But understanding why he'd done it was another thing entirely. *And I still don't know where the gun went.* She switched the camera to record and sat down opposite him.

His first confession, though captured on camera, was given while heavily intoxicated; Phoebe needed him to confess again, this time sober. One of her team had brought him food; its smell almost overpowered the awful smells coming from Taylor. He looked just as haggard and filthy as he had the day before.

"Michael," she said, "now that you've slept off the alcohol, I'd like to talk to you again."

He didn't answer. Phoebe glanced back at the camera; she needed this. More than just professionally. She needed to know why he killed a child, and where the gun went.

"Do you remember our previous talk?"

Taylor nodded absently, his eyes fixed on nothing.

"I need you to speak, Michael. We need your participation."

For a long moment, he kept staring. Phoebe couldn't tell if he was performing, or genuinely traumatised by what he'd done. Crimes of passion usually ended with the perpetrator acting the way Taylor was now. But something about the crime, the series of events that lead up to it, and Taylor himself, led Phoebe to believe the shooting was planned.

"I remember, mostly. I drank a *lot* though."

"You did. Were you drinking so much to make it easier to kill Jacob Turner?"

A heavy sigh came from Taylor. Sober, he was a different man. Phoebe had seen the same transformation thousands of times. But fights were easy to blame on alcohol, as well as any number of stupid, mostly harmless decisions; murder was not.

"I had to do it," he said, "I *had* to. And yeah, the alcohol helped a little. If I had drugs, I would have taken them too. Have you ever had to shoot someone?"

"No, I haven't."

"Then you have no idea how terrifying it is. How *horrible*."

Phoebe leaned back, unable to stop the frown creasing her face as she stared at him.

"So why shoot him, then?"

"I told you, I *had* to. He deserved it."

"He was a *child*."

"You have no idea," he said, "you'd never understand."

"Help me to understand, then," she said, leaning forward, "you're not making anything easier on yourself by being uncooperative."

"It doesn't matter. You won't solve this, detective. I'm sorry. Even with my confession, there won't be any closure."

She shut her eyes, hard, for a moment. Anxiety buzzed in her chest, and rage just below that. *It can't be this complicated. He's insane, it's the only logical explanation.* He was speaking as though there was some great conspiracy.

"Why did you shoot Jacob Turner?"

Another long stretch of silence filled the room. He shook his head, a pained, humourless smile pulling at his lips.

"You won't believe me. It doesn't matter anyway, there's no way I come out of this alive."

What the fuck does that mean? She thought. *Damn it, it's like he enjoys the mystery of it.* She had no idea what could possibly make him think he would be dead because of the shooting. Jacob's parents wouldn't retaliate so extremely, at least not with Taylor in custody, and nowhere in Australia carried the death penalty.

"Just tell me," Phoebe said. "I need to understand why this happened."

He sighed again, rubbing his forehead with his palms.

"Jacob Turner is Australia's most prolific serial killer. I had to stop him."

She almost laughed. But a cold, sick feeling gripped her stomach, and no part of her found the situation funny. *He's speaking so normally now that he's sober,* she thought, *but he's clearly delusional.*

"Jacob was eleven years old. What on earth makes you think he was a serial killer?"

"Well, he's not. Not anymore."

She could have screamed. Her hands were balled into fists; when she noticed, she moved them under the table.

"I need you to speak plainly, Michael," she said, her voice wavering just a little, "answer my questions as directly as you can. I need facts, not mysteries."

"You already think I'm crazy, don't you?"

"I'm not here to judge, Michael, but you need to work with me here."

He sighed yet again, staring at the table. Phoebe could see him thinking through something. *Is he finally going to come clean?* Either way, they would need to have him psychologically evaluated; he clearly believed that Jacob's shooting was deserved.

"Michael, I'll ask one more time," she said, as gently as she could, "why did you shoot Jacob Turner?"

Phoebe watched him carefully as he stared at the table. A frown pulled at his face, but in his eyes lay a deep sadness. There was guilt there, too. His breathing grew deeper, more deliberate, and she knew he was about to speak. Electricity spread through her chest like pins and needles, almost replacing the anxiety and rage she felt.

"Okay, here it is."

He rubbed his forehead with his palms again, took a deep breath, and looked her in the eyes.

"I'm from the future," he said, "I came here to kill Jacob Turner before he kills anyone."

Time travel. So, he's really insane, then.

She sighed; he noticed.

"I know you don't believe me," he said, "but check the books, that might help. I brought one back with me."

"What books?" she asked.

"You'll see."

The best they could hope for was some hard evidence from the lab; the interview revealed nothing but mental instability. The fact that he displayed remorse and understanding of his actions meant that he wouldn't get off on a defence of mental illness plea. He knew exactly what he was doing when he did it, despite being drunk. His reasoning was less important than his actions, but they would still need proof. And besides a legal need for proof, Phoebe needed to understand.

"Where did the gun go?"

Taylor shook his head again, maintaining eye contact with the same pained smile.

"It's just gone, detective. I can't explain it any more than you can."

"That's not good enough, Michael. You're the only person who can tell me where it went. Other people could be in danger. If someone finds that gun, you could be responsible for more innocent people's deaths. Do you really want that?"

"It won't happen," he said, "I can promise you that. The gun is gone. It will never be found."

Phoebe felt an almost overwhelming urge to either cry or scream; or both. Taylor lowered his eyes to the table again. He wasn't joking, or playing with her; she had no doubt that he believed every word he'd said. It was up to her to find the gun without his help.

22 May 2008 10:48am (Thursday)

"Phoebe Wilson?"

Her head snapped up; she felt like she was about to undergo an invasive, risky operation. *It's fine,* she thought, trying to channel Ben's soothing voice whenever he comforted her, *there's nothing to be nervous about.* He didn't say anything reassuring as they rose from their chairs; instead, he simply gave her a warm smile.

The room they were led to was completely white; even the furniture. The ultrasound equipment itself was a pale blueish-grey that almost blended in with the white anyway. In the middle of the room, a narrow medical bed sat waiting for Phoebe. Next to it was a small TV monitor; where the baby would appear soon.

"Sit up here, and let's take a look," the woman who'd called her name said.

Phoebe sat on the bed and tried to get comfortable as the woman prepared the scanning device. *First ultrasound,* she thought, shaking with nerves. She knew there would be nothing wrong, but there was something about all the medical equipment that filled her with doubt. At the sonographer's instruction, she pulled her shirt up and unbuttoned her jeans.

She gasped as the woman poured a cold jelly-like substance onto her stomach. She'd seen enough movies and TV shows to know what to expect, but the temperature still shocked her. Ben stood next to her, staring at the monitor and holding her hand.

A strange and rapid whooshing sound filled the room, and Phoebe glanced at the sonographer; her face was serene and patient, and Phoebe tried to calm herself.

"What's that?" she asked.

"That's the heartbeat," she said, smiling at Phoebe and Ben.

"Why is it so fast? Is the baby okay?"

"It's totally normal."

The sonographer spent several minutes maneuvering the scanning tool around her belly, staring intently at the screen.

"The sac is well attached," the sonographer said, "and baby is measuring in line with your dates. Your due date will stay the same. Everything looks the way it should."

"Do you know if it's a boy or a girl?" Ben said.

"No, we won't know that until the second scan. Not until nineteen or twenty weeks, roughly."

He nodded, his eyes never leaving the monitor. Phoebe found herself staring too. *She said it looks the way it should,* she thought, *but it looks like nothing to me. Where's the baby?* She didn't say anything out loud, but the thought left her feeling strange. *I should just be feeling happy right now.* And she did; but the jumbled black and white on the monitor looked like nothing at all, and it scared her.

As though she read Phoebe's thoughts, the sonographer pointed at a black circle with a small white blob inside it, smiling.

"That's the baby," she said, "in case you couldn't make it out."

Maybe it's normal for first time mums to not see anything after all, she thought, a weak flash of relief pushing back some of the anxiety in her chest.

"How are you feeling?" the woman asked.

"Umm," Phoebe said, "good. Scared. Nervous, really."

"That's normal. But everything looks like it's developing normally."

Ben squeezed her hand, and warm comfort spread from him to her. *I don't even know why I'm so scared of this,* she thought, *everything is fine.* She was certainly not the first woman to be scared during pregnancy.

"You okay, babe?" Ben prompted.

He can always tell what I'm thinking.

"I'm fine," she said, "of course! I'm so excited."

And she was; but she was also scared. *So is Ben,* she thought, *he just hides it better.* But his smile was steady, his eyes warm, and her heart calmed again as they stared at each other. The quiet whoosh of the baby's heart beat played from the monitor, and Phoebe's fears disappeared.

She climbed off the bed, and the sonographer gave her a white towel to wipe off the gel. Ben tried to help her, but she waved him off. Instead, she wiped up as much of the gel as she could herself and set her clothes straight. Her stomach still felt a little sticky, and she promised herself she would shower as soon as they got home.

"What's the next step?" Ben said to the sonographer as Phoebe tugged on her jumper, "with you guys, I mean."

"Well, the next scan won't be until about twenty weeks. You can book in on your way out. Other than that, just stay happy and healthy."

Phoebe nodded, most of her anxiety draining out of her like she'd pulled the plug out of a bath tub. Going into the appointment, she'd known nothing bad would happen and that there'd be nothing wrong; but there was still a swell of relief now that it was done.

She couldn't have been more thankful for Ben; he was always thinking ahead, always planning the details that seemed to slip her mind lately. She shot him a loving glance. He returned it in kind. They thanked the woman, and left down the hallway. Phoebe headed down the corridor back the way they'd come in from. Ben kept pace beside her, his presence warm and comforting even when they weren't touching.

When they reached the front desk, Phoebe stood back and watched Ben make their next appointment. He stood with a calm confidence, and it was easy to see him as a father already. She smiled as she watched him interact with the young woman behind the counter. *He's always so nice,* she thought, *to everyone.*

In that moment, she saw why some people gave their children the same name as the father. She briefly considered naming the child Ben Junior, if it was a boy. *Ben would just laugh at that,* she thought, almost laughing herself. *No,* she thought, *not Ben. He can keep his name.*

She loved the idea of naming the child after someone, though; *I'll just have to think of a few potential people to name it after. I'll have to run it by Ben, too.*

"Alright babe, let's go," Ben said, "we're all booked in for the next appointment."

"You know I'll be just as nervous next time as I was this time, right?" she asked.

"Yeah," he laughed, shaking his head with a gentle smile, "I wouldn't have expected anything else."

28 November 2019 5:41pm (Thursday)

Brouwer handed her a folder as soon as she walked out of the interview room. She'd almost forgotten about the CCTV footage he promised her. *Hopefully this is more useful than Taylor was,* she thought.

His words stuck with her, and the sheer certainty with which he said them. *I'm from the future.* He'd been staring into her eyes when he said it, with no trace of mocking. She couldn't blame it on the alcohol, not this time. *Mental illness is still a strong possibility,* she thought, *but there's no way to tell without a full psychological analysis.* Phoebe had never heard of such a specific delusion before, paired with otherwise complete awareness of reality.

Sitting back at her desk, she opened the folder and pulled out a pile of A4 printed screen shots. They were grainy, barely discernible shots from down the road. *I can't even tell where Taylor is,* she thought. CCTV footage was always a gamble at best, unless a crime took place somewhere security was more full-on; she knew it, and she'd tried not to get her hopes up. But as soon as Brouwer gave her the folder, her excitement rose.

It took her a while, staring hard at the static-filled first page, before she finally made sense of it. When she flipped through the pictures, knowing what to look for, she could follow along with what was happening. *There's Taylor,* she thought, *and there's Jacob walking in from down the street. Does he talk to Jacob before shooting him?* None of the witness reports she'd read mentioned a conversation, but as far as she knew none of the witnesses saw anything before the first two shots were fired any way.

The footage should be in the system now, she thought, *I wonder if watching the video is easier than looking at stills.*

She could bring the screen shots home and look at them later; but the footage would stay at work. Opening the folder on her computer where it was uploaded, Phoebe clicked play.

Constable Brouwer, or whoever edited the footage, had placed a bookmark at the point that Jacob entered the park. There was no sound. A pixelated, grainy black and white copy of Alpha Park's entrance appeared, the trees flickering slightly as they moved faster than the camera could focus. Phoebe identified a dark shape as Taylor, standing still as the smaller shape of Jacob Turner shuddered towards him in the stop-start way CCTV footage played.

Taylor was already facing Turner. *Definitely premeditated,* she thought, *he even knew which direction Jacob would approach from.* He remained still until Jacob was close enough that there was no escape, then moved towards the child. Though he lurched and moved like a drunk—it was even obvious on the blurry CCTV footage— Taylor moved with purpose and conviction.

Two sudden flashes came from Taylor's outstretched hand, and suddenly Jacob was on the ground. Four more flashes, only just bright enough to see on the footage, appeared as Taylor stood over Jacob and fired into his body and head. He swayed, though Phoebe wasn't sure if that was just the natural static of the camera, and then threw up and fell over. If she hadn't known that's what happened, she wouldn't have recognised it in the footage; all she could say for certain just from the video was that he fell to the ground as suddenly as Jacob did.

A sickening flutter began in her stomach as she watched the footage again. By the time she arrived at the crime scene, Jacob was well and truly dead, but seeing him alive and moving in the seconds preceding his murder made her heart break all over again. She stared hard at the footage, forcing herself to watch it as Jacob died again, focusing as intently as she could on the moment Taylor passed out.

It's too blurry, she thought, *I can't see what's really happening.* The actual crime was clear as day; any jury would agree that the man in the footage shot Jacob. But there was no way to identify the shooter from so far away, and she couldn't see what happened to the gun. *Tonight is going to just be me staring at the screen shots,* she thought, *I know it.*

The footage went far enough that she saw the police show up. A few minutes later, she saw herself walk into the park entrance. Shortly after that, the video cut out. They had hours of footage leading up to the shooting; it might help to know which direction Taylor had come from, or if he'd spoken to anyone before the shooting. *I'll have to remember to get one of my team to go through all of that video,* she thought, *I doubt we'll find much, but at this point anything will help.*

28 November 2019 9:00pm (Thursday)

Phoebe sat at home, trying to focus on the case without thinking too much about the details. Despite the heat, a light rain pattered against her living room window. Heavy enough to make the air humid, but not heavy enough to give any relief. Phoebe's one-bedroom apartment had no study and was too small to fit a work table, so she sat on her lounge to work.

Copies of all the existing information on the murderer were piled on her lounge. It was a small pile. There were pictures and photocopies of everything found on his person, transcripts of the witness reports, screen shots of the CCTV footage, and the police photos of the crime scene.

The crime scene photos were face down at the bottom of the pile on her lounge; she didn't need to see them again. What interested her most at the moment were the witness reports.

Witness interview – Daniel Knight – Wed. 27 Nov 2019
Const. Wilks: Did you see the incident?
Knight: Yeah.
Const. Wilks: What happened?
Knight: The kid was walking up to the park, and the guy was already there. He was standing there waiting. He walked over before the kid got... Before he got to where the man was, and he just pulled out a gun and started shooting.
Const. Wilks: Did you see where the man was before the park?
Knight: No, I was walking down the street towards him and he was already there.

Const. Wilks: Did you see anyone else there before the police?

Knight: No, the police got there pretty fast.

Const. Wilks: There was no one there other than the victim and the shooter?

Knight: No.

There had been no weapon at the scene. No spent bullet casings. But there was also no one else present who could have taken them away before the police got there. What should have been a very straightforward—though terrible—crime, was quickly becoming far too mysterious for Phoebe's taste.

At the time he was found unconscious, the murderer was carrying a small set of keys, a mostly empty wallet, a black ball-point pen, and a piece of crumbled paper covered in crudely scrawled numbers. Photos of each sat balanced on her lap, along with photocopies of the contents of his wallet; a bus card, a library card, and five dollars in cash.

"Who has a library card?" She said.

Living alone meant she often spoke to herself. The tricky part was trying to remember not to talk randomly out loud when in company. It helped her sort through her thoughts, and focus on important things.

Other than his wallet, in his pockets he'd had about seven dollars in coins. Phoebe didn't know anyone else who carried so little on their person. Then again, she didn't know this guy either; yet.

"Who the fuck *are* you?"

No ID of any kind, other than the library card. Barely any cash, and no other clues. When the suspect was found still at the crime scene, everyone assumed it would be a straightforward case. The murderer was at the scene, witnesses saw the shooting. But she would have preferred the murderer fleeing, to be caught by solid police work, over this. It was an absolute headache.

Michael Lee Taylor had no criminal history. Phoebe had searched shortly after he'd given them the name. She'd checked all the usual avenues too; births deaths and marriages, electoral enrolment, vehicle registration. Now, she was entering Taylor's name into every social media platform she could think of. Facebook; nothing. Instagram; nothing. Twitter; nothing. She Googled his name; nothing.

Searching every variant of his name only returned strangers. Mike Taylor, Michael Lee, Lee Taylor, Mike Lee... she tried everything, staring closely at every profile picture for his face. He just didn't exist. She'd never seen anyone who had absolutely no social media presence.

He's either used an alias on social media since day one, she thought, *or deleted it, or just never bothered with it in the first place.* Both options sounded very odd to her. She knew a few people who used a fake name on Facebook, mostly to avoid stalkers or creepy colleagues, but no one who had absolutely no presence. He didn't have a mobile phone on him either, so they couldn't check his contact lists for family or friends to interview. Michael Lee Taylor could have been a fake name; but they'd taken his finger prints and photo upon taking him into custody, and no results came from searching their system. As far as she could tell, he simply didn't exist.

She read the other witness reports, trying to form her own image of the event. All the accounts were more or less identical, though some witnesses hadn't been looking until the shooting started; other than the lack of a weapon, it was very clear what had happened.

The security camera footage was unclear at best, and definitely couldn't be used to ID the suspect. But Jacob's face was relatively clear, and there was one screen shot that showed him approaching the park before he was killed. Despite the grainy quality and the distance, his innocent smile was clear as day.

Forcing herself back on track, she busied herself by reading all of the witness reports yet again. There were almost two dozen in total; it was a relatively busy area, right next to a shopping mall in the early afternoon.

Witness interview – Jake Hall – Wed. 27 Nov 2019

Const. Wilks: Tell me about what happened.

Hall: I didn't see much. I was walking the other way, and then I heard a bang, I turned around, and there was some dude shooting a kid on the ground. I didn't really believe it at first, y'know? Not until the police and the ambulance got there.

Const. Wilks: Did you see anything unusual after that?

Hall: What, like other than a kid getting shot?

Const. Wilks: Yes, other than the incident itself.

Hall: Not really, no. I guess... I mean, I was facing the sun, but I think I saw a flash of light just before the guy passed out. Didn't really look like a gunshot or whatever. Weird. Him passing out counts as unusual too, right?

Const. Wilks: I suppose so. Thank you for your cooperation.

Phoebe frowned, shuffling through the screenshots of security camera footage. They had the footage itself saved digitally, but for now she wanted to see if the screen shots captured a flash of light like the witness described. A few dozen screenshots had been printed, most of them looking more or less exactly the same. There was one good one before the shooting, and the rest showed Jacob on the floor and the shooter standing above him.

One screenshot showed Taylor doubled over and vomiting though it was very unclear, and then the next showed a blurry shape as he fell to the ground. The last two were Jacob's body and the killer lying next to each other. There was no gun in sight in either of them.

She looked back at the image of Taylor throwing up; the gun was in his hand. In the shot of him mid-fall, it was impossible to tell, but she thought she could see both his hands empty. It could have easily been an optical illusion or just her mind deciphering blurred images incorrectly. His arm was blurred, though; as if he'd swung it as he fell.

"It has to be nearby. He threw it. He must have."

None of the witnesses had seen anyone else nearby between the shooting and the police showing up; at least not that she'd read so far. Shuffling back to the witness reports, she scanned the rest of them.

Witness interview – Jessica Brown – Wed. 27 Nov 2019
Const. Wilks: Did you see what happened?

Brown: Yeah, I was sort of eyeing off the dude at the park already to be honest. He looked pretty dodgy even before he killed the kid.

Const. Wilks: Did you see where he came from?

Brown: Nah, he'd been there a while. One of the things I thought was dodgy about him.

Const. Wilks: Was he doing anything before the victim arrived?

Brown: Not that I could tell, just standing there looking around. He might've been talking to himself, but I was too far to hear anything.

Const. Wilks: Did you see anything suspicious after the incident?

Brown: I kinda turned away to be honest. As soon as I saw the first shot, it freaked me out too much. When he stopped shooting, I looked back. I think someone took a photo or something, there was a camera flash. Then he just threw up and passed out.

Const. Wilks: Thank you for your cooperation.

That's at least two witnesses who mentioned a flash, she thought. It could have been a camera flash; but Taylor had no device capable of taking photos on him, and no one else was close enough to cause a flash that other witnesses would see. *Even if it was a camera*, she thought, *why wouldn't the person who took the photo come forward?* The witnesses were listed by name and contact details in the case file. If she needed to speak to them again, she could. But what she really needed

74

was more proof. Actual evidence. *If someone took a photo, I need to see it.*

There was no gun. The witnesses seemed confused, the security footage was terrible and the lab hadn't come back with anything yet. He'd confessed, but was intoxicated when he gave it, and might possibly have been on other substances too. It would explain his erratic behaviour, and would go a long way towards soothing her disquiet about him.

The second confession was far more coherent, but just as unbelievable; it wouldn't help her case. There was still far too much they didn't know, and a lot of work ahead of them. Mostly, she just wanted the lab to return their results. It would at least give them something specific to focus on. She would get the rest of her team out investigating other areas too. If there was anything they could find, her team would find it.

Chapter Two: Complications

Her favourite coffee place was near the station. She usually parked at work early and walked to the cafe and back before her shift started. They would have to let Taylor free, until the court proceedings began; Phoebe wasn't thrilled about the idea. Even if he didn't want to kill anyone else, he was disturbed and unstable enough to be a danger. Now that he was sober and calm, and with no evidence, he'd be able to leave the station.

Someone shouted her name and she snapped out of her thoughts. Without realising, she'd reached the cafe and ordered her usual, and it was already ready. She took the cardboard cup with a blustered thanks and headed back towards work. By the time she walked through the station doors, she'd almost finished her coffee.

Logging in to her computer, Phoebe sipped the last of her coffee and threw the cup into the tiny recycling bin under her desk. There was still no new evidence or information, but she planned on going through everything once again. By the time the case was closed, every single detail of it would be burned into her brain forever; it was not a comforting thought.

"Sergeant," Constable Wilks said, "I've got some... upsetting news."

What now? She thought. *This case just keeps getting worse.*

"What's happened?"

"I think we should talk in the debriefing room."

Her heart sank. *What could be so bad that Justin can't even tell me with people around?* Anxiety threw her brain into overdrive, and a hundred horrible scenarios swept through her mind as her heartbeat sped up. Wilks led her to the debriefing room, and closed the door behind her when she entered.

"What's going on?" she asked, the question tumbling from her before she even thought the words.

"Before I say anything, we can still close this case. I'm not sure how to tell the Inspector, but I know he'll want us to finish it either way."

"Justin, what happened?"

He exhaled sharply, watching her as though he expected her to faint.

"Michael Lee Taylor is dead. It happened just now, just before you got here."

Phoebe's heart stopped cold for a painful moment. *He's dead?* They didn't even have all the evidence yet. He'd told them almost nothing. Now she'd never truly understand why he shot Jacob Turner. His two confusing confessions were all they would ever find out from him.

"I... I see."

They stared at each other for a moment; neither knowing what to say. Even if they gathered the evidence they needed and could prove Taylor's guilt without doubt, there would be no justice. They would be investigated by the Law Enforcement Conduct Commission, as all deaths in custody were. Although she had nothing to hide, it might distract from the case and slow her team's ability to find more evidence. Her only avenue now was to gather as much information as she could for the coronial brief of evidence they would be required to put together, and hope Inspector Rogers didn't shut them down too early.

"Report it to the coroner," she said, "and contact the morgue. I'll tell the Inspector."

She already had a meeting scheduled with Inspector Rogers that afternoon; she wanted to wait until then. It wasn't an option, of course, but she couldn't help wishing it was. *That conversation isn't going to go well,* Phoebe thought.

The forensic examination would be performed by a forensic pathologist at the Department of Forensic Medicine in Lidcombe. They were usually able to return basic results back to the police the day after they received the body. Though examinations were performed relatively quickly, a full report would take a while, and Phoebe had no doubt the coroner would order an inquest into Taylor's death. Inquests took longer, and Phoebe was not looking forward to it.

Something tells me there won't be any easy answers from the report or the inquest, she thought, *and we still don't even have the crime scene details back from the lab.*

Constable Wilks made to leave, but she stopped him.

"Wait," she said, "is there any indication of how he actually died?"

"None," Wilks said, "no obvious injuries, no signs of struggle. He was sitting up, eyes closed, like he just fell asleep."

It wasn't possible. Unless he had a fatal illness and went too long without treatment. But even then, he hadn't looked ill; other than being very severely intoxicated. Her mind conjured his haunted face, and something he said came back to her; *It doesn't matter anyway, there's no way I come out of this alive.*

"Tell the hospital to put a rush on the autopsy. I need to know how our only suspect died."

Phoebe rushed into the Inspector's office, barely registering the fact that she'd interrupted a meeting. Inspector Rogers, to his credit, kept patience as his sentence cut off abruptly.

"Sergeant Wilson," he said, "what is it?"

"Michael Lee Taylor, sir," she said, breathing heavily from her rush to his office, "he died in his cell. Barely an hour ago, from what we can tell. He was only just found."

Inspector Rogers stared at her, his face still a mask of controlled patience. Phoebe's breathing was back under control by the time he spoke again.

"Alright," he said, "thank you, Sergeant. An autopsy has been ordered, yes?"

"Yes, sir."

"Good, good. Prepare a statement to the media. As soon as we know how it happened, we can update our media team. For now, focus on the case as is."

She nodded, information and thoughts flooding her mind. Of all the things that could have happened, this was by far the biggest road block she could imagine.

29 November 2019 4:24pm (Friday)

Alpha Park loomed before her in the afternoon heat. The entrance had become something sinister, as though the echo of Jacob Turner's murder remained. Phoebe didn't believe in ghosts, but she felt something as she stood at the park's entrance that she'd never felt before.

She could see its beauty; visually, nothing had changed. But something lay underneath, like an inaudible whisper in the back of her head. Jacob's body flashed into her mind again, all bright red blood and twisted limbs. Taylor's cackling laugh surfaced from somewhere, and heat waves rising from the pavement made the ground spin in front of her.

Phoebe sent her team to look through the park, and she trusted them to find anything that could be found. She'd only returned for her own peace of mind; *I have to see for myself,* she thought, *I have to know for sure that there's nothing here.*

The afternoon sun beat down on her. Sweat trickled down her sides and back. Down the back of her neck. Looking at the park proper, she was struck by the uncomfortable sensation that she was looking at a painting. Somehow, it didn't feel real. All that did feel real was the shooting; Jacob's death, his body, the blood. Michael Lee Taylor laying unconscious right next to the child he killed.

If she hadn't seen the CCTV footage herself, she would have entertained the idea that Taylor had been framed. *Or covering for someone else*, she thought. Not only had she never seen a suspect passed out at the scene of such a violent crime before; she'd never heard of it in any other case.

"You came from the pub," she said, "but where before that? And where would you have gone if you hadn't passed out?"

Taking a deep, steadying breath, she headed into the actual park. *Was Taylor aware he would pass out? Or did he have an escape plan that didn't go through?* He clearly couldn't have driven anywhere; even a functional alcoholic wouldn't have been capable of driving with as much alcohol in their system as Taylor had.

"So," she muttered to herself, "you live nearby?"

Alpha Park was fairly large, surrounded on two sides by shopping centres and on the other two by homes. He wouldn't have dared commit a murder in a park right next to his own house; but there were endless residences within easy walking distance. She sighed as she walked through the trees.

"Couldn't you at least have *tried* to run, before you passed out? Taken a few steps towards home?"

If Taylor had at least been heading in the rough direction of his house, she could have a vague idea of where to start looking. But he didn't even take a single step after shooting Jacob. She would still organise a search, but it was unlikely they'd ever find his residence without more information.

Not knowing what to do, or what she was actually looking for, Phoebe wandered through the park. She knew what she wanted to find; the gun. But it couldn't be this far into the park. No one approached the scene after the shooting other than the police; she'd seen the CCTV footage herself.

She threw her hands up, glancing in every direction. She'd hoped physically being at the park would help somehow. Instead, she felt even further from the answers she needed.

"How did this happen?" she asked. "How are you getting away with this?"

At least the autopsy results will come in tomorrow, she thought, *there might be some information his corpse can tell us that he didn't.* Phoebe was still reeling from his death; it felt now as though none of her questions would be answered.

25 May 2008 10:21am (Sunday)

Heavy rain pattered against the bedroom window, and the cold outside threatened to invade. Phoebe felt the cold, a subtle aura that glowed from the glass, even as their heater fought it off. It was her idea of the perfect Sunday, though Ben would have preferred a hot summer day outside.

Despite the cold, they were naked, half covered by the sheets and thick blanket of their comfortable bed. Neither of them liked pyjamas, even in winter. Phoebe watched as thick raindrops splashed the window, and rivulets of water slid down the glass. They'd been silent for a while, comfortable in the aftermath of their lovemaking.

Though they hadn't spoken a word since moments before they made love, Phoebe knew they were thinking the same thing. *Names*. Some couples found baby names easily; for some it was a source of argument. Phoebe and Ben somehow found themselves in the limbo between both ends of the spectrum; though it caused no arguments or fighting, they simply couldn't agree on any names.

She ran her hands over his chest slowly, smiling as his muscles gently tensed at her touch. Tracing her fingers lower, she drank in his reactions, watching his face and listening to his breaths. He stirred as her fingers reached him, gentle and teasing, and he kissed her head and held her close.

"How do you feel about Matthew? If it's a boy." She asked, her fingers still running gently over him.

"I don't mind it," he said, his breathing a little jagged each time her hand changed direction, "it's a little generic though."

"Hmm. Patrick?"

"Too Irish," he laughed.

"Is that really such a terrible thing?"

"Only because neither of us is actually Irish."

His eyes gleamed as he said it. They seemed to sparkle when he joked, and Phoebe fell in love with him again every time she saw it.

"William?"

He paused; his eyes narrowed as he weighed the name by whatever criteria he'd been using.

"Not bad," he finally said, "Will. That's a maybe."

"Babe!" she said, almost squealing in her excitement, "we have our first maybe name!"

She planted rapid kisses on his shoulder and neck, up to his cheek. By the time she reached his lips he was ready, and kissed her back. Before their passion built too much again, she pulled back.

"What if it's a girl?"

Ben laughed, shaking his head. Though he was only mocking frustration, she could tell there was a tiny amount of real frustration under the surface. They'd never fought about names, but Phoebe had brought it up many times by now, and they never agreed.

"Babe, do we really need to be ready to go with names right now?"

As always, when he countered with a rhetorical question, Phoebe deflated a little. *It's like it won't feel real to him until there's a name,* she thought, *so he's avoiding it for as long as possible.* She nodded, unable to stop a disappointed frown.

"I guess not. I like Emma though, just so you know."

"Let's put that in the maybe pile too then," he smiled, kissing her forehead.

She knew he was just humouring her to avoid an argument, but she let it slide. *If I keep pushing,* she thought, *I'll just end up upsetting him.* Becoming parents was a big deal to both of them, and she didn't want to overwhelm him. Although he'd wanted it as much as she did by the time they decided to try, before that it took him a lot longer to decide he was ready to be a father. The idea that he might change his mind scared her more than even having the baby itself.

Phoebe's method of dealing with the stress and fear was analysing, planning and preparation. Ben's was dropping the stress under an avalanche of denial and charming smiles. Sometimes, his method worked so well that Phoebe found herself charmed out of her own stress; but more often than not it just piled on. *I'll be the one to decide on names,* she thought, *in the end he'll probably just agree to whatever I suggest. If I like the name enough, anyway.*

It was frustrating, but not enough to ruin her mood. Lying in bed with Ben on a cold, rainy Sunday was her idea of heaven. They settled into a comfortable silence again, and Phoebe resumed tracing her fingers over his body while she listened to the rain outside. Eventually, he spoke again, his voice gentle and loving.

"We've got a while to decide on names," he said, "how about we decide on the day it's born? Maybe when we see its face, we'll know what to call it."

She thought about it. The idea was romantic, and probably easier said than done. But they had a couple of maybe names, and that was good enough for her. *For now.*

"Okay," she said, "but I'm probably going to come up with a bunch more when we find out the sex, just so you know."

He laughed.

"So, we'll have a bigger maybe pile, then."

29 November 2019 5:56pm (Friday)

"... And in local news, the man who allegedly shot eleven-year-old Jacob Turner was found dead in police custody this afternoon. Sources indicate he remains unidentified, and the police investigation into the shooting will continue. So far, the police have not disclosed any more information about the shooter or the incident..."

29 November 2019 7:20pm (Friday)

"So... what, he just died?" Claire said, a bemused frown creasing her forehead as she took a sip of wine, "just like that?"

Phoebe nodded, took a sip herself, and then shook her head.

"I mean, we won't get the autopsy results until tomorrow, but as far as we can tell, there was no cause."

The sun still hadn't gone down, but despite the warmth, they sat outside on Phoebe's tiny balcony.

"I don't get it," Claire said, "you can't just *die*."

She leaned in close, an evil smirk twisting her lips.

"What if someone framed him, then snuck in and killed him so no one would find out?"

Phoebe shook her head again.

"It definitely wasn't murder."

"You said no one knows how it happened."

"You watch way too many serial killer movies." Phoebe said, laughing and taking another sip from her glass. "this isn't some convoluted murder conspiracy."

As she said it, the thought occurred to her that a murder conspiracy might be exactly what it was.

"Any way," she continued, "just because you're my best friend, it doesn't mean I'm going to tell you every little detail of my cases."

"Oh, come on Pheebs, we always talk about that stuff."

"This one's different," Phoebe said, "besides, it's been ages since I heard about your latest boy toy. Any more fun stories for me from the dating world?"

Claire laughed, snorting and almost tipping some of her wine out.

86

"You know, you could just date people yourself and make your own stories?"

"Sure, but then we'd have nothing to talk about except my boring cases."

"Ouch. My conversation isn't good enough without talking about the dumb guys I date?"

"You know your horror stories give me life," Phoebe said, "besides, hearing all this shit from you saves *me* from going through it. Why would I want to date after all the idiots you've told me about?"

"If you really don't know the answer to that," Claire said, "you haven't been listening to my stories."

Phoebe rolled her eyes, laughing as she stared into her wine glass. She couldn't stop her cheeks from burning into twin pink clouds; Claire's stories were often incredibly graphic. Phoebe didn't think of herself as a prude, but she'd always been uncomfortable talking about sex with anyone other than Ben. After being friends for most of their lives, Phoebe could at least listen to Claire's outrageous stories. But Claire still knew very little about her sex life.

"Oh, I've been listening," she said, "I'd still rather have nothing to do with the idiots you date."

"Who said anything about my idiots?" Claire said, "get your own idiots."

The idea of dating one of the same men Claire had dated made her shudder; most of her stories really were unappealing.

"Are there any men out there who *aren't* idiots?"

"Honestly, no. Some of them are great in bed though."

Phoebe laughed, and finished her wine. Claire finished hers off a few seconds later, and Phoebe went back into the apartment to get the bottle. From the fridge, she heard the sliding door open and close, then Claire sighed as she settled on the couch.

"Too hot out there," she yelled, "I'm gonna put a movie on."

By the time Phoebe brought the bottle down to the couch, Claire was scrolling through Netflix. She picked out a crime thriller, and Phoebe cleared her throat.

"I deal with enough of that at work. How about a comedy?"

"Oh, come on," Claire said, "you won't tell me anything interesting about your case, I need *some* kind of excitement."

"I've told you more than anyone is supposed to know."

"And I still don't know anything!"

"I don't know anything either; none of us do." Phoebe said, and ran her fingers through her hair. "I feel like I'm trying to solve a puzzle with most of the pieces missing."

"Alright, I get it Pheebs. We won't talk about it any more."

"Thanks."

Claire held the remote for a moment, staring at the TV screen with a frown.

"You're okay, aren't you Pheebs?" She said.

She sighed, closing her eyes. Sorting through the last couple days in her mind was a chore on its own.

"No," she said after another breath, "I don't think I am."

"Is the case really affecting you so badly?"

"Yeah. It's not just the case though." She looked at Claire briefly, then focused her eyes on the TV.

"Your grandfather?"

Phoebe nodded. She felt tears coming, and fought them back.

"He's not going well."

"When's the last time you saw him?"

Too long ago now, she thought.

"It's been... a little while."

"You should visit him, Pheebs."

Claire's grandparents had both passed away several years before. She had a habit of getting pushy with life advice; but in this case, it was understandable. If Claire's grandfather was still alive, Phoebe had no doubt she'd be visiting him as often as she could. All it did was make Phoebe feel more guilty.

"I know, I know. I'm just... scared. Last time I saw him, he didn't recognise me. He's getting worse every day. I don't know if I can deal with it."

She poured the last of the wine into their glasses. Her hands shook as she did it; she hoped Claire didn't notice.

12 July 2008 11:19am (Saturday)

Phoebe was in the kitchen, waiting for the kettle to boil for a cup of tea, when the baby kicked for the first time. For the last week or so, she'd felt small movements; but nothing she would have defined as a proper kick. Besides, none of the previous times had been big enough for Ben to feel. Now, the feeling was far stronger. She gave a gentle scream, and Ben came running.

"What's wrong?"

"Come here, now!"

He moved straight away, eyes wide with questioning fear.

"Put your hands on me," she said, her words barely a whisper, "there. Just wait."

"You felt it move?" he asked, staring at her belly.

She only nodded, waiting for another kick. Nothing happened for at least a few minutes; Ben shifted his stare from her belly to her eyes. Finally, she felt it nudge her again, and moved his hand to the spot. Another long moment passed, and then he felt it too.

"Holy shit."

He looked as excited as he did terrified. She laughed and kissed him. They stood together like that for a while, glancing at each other and smiling every time they felt a kick. The kettle boiled and cooled again, forgotten.

After the initial excitement of the baby kicking died down, Phoebe returned to the couch, clicking on the TV. It wasn't for another twenty minutes that she realised she hadn't actually made herself any tea.

"Babe!" she called.

Ben was working in his study. It was really a second bedroom, but before they'd planned on having kids, he turned it into a study for work, as well as a games room. He spent a fair amount of time in there, especially lately. *Trying to make the most out of it,* she thought, *before the baby comes and it goes back to being a bedroom.* They'd talked about it, and when the baby was born he planned on using a small chunk of the lounge room for his study.

"What's up, babe?" he called back.

"I need a cup of tea!"

"You know where the kettle is."

Phoebe groaned loud enough for Ben to hear, though it was mostly sarcastic.

"Babe, I'm gonna play the pregnant card."

She heard his laugh ring out from the study. *Ugh, his laugh is even hot when he's being a jerk,* she thought.

"Oh, come on," he called back, "isn't it a little early to play that card?"

"It's never too early. I'm pregnant, aren't I? One cup of tea, come on!"

Ben shuffled out of the short hallway, a sardonic smile painted on his face. He flicked the kettle on, saw that she'd already put a teabag in a mug, and leaned against the kitchen counter.

"So the rest of the pregnancy is going to be you just ordering me around, huh?"

"Well," she said, "I need to practice being a mum, right? That means I need some practice being in charge."

"Remind we why I agreed to this again?"

"Shut up."

Phoebe flicked through channels, smiling at Ben as she did. Part of the kitchen could be seen through an enclave where the breakfast bar was. He gazed at her, admiration and love making his face glow. Moments like these eased the stress of knowing she would be having a baby soon; Ben was always a soothing presence.

The kettle began rumbling, and Phoebe gently rubbed her belly as she waited. *Some chamomile tea will really help,* she thought, *I feel like I'm just constantly cramping.* She would've loved some pain meds or even some wine, but that wasn't an option. The advice differed depending on which doctor gave it, but Phoebe wasn't willing to take any chances. She avoided alcohol, medication, and all the foods she'd discovered were potentially damaging.

Tea was one of her only remaining vices, and even then, she had to stick to variants she knew had no caffeine in them. *Not like it's even a vice,* she thought, *I'm pretty sure it's good for me.* It certainly made her feel better.

She watched him carefully pour boiling water into the mug she'd prepared. He dipped the bag of tea in and out of the water, staring as he did. *He's always so focused,* she thought, *and so careful.* Even doing things that most people barely paid attention to, he seemed to take some kind of pleasure from being precise. Watching him give all of his attention to a mug of tea, all she could think was *I hope he approaches fatherhood the same way.* But even as she thought it, she knew he would.

30 November 2019 11:22am (Saturday)

It will be okay, she thought, *just get through it. He might even recognise you.* She stood outside the retirement home, on the pavement in front of her car. It was late morning, and the heat was already intense. Her heart beat quickly, hot air clawing at her lungs as she tried to prepare herself.

It will be okay.

The conversation she had with Claire the night before pushed her into visiting. She wanted to see him; but she wanted to see the *real* him, the man she'd grown up adoring. The man she would see today wouldn't know her; wouldn't *see* her. His mind was disappearing rapidly. It scared her more than anything.

"Damn it," she said, "it'll be okay. Just go in there and see him, say hello, smile and get through it."

She had the weekend off. *Not like it feels that way,* she thought, *this is stressing me out more than work.* The hardest part would be stopping the tears while she was with him; if she cried, it would just confuse and upset him. She had to be a positive presence, so that he'd be comfortable even if he didn't recognise her.

Maybe he will recognise me, she thought. But she pushed the idea away; getting her hopes up would only break her heart more. Taking three slow, deep breaths, she forced herself to walk into the building. The heat of the day melted under a forceful but quiet air conditioner above the entrance.

"Morning," the woman behind the desk said, "here to visit someone?"

Although she had kind eyes and a soft smile, the woman looked bored and distant. Her name tag said Sheryl. In her mid-forties at least, unfit, and probably not paid enough. *It wouldn't surprise me if she was working the day Grandpa escaped,* she thought.

"Yeah, my grandpa."

"What's his name?"

Phoebe had to clear her throat; tears were threatening already. *I'm not ready for this.*

"Charles Wilson."

The woman's eyes went wide for just a second, then she forced herself back into a placid expression. *I knew it.* Unlike her mother, Phoebe didn't blame anyone for the escape. *Lucky for you, Sheryl. If I was my mother, you'd be copping an earful right now.*

"Great, sign in with this form, and I'll give you a visitor's badge."

She had to write her name slowly to stop her hand from shaking. Her signature ended up a scribbled mess. Sheryl didn't check it when Phoebe handed it back to her. She didn't ask for Phoebe's ID, either. *They run a tight ship here,* she thought, and couldn't quite hold back a frustrated sigh as she walked past the desk.

"He's in room two seventeen," Sheryl said to Phoebe's back; her voice was as lazy and bored as her expression had been.

He won't know you, she told herself. *Be prepared, Phoebe, he won't remember you.* Tears started slipping down her face before she'd reached his room, and she palmed them off her cheeks impatiently. *Don't cry in front of him. Be happy and calm.* Her breath was ragged, shaking like her hands. The air conditioning made her sweat cold against her skin.

The door to his room was old, relatively clean but worn down. A vague, ominous aura spread from it; the way unknown adults were scary to a child. Completely the opposite to how she'd felt about him when she was little. She realised that she wasn't just upset about his declining health, or his mental state; Phoebe was actually scared of him. Not because he didn't recognise her, but because what was happening to his mind was ugly, and undignified. It was unfair.

She was scared because if it happened to him, it would probably happen to her too. The world would pull away, subtly at first, until it was mostly gone. She would be surrounded by family one day, then strangers the next. Simple things would become alien, and she would never understand what was happening to her.

In the centre of the door, the room number was chipped and faded. She wondered how many people had withered away in this room, fading and chipping down to nothing like the number on the door. Their decline couldn't be stopped, or avoided, or even treated. *Like death itself,* she thought.

In that moment, wishing she was anywhere else, she felt a stab of envy for Jacob Turner, and even for Michael Lee Taylor. They'd both died quickly, without warning. Without years of suffering and confusion.

As she reached for the door handle, breathing became more difficult. She wanted more than anything to see her grandfather the way he used to be. *I took him for granted when I was little,* she thought, *he was so... solid. Reliable.* He never seemed to age; until suddenly he did.

She turned the handle. Her heart stopped. She pushed the door open slowly, trying to control her breathing and her tears.

"Is that Michelle?" her grandfather asked.

His voice was weak. Phoebe entered the room proper, and saw him lying in bed. He was thin; painfully thin. His eyes were glassy and faded, and looked at her with no recognition. A vaguely friendly smile lay on his face, as though he was in the middle of a pleasant, meaningless dream.

Phoebe approached him slowly, smiling and trying not to cry.

"Hello, Michelle," he said.

"I'm not Michelle," Phoebe said, "I'm Phoebe."

"Oh, are you new here?"

He thinks I'm one of the carers. His smile, though tired and unknowing, was warm, and she saw a hint of the man he once was.

"I'm... no, I'm your granddaughter. Phoebe."

"Oh. Well, that's nice. How are you?"

"I'm okay."

She sat next to the bed; there was one small chair that she dragged over.

"I've been dealing with a lot at work."

"That sounds exciting. What do you do?"

"I'm a detective Sergeant with the New South Wales Police."

Her grandfather nodded politely, with the same vague smile.

"How lovely. You must be proud."

He was the one who convinced me I'd be a great detective, she thought. He used to read her Sherlock Holmes when she was younger, and she would constantly try to guess who'd committed the crime. The memories were only hers now; gone from his mind, his world.

"I am, Grandpa," she said.

"You know," he said, leaning close with a grin, "they have biscuits here. And tea. Would you like some?"

She smiled, unable to stop a tear from falling.

"That sounds lovely, thank you."

"I'll call someone in. I have a little button I can press."

He busied himself finding the remote on the other side of the bed, and spoke over his shoulder as he did.

"Now I'm sorry, but I can't remember; are you one of the neighbour's kids? Sandra and Peter, I think. They live next door, lovely couple."

"Grandpa, it's me, it's Phoebe. I'm Nicholas' daughter."

"Oh Nicholas! I have a son called Nicholas, he's a good boy."

"I know," she said, "he is. Are you enjoying it here?"

"Oh yes, it's quite nice, isn't it?"

"It certainly seems nice. I'm so glad you're happy."

"You're a lovely girl. Look at me, making new friends at my age!"

Phoebe laughed, then let out a choked sob.

"I'm sure you don't have any problems making friends."

"Oh yes, everyone here is very lovely. They take care of me very well."

He leaned in again, another grin lighting his face up just a little.

"I can call them in you know, for tea and things. Would you like some tea? They have biscuits too."

Chapter Three:
Reaching Out

02 December 2019 10:32am (Monday)

"I'm so sorry," the pathologist said, "we're still working on it. I've never seen anything like this. We'll have the results to you as soon as we can, but it'll be another day or two."

"Anything you can tell me now?" Phoebe said.

"At the moment, it's better to avoid speculation. I don't want to give you any information that may be wrong."

"I understand. Thanks for letting me know."

She hung up and scrunched her eyes shut. Nothing was going her way lately. *At least by Wednesday I'll have the autopsy* and *the lab results,* she thought. *I just need to wait until then.* She knew there wouldn't be any further information or evidence; it all came down to the lab.

Even the autopsy wouldn't actually help with the case. It was just standard procedure when a person died under unusual circumstances. *And I need to know how and why he died for myself, too.* If she couldn't solve the mystery of how he shot Jacob Turner with no gun or trace evidence, she would at least understand what killed him.

Some consolation prize, she thought, *but it'll have to do.* In the meantime, all she could do was wait. If she at least knew who he was, or anything about him, she'd have a starting point. But as far as Phoebe could tell, 'Michael Lee Taylor' had appeared from nowhere, killed a child, and then died without any obvious cause.

They had nothing on him. Absolutely nothing, but his face and the name he'd given them. Phoebe wouldn't assume his name was real; the way he'd said it during the interview wasn't exactly convincing.

His face. They had photos, at least. State Police didn't often communicate, but in situations that called for it, they shared files and evidence. *Why didn't I think of it before?* She thought. He had no ID, gave a most likely fake name, and no records or social media presence. His accent was definitely Australian, but Australia was a big place. *Maybe he's known in a different state. Even if we don't have his name, another police department might recognise him.*

"Wilks, Brouwer, Dennis," she said, "get Taylor's photo sent to every other department you can. See if he has a criminal history anywhere else."

They each nodded and set to work without a word, frowning at their screens. Satisfied that they would get it done, Phoebe turned her attention to the facts they currently had. She flipped her notebook open and wrote them down as a list:

-MLT seen at nearby pub before shooting
-Several witness statements
-CCTV footage of shooting (blurry, from a distance)
-Confession from MLT
-Belongings and crime scene evidence sent to lab
-Waiting on autopsy

It was everything they had. They had no actual physical proof, and depending on what came back from the lab, they still might never have any. She felt herself becoming obsessive, and didn't even try to stop it. *I have to know. I have to understand this case.*

Before Michael Lee Taylor, she'd worked on a seemingly endless string of thefts and similar crimes. A lot of thefts went unsolved, but Phoebe had begun to make a name for herself bringing the numbers up for Rosetown almost single-handedly.

Sighing, Phoebe stared hard at the list in front of her. Even the thefts that she couldn't solve bothered her; a mystery this infuriating was going to drive her insane. If he'd lived, she could have kept interviewing him, adding pressure as they found more evidence, until she finally understood.

I at least need to know who he is, she thought, *where he came from. And where that fucking gun went.* She sent an email to the Inspector requesting a meeting. His assistant Sarah would get back to Phoebe shortly; she always did. It was time to use the one thing she had against Michael Lee Taylor.

02 December 2019 11:45am (Monday)

Inspector Rogers was a practical man; his office was large, but mostly bare, and meticulously clean. His assistant's work area, just outside his office, was quite the opposite; though she was as dedicated and hard-working as her boss.

"Hi Sarah," Phoebe said, "Is Tim ready?"

"Sure is, Sergeant. He's got a meeting at twelve though, so it'll have to be quick if that's okay."

"Yeah, just a chat."

The Inspector wasn't sitting at his desk when she entered. He stood at the bookshelf that covered most of the far wall.

"Sergeant Wilson," he said, "what can I do for you?"

"Michael Lee Taylor," she said, "I'd like to spread his photo through the media."

"Is there a hotline set up yet? You know how many people call about these things."

"Not yet. I mentioned it to my team, but we've been chasing information. I'll get on it."

"What are you hoping to find by spreading his face around?"

"At this stage," Phoebe said, trying not to sound too frustrated, "anything. He gave us a name, but there's no trace of it online or in our files. I want to identify him properly, and then we might be able to get somewhere."

He stared at the books on the shelf in front of him for a moment. Phoebe could never tell if he was angry or upset; his tone was always neutral and he often let long silences drag out in conversation.

"If it means the case gets closed, you have my approval. Submit it in writing, and I'll have Sarah put you in touch with the policing media unit."

Phoebe thanked the Inspector and left his office, waving to Sarah as she passed. As soon as she reached her desk, she filled out the submission to gain approval for media release. Within five minutes of the meeting, she'd emailed it to Sarah for Inspector Rogers' signature.

"Guys," she said, waiting for her team's attention, "we're going to set up a hotline and send out photos of Taylor for media circulation. Simpson and Timms, I want you to liaise with Crime Stoppers and the Police Assistance Line. We don't know how many calls we'll get yet, but expect a lot."

Her team nodded; there was some grumbling, but they'd do what they were told. Crime Stoppers and PAL would take the vast majority of the calls, but anything important would be transferred to them. As well as that, all the information from the most likely helpful calls would be disseminated to her team to be followed up. Calls from the public weren't pleasant at the best of times, and she didn't envy them.

"Timms, get in contact with those teams, and set it up with them."

"On it, Sergeant."

It felt good to be doing something. Acting, instead of sitting around waiting for the lab. They still might get nowhere with it, but at least Phoebe and her team were moving forward. If anyone recognised him, they might be able to find out where he worked, or his address, or family members; at this stage, she would take anything that came their way.

18 July 2008 11:06am (Friday)

How has it already been twenty weeks? Phoebe thought. Her belly had grown a lot, and for the last little while she really felt pregnant. A heaviness sat in her belly, and her bladder was constantly under stress. As always since first finding out about the baby, she remained perpetually full of both fear and excitement.

Her second ultrasound was booked. They were on their way now; Ben drove, and Phoebe tried to relax in the passenger seat. For some reason, ultrasounds made her nervous. She knew there was nothing wrong, and they weren't exactly invasive.

"You okay?" Ben said.

"Yeah, yeah. Just nervous, I guess."

"You're always nervous about this stuff. It's weird." he laughed as he said the last two words.

"And you never are. *That's* weird."

"It's just a test, babe. It's not surgery or anything. We're just saying hi to the baby."

She knew he was just trying to make her smile. It almost worked, too. But she wouldn't relax until the baby was born healthy. *And even then,* she thought, *I'll just be stressed about raising it properly... and being a good mum.*

"As long as it's healthy, I'll be alright," she said.

"Of course it's healthy. Why wouldn't it be?"

"Can you stop acting like I'm crazy for being nervous, Ben? This is kind of a big deal."

He laughed again, shaking his head and glancing briefly at her.

"You're not crazy, Pheebs. I never said that."

It was a clear day, but on the cold side, and Phoebe wore three layers; she always felt cold. Ben wore a long sleeve

103

shirt; no jumper, no jacket. Not even a singlet underneath. He baffled her sometimes. Phoebe shivered just thinking about the gel they would spread over her stomach for the scan.

"We left the heater on, right?"

This time Ben's laugh rang out, loud and genuine, and Phoebe couldn't stop a small giggle of her own.

"You make it hard to say you're not crazy sometimes."

"If you were as cold as me, you'd be wondering the same thing."

"Yes," he said, humour still brightening his voice, "we left the heater on. When we get home, we can lay on the couch and bury you in blankets as well."

She knew it was stupid, but the idea brought an overwhelming wave of happiness pulsing through her. It almost outbalanced the anxiety swirling through her stomach at the prospect of her second ultrasound. She hadn't been overly hormonal during the pregnancy so far, at least not that she noticed; but lately anything nice that Ben did for her brought tears to her eyes and a swell of powerful love in her heart.

They arrived at the hospital, and a breeze blew past Phoebe as she opened the car door. Its cold somehow reached straight past her layers, grabbing her skin and sinking deep. Shivering, Phoebe walked as quickly as she could to the front doors. Ben's footsteps thumped into the concrete behind her as he raced to catch up.

"Remember," he said, "nothing to be nervous about. Just another check in with the baby."

Phoebe didn't answer. The cold, the nerves; her mind was too scattered. Another gust of wind slammed into her, and her shivering grew even more intense. Ben put his arm around her. The thought warmed her more than the actual embrace did, but she tried to control her shivering as they approached the doors.

They were led to the same room as last time. It was laid out the same way, all white and grey except the monitor. Phoebe sat on the medical bed, settling into a semi-comfortable position. It was almost the exact same experience as the first time, and Phoebe's head swirled; she knew it was just that she'd done it before, but somehow it felt unreal, like deja vu but in a dream.

"How've you been feeling?" the same woman asked as she rubbed cold gel onto Phoebe's stomach.

"Not too bad," Phoebe said, hearing the words come out of her mouth from a distance, "I'm just tired, and I need to pee all the time."

"If I had a dollar for every time I heard that in this room," she said, and then smiled at Phoebe, "it's perfectly normal, I promise."

The heartbeat sounded strong, even to Phoebe. Ben and the woman talked a bit, but their voices blurred into white noise which Phoebe barely heard. As she sat there, not hearing the two talk, it occurred to her that she couldn't remember the woman's name, or if she'd even introduced herself. *Maybe that's part of what people mean when they mention pregnancy brain*, she thought, *but I don't think I've been that bad.*

"Babe?"

Phoebe snapped back to the moment, glancing around the room as Ben laughed.

"Is that normal, too?" he asked the woman, "she's been doing that a lot."

"Oh yeah, it happens all the time. Pregnancy takes a lot out of a woman."

"Sorry," Phoebe said, "what were you talking about?"

"Well," Ben said, "Stephanie just asked if we'd like to know the sex of the baby."

A cold weight dropped into her stomach, and just like that the fog in her mind cleared. At the same time, her chest fluttered with pure, joyful excitement. Knowing the sex of the baby was always something she'd looked forward to, but now that it was right in front of her it felt too big, too real. *Our maybe pile is about to get cut in half,* she thought, *now we have to start thinking seriously about names, I guess.*

"Phoebe? Are we finding out the sex?"

Phoebe breathed deep, trying to clear her head. Her heart still thumped erratically, a tingling feeling spreading through her entire body as excitement took over.

"Yes," she said, "yes, let's find out."

The woman—*Stephanie*, Phoebe thought distantly—smiled and double checked the monitor, looking closely with a slight frown. Phoebe grabbed Ben's hand, squeezing with more strength than she meant to. *Why is she frowning? What's wrong?* Something bothered her, and she tried to force her fears down underneath the excitement.

"Okay," Stephanie said, "you ready to find out?"

Beyond words, Phoebe simply nodded. She'd stopped breathing. Ben brought her hand up to his mouth and kissed it, fixing her with a reassuring glance. There was no anxiety in his eyes.

"Yep," Ben said, "what are we having?"

"It's a boy," she said, "congratulations!"

02 December 2019 8:26pm (Monday)

At home again, Phoebe sat on the couch, trying not to look through the folder she'd kept on Taylor. The main menu of Netflix was running on her TV. She stared at it, not seeing any of the titles. *There's no new evidence since the last time I looked,* she told herself, *just watch TV and take your mind off it until we hear back from the lab.*

But she sat, staring, the remote forgotten next to her leg. The few tiny pieces of evidence she had were surrounded by a swirling, smoky void. They wouldn't leave her mind; they couldn't fit together. *His face will be all over the news soon. Someone will call, we'll find out who he is. Just watch TV. Unwind.*

Without checking what movie she'd selected, Phoebe pressed play. Then she opened the folder in her lap, and started reading again.

Her phone rang, and she almost spilled the folder off the couch.

"Fuck," she said; it was her mother.

"Hey mum."

"Hello, Phoebe. How are you?"

"Stressed. Exhausted."

"What are you up to now?"

Obsessing over an unsolvable child murder.

"Sitting at home," Phoebe said, "trying to relax."

"Well, that doesn't sound very stressful."

"I'm stressed from work, mum, it doesn't just go away as soon as I sit on the couch."

"But you are resting though, right? So you won't be stressed for long."

Dear God, she thought, *I don't think mum has ever been stressed in her life.*

107

"What's up, mum?"

"I just wanted to check in, see how you're doing."

Yeah, right. Her mother had not once called simply to check in; there was always an ulterior motive. Usually, it was to guilt her into doing something, or pressure her into an awkward family gathering.

"Well I'm getting there. Work is difficult at the moment."

"What about the weekend? Did you do much with your free time?"

"I visited Grandpa, actually," Phoebe said.

"Oh, I'm so glad to hear that! I know it's been a long time since you saw him. It would be nice if you saw him more often, darling."

So that's what it is. Visiting Grandpa. They'd already spoken several times about it, and lately her mother was becoming even more insistent.

"I visit when I can, mum," she said, "it's not always easy."

"I know Phoebe, but you have to make the time. For him. It's stressful for everyone, and we all have other things to worry about. But he needs his family."

He didn't even know who I was.

"He's being taken care of, mum. He's happy and comfortable. That's the best we can hope for."

"Darling, he may not... he doesn't have much time left. He needs us, he needs you. I'm sure he misses you, don't you miss him?"

She felt her heart speeding up, felt the tingling and pressure in her chest that meant a panic attack. *I don't need this kind of guilt right now.*

"Of course I miss him," she snapped, "every day. But don't tell me he misses me, or needs me. He has no idea who I am, mum. He thought I was one of the nurses. They're the ones he needs."

There was a brief moment when Phoebe thought she'd made her mother cry, but when her voice came back there was no hint of tears.

"You should still be there for him, Phoebe."

"I want to be, I do. But... I don't think I can."

Don't cry, she thought, *stay strong. She won't listen to you if you cave.*

"Why, because of your police work? You know I've been working too. We *have* to make the time."

His blank, friendly smile swam into her mind. She'd been a stranger to him. No one. Decades of love and laughter swept away, leaving her alone with the memories of who he used to be.

"It's not about the time, mum. I am busy, but that's not... it's too painful."

Her voice hitched on the last word, and she forced herself back under control.

"You think it's not painful for me?" her mother said, "he's my father-in-law, Phoebe. I've known him since before you were born, and he doesn't know me either. You'll just have to find a way to deal with it. For him."

Her chest buzzed, thumping painfully with her heart beat. *Just deal with it,* she thought, *like it's so easy.* Breathing was becoming difficult; she felt her lungs closing up, only taking in a fraction of what she needed. *I can't do this. I could barely unwind before mum called.* Pushing herself into Sergeant mode, she used her best police voice.

"I'll see what I can do."

She hung up the phone before her mother responded. Before she realised what she was doing, she opened a new bottle of wine and poured a large glass for herself.

03 December 2019 3:32pm (Tuesday)

The day dragged on. Phoebe spent it looking over the evidence yet again, and waiting for news that might help. *Not that I expect anything to help at this point,* she thought. Waiting was bad enough, but knowing anything useful was unlikely made it far worse.

Staying focused was becoming difficult; going so long without a win or any progress left her feeling like she was stumbling through a pitch-black room. The unanswered questions of the case stuck out like broken shards of glass, glittering dangerously in her mind.

Gathering them up and putting them back together wasn't just a desire; it was a *need.* Even if she cut herself to do it, even if it killed her, she had to answer the questions. *I need to understand.* If Taylor had confessed to it being a crime of passion, she might have been able to let it go. If Jacob was in the wrong place at the wrong time, just happened to walk by a mugging or a fight, maybe it would've made sense.

But it wasn't like that, and she knew it. From the few facts available to her, it was clear that Michael Lee Taylor intended to shoot and kill Jacob in advance. His confession might have come across as insanity, but he clearly believed that killing Jacob was his only choice. When he confessed the second time, he was sober and coherent. What he actually said was impossible, but the way he said it and his behaviour led her to believe he was in control of his mental faculties.

When Phoebe questioned him the first time, he was erratic and unstable. The second time, he was almost a different person. She'd never seen a mentally unstable violent person speak so rationally, and she'd watched hundreds of hours of police interview footage. If he was sane, she had to understand what was going on. And if he wasn't, she needed proof. *But that's almost impossible now.*

"Boss," Constable Dennis said, yanking her from the depths of her mind, "we've heard back from a few of the other departments. They're still looking, but so far nothing."

She sighed, nodding; it was pretty much what she'd expected.

"Keep me updated. Don't be shy about chasing them up."

"Will do, boss. I'll keep on them"

No interstate criminal history so far. It felt like she'd been waiting a month for the lab; they had to be almost done.

"Oh, and we're halfway through getting the phone line set up."

"Great," Phoebe said, "as soon as it's ready to go, I'll send out Taylor's photo to the media."

She was trying to keep her expectations low, especially about the hotline. If their witness statements were near useless, phone calls from random people would be even worse. People would be reporting their neighbours, acquaintances, and anyone they saw who even remotely resembled Michael Lee Taylor.

They would receive phone calls from people asking stupid questions about the case, double checking that he was really dead, and abusing the police for not working fast enough.

"Hey, Sarge?" Dennis said, "are we gonna be receiving transfers from Crime Stoppers and PAL? They have a habit of transferring anything they feel like not dealing with. It's already on the news, I think we're gonna be overrun pretty quickly as soon as there's a public number."

It was a good point. Phoebe was already expecting a lot of calls; the idea that she was underestimating the number they'd get wasn't out of the question.

"Check around the station," she said, "if anyone can spare people, get IT to connect them to our team's line."

Dennis left straight away. A quick glance around her team showed the same grim determination on every face. *They all know the next couple weeks are going to be brutal*, she thought. There was no way to know when things would calm down again; Taylor was dead, but the case was open and the mere presence of a public phone number guaranteed endless calls. Even after the case was eventually closed, they'd continue receiving phone calls until they shut down the link between them and Crime Stoppers.

I won't blame them, either, she thought, *I need to know what the hell's going on more than any of them.*

22 July 2008 10:13am (Tuesday)

A few days after her second ultrasound, Phoebe and Ben went to the doctor to discuss the results. Still, underneath her excitement, a low anxiety pulsed away in her stomach. *I'm not even here for a scan or anything,* she thought, *why am I always so nervous about this stuff?* Ben's presence was calm and reassuring, as always, and for that she was grateful.

They'd only dealt with the woman who performed the scan so far, but the appointment they were waiting for now was with Phoebe's GP. He called them in from the waiting room, and Phoebe fought to keep calm. Ben squeezed her hand as they stepped into the small doctor's office.

"Phoebe," Doctor Hatzis said, "how are you feeling?"

Phoebe glanced at Ben, and he smiled. *I would be lost without you,* she thought. His smile grew a little as though he knew exactly what she was thinking.

"A little nervous, but otherwise okay," she said, "the sonographer said everything is fine, that's right isn't it?"

"Well, let's take a look at the results, and I'll tell you."

Doctor Hatzis stared at his computer screen, clicking the mouse and frowning. Phoebe's anxiety peaked; *why is he frowning so much?* she thought, *it's supposed to all be fine.* She looked at Ben; as always, he looked unbothered. *I wish I could be as calm as he is, even just half the time.*

They sat in silence, Phoebe growing more and more nervous as Doctor Hatzis kept staring at his screen. She knew it was fine, deep down, but in that moment every possible worst-case scenario ran through her mind at the same time. *It's okay,* she forced herself to think, *the baby is fine.*

"Alright," Doctor Hatzis said, dragging the word out for way too long, "yes, yes. The baby is fine, it all looks fine."

"Are you sure?" Phoebe asked, squeezing Ben's hand hard, "you were really staring for a while."

"Just like to make sure," he said, finally looking directly at her, "it looks like the baby is developing normally. You can relax."

She nodded, breathing as slowly as she could.

"Really," the doctor said, "it's really fine. You can calm down now."

Ben drew her into a hug, and her heart started to slow down again. *My baby boy is going to be fine.* Every time she thought it, it felt that much more real. *I have a son.* She felt him growing, becoming a real person each day. Having Doctor Hatzis confirm the baby was fine drove the fear away. *Almost,* she thought; there would always be some fear.

After they left the doctor's office, Ben drove them home, and Phoebe stared out the car window.

"I'm glad to see you're feeling happier, babe," he said.

"What? Oh, yeah."

I didn't even realise I was smiling. She'd been thinking about her son, and trying to land on a name. *Obviously, it'll be a joint decision with Ben,* she thought, *but now we know the sex I can at least narrow things down a bit.*

"What are you thinking about?"

"Baby names."

Ben laughed and nodded.

"Yeah, I should've guessed. Any new ideas?"

She shook her head, frowning a little as she mentally scanned through their maybe pile.

"Mostly just thinking about the ones we already like. Do you have a favourite?"

"I like William. Or we could always just go with Ben Junior."

Phoebe shot a glance at him; a sarcastic smile lit his face.

"Oh my god babe," she said, an incredulous laugh almost overtaking her words, "I was thinking the same exact thing a while ago!"

"Why didn't you say anything? I would've said yes to that straight away."

She laughed, and he laughed with her. *I can't believe him sometimes,* she thought, *I really thought he would have laughed and said no way.*

"You're joking," she said, "right?"

"Well, kinda. It would be pretty great, I'm not gonna lie."

"Okay, well maybe it can be in the maybe pile."

His eyebrows shot up when she said it; a glow brightened his eyes. She couldn't tell if it was humour or excitement.

"Right at the bottom," she added.

Ben gave a long sigh, shaking his head slowly. Phoebe tried to hold in her laughter.

"Can't you just let me have this?" he said, "even just until he's actually born?"

"We're not naming him Ben, babe," she said, "I thought about it, but I don't think it would suit him."

"You realise that makes no sense, right? He's gonna be half Ben anyway."

He actually wants this. Phoebe stared at him as he drove them home. Sometimes, she couldn't tell when he was joking. He could be a little too hard to read; it really seemed like a joke at first, but now it felt like he was actually a little disappointed.

"Well by that logic," she said, "you should be named Eric Junior."

"Oh please," he said, rolling his eyes, "I don't think that would suit me at all."

She laughed again; she couldn't help it. Still, he went quiet after the joke, and she let the silence settle in for the last few minutes of the drive. Though they got along well whenever they saw each other, Ben and his father barely spoke. It upset him sometimes, but usually Ben was the first one to make a joke about it. *He doesn't look upset,* she thought, *but he's usually pretty closed off when it comes to his dad.*

They got home, and Phoebe went straight to the bedroom; lately she'd been spending as much time in pyjamas as humanly possible. She was getting bigger, and though it would have made sense to just wear comfortable clothes out in public, she couldn't bring herself to go out in her pyjamas.

Ben walked in after her, just as she stepped out of the pants she'd worn to the doctor's. He moved right up behind her and pulled her into an embrace. Leaning back against him, she closed her eyes.

"I love you," he said. His voice was quiet; not quite restrained, exactly, but something felt off.

"I love you too, Ben."

He squeezed her gently, then ran his hand over her belly. *Even when I'm huge, he makes me feel beautiful.*

"This is so nice," she said, "but can you let me get some pants on now?"

Chapter Four:
Progress

04 December 2019 9:10am (Wednesday)

Shortly after she arrived at the station, an email came through notifying her that the lab in Lidcombe had sent back the results. Almost an hour after the email, a courier arrived with the sealed parcel. Phoebe had to stop herself from snatching it off the man; she brought it back to her desk as fast as she could.

"Is that the Alpha Park evidence, boss?" Constable Brouwer asked.

Phoebe nodded, and the rest of her team gathered as she tore the seal and slid the contents onto her desk. Several folders were arranged by evidence type. She flipped straight to the chemical tests on his skin and clothing.

"There's... no trace," she said, "no trace of residue on his hands from firing a weapon."

Her team stood in silence. *It's not possible,* she thought. *It couldn't have been anyone else. He fired that gun. He shot Jacob Turner.*

"It doesn't make sense," Wilks said, echoing her thoughts, "no one else could have done it."

She kept flipping through the folders. It was even worse than she'd thought. *I was hoping for something, anything, that could help. Can't I just have one thing in this case that makes sense?*

"Okay guys," she said, "back to work. Let me go through this properly."

They left her to the folders. Chemical tests on Jacob's blood, Taylor's vomit, and samples from the crime scene all showed nothing out of the ordinary. Not surprisingly, Taylor's blood did show that he'd been heavily intoxicated; enough to cause alcohol poisoning, in fact. *It's a wonder he didn't die from that,* she thought, *but he'd mostly sobered up by the time he died.*

The forensic autopsy on Jacob Turner revealed the type of gun used to kill him, not that it helped Phoebe find it; a .44 revolver, the kind with a six-shot cylinder that only expelled spent rounds if you unlocked the chamber and tipped them out. *That explains the missing bullet casings,* she thought, *but not the missing gun.*

As frustrating as the missing gun was, the fact that the bullets existed and could be identified gave Phoebe a tiny glimpse of hope. *I was beginning to think this really was some kind of insane conspiracy.*

Even as a child, Phoebe loved mysteries and crime stories. Sherlock Holmes had been her first experience of mystery, and from then on, she was obsessed. She'd read some truly bizarre stories, fiction and non-fiction, but even the convoluted fictional mysteries she scoffed at didn't present unanswered questions like the ones she was dealing with now.

I suppose no matter how ridiculous those mysteries are, they're designed with a neat ending in mind, she thought. Unfortunately for her, real life didn't always pan out that way. The number of cold cases she'd studied throughout school were a testament to the fact that sometimes, there were no answers.

For a while in university, Phoebe had become drawn to reading about not just cold criminal cases, but unsolved mysteries in general. Even in Australia, there were some truly unbelievable cases. As horrifying as it was, Phoebe was beginning to suspect that the shooting of Jacob Turner would be counted among them. Even worse, her name would be attached; she was the detective Sergeant in charge, after all.

She wouldn't be fired for not conclusively solving such a mystery; it wouldn't even be a mark against her career. It would just bother her personally. She would always know that she'd failed to answer the questions raised by Michael Lee Taylor. The mystery would endure, and she would never fully understand what happened.

Her desk phone rang; *the front reception,* she thought as the caller ID appeared, *what now?* Putting the evidence folders away, she hurried to the lobby. Another courier stood near the desk, clutching a folder to his chest.

"Is that the Taylor autopsy report?"

He nodded, and practically shoved the folder at her face. Phoebe hadn't seen anyone look so nervous about delivering something before. *Bad news, I guess.* She was assuming as much; *every other aspect of the case is a mystery, so why should Taylor's death be any different?*

"Thanks," she said, "hopefully this will help our investigation."

Blushing, he fixed her with an apologetic stare that said *don't get your hopes up.* Before Phoebe could move, he was already halfway to the door. She shook her head, sighed, and went back to her desk.

"Autopsy results," she said to the team as she sat down.

She scanned the report as quickly as she could. *Damn it,* she thought as she read the words:

Manner of death: heart failure.

Cause of death: undetermined.

"Shit."

"What's up, Sarge?" Timms said.

"They didn't find a cause of death."

"Oh, come on!" Brouwer said.

"Yeah, you said it," Phoebe said, "this case is a complete disaster."

As her team kept talking, she read more of the report. *Spleen is abnormally large,* it said, *about 3 times normal size. Heavy congestion throughout most organs including the brain. No foreign substance found, though internal damage to organs is consistent with poisoning.*

Something about the report echoed in her mind, almost sparking a memory. *Have I read something like this before?* She thought. It would bother her until she remembered. But if the memory came, and if it was a recent case she'd worked on, it might help her make a connection.

Poisoned, she thought, *but with no trace of poisons in the blood. Massive spleen. I know this from somewhere. I've read it in a report, in a different case, I know I have.*

The frustrating thing was that it may not have been her own case; she'd read so many historic criminal cases, so many recent solved and unsolved Australian case files, that it could've been anything. It stuck out in her mind though, glowing and flickering like a neon sign, and she knew she wouldn't be able to let it go.

06 December 2019 4:03pm (Friday)

Two days after the autopsy and lab results came back, Phoebe was still no closer to answering any questions. She'd taken to patrolling the area around the park, looking for nothing specific but looking nonetheless. The phone line was up and constantly ringing, and Taylor's face appeared on the news several times a day.

There was nothing else left; no leads to follow, no contacts to interview, no forensics to lead them to the next clue. All she could do was wait for someone to hopefully recognise Michael Lee Taylor and call the hotline. The phones rang far more than they should have, and it didn't take long for the sound of ringing to push her into anxiety. *Why do Crime Stoppers bother taking calls if they just transfer to us most of the time anyway?*

Listening to half conversations was no better; her team kept repeating the same phrases.

"Could you describe him in detail?"

"Where and when did you see him?"

"We're doing everything we can."

"Thank you for your help."

"No, there is no reward for information."

She tried to tune it out, tried to focus on something positive, anything at all. Several times that day, she'd left the office to either sit in the break room, or walk slowly to the park and back. Her team remained at their desks, taking phone calls and working as hard as they could. *After this is all over, I'm taking them for dinner and drinks,* she thought. *If it's ever actually over.*

Sighing and rubbing her temples against the headache that threatened, she left her desk again, heading for the door outside.

"Wait, Sarge!" Timms said, the excitement in his voice stopping her cold.

He put the phone back to his ear, listening intently but staring at Phoebe with wide eyes.

"You definitely knew him? You're sure?"

Phoebe's heart stopped for what felt like an hour, then thudded painfully against her chest.

"Put them through to me," she said, rushing back to her desk.

Timms nodded, but kept listening to the person as they spoke. Phoebe's patience had disappeared; all her focus was on the phone call. *If they really did know Taylor,* she thought, *this is it. This is the lead that could close the case.* She tried not to get her hopes up, but it was too late.

"Timms," she said, "put them through."

He squinted through her words, hunching and pushing the phone hard into his ear.

"Okay," he said, "I understand it might be difficult, but you will need to come in to the station as soon as possible. Can I have your name and phone number please?"

Grabbing a pen, Timms scribbled quickly, checking the spelling and the number twice. Phoebe listened to the name, and watched Timms write it down. *Jessica Bloom.*

"Five minutes? Great, we'll see you soon. Ask for Sergeant Wilson when you get here."

Five minutes. The last few days had crawled by so slowly, and now she only had to wait five minutes for a potentially huge lead. *The next five minutes will probably feel even longer than all of today so far,* she thought.

The phones kept ringing, but Timms left his for a moment and stared hard at Phoebe.

"Sarge, you need to know something before she gets here," he said, "she told me she was Michael Lee Taylor's girlfriend."

Oh shit. All she could think of in that moment were the women who'd been in love with Ted Bundy; they either had no idea what he was doing, or point blank refused to believe it. *If she's anything like them,* she thought, *this is just another dead end.*

"We better hope she can give us something," she said.

The five minutes actually passed quite quickly; she had one of the interview rooms made ready, and by the time she'd mentally prepared herself for the woman's arrival, her desk phone rang.

"I have a woman here to see you, Sergeant," the Constable working reception said.

In a daze, Phoebe practically ran to the lobby. The young woman waited for her near the chairs against the wall. She wasn't seated, just standing close as though she was too nervous to sit down. The lobby was almost full of people, but Phoebe spotted Taylor's girlfriend at a glance. She had the same haunted look in her eyes that Taylor himself did during his interview.

"Miss Bloom?" Phoebe said.

"Are you Sergeant Wilson?" she asked.

Phoebe nodded.

"I'm Detective Sergeant Phoebe Wilson, yes. Please come with me, we'll have a chat somewhere more private."

She led the girl to the same room where she'd interviewed Taylor. They sat opposite each other, with Jessica sitting in the same chair her boyfriend had not long ago.

"Okay, Miss Bloom," Phoebe said, trying to make her voice as gentle as possible, "I need you to tell me everything you know about Michael Lee Taylor."

Silence fell over them, and Phoebe watched the girl think about how to start talking.

"We met about a year ago," she said, "at the... at the park."

"Alpha Park?"

She swallowed, her face turning white.

"Yeah. He was so lovely, he was bird watching, and we just hit it off."

"He was bird watching? Like with binoculars?"

"Um, yeah."

"What did you two do together?"

"Well, um..." Jessica blushed, avoiding eye contact.

123

"Besides that."

Her eyes never left the table in front of her.

"We just hung out. Watched TV, ordered in. He's not really... He *wasn't* really the going out type."

"Where did he live?" Phoebe asked.

Please have an address, she thought.

"We only ever hung out at my place."

Shit.

"Did you go out at all? Even once?"

"A couple times, we hung out in the park. He said he liked it there."

"Did he mention any friends or family?"

She shook her head, her face still ghostly pale. Phoebe couldn't imagine how it felt to be her. *All these red flags that went unnoticed. She must feel like an idiot for not seeing anything strange.* It meant he'd been hiding himself from her. For a whole year. He couldn't possibly have been insane; the level of deception and control it took to keep up appearances for a girlfriend over that amount of time meant he was definitely, fully aware of what he was doing.

"Do you know if he had a job?"

"He never mentioned it."

Phoebe frowned.

"And you didn't think that was strange?"

"I don't... We never talked about it. I guess I just assumed he did or something. Or maybe that he lived with his parents, and he was too embarrassed to say."

She did half the work herself, Phoebe thought, *he wouldn't have had to try hard to fool her.*

"Did he behave strangely at any time?" she asked, "especially in the last few weeks?"

"Well, he was drinking a lot more than normal," Jessica said, "and he was a bit moody. But other than that, he was always a great guy to me."

"Did you ever see him with a weapon? Or acting violently in any way?"

"No! God, no. He was so tender. Even, um... you know."

"Even in the bedroom?"

She nodded, her lips drawn to a thin line. She looked as though she was about to faint. *I'd feel the same way if I found out I'd been dating a murderer,* Phoebe thought.

"Did he ever say anything strange, or anything that made you uncomfortable?"

"No."

Phoebe watched her think. Her eyes narrowed, mouth still pressed tight.

"Actually..."

Phoebe let the silence stretch a little, looking directly into Jessica's eyes.

"About a month ago," Jessica finally said, "we were hanging out, watching a movie, and he said something like 'I'm glad it wasn't you'. He started crying, and he said something about how he was sorry that it wouldn't last, and that he hoped I could forgive him for being a monster."

"Did he say anything more specific?"

"No, he shut up after that and wouldn't talk. He never mentioned it again. It scared the hell out of me. Now I finally know what he was talking about. He'd already planned to shoot that kid."

25 July 2008 2:08pm (Friday)

A full week after her second ultrasound, Phoebe was finally feeling less anxious about the pregnancy. She'd read about a thousand books, and talked to as many people as she could. Ben was as calm and collected as ever. He converted his study into the baby's bedroom, just like they planned.

They still didn't have a name; both agreed on waiting until after he was born to decide what his name would be. Names were always on her mind, though. Every name she heard lit up in her mind like a buzzing neon sign; *Mason? Michael? Frank? Bruce?* It seemed like she heard a hundred boy's names every day.

Phoebe had been on maternity leave for a little while now; she wanted to start early, and a heavily pregnant police Constable wasn't exactly an efficient police Constable anyway. It was her own choice, but the station had been supportive. Her boss even sounded quite relieved when she suggested it.

She was a little nervous about going back to work after the baby, but that was future Phoebe's problem. *I need to focus on the baby for now,* she thought, *nothing else.* Ben worked from home most of the time, so he would be around as well, but she was always going to take at least some time off from work.

It was just past two o'clock on a cold Friday afternoon when the first cramp hit Phoebe. She was on the couch, watching TV and absently running her hand over her belly when a sudden, blinding pain sliced into her. At first, she couldn't make a sound, not even to breathe. Leaning forward, eyes screwed shut, she tried to break through the pain just enough to take in some air.

Ben, she thought, *I need Ben.* He was in the baby's room, cleaning or putting things away. She couldn't get any words out; when she tried, all that escaped her was a low wheezing sound. The baby kicked, over and over, and she finally drew in enough air to scream.

Ben came rushing down the hallway, eyes wide and face pale. He ran to her, dropping to his knees on the floor in front of her.

"What's happening?" he said, placing his hands gently on her shoulder and knee, "what's wrong, babe?"

"I—" she started, before another cramp choked the words away.

He rubbed her back, staring with a fear in his eyes that terrified her more than the pain itself. *He's really scared,* her racing mind said, *that's not good. He's never scared.*

"Should we go to the hospital?" Ben asked, panic breaking his usually smooth voice.

Phoebe shook her head, moaned through another cramp, and grabbed his hand. *It'll pass,* she thought, trying to say it out loud and failing, *it's just the baby kicking really hard.* She wasn't convinced that was true, but her desperate hope that it was kept her mind off any other possible cause.

Ben rushed off to the kitchen, and Phoebe breathed as the latest cramp died down. She heard the kettle rumbling, and could only think *this is hardly the time for tea. I won't even be able to hold a mug.* A few minutes later, the cramps seemed to have stopped, and Ben returned from the kitchen holding a hot water bottle. She giggled, and Ben stared at her with an eyebrow raised.

"I thought you were making tea," she said.

"This isn't really a good time for tea," he said, a low chuckle cutting the panic from his voice.

"That's what I thought."

And all at once, the panic passed. She was still anxious about feeling that much pain during a pregnancy, but she'd heard of cramps and other soreness being quite common, and she was determined not to worry too much. Ben sat next to her and put the hot water bottle against her lower back, and gently rubbed her belly as she settled back into the couch.

For a little while after that, the baby kept kicking. Every now and then Phoebe let out a little groan or a sigh, and Ben reacted when he felt it too. Eventually, the kicking stopped, and they watched TV while Phoebe tried not to think of the worst-case scenarios. *It's a healthy baby,* she thought, *Doctor Hatzis and the sonographer both promised.*

Ben went straight back to being his usual calm self, and Phoebe tried to soak up some of his confidence. She held him close, and he squeezed her hand and kissed her nose.

"It's going to be okay," he said.

I swear, sometimes he can read my mind.

"I know," she said, though they both knew she was lying.

"Are you sure you don't want to go to the hospital, though?" Ben asked, "just to make absolutely sure there's nothing wrong?"

"I feel fine now. I really think it would just make me anxious right now. Maybe tomorrow, or after the weekend, or something."

He nodded, his hand still tracing gentle circles over her belly. A part of her wanted to go and get checked out; but it was a small part. The rest of her was simply too scared. *If we get it checked out and there's a serious problem, it'll break my heart,* she thought. Knowing was better than not knowing, but Phoebe's mind wasn't being run by rational thinking. Ben would have pushed harder, but he knew the state she was in, and he'd never been one to push for anything she didn't want.

For the rest of that day, they stayed on the couch. Ben had work to do, but he always knew when she needed him and he was always there when she did. He ended up making tea after all, and she laughed when he walked in with two of their biggest mugs. *He only drinks tea with me when he knows I'm really upset.* He was a coffee fiend, and she'd never seen him drink tea outside of when he made some for her when she was down. Somehow, that small gesture made the tea taste better than anything she'd ever had before.

They watched TV together, and Ben held her until she finished the tea. Then he brought the mugs back to the kitchen sink, returned to the couch, and held her even tighter. Phoebe stopped hearing the dialogue on the TV, content with letting her mind wander and feeling Ben's soothing presence.

I don't know how he does this, she thought, *but he always calms me down.* The cramps and the panic that followed felt like a previous day's problems as Ben kissed her and held her close. By the time she was tired enough for bed, she'd almost forgotten about them. She drifted into sleep thinking about what a great father Ben would make.

07 December 2019 6:30pm (Saturday)

"She had no idea," Phoebe said, "no idea what he did, until she saw his face on the news."

"That's rough," Claire said.

"She couldn't give us anything useful. I need to speak with her again. Maybe she knows something, but doesn't *know* she knows it."

"Pheebs, listen to yourself. You're diving too deep. Leave the poor girl alone."

She doesn't understand, Phoebe thought, *she works at a clothing store; her worst day at work is some idiot making a scene over the price of pants.*

"I need to close the case, Claire," she said, "I can't leave it open."

"Sure, work the case. But don't push that girl any more than you have. She's grieving, and she just found out her dead boyfriend was a murderer. Leave her out of it."

"She's the only lead we've had. The only one. Forensics and the autopsy gave us *nothing*."

"That can't be true. Maybe there's something there, but no one's made a connection?"

Phoebe sighed. She almost snapped, almost lost her cool. Instead, she took a long sip of wine. *I've looked at every detail a thousand times*, she thought, *if there was something to see I would have seen it*. As much as they'd spoken together about Phoebe's cases, Claire still had no idea what was involved in the work.

"Trust me, Claire," she said, "there's nothing. I've looked at it all, again and again. It's all I can do."

She emptied her glass, and got up to refill. They'd only just opened a new bottle, and Phoebe brought it down to the couch with them. *It won't last long*, she thought, *I could use a whole bottle myself.*

"Hey, Pheebs?" Claire said.

"Hm?" She filled her glass as much as possible.

"Are you... seeing anyone?"

Ugh, not this again.

"I told you I'm not interested in dating anyone right now, Claire."

"No, I meant, well… professionally. A psych?"

"You think I need help?"

"Well, your job is intense. Look, I'm not trying to offend you, but that kind of stress can be really dangerous. It's obviously affecting you."

I can't believe this. My best friend thinks I'm losing it. If anything, Phoebe was the only one who took the case seriously enough. *And Inspector Rogers.* If not for him, the case would've been shelved by now. If Taylor was still alive, everyone would see it the way Phoebe did; it seemed insane to her that the shooter's death made everyone stop caring about the fact that it was still unsolved. *There are so many unanswered questions*, she thought, *he may not even be the shooter at all.*

"Can you at least think about it, please? For me?"

"Claire, I'm fine. I just need to solve it, and then things will go back to normal. I just need answers."

Claire looked at her as though she was lying in a hospital bed. A deep sadness made her eyes shine. It scared Phoebe; she'd never been looked at that way before. *Am I really spiraling so badly?* She thought. *I don't feel any different. Stressed, sure, but no more than usual.* Police work was never easy. But the way Claire looked at her then was alien; unlike anything she'd felt before.

Her best friend shuffled uncomfortably, still staring at her in that strange, sad way.

"And what if you never get any answers?"

12 December 2019 10:08am (Thursday)

"We've still only had one genuine call so far," Phoebe said, "from the shooter's girlfriend. She didn't know much, but I'm sure it'll lead somewhere."

Inspector Rogers nodded slowly, his normally friendly face punctuated by an intense, cold stare.

"Keep the phone lines up for now then," he said, "but we're reaching the end of our resources, Sergeant. Every day that passes costs us, and I haven't seen any progress."

"I promise, I will close this case," Phoebe said, "I just need time. There's more to this than we thought."

"It seems pretty simple to me, Sergeant. Sometimes the evidence is a little misleading, but that doesn't mean the simplest explanation doesn't apply."

"With all due respect, sir," Phoebe said, "the evidence isn't misleading. It's non-existent. If there's absolutely nothing to tie the dead man to the shooting except his confession, there may be something else at play."

"I'll give you another week. If nothing comes to light, the case is closed and I'm putting your team on cases we can actually solve."

"Thank you, sir."

She forced the anger from her voice, but couldn't keep it from bubbling in her chest as she walked back to her desk. The last time they hung out, Claire had asked her what she'd do if there were no answers. She didn't have an answer, but it looked as though she'd find out soon enough.

It's done, she thought, *I haven't found anything so far, why would the next week be any different?* Despite the looming certainty of failure, Phoebe couldn't shake her need to solve the case. *This must be how detectives felt who worked on the cold cases I've read. I wonder if they ever really moved on.*

After she sat back at her desk, she opened the case file and pulled Taylor's evidence folders from her drawer; it was an unconscious habit now. Looking through the evidence, re-reading the reports, she'd stopped absorbing the information a while ago. The sound of the phones ringing and her team speaking buzzed in the background.

Maybe it's true, she thought, *fuck it. Maybe he is a time traveller. It makes more sense than anything else at this point.* She couldn't accept that; not without proof. *I feel ridiculous for even thinking about it.*

"Boss," Brouwer said, "We've got another one on the phone."

She slammed the folder on the desk, her heart thudding hard and fast.

"Put them through to me. Now."

Her phone rang a moment later, and she picked it up before the first ring ended. A click and a beep followed, and then she heard breathing.

"Hello," she said, "this is Detective Sergeant Phoebe Wilson. Who am I speaking with?"

"My name's Dan Morris. I recognised Michael on the news."

"How do you know him?"

"He's one of my tenants."

Her breath caught in her throat. *Taylor's landlord... We have an address!* She tried to start breathing normally again, but her lungs hitched. *It's almost too good to be true.*

"What's his address?"

She wrote it down, double checked it, and took his contact details as well.

"Will you come in to the station and give a statement about Michael Lee Taylor?"

"Okay," he said, "but I didn't know him personally."

"But you have his renting history, identification documents, credit card, things like that? All of that can be very useful to a police investigation."

A few seconds of silence followed, stretching into what felt like hours. Only the faint buzzing static of a bad phone line broke it. Phoebe still couldn't breathe properly; *so close,* she thought, *this could be all it takes.*

"Well, look, I hope I don't get in trouble for this," he said, "but no, I don't have any of that stuff."

Phoebe almost threw up as a surge of disbelieving rage slammed into her chest and stomach.

"Why not?"

"He, uh, paid in cash. A *lot* of cash."

Shit. Of course he did.

"Do you have anything? *Any* information about him?"

"I'll take a look around," he said, "I haven't been to his apartment since the news. I didn't know if I'd be allowed to."

"Leave his apartment alone," Phoebe said, almost shouting, "we're going to check it as soon as we can. It's a possible crime scene, don't even go near it."

She ended the call and sprinted to Inspector Rogers' office. Sarah tried to wave her away, but Phoebe knocked on the door. Muffled voices in the room suddenly stopped, and she heard Inspector Rogers call out.

"Come in."

He was sitting with one of the other Sergeants. Phoebe nodded to him, then addressed the Inspector. *No time for pleasantries.*

"Sir, we have Michael Lee Taylor's address."

His brows raised, the expression of pleasant surprise making his friendly face even friendlier.

"Good news," he said, "get a couple of your Constables together and check it out."

12 December 2019 11:02am (Thursday)

At university, Phoebe studied crime, and took a particular interest in serial killers and mass shootings. After researching countless planned shootings and their aftermath, Phoebe wasn't looking forward to seeing whatever they'd find at the apartment.

Taylor's apartment was smaller than Phoebe's, and a great deal shabbier, in a part of Rosetown reserved for Government Housing. She'd been there many times before. Usually domestic dispute calls, often drug related offences. Michael Lee Taylor certainly wouldn't be the only tenant paying cash and keeping their identity secret.

A sense of dread had settled deep in her gut by the time they'd approached his door. There were three of them; Phoebe, Brouwer, and Simpson. Taylor's keys sat in her hand, feeling heavy and dangerous.

"Okay."

She wasn't speaking to the men with her, but they nodded to show their support.

"Alright. Careful in here, okay?"

They nodded again.

"Check everything, don't step anywhere unless you can see the floor. Don't touch anything unless you can see it's safe. We don't know what this guy might have set up in here."

She counted down from three in her mind, breathed deep, then gave the signal. Simpson and Brouwer brought their guns up. Taylor hadn't given any indication of involvement from other people, and there was no evidence to suggest this was anything other than a one-off attack; but they couldn't be too careful.

Taylor's keyring only had four keys on it; she'd identified three as being standard with any apartment lease. One for the windows, one for the mailbox, and one for the front door, which she slid into the lock. The last key was a mystery so far.

His apartment was bunched tightly into a group of six or so, tiny places that were probably far more expensive than they had any right to be. The entrance space was a cramped corridor with a built-in kitchenette. Beyond that, a filthy little room waited for them to enter. Just as she feared, she could smell it from the doorway.

They moved into the apartment, single file in the tiny space. One floor length window covered most of the left wall, a thick curtain closed over it. The darkness was stifling. Simpson pulled it open, slowly, as Brouwer and Phoebe covered the room.

As sunlight flooded the space, she understood why Taylor had elected to keep the curtains closed. In broad daylight, it was revolting. *How could someone live like this?*

A futon squatted in the centre of the room, lumpy and torn. Paper plates and plastic cutlery were heaped randomly on the floor. They were covered in half eaten food, and more food was scattered on the carpet itself, rotting before their eyes.

Empty bottles of cheap whiskey lay wherever he'd thrown them after drinking, some broken and one completely shattered. The carpet glittered in places like it was pretending to be clean.

The window doubled as a sliding door, and beyond it was a walled courtyard even smaller than the living room. A large tree overhung the space, dead leaves dropped from its branches forming a decaying mountain in the courtyard's centre. A few old moving boxes were piled against one of the brick walls, water stained and covered in flies.

Other than the futon, there was no furniture. A cupboard built into the wall stood slightly ajar. A stained pile of pale blue bed sheets spilled out at the bottom.

Another door stood in the corner of the room, next to the entrance through which they'd come. Phoebe stepped gingerly over the stains in the carpet, glancing at everything and trying not to breathe.

It was a bathroom, just as filthy as the living room. A beat-up washing machine sat on one side, and a muck-encrusted toilet on the other. The shower stood in the far corner. At the top of the back wall, next to the shower, a tiny window dragged in a pathetic beam of sunlight. There was no glass, just a torn sheet of fly screen.

"Clear," she called to the others.

No accomplices, no booby traps, no other dead bodies. Yet. They still didn't have enough to convict him without the murder weapon. There had to be something here that would incriminate him. But other than the filth, there was nothing. No computer, no phone. He hadn't been in possession of a phone when arrested, either. And there was no charger in the apartment.

She moved to the cupboard, not particularly wanting to explore further. But she had to be thorough; if she missed something serious just because she was a little grossed out, she'd never live it down.

There were clothes piled on the shelves. She couldn't tell if they were clean or dirty, but she wouldn't be willing to bet they were clean. A few books were strewn about one of the shelves. Other than that, there was only the pile of bed sheets at the bottom.

Paying a little more attention, she realised all his clothing was the same. Not that there was much of it. Three identical shirts, four pairs of identical underwear and socks, and a pair of pants which looked to be the same design he was wearing at the station. The shirts matched the one he was wearing when he'd been arrested too.

Constable Brouwer took photos, the flash of his camera pulsing in the corner of her eyes. She called him over to take photos of the cupboard's contents so she could move them; they had to make absolutely sure he wasn't hiding anything.

He moved off to the bathroom. She snapped on a pair of forensic gloves with a rush of relief, and went through the cupboard properly. The clothes weren't covering anything up.

There were four books. Among them was a battered, old journal. Breath caught in her throat, she reached straight for it. It was thick, and used, and a faded label was printed on the front:

2017 DIARY

Forcing herself to breathe, she opened the journal and began to read. She scanned through the first page, then picked out two random pages further in; she knew she'd have to read the whole thing later anyway.

As far as journals went, it was fascinating, but absolute nonsense. For one thing, none of it could even slightly be used as evidence in court. For another, it didn't help to establish his movements leading up to the crime.

The only thing it did do was solidify the theory that he was insane. Other than that, it just raised more questions. Where had he been before 2017? Where were his friends and family? With no social media, or any other means of determining his movements, he may as well have been a ghost.

She could readily believe he had no friends, but she was less convinced he had no family. They likely wouldn't live in Sydney; if they did, he probably would have been staying with them. But with some digging, she'd find them. She called for Simpson and Brouwer to pack up and get ready to leave; the journal was as useful as this place was going to be.

27 July 2008 4:12pm (Sunday)

Ben's keyboard clicked away in the corner of the room. Phoebe still heard it through the headphones she'd started using, though she didn't mind. He offered to buy her noise cancelling headphones, but the sound of him working somehow soothed her.

Claire had laughed when she found out Ben's study would be moved to the lounge room. She was convinced that Phoebe and Ben would grow to argue constantly. *I can't wait to tell her how wrong she is,* Phoebe thought. Ben and Phoebe made the perfect team, and spending most of their time together didn't change a thing.

Once the baby was born, it was going to be more difficult to maintain the same level of calm; but they were both as prepared for that as they could be. Ben's patience was almost limitless, and Phoebe had read as many books and done as much research as she could.

Phoebe went to the kitchen, cradling her belly as she flicked the kettle on. She glanced at Ben through the kitchen enclave, smiling as he frowned at his screen and tapped away at the keyboard. She loved seeing him in the zone; he was focused, passionate, and hard-working. It was incredible to watch. She loved his books; his creative talent was one of the things that drew her to him in the first place.

As much as she loved his focus, a small part of her was worried that the baby would take too much time away from his writing. She would hate to feel like their relationship and the baby were stopping him from what made him happy. When she started going back to work, most of the responsibility would be on his shoulders. He was confident he could handle it, but she knew how much things could change after a baby.

The kettle rumbled and the switch flicked off. Phoebe took out a mug and a teabag and watched the boiling water swirl with dark colour. She stood at the kitchen bench for a little while, taking in the smell of brewing tea. Her hand rested on her belly, and it occurred to her that she hadn't felt the baby kick in a while.

Two days had passed since the cramps. *It's strange the baby hasn't kicked,* she thought, *but I'd rather no kicking than whatever the hell that was two days ago.* Frowning, she went back to the couch, staring at the mug in her hand as she went. *Is two days with no kicking normal?* She couldn't remember. Faintly, in the part of her mind that was always picturing the worst, alarm bells echoed. She barely heard them, focusing instead on the doctor's promise that everything was fine.

I'm going to feel so much better after this baby is born, she thought, *even if it means a whole bunch of work.* There was a strange and horrifying pressure on her that she'd never really thought about before becoming pregnant; *I'm creating a life right now.* It wasn't just that she was responsible for his well-being after he was born. It was that right now, inside her, was a fragile and helpless baby that couldn't do anything but rely on her to grow. *At least when he's born, I can see him and take care of him directly.* Before that, she just had to hope for the best and assume it was okay in there.

Phoebe had never dealt well with uncertainty. Even small things became ominous and scary when there was no clear answer. *I just need to wait a little longer,* she thought, *and then things will be different. He'll be in my arms, I can hold him and stare at him, and we'll be a family.* She couldn't wait. Ben couldn't either; through his endless confidence, Phoebe felt his excitement just as intensely as she felt her own.

"Babe," she called over her shoulder, "haven't you worked enough today? Come and sit with me."

She took off the headphones she'd been wearing, ignoring the TV for the time being. Ben tapped away at his keyboard for a moment longer, and then the rhythmic sound stopped and she heard a grunt as he got up from his work chair.

"You know, I think you're right," he said, "I've done a couple thousand words already."

Phoebe beamed at him, and kissed him when he sat next to her.

"Well done," she said, "I have no idea how you do that. A couple thousand words was hell to me at school, it used to take me ages."

Ben laughed.

"Well, essays and assignments weren't exactly fun for me either, back in those days. Writing an essay and writing a thriller are pretty different things."

She kissed him again, and he threw his arm around her shoulders.

"True," she said, "but I still have no idea how you do it."

His answer was a nonchalant shrug, and Phoebe scoffed and kissed his cheek. She stared at him a little longer, but his eyes were already fixed on the TV. Shaking her head, she unplugged her headphones so that they could actually hear the dialogue. Despite instantly becoming a TV zombie, Ben held her close, and his presence was as soothing as ever.

As they watched and held each other, a barely coherent thought whispered in her mind. It was so faint that she almost didn't register it, but it was there, worming its way up into her consciousness; *the baby hasn't moved or kicked,* it said, *what if there's something really wrong?*

12 December 2019 12:41pm (Thursday)

After the apartment, they sent the camera and the journal off to the lab in Lidcombe and Phoebe returned to her desk, exhausted despite the full night of sleep and the fact that it was still before her lunch time. Simpson stepped up behind her, grabbing her shoulder and making a grumbling sound; an old inside joke.

"Want a coffee, Sarge?"

She nodded.

"Hell yeah. Thanks."

He gave a smile that said he knew exactly how important coffee was right now. She was his boss, but she'd built a great relationship with her team members, and in the office their conversation was relaxed and casual.

Inspector Rogers wasn't a fan of the way her team behaved, but they worked well and he wasn't about to shut them down for getting along. Despite several heated conversations about it between Phoebe and Inspector Rogers, her team were allowed to keep up their unorthodox behaviour.

Office politics had never been a strength of Phoebe's. She just wanted to get things done, and if her team needed to have a fun atmosphere to do it in, she was all for it. Outside the office, they had to be professional; but she didn't think it should matter when there were no members of the public around.

Simpson returned a short while later with coffee, and she took the black plastic lid off, breathing in the smell with her eyes closed.

"Thanks, Matt."

Seeing Taylor's apartment felt surreal. The journal was a great find, and she was excited to see if it answered any of her questions. But overall, his residence was more of a disturbing look into his day-to-day life than a solid lead in the case. *At least, from what we can tell so far.*

Simpson returned to his desk, and Phoebe drank her coffee slowly, trying to focus as she did. It would be a little while again before they could properly peruse the evidence they'd found, and there was nothing more she could do at the moment. But she could at least theorise. *Not that that'll do me much good,* she thought.

Looking back on the raid of his apartment, she found the details getting fuzzier; *must have been adrenaline.* At the time, every inch of the apartment stood out to her like a million bright lights. She'd noticed everything, every separate glint of shattered glass and every old, tired stain. But now that the moment had passed, it all melded together into one uncomfortable blur.

The only memory that stuck in her mind, lingering like smoke, was the smell. Michael Lee Taylor was filthy, and his apartment was just as unclean as the man himself.

"Of all the things to stick in my head, it had to be the smell," she mumbled to herself.

"I know what you mean, Sarge," Simpson said, "that place was disgusting."

"Hopefully it was worth the visit," Brouwer called from his desk, "otherwise I'll have that smell stuck in my nose forever for no reason."

Chapter Five:
Dead End

18 December 2019 11:27am (Wednesday)

Almost a week passed; the Inspector allowed Phoebe the extra time thanks to the new evidence found in Taylor's apartment. Waiting for the lab to come back with results had been difficult the first time; this time it was like torture. When she received the parcel back from Lidcombe, she tore it open and scanned it quickly. She had to remind herself to slow down so she'd actually comprehend what she was reading.

It was mostly just descriptions of everything they'd found, along with results from forensics testing on anything they could test. The lab had saved Taylor's DNA, and it was present all through his belongings. No other DNA was found. *Definitely no accomplices then,* she thought. She couldn't tell if that disappointed her; though an accomplice would mean more leads, someone else to find and question. Someone to take the blame.

After her initial frantic scan of the reports, she settled down and properly read through everything. Nothing seemed out of the ordinary. There were a handful of books found; other than the journal, Phoebe hadn't paid attention to them at the time. She read through their descriptions.

One 2017 journal, containing hand writing and finger prints of the suspect.

One copy of '11.22.63'.

One copy of 'The Last of the Vothuin'.

One copy of 'The Rubaiyat of Omar Khayyam'.

The last one forced an electric jolt down her spine, but she couldn't quite understand why. *I've read that somewhere before.* She didn't know what it was about, but the title buzzed in her mind like an alarm clock dragging her out of sleep. *Something more to focus on,* she thought.

The novel called 'The Last of the Vothuin' didn't mean anything to her; it looked like a pretty standard fantasy novel, and she didn't read fantasy. But she'd heard of '11.22.63'. *A Stephen King novel,* she thought, *about time travel. Of course.*

Her interview with Taylor surfaced in her mind again. He'd mentioned books. *There must be something here,* she thought, *something that he believes proves him right.* Now that they'd been processed and tested, she would be able to look at them herself. Read them, if she had to. Other than the journal, the lab hadn't found any hand writing in the books, but Taylor obviously thought there was something for her to find.

Out of the books, the journal was obviously her first priority. Though 'The Rubaiyat of Omar Khayyam' came a close second; there was definitely something about it that set off alarms in her mind. She saw the connection to be made with the Stephen King book, but if there was no hand writing from Taylor inside, there was nothing useful she'd find. The last book was the least interesting, and certainly wouldn't contain anything useful. *It's probably just got something about time travel as well,* she thought.

A little while after the reports arrived, Phoebe went to the records team; all the physical evidence taken from Taylor's apartment went back to them after Lidcombe was finished with it. She spoke to Les again, who was sitting at her computer looking bored.

"Hey Les," she said, "can I take a couple of the books found at Taylor's place?"

"Absolutely. Guess you're pretty stoked that more evidence has come up, right?"

"You can say that again."

"Pretty spooky though, that book."

She must be talking about 'The Rubaiyat of Omar Khayyam', Phoebe thought, *although the journal is pretty spooky too.*

"Yeah, there's something about it. I know I've seen the title before. I have a feeling it was mentioned in another case I've read about, but I can't remember which one."

"Now that would be something. Considering it doesn't exist."

Phoebe frowned.

"What do you mean?"

"The fantasy book. The last of the... whatever."

"Wait, what are you talking about?"

Les laughed, shaking her head.

"You're not gonna believe it. I searched for it, tried everything, and there's absolutely no trace of it anywhere."

Les brought the books out from a box, placing them on her desk. She picked up the fantasy novel, and flipped the first couple pages.

"Here's the kicker, though. Look at the published date."

Les handed the book to Phoebe. She almost didn't want to look, but she couldn't stop herself. A copyright symbol was followed by the author's name, and then the year that it was first published. *2024.*

"I don't..." she said, staring at the numbers as though they'd somehow begin to make sense.

"It has to be a fake, or something."

"Well, yeah. He probably ordered it online somehow, there are websites that print off custom books. Didn't he tell you he travelled from the future? It's probably his insane idea of proof."

Phoebe nodded, still staring at the copyright information.

"Yeah, he did. Wait, how did you know that?"

"My team processes and archives the interview footage, Sergeant. I saw the whole thing."

2024. This is insane. There was a part of her, just a tiny part, that almost believed it. But Les was right; there were ways to have a custom book printed. It wasn't even close to proof. *But why would he bother?* She thought, *surely, he'd*

146

know it wouldn't hold up as a defence. He couldn't have expected anyone to genuinely believe him.

"Can I take all of these?" she asked, gesturing at the books on Les' desk.

"Yeah."

Phoebe brought them back to her desk, stacking them next to her computer. She Googled each of the three novels, starting with the Rubaiyat of Omar Khayyam. *It's not exactly a standard book,* she thought, *not the kind of thing most people have laying around.*

She read through the entire Wikipedia entry; nothing useful showed up—until near the end of the page. Under a list of its influences on other literature and culture, an "other" tab listed miscellaneous facts. The first dot point sent an icy rush through her entire body, forcing the breath from her lungs.

In Australia, it said, *a copy of FitzGerald's translation and its closing words, Tamam Shud ("Ended") were major components of the unsolved Tamam Shud case.*

She clicked the link to the Tamam Shud case, and all at once the details returned to her. She'd read about it years earlier, and had been both fascinated and frustrated by the unsolved mystery. She read through the entire entry, and another cold shudder swept through her as she saw the details of the autopsy:

The stomach was deeply congested... There was congestion in the second half of the duodenum. There was blood mixed with the food in the stomach. Both kidneys were congested, and the liver contained a great excess of blood in its vessels. ...The spleen was strikingly large ... about 3 times normal size ...

How is this possible? She thought. The details matched almost exactly; the only difference was that the man found in Somerton hadn't been convicted or even suspected of a murder. *That doesn't mean he didn't commit one, though,* she thought, then shook her head. *I'm going crazy. This has to be a coincidence.* But she couldn't quite convince herself to let it go.

Further down the entry was a segment on the case's connection to the Rubaiyat of Omar Khayyam. It mentioned another fact that Phoebe had forgotten; a hidden pocket in the mystery man's trousers that contained a piece of paper torn from the Rubaiyat's last page. It contained the words that the case would be named after: *Tamam Shud*, which was apparently Persian for "finished" or "ended".

Phoebe leapt from her chair, and ran to the records room again. Les still sat at her desk, and Phoebe wasted no time on conversation.

"Do we have his clothes?" she asked.

"His... uh, yeah. Yes. Somewhere."

"I need them. Now."

Les took a few minutes searching on her computer's filing system, then retrieved a box from one of the shelves. Phoebe tugged on a pair of gloves, pulled the box open, rummaged through to his pants, and yanked them out of the box.

"If there's a secret pocket in here, I'm..." She trailed off, turning the pants around in every direction. Finally, she shoved her hands into the legs and pulled them inside out. Nestled under one of the actual pockets was a small sewn-on fob pocket.

"What the fuck is going on?" Les asked.

Phoebe opened the pocket, and pulled out the tiny piece of paper hidden inside. Unrolling it, she read the words she knew would be written there:

Tamam Shud.

Her team were as baffled and disturbed by Taylor's link to the Tamam Shud case as Phoebe was.

"And they never discovered what that piece of paper meant?" Wilks asked.

They were gathered around Phoebe's desk, silent and pale after she'd briefed them on what she found.

"Other than translating it from Persian to English," Phoebe said, "no. The significance of it and why he had it is unknown."

"What does it mean in English?"

"It translates to 'finished', or 'ended'."

"Oh shit," Wilks said, "okay, so hear me out. He said he came back from the future to kill a serial killer, right?"

"Wilks..."

"No, I know, but seriously; what if it's actually true? And that other guy from the 40's did the same thing, but he just wasn't caught?"

"Shut up, Justin," Simpson said, "you're not helping anyone."

"At this point, I'll hear anyone out," Phoebe said, gesturing for Simpson to quiet down, "Wilks, what's your point?"

"Well, okay, so what if they work for some kind of organisation that can send people back in time, and when the mission is done, they use that little slip of paper to somehow signal that they're finished?"

"How would that even work?" Brouwer said, frowning, "it's just a piece of paper."

As much as she hated the mystery, Phoebe loved seeing her team talk things through. Even if it was just stupid conspiracy theories. *At least they're thinking.*

149

"I don't know, but it kind of explains why they both had it, and why no one can find any information about either of them. And why the word 'finished' was chosen."

Wilks loved conspiracy theories. The number of times he'd ranted about the pyramids, or Roswell, or any other inexplicable events or objects, was beyond count. He was always quick to say he didn't genuinely believe in them, but his fascination and passion for them were undeniable. Phoebe had to fight to avoid rolling her eyes. She had to admit, she was drawn to the possibility that Taylor might have been telling the truth. *Somehow, something about it might be true, anyway,* she thought.

"He probably just read about the Somerton Man somewhere else, and decided to copy the note to confuse the police," Brouwer said.

"That makes sense," Simpson said.

"Did he decide to copy the guy by making his spleen three times too big as well, then? And what about the gun? Did he just disappear it away?"

"Well how do *you* explain the gun, Wilks?"

"Maybe the organisation can bring weapons or small things back to their own time."

"Listen to yourself, mate," Brouwer said, "this isn't some B-list sci-fi movie."

"I don't hear you coming up with any ideas."

"How about this one: it's a coincidence."

"I don't agree with that, Aaron," Phoebe said. Her team, Wilks included, stared at her as though she'd dropped a live grenade in front of them.

"I don't necessarily agree with Wilks, but... there's more to this than coincidence. The details are too similar, and some of them are both uncommon *and* can't be faked."

"Is there anything in the journal, Sarge?"

She threw it to Wilks, who flipped it open and busied himself reading.

"It's mostly total gibberish," Phoebe said, "but some of it is pretty spooky. I haven't actually read the whole thing yet."

"Lotta numbers in here. That could mean something. Mind if I read it all?" Wilks said.

"Go nuts, let me know if you find something useful. Just have it back to me by the end of the day. I want to read it too. And send the photocopied file to whoever works on codes and stuff."

Wilks nodded and returned to his desk, barely looking up from the journal as he walked. The group dissolved, and Phoebe wandered to Sarah's desk.

"Hi Sarah," she said, "is the Inspector free?"

"Only for the next two minutes or so."

"That's enough, thanks."

She knocked and entered, and Inspector Rogers stared as she walked in. After she told him about the Tamam Shud case, his expression didn't change. *He thinks I'm crazy now,* she thought, *or stupid. Too late now; I believe there's a connection, and I need him to understand.*

"It cannot *possibly* be a coincidence," Phoebe finished.

"What else would it be, Sergeant Wilson?" the Inspector replied, "there is literally nothing else that connects these cases. And even if there is, how does it help us solve this one?"

"I don't know, but they have to be connected," she said, "they have to be."

"I don't care about the Somerton case, Sergeant. Solve the Alpha Park case, or it gets frozen."

"Yes sir."

She returned to her desk, mind racing through a thousand connections that meant nothing. *Somehow, there will be a connection between the two cases that makes sense.* It was all she had.

18 December 2019 8:21pm (Wednesday)

Wilks finished reading the journal shortly after borrowing it; as it turned out, almost all of the pages were taken up by numbers instead of actual journal entries. The significance of the numbers was lost on Phoebe, and on Wilks too, though she imagined he would come up with a convoluted theory soon. For now, she skipped most of the number pages.

He might just have done it to confuse or fool the police, she thought, *after all, he had to know he'd be caught*. But that still didn't explain why so much of the journal was carefully written numbers laid out in apparently precise lines. Although she couldn't see a pattern in the numbers themselves, Taylor was clearly following some kind of format.

No one would go to this much effort just to confuse police a little. It had to be a code. A method of communication. It had to mean *something*.

Focusing as intensely as she could, she read every page. As she read the words, his presence came back to her from the depths of her mind. Reading his strange thoughts was as uncomfortable as speaking with him, but she pushed herself to finish every page:

The journal is their idea. I said it would be evidence if I get caught... WHEN I get caught, more like.

None of us come back, not on these missions. Thomas didn't come back, but at least he died on a beach. Looking out at the ocean.

I envy him. 1948 was far easier to get this kind of mission done without being caught. Still, he died. And so will I, even if they assure me I won't.

But they said evidence didn't matter. I have to keep a journal. So that's what I'm doing.

If evidence doesn't matter, I'm taking some other books too. The poetry is required, obviously, but the others are for me.

4 25 17 1930
33-52.1S 151-11.7E
18 3 6 30 9 12 22
24 2 6 23 14 3 17

Took a while to find it.

First identify, then exploit.

Should do the trick. Gonna need more though.

M.L.T.

March 20 2041

The spiral itself is weird. I'm not a fan of the purple lights.

Flashing and spinning. I feel sick just watching.

But they said I have to. There's no one else.

Well, here goes nothing.

M.L.T.

April 22 2041

24 11 35 5316

1 53 2334 35

53 735 54 22

12 48 334 21

34343 53 12

REOGEOHAG

OTAHJTEOO

TPHEETH

BLMOETWDSARP

RWTOBFKDOS

WRGOABABD

~~*MLIAOI*~~

WTBIMPANETP

MLIABOAIAQC

ITTMTSAMSTGAB

Thomas' instructions.

Here now, Sydney. The trip was crazy. Arrived in the park near where it'll happen. Such a bright flash, and heaps of wind. Not sure how no one noticed, even with the sunlight.

I'm confused and can't remember much. Just the mission.

I don't want to do it.

Who would, really? Everyone said they would, but going through with it is something else. It's fucking terrifying.

M.L.T.

October 16 2017

I miss Taured. Australia is terrible, especially in 2019. It's all fires and politics. So depressing.

Vacation in Taured... best 2 months of my life.

The memory is keeping me going.

January 8 2018

11 20 19 1930

23 10 12 27

3 22 22 28

14 5 12 27

16 4 18 22

I keep forgetting what year it is. I can't draw attention to myself, but I keep getting strange looks for saying things. Then I realise I've said something no one in 2019 would know.

Can't get locked up before the mission is done.

May 4 ~~2041~~ 2019

MLTITTT

EROJAPTT

TEAOHQWRHGTO

QPTJQWPTJ

JPJOEEPHPTH

School lets out at 3. Bus stop next to the park at 3:15 or so.

Bar nearby. Drinking helps, drugs are better. Just need a bit of help before the big event.

CAN'T BE LATE.

September 7 2019

23 236 65 356

256256 6535

223 54 66 6542

26 543 23 22 12

26 65 28 15 34

There's no such thing as innocent. He has to die.

There's no such thing as innocent. He has to die.

There's no such thing as innocent. He has to die.

There's no such thing as innocent. He has to die.

There's no such thing as innocent. He has to die.

HE'S NOT INNOCENT!!! HE HAS TO DIE

FSHOSEGEA

PAEJOJGAP

PAPJPGEAEWO

BTRKLDDOS

WSDICFLWRJB

Tomorrow.

He dies tomorrow.

What first stuck out to her, of course, were the dates; several journal entries in the early pages of the book included dates from 2041. Given that the diary itself said 2017 on the cover, it was hardly believable. *But why bother writing something like that,* Phoebe thought, *if it's so easily dismissible?*

The first few pages left a strange echo in her mind. Taylor mentioned a friend, Thomas, who apparently had a 'mission' in 1948. She scrolled through the Somerton Man case on Wikipedia again, until she found what she was looking for:

"All identification marks on the clothes had been removed but police found the name "T. Keane" on a tie..."

T. Keane, she thought, *Thomas Keane?* A few minutes of frantic searching confirmed that there had indeed been a man named Thomas Torance Keane alive in Australia at the time. He had died in 1949; but that may have been an error. Almost nothing was known about him, and other than the name he had no clear link to the Tamam Shud case, but it was enough to send a cold chill down her spine.

Taylor mentioned Thomas by name, and said he died on a beach during a mission like his but in 1948, she thought. The body of the Somerton man had been found at Somerton Park Beach, lying back against the seawall and facing out at the ocean. It was publicly available information, so it didn't prove anything. But the way Taylor wrote about it made her question his statements.

Opening her notepad, she made another list:

MLT and Somerton Man
-spleen 3x too big
-no cause of death
-same poetry book found
-secret pocket with tamam shud note
-unconfirmed identity
-very little evidence

There were so many similar elements between the two cases that Phoebe found herself almost believing Michael Lee Taylor's insane confession. Despite the fact that the two cases were separated by seventy years, she was convinced they were related.

Even laying aside similarities to the Tamam Shud case, every single page of Taylor's journal disturbed her more than she thought possible. When she was done reading, her hands shook. She felt as though she was about to throw up. A lot of it didn't make sense, but the parts that did were horrifying. Especially the final page; *He dies tomorrow.*

At least there's proof the murder was premeditated, she thought, *though it's vague enough that it may not constitute solid evidence.* It was as close as they would get to proper proof, and Phoebe just hoped it would be enough.

She flipped through the journal again, glancing over the pages full of numbers and gibberish. *Who fills a journal with stuff like this?* She thought, *it has to mean something.* But no matter how hard she focused on the numbers, no pattern presented itself.

There were lines of seemingly random letters, which also followed no discernible pattern. They did look familiar, though, and an uneasy foreboding settled over Phoebe. *I've seen these before,* she thought, *maybe not the same letters, but this kind of pattern.* No associated memories surfaced, but she kept mulling over it in the background of her mind as she re-read the journal.

No piece of evidence had ever frustrated Phoebe more than Michael Lee Taylor's journal. It said nothing of value, but somehow there were a hundred tiny pieces of information that stuck out as familiar in her mind. *There's no way to know where I've seen this stuff before,* she thought, *hopefully I'll remember.* In the meantime, all she could do was try to figure out what Michael Lee Taylor's codes and riddles actually meant. *I'll get you,* she thought, starting the journal from scratch again, *it's just a matter of time.*

20 December 2019 11:08am (Friday)

"Are you seriously saying you think Wilks is right?" Brouwer said.

"I'm saying there's some stuff in that journal that makes me think twice about it," Phoebe said, "not to mention the links between the Somerton Man and Michael Lee Taylor."

"C'mon Sarge," Brouwer said, exasperation pulling at his voice, "you can't be serious. You're talking about time travel."

"Look at this," Phoebe opened the journal, flipping to the pages that mentioned the murder, "School lets out at 3. Bus stop next to the park..."

She turned a few more pages, towards the end of the journal.

"There's no such thing as innocent. He has to die."

The last page still haunted her; such a short entry, but it left cold goosebumps all over her skin.

"Tomorrow," she read, "he dies tomorrow."

Constable Brouwer stared at her, any trace of mocking vanished from his pale face.

"That really doesn't mean—"

"It doesn't prove time travel, obviously," she said, "but there's more to this than a simple shooting, and this at least proves that it was premeditated."

"Where do we go from here?"

"I don't know," Phoebe said, "we can't use a journal entry as hard evidence, especially without a gun to tie forensics to Taylor. There's got to be something. I want you all on this. There are copies of every page of this journal, and I've added as much relevant info as I can to the case file. Read everything you can, and try to keep an open mind."

Her team went back to work, and Phoebe busied herself with more research on the books found at Taylor's apartment. In cases like this, with no conclusive evidence, every tiny piece of information added up to a big picture. If the big picture was convincing and damning enough, they might still be able to close the case in a satisfying way.

A short while later, a young man with an over-confident expression strolled up to her desk. He smiled, and Phoebe raised her eyebrows in response. After a few seconds, his cocky smile faltered, and he stood up a little straighter.

"Detective Sergeant Wilson?" he said.

"Yes," Phoebe said, "how can I help you?"

"I'm the cryptologist your team sent that diary to. I've finished looking through it."

"That's great," Phoebe said, "any good news?"

"I'll end my full report by email soon, but I just wanted to tell you in person… unfortunately, there's no known code or cypher used anywhere in that book. As far as I can tell, it's just random letters and numbers."

20 December 2019 2:12pm (Friday)

Phoebe was pouring over evidence, at what felt like an impasse, when her desk phone rang; Sarah's name appeared on the caller ID.

"Hi Sarah, what's up?"

"The Inspector wants to speak to you, Sergeant." she said.

"Good news, I hope?"

"He didn't say."

"Sounds about right," she said, her stomach plummeting, "I'll be there in a sec."

He's going to freeze the case, she thought. She gathered the folders of evidence she had, determined to at least fight for what she had so far. It wasn't much, but if she could show him that they were finally beginning to make connections, he might give her another few weeks.

Walking straight past Sarah's desk, Phoebe opened the Inspector's door without knocking. *I will finish this,* she thought.

"Sergeant Wilson."

"Inspector Rogers. You wanted to see me?"

He nodded, looking directly into her eyes and frowning.

"I'm sorry, Sergeant Wilson, I really am. The Alpha Park shooting case is being frozen as of today."

I knew it. I knew that's what he was going to say. The words still rang viciously in her mind; though it wasn't a surprise, it hurt. *It's done. That's it; I have to give it up.* There were always more cases, more problems to solve. But Phoebe wasn't sure she could deal with never knowing what happened with Michael Lee Taylor. Technically speaking, 'freezing' a case was simply slang for it becoming a cold case. *Just like the Somerton Man,* Phoebe thought, *people will*

173

still be looking into this in seventy years… but no more police resources will go towards it.

"Okay," she said, "I knew it was coming. I really think I could've solved it with enough time."

"I think you could have too, Sergeant. But there are cases that need your attention, and with the suspect dead and no evidence on our side, Taylor is a lost cause."

"Have you seen all the most recent information, at least?"

"I know about the journal. I haven't read it myself, but I've been briefed. There's nothing there, Phoebe. We've hit a dead end. I'm sorry, but it's done."

She nodded. But deep down, an empty space where the answers should have been sat waiting. It felt like hunger; sharp, aching, gnawing at her mind until it could be fully satisfied.

Just because the case is frozen, she thought, *doesn't mean I can't do more research in my own time.* She wouldn't be able to add more evidence to the case, and if she discovered the truth, it would only be for herself. *But I can't let it go.*

"I have a series of assaults I want you to look into," Inspector Rogers said, "I suggest you focus on them and get your mind off Taylor."

20 December 2019 6:02pm (Friday)

"...The police have officially stopped investigating the murder of eleven-year-old Jacob Turner last month, blaming a lack of evidence and the death of the only suspect. The victim's family have declined to comment, and no further information has been given by the police. A hotline set up for information about the suspect was closed. Sources say a small group of people, led by friends and family of the victim, is campaigning for the investigation to be re-opened, but so far police are ignoring the campaign, and have not responded to any complaints..."

28 July 2008 9:16am (Monday)

At Ben's insistence, they went to the doctor the day after Phoebe noticed there had been no kicking. A strange numbness settled into her mind; by the time they arrived at the doctor's office, Phoebe felt almost nothing. She would normally have been anxious, borderline panicked, but for some reason her mind simply shut down as they walked to the office.

"Phoebe, Phoebe," Doctor Hatzis said, "let's see how things are going."

Ben squeezed her hand as they went into his office. She sat down, her mind still blank, and looked at the doctor as he brought up her file.

"Ben said you were having some problems a few days ago?" Doctor Hatzis said.

"Yeah," Phoebe said, "really bad cramps. Then no kicking or movement at all."

The words sounded flat and distant, and Phoebe wondered if it was some kind of defence mechanism. *I know there's bad news coming.*

"I see. Well, I'm glad you came in, it's always better to know what's happening. What we'll do is go over to the sonographer and do another scan. I'll be there too this time, and we'll go over the results together. How does that sound?"

She nodded, and Ben did too. They followed Doctor Hatzis to the room she'd been in a couple times before, where the same sonographer was already waiting. *Jennifer?* Phoebe thought, *Jessica?* She couldn't remember. *Ben probably remembers.*

She climbed up onto the bed, the numbness finally giving way to cold fear. Glancing at Ben, who gave her the same confident, reassuring look he always did, Phoebe tried to hold

176

onto the numbness. Cold wetness touched her stomach, and she yelped.

"Sorry," the sonographer said, "I thought you knew it was coming."

Phoebe saw Doctor Hatzis shake his head from the corner of her eye, as Ben laughed and squeezed her hand again. He said something reassuring, but she didn't hear it. The scanning wand took her attention as the sonographer pressed it against her stomach. She couldn't look at the monitor. *I wouldn't know what I was looking at anyway,* she thought, *but it's still too much.*

"Okay." Doctor Hatzis and the sonographer spoke at the same time.

Phoebe shut off again, her mind closing as the room washed out into shades of grey and white. Distantly, she felt Ben put his hand on her shoulder. No words came to her, though she heard voices in the room as the professionals spoke with Ben.

After a short time, Phoebe was ushered off the chair by Ben, gentle and careful. With his arms around her, he guided her back to the doctor's office. She sat down, empty and cold. A part of her knew something awful was coming, but her dull, aching mind couldn't provide any more concrete thought beyond a distant sense of dread.

Gently but firmly, Ben shook her knee with his hand, and she was wrenched partly back into the moment.

"What?" she said, looking from Doctor Hatzis to Ben and back.

"Babe, did you hear Doctor Hatzis?"

"Yeah," she said out of instinct, before shaking her head and frowning, "umm, no. What's happening?"

"I'm sorry for your loss," the doctor said, "but the baby is gone."

A wave of cold sickness rushed up from somewhere deep inside her. For just a second, she didn't recognise the faces of the men in the room. As quickly as the cold washed over her, it disappeared, and Doctor Hatzis' words lost their meaning.

The room disappeared in a fog again, and Phoebe embraced the void; there was comfort in that nothingness.

"Now," Doctor Hatzis continued, "I understand this is going to be a very difficult time, but there are still some decisions to make."

"Doctor," Ben cut in, "maybe it's best if you speak with me, and I can speak with Phoebe in private?"

"I really think she should be here to at least hear it all from me."

They both glanced at Phoebe, but all she could do was nod. She knew what was happening, but only in the way that she was sometimes dimly aware of when she was dreaming. The doctor's office felt surreal, somehow unsolid. *This can't be real,* she thought. *It's not real.*

"Phoebe," Doctor Hatzis said, "as awful as this is, in situations like this there still needs to be a labour and birth. It can happen naturally, but we recommend inducing labour as early as possible."

Phoebe nodded again, though the words drifted like smoke in her mind. She stared at the paperweight on Doctor Hatzis' desk. It was a glass globe, with swirls of blue and purple forming suspended tornadoes that were somehow soothing. She wondered how something like that could be made. *Don't think about anything else,* a dark corner of her mind warned, *everything else is far too dangerous right now.*

"... Phoebe?"

Phoebe shook her head, tears falling as she fought to stay distant. *This is a dream. It has to be.*

"Phoebe, I need your permission to go through with inducing the labour," the doctor said, his voice gentle but firm, "for your own health, it should be done as soon as possible."

Taking a deep, shaky breath, Phoebe tried to speak. At first, nothing happened, except more tears slipping down her face. Finally, after a jagged sigh, the words came.

"Okay," she said, eyes still fixed on the paperweight, "whenever you want to do it, we'll do it."

"Are you sure you're up to it, babe?" Ben said, pulling her close.

"It doesn't matter," she said, "it has to be done, right?"

I didn't mean to sound that cold, she thought, *I hope I don't sound like a bitch.* But Ben kissed her forehead, squeezed her hand, and kept talking with the doctor. She distantly heard them organize the procedure, though the details escaped her. They spoke about other things too, things that Doctor Hatzis insisted were essential. Phoebe drifted back into that grey nothingness for the whole conversation, only responding when Ben shook her knee or when she heard her name.

The truth still hadn't settled into her mind, she knew that. It loomed below her conscious thoughts, cold and destructive, waiting for her numb shock to abate before it struck. She could feel it. On some level, she knew what had happened. But for now, there was no feeling or understanding. She realised, in a strangely matter-of-fact way, that this was what it meant to go into shock. *When the shock dies down,* she thought, *that's when I'm in trouble.*

25 December 2019 4:46pm (Wednesday)

Christmas day; why doesn't today feel like a holiday? It was hot, and quiet, and Phoebe would have preferred to be going anywhere else. Her mother sat in the passenger seat, a slight sheen of sweat covering her face and neck. Phoebe drove, sweating just as much; her car was usually cool, but she'd parked outside her mother's place the previous night, and it spent the whole day baking in the sun. The bushfires were at their height too; on top of the heat, smoke covered everything in a sickening orange glow.

The nursing home was just as cool as ever, though the smell of smoke lingered underneath the refreshing temperature. Their air conditioning was one of the few things that seemed like it would never fall apart.

"Where's your grandfather's room?" her mother asked.

"You mean you haven't visited?" Phoebe said, "after all the crap you gave me?"

"Oh, please Phoebe, don't start an argument when we're just about to see your grandfather. He doesn't need this kind of stress."

She couldn't stop a sigh escaping; her mother scoffed and shook her head.

"It's Christmas, Phoebe. Let's try to have a nice family gathering without the attitude."

They reached the reception desk, and the same woman greeted her. *She doesn't even recognise me. It's a wonder she hasn't been fired yet.*

"Are you here to visit someone?"

"Yes, Charles Wilson."

"Oh, hi! Sorry, didn't recognise you. One of those days."

She laughed, no trace of regret in her expression.

"He's in 217."

"Yes, thanks."

Phoebe filled in and signed the form, then handed it to her mother. After she signed, Phoebe led her down the corridor to her grandfather's room. The same heavy anxiety built in her chest, the same fear and sadness. *It is a little easier though, with someone else here.* She looked at her mother; her eyes were glassy, her mouth pinched into a thin, tense line.

This is just as difficult for her. Somehow, the realisation hit her as hard as the situation itself. Her mother never admitted to vulnerability, and Phoebe had almost never seen her cry. Seeing her struggle with it brought another level of reality to her grandfather's illness. They stood outside his door for a moment, and Phoebe put her hand on her mother's shoulder.

"Are you ready?"

Almost imperceptibly, she nodded.

"It'll be okay, mum."

"I know, I just... I'm sorry."

"It's fine, mum. Let's go in and say hi."

Gently, slowly, she opened the door. Charles Wilson sat in his bed, a small smile lighting his face as his eyes stared at nothing. Phoebe's heart ached for him in that moment; he used to read massive books back-to-back, complete puzzles and research complex topics just for fun. Now he simply sat and stared, the world outside his room lost to him.

"Hi grandpa!" she said, smiling and waving.

His attention turned to her, slow and unfocused.

"Oh, hmm. Hello there."

"Grandpa, it's Phoebe."

"Oh yes, Phoebe. How are you?"

"I'm good, Grandpa. Is it still nice here?"

"Oh yes," he said, "it's lovely."

Phoebe's mother stepped closer, her movements hesitant. "Hi, dad."

"Hello," he said, "you look familiar."

She sobbed, and Phoebe put her arm around her shoulders.

"This is your daughter, Grandpa."

181

"Oh my, yes of course. How are you, sweetheart?"

"I'm..." her mother took a deep breath, "I'm good, thanks dad. I wanted to say, um... Merry Christmas."

He smiled, warm and genuine, though with a slight frown, as though he didn't know what Christmas was; Phoebe had to force herself not to cry again. *Does he recognise us? Or is he just being polite?* She was good at detecting lies, but with her grandfather she couldn't tell.

"It's Christmas, is it?" he said, "Well that's lovely. I hope my family visits, it would be so nice to see them again."

"We're here, Grandpa. We're right here."

He kept smiling, but her words evaporated before any meaning or memory came to him. Her mother shook slightly, holding back tears with her typically resolute stoicism. Phoebe wanted nothing more than to reach both of them, break through the fog of his mind and the wall she'd put up, and join them again.

"Would you like some tea?" he said, reaching for the button to call a nurse.

"That sounds lovely," Phoebe said.

Her mother still shook, her breath hitching silently. *I keep forgetting he's basically her dad,* she thought, *I grew up with him too, but it's different for her. Harder.* She led her mother to the chair, smiled at her grandfather, and they waited for the tea.

02 January 2020 09:12am (Thursday)

During the week or so between Christmas and New Year's, Phoebe took paid leave, though she never stopped reading and re-reading the details of the Michael Lee Taylor case. Claire had begun to berate her for her obsession every time they saw each other; they started seeing each other less often.

There were still protests against the police for dropping the case. Phoebe agreed with them, though they hated her as much as anyone else. Her name hadn't been publicly linked to the case, but people protesting outside the station shouted at her whenever she showed up outside.

They'd closed the hotline, but the station itself still received a lot of phone calls; almost all of which were angry calls about the case being frozen. *I can't even tell them I agree,* she thought, *we have to use some stupid vague lines.*

"I understand that Jacob's parents are upset, but we have insufficient evidence, and we no longer have the resources we need to pursue the case."

She heard it at least a hundred times when she returned to work, and some of her team hadn't taken any time off; they'd been repeating it every day for the last week. It didn't calm anyone down or fix anything, but it was all they were allowed to say.

Phoebe only dealt with it by diving into her work; there were always new cases to close, new suspects to find. She was grateful for that much, at least. Her time off hadn't been restful or relaxing; it had been spent obsessing over Michael Lee Taylor. Coming back to a workplace full of public resentment and protesting, she felt a surge of burning frustration at herself.

Why didn't you just relax when you had the chance? Go to a spa, get a massage, watch movies? But even as she thought it, she knew she wouldn't have been capable of simply letting Taylor go. Even now, she felt the overwhelming urge to know and understand what really happened. It was so obviously more complex than Inspector Rogers would admit; even if it wasn't as crazy as Taylor wanted her to believe.

Although the evidence they had was almost entirely useless, they had a lot of it now. But none of it could be linked together to create an airtight case, or to solve the crime with complete certainty. The only theory that made sense was that Michael Lee Taylor was unstable enough to kill, and all the evidence that seemed to lead nowhere did so because of his instability.

Even then, she thought, *there are too many unanswered questions. Too many blank spaces and coincidences*. Michael Lee Taylor's death was just another one of the endless questions, with no evidence to clarify.

With what felt like superhuman effort, Phoebe wrenched herself out of the spiral of frustration, and opened the file she was supposed to be working on. A series of assaults occurring at the train station into the city centre. All the witness and victim statements gave matching descriptions of the attackers. They all happened within a hundred metre radius at the same station, and all occurred over the last two weeks. A lot of the work had been done by her team, but now that she'd returned, she took the lead once more.

Such straightforward cases wouldn't be difficult enough to fully distract from Michael Lee Taylor, but at least it was something. *At least I have someone to track,* she thought, *and someone to bring to justice*. Other than the mystery, and the senseless death of a child, what bothered Phoebe was that Michael Lee Taylor was never properly brought to justice.

Some might say his death was justice served. Phoebe disagreed. As unstable as he was, there was clearly some remorse in his eyes, and his words. He knew what he'd done, and he knew how horrific it was, and he did it anyway. Jacob couldn't be brought back, and now his killer would never be punished either.

But the person—or people—assaulting victims at the train station... they would be punished. There would be no mystery, no random, inexplicable death. *They'll be caught,* she thought, *I'll make sure of it.*

FOUR YEARS LATER

Chapter Six:
Anonymous Help

10 April 2024 2:24pm (Wednesday)

Jacob Turner would be fifteen now, if he was still alive. Phoebe found herself thinking about him often, and Michael Lee Taylor. *Not to mention the missing gun.* It still kept her up some nights, even after four years. *My son would be fifteen too.* An old, nasty pain flared up in her heart at the thought. It was all too familiar to her, something she felt most days. It would never completely go away. But after the Alpha Park case, the pain of losing her son had been inexplicably linked to Jacob Turner's murder. They would have been the same age, and might have even gone to the same school. *And both were lost without reason,* she thought, *and no answers.*

The coronial inquest into Taylor's death had dragged on for almost a year, as had the investigation by the Law Enforcement Conduct Commission. Phoebe was heavily involved in both, and neither one wrapped up with much closure. As Phoebe predicted before they began, there simply wasn't enough evidence to draw any conclusions. None of her team, nor Phoebe herself, were found liable; a surprise to no one. Michael Lee Taylor's cause of death was ruled as undetermined, and with the sole suspect dead, the matter was dropped.

In 2022, two years ago and two years after the case was frozen, Phoebe was assigned an intense new case; an actual serial killer had plagued Rosetown. *At least that case made sense,* she thought, *as disturbing as it was.* She worked hard on it, and eventually brought the killer down. Yet even the biggest victory of her career couldn't drive away her need to

187

solve the Alpha Park shooting. *At least I was distracted by it,* she thought, *I barely even thought about Michael Lee Taylor during that case.*

Once it was over, and the serial killer was caught, Taylor had slowly seeped back into her mind. Memories of her interviews with him, of his journal, of seeing Jacob's body, all gradually returned. And after the accomplishment of catching a real serial killer began to fade, the same empty craving set it; she *still* needed answers. The only thing that seemed to dull the craving was alcohol. She kept it under control, but a water bottle full of vodka in her work desk drawer waited for the particularly difficult days. A bottle of wine, sometimes two, after work, meant she could blot out Taylor's grating laughter and get to sleep. She forced herself to stay sober during work hours, other than the occasional nip from her hidden vodka bottle.

Now, she was working on a much simpler case; the armed robbery of a jewelry store. They had witnesses, CCTV footage, and enough evidence to track down the suspect. Far more than they'd had with Michael Lee Taylor. *Simple,* she thought, *easy.* She'd narrowed the suspects down to two. *It won't be long until we get him.*

"Sarge," Wilks said, "we've identified the suspect."

Any progress in a case lately filled her with energy; she felt the warmth spread through her in a sudden wave, and beamed at Wilks as he handed her a stack of printed CCTV screen shots.

"Thank you, Senior Constable," she said.

Wilks was promoted to Senior Constable in 2022 after his work with her on the serial killer case. It had been two years, but it still felt strange to say his title out loud. Not that he didn't deserve it; she'd just never thought of him as a higher-ranking member of the team. Out of all of them, he was perhaps the least professional, and his keen interest in conspiracy theories should have killed his credibility. But he'd proven himself, and Phoebe was happy for him, as odd as it felt to address him by his title.

She looked closely at the screen shots, turning her attention back to the case at hand.

"This is further down the street?"

"Yep. He couldn't help himself, apparently. Probably adrenaline, or inexperience. Or both."

The suspect had run down the street a few blocks, to a car he parked in preparation for his escape. But before he got in the car, he'd removed the mask he wore during the robbery. His face was as clear as a mugshot; the CCTV camera was positioned perfectly. *It's almost too good to be true,* she thought, *but then again, it's not like we're dealing with an insane mystery here.*

"Wait. That's Dan Reeves, isn't it?" Phoebe asked.

"Yep, clear as day."

Reeves was one of the two suspects Phoebe had narrowed their search down to. The swell of pride and satisfaction filled her chest with a lightness she hadn't felt in too long. Those positive feelings never lasted long anymore; even solving cases only gave her fleeting moments of victory. She tried to enjoy it while it was there.

"I never get sick of being right," she said, "do we know where he is?"

"Shouldn't be long. I'll send a KALOF to active patrols, they'll bring him in if they see him."

KALOF orders—'*Keep A Look Out For*'—were one of the most common ways the police ended up finding wanted suspects.

"Good job, Wilks. Work on locating him, and we'll bring him down today if we can."

"On it, Sarge."

Most cases were quite simple, once the work was done. But lately cases that didn't leave her questioning everything seemed... *too* simple. She still felt the same rush of warmth and energy when she solved even the simplest cases; but it would've been so much more powerful, and so much more permanent, if she'd solved the Alpha Park shooting.

I need that feeling. More than anything, I need that. She knew it was bordering on an addiction, but she couldn't help herself. Claire had tried to push her away from the case at the time. Phoebe didn't listen, and she'd tried to keep her continuing obsession a secret from her best friend since the case was frozen. But it cost her the friendship itself; they hadn't spoken in years.

Occasionally, Phoebe still opened the archived case and read through the details. She had photocopies of the evidence in a folder at home; it wasn't strictly allowed, but it wasn't specifically against the rules either. Actual evidence couldn't be taken without approval, especially after a case was frozen, but Phoebe only had a folder of photocopied pages.

"Hey, Sarge."

Michael Lee Taylor's journal was up on her computer screen; she hadn't heard anyone approach. Minimising the window as quickly as she could, Phoebe swept around to see Constable Brouwer.

"Reading Taylor's journal again?" he asked.

"You know me, Brouwer," she said, "can't let a good mystery go."

"If you keep reading it, you'll end up as crazy as he was."

She shook her head.

"I think I already am. What sane person would still be investigating a case four years after it gets frozen?"

"I wasn't gonna be the one to say it," Brouwer said, "but uh, yeah."

"Careful, Brouwer. Calling your boss crazy is a dangerous move."

"Did you hear me say that?"

"Get to work," she said, laughing.

"Yep, yep. But I did bother you for a reason, Sarge; I've seen some CCTV footage that shows a second suspect in the robbery. No ID yet, but there were definitely two people involved."

"We've ID'd one of them," Phoebe said, "Dan Reeves. Go over his associates and check alibis, whatever you need to check."

"Reeves..." Brouwer said, "I remember that name. He stole a few cars a while back, didn't he?"

"That's him, yeah. He's never committed this kind of robbery before, so I'd say his accomplice is probably more experienced. Someone he brought in to help him with the details. They had to have known each other somehow, so start with Reeves and work your way to whoever could be the second man."

Brouwer nodded and left for his desk. *Two for the price of one. This case is a little more interesting than it seemed after all.* After Brouwer returned to his desk, Phoebe opened Taylor's journal again, scrolling through the scanned pages as she had countless times before.

The numbers have to mean something, she thought, *no one would write all this down unless it meant something.* No matter how many times she looked, there was no pattern. The format was mostly consistent, but she still couldn't see anything that linked the numbers. It had become almost like a ritual; an automatic habit, like checking the time or mindlessly unlocking her phone whenever she wasn't doing something else.

She'd stared at the numbers so many times that she was beginning to think she'd never see their meaning. *Maybe he just believed they had something to do with time travel,* she thought, *some kind of formula. Part of his delusion.* She still struggled with disregarding his statement. As insane as it was, some of the things he'd said—and some of his journal entries—were just a little too convincing.

If anything he'd written could be linked to the real world, in any way, Phoebe could bring it to the Inspector. *He'd hate me, but if it's convincing enough, he might listen.* A small part of her, a *very* small part, actually hoped that Michael Lee Taylor had been telling the truth.

11 April 2024 3:52pm (Thursday)

A day after identifying Dan Reeves as the jewelry store robber, Phoebe's team found the address where he was hiding out. They'd checked his actual listed address first, and found nothing. A run through his known associates had found his girlfriend, Teagan Lee, and a covert drive past her place revealed his car in the doorless carport. Wilks advised her as soon as he returned from the drive.

Too easy, she thought. Their search through his associates also highlighted several potential suspects for the second man. No clear leads yet, but it was only a matter of time.

"Well done, Wilks," Phoebe said, "now let's go get him."

He was armed, and they had no way of knowing if the second man was there too, so the whole team prepped and left the station with her. These were the most dangerous situations; apprehending armed criminals in their own dwelling. They were far more likely to fight back, and since they were often taken by surprise, far more likely to use firearms in the heat of the moment.

Phoebe let Wilks drive; he'd only just been there. During the trip, her mind kept dragging back to Michael Lee Taylor. Even the potential danger they faced didn't entirely pull her out of it. *Come on, Phoebe,* she told herself, *focus.* She'd seen the numbers in his journal so many times now that she could recall a lot of them perfectly. Not every page, but quite a few of them; they swam in her mind's eye whenever she wasn't focused on something else, along with all the other details of the case.

When they arrived at the house, Brouwer had to shake her by the shoulder to bring her back to reality; She blinked the ghostly numbers away, and stared back at him.

"You good, Sarge?"

192

"Yeah, just tired, I guess. Let's do this."

He didn't argue, but he gave her a doubtful look before following her out of the car. *No lights, no sirens,* she'd said when they left the station, and they approached the front door silently. Faint music reached them from inside. The place had a backyard, but no way to escape other than around the sides to the front where Timms and Simpson stood waiting.

Glancing at each of her team, she checked they were all ready. They each reacted with silent nods, and she knocked on the door. A few seconds of silence followed, other than the faint music. Then she heard footsteps, and a cold voice shouted from somewhere inside.

"Who is it?"

Phoebe raised her voice, keeping it as stern and confident as she could.

"New South Wales Police, open the door now."

Again, a brief moment of silence followed. Then, the dry bang of a door slamming rang out from the other side of the house.

"He's going around the back," Phoebe called, "Brouwer stay here, Wilks and Dennis with me."

They sprinted around towards the backyard, and met Dan Reeves halfway there.

"Stop!" she couldn't regulate her voice anymore; it came out as a panicked shout as she drew her gun.

He wasn't armed. Somewhere in the depths of her adrenaline-fueled mind, she thought *at least that's something.*

"On your knees," she said, her voice already steadier, "hands behind your back."

He obeyed, though for a moment it looked as though he wouldn't. Dennis swooped in behind him, snapping handcuffs on his wrists and pulling him back to his feet. He brought the captured man to the second car, and stood waiting as Phoebe and the team entered the house.

It was more or less what she expected; messy, a little neglected, and full of drug paraphernalia. Reeves' girlfriend apparently wasn't home. Brouwer took photos, and they searched for any jewelry Reeves might have hidden. Phoebe ran through a mental list of all the standard hiding places, but her team was already on it.

Phoebe scanned under the bed, lifted the mattress, and rifled through the drawers and cupboards in the bedroom. It was clear. She was about to search the bathroom when Timms called from the kitchen.

"Brouwer, get the camera over here!"

The rest of the team kept searching, and Phoebe smiled. *Some other teams would stop searching as soon as they found the first evidence,* she thought, *but my team know better.*

By the time they were done, they'd found three separate lots of stolen jewelry. Brouwer photographed them, then Phoebe bagged them separately. They still had a second suspect to find, but Phoebe couldn't have been any happier as they drove back to the station.

11 April 2024 5:14pm (Thursday)

"We found the stolen jewelry."

His eyes projected defeat, but a defiant stubbornness as well; *he won't make this easy,* she thought, *there's more to the case still; more jewelry.* It must have been split between Reeves and the other man. *Makes sense. Two robbers, two cuts.*

"We know you worked with someone," she said, "we're closing in on them now."

"But you don't know who it is yet?" he said, his eyes sticking to the table in front of him.

That was a question. There's hope in his eyes too; he's invested in whoever helped. His certainty had all but disappeared when Phoebe mentioned them going after his partner. *It's almost like he wanted to get caught so we wouldn't look for anyone else,* she thought, *as though he hoped we would assume he worked alone. He has a reason to want to protect whoever he worked with.*

"We have a few leads. It's only a matter of time."

A cold rage settled into his eyes at that. His defiance came back, and he sat back against the chair.

"If you assist in the rest of the investigation, it'll go a long way towards your case in court."

A sharp, exhaled scoff was his only response, and Phoebe stared hard at him.

"Look, Dan," she said, shifting her tone to gentle and compassionate, "I know you've never done this kind of thing before. You've got a history, but it's way less than armed robbery. We can use that in your favour. It's your partner who's had experience."

And I think I know who it is now, she thought. His face remained impassive, staring at the table as though his gaze would set it alight.

"We can argue that your partner is the one who planned it all, that they forced you to join in." She took a deep breath, as silently as she could, prepared for the gamble.

"We can argue that... *she* forced you to rob the place with her."

His shoulders fell, his nose curling into a derisive snarl. *There it is,* she thought, *I knew it.*

"It was my plan, though," he said, "she just knew how to pull it off."

"I'm trying to get on your side here, Dan. Teagan is clearly the one with experience and knowledge, and your history reflects that. If you help us, it'll only make you look better."

For a full minute, he continued staring at the table, unmoving. Finally, he met her gaze with his own.

"I can't help you find her," he said, "she didn't tell me where she would hide out."

"Will you testify against her though?"

He sighed, and frowned as though he was really thinking it over. Phoebe let the silence build, her patience growing thinner as she watched him think. *Either way, we have him. Either way, we'll catch her too.* He most likely realised he wouldn't actually gain much from turning on her. Phoebe just wanted to be done with it now that the questions had been answered.

"I can't. I can't do that to her."

Phoebe nodded; she expected as much. She watched him a moment longer, then nodded again.

"Okay, Dan. You'll get no lenience in your case. We caught you first, and you're the one on the bulk of the CCTV footage, with your face clearly seen. We've got all the evidence we need. Teagan is going down too, whether you help or not."

Before she left the interview room, she took another close look at his face. His stubbornness and defiance still glowed behind his eyes, but to Phoebe he looked like every other criminal did after she'd caught them; defeated and resentful.

There was an exception; one man who never looked the way Dan Reeves did now. *Michael Lee Taylor was never defeated,* she thought, *that's why. He was ashamed and remorseful of his actions, but even being arrested wasn't defeat; not for him.*

31 July 2008 3:26pm (Thursday)

She sat in the shower, arms wrapped around her knees, not feeling the scalding water. Though she couldn't feel them either, tears streamed down her face. One word wavered in her empty mind, a word that had new meaning. It echoed, glaring and mean, and she never hated a word in the English language as much as she did the one repeating in her head. *Gone.*

Her mind reeled. Shock seeped into every cell of her being, wringing out her thoughts and leaving her an empty shell. *He's gone.* Knowing she had to go through with it was one thing, but the actual experience would never leave her. What should have been the most beautiful day of her life was now going to be a recurring nightmare.

Phoebe tried to forget. She tried to feel the hot water falling on her, running down her skin, and imagined it washing her memories away. It didn't work, but she kept her mind as blank as possible.

Ben was in the bedroom they set up for the baby. He'd been quiet since they got back from the hospital. She wanted him with her now, but they were both reeling. *I don't even know what's going through his head right now.* Of all the times for him to shut down, now was the worst. *I need him more than ever.*

She opened her eyes, staring at the blank wall of the shower. The hospital was a distant, cold memory, but at the same time it felt like she was still there. She couldn't remember if it was earlier that day, or a week ago. All she knew was she was still in pain. *Exhausted, too,* she thought, *I could fall asleep right now if I wasn't so upset.*

A blast of cold swept over her and she gasped. Ben stood at the glass shower door, looking down at her with red, puffy

198

eyes. He was naked. Stepping half into the shower, he held his hand out to her and she took it. She was still numb, but letting him guide her to her feet and step into the shower with her gave her a distant comfort.

He held her, standing so that the water fell on her instead of him. He always did that when they showered together; it was a small gesture of selflessness, but one that made her feel loved. She couldn't tell if she began crying again, or if she'd never stopped.

For long time, they simply stood together, holding each other under the water. His shoulders shuddered a little, and she pulled away to look at him. His eyes were still red. Even though the shower water made it impossible to see, she knew he was crying too.

"I love you," he said.

Phoebe nodded and buried her head in the space between his neck and shoulder. *This is the first time he's cried in front of me,* she thought, *what do I even say to him?* He'd always been the one to comfort her. He still was. But right now, not knowing what to say to comfort him just made her feel more helpless.

She sobbed, moaning and squeezing Ben as tightly as she could. He gave a heavy, ragged sigh, his mouth close to her ear. Her mind was blank. Pain throbbed in her belly, all through her insides. She'd expected pain; she'd given birth. But it was far more difficult to deal with than she thought it would be. It was a constant reminder of what she went through; what she lost.

Ben kissed her forehead, then her lips. Despite their tears, and her trauma, she felt him swell against her. She knew he wasn't doing it on purpose, but it sparked a low anger deep in her mind. Not at him, exactly; it felt more like it was directed at the concept of sex itself. In that moment, his member pressing against her belly with its crude urgency, the thought of sex made her almost throw up.

She was attracted to him; that had never changed. But right then, nothing could have made her want him in that way. His embrace was an intimacy and a comfort she desperately needed, so she tried to ignore his arousal and kept holding him close. He pulled away, cupping her face in his hands as he looked into her eyes.

"Are you okay?"

Phoebe shook her head. There were no words to describe how she felt, so she pulled him close again. He stroked her hair, gentle and loving. Though he made her feel safe, she also felt pressure to please him. He'd never once pressured her in that way, but she felt it nonetheless.

He stirred again, shifting against her in the way he sometimes did when he was hard and she wasn't showing interest. She could never tell if he was trying to signal her, or if he was simply uncomfortable. Not knowing what else to do, she squeezed him tightly, her arms around his broad chest and back. She felt more movement, and he pushed his hips forwards slightly, rubbing against her belly.

He actually wants to fuck me, she thought, *I can't be here right now. I can't do this.*

"Ben," she said, pulling away from him, "I… I can't."

He nodded, but didn't say anything. He stopped looking her in the eye. Phoebe got out of the shower, drying herself off as she tried to control her breathing. She didn't feel unsafe, she just felt... objectified. By her own husband. *I thought he was as upset as me,* she thought, *but he just wants sex. I can't believe he's even thinking about sex right now.*

Phoebe left the bathroom as soon as she was dried off, trying and failing to hold back more tears. For the first time in their relationship, she felt like she couldn't go to Ben for comfort. *I really thought he was just comforting me,* she thought, *who can I talk to now?*

13 April 2024 10:48am (Saturday)

Charles Wilson looked like a living skeleton. Phoebe looked at him, shaking with grief, as he sat in his bed. He barely moved, didn't speak, and didn't acknowledge her presence. *He should have died years ago*, she thought, *no one deserves a life like this*.

He was being taken care of; Phoebe was grateful for that much. But seeing him waste away like this... *I'm not sure I can visit again.* Her mother hadn't visited in a while, and she understood why. *He's barely alive.* When she arrived, she said hello; he didn't move. Sitting next to him now, she felt utterly alone.

"Hey, Grandpa. I brought something for you."

Rummaging through her bag, she brought out an old, battered book. Her grandfather continued staring into nothing, a faint smile on his gaunt face. As always when she opened the book, she read the handwritten note on the cover page with a smile; *To my little detective, never give up on the mysteries of life. If anyone can solve them, you can! Love, Grandpa.*

Tears slipped down her cheeks as she flipped to the beginning of the story.

"One of your favourites," she said, "A Study in Scarlet."

She began reading out loud, as clearly as she could. There was no way to tell if he was hearing her, or understanding the words, but she had to try. Her grandfather read this copy to her dozens of times; if not hundreds. She could have recited it almost word for word, but holding the copy her grandfather gave her was a comfort she desperately needed. It also gave her something to look at, something to focus on, other than his listless stare and vague smile.

The words flowed through her, familiar and warm, and she disappeared into the story as she read. *The clues are so obvious to him,* she always thought, *and the answers appear to him as obviously as the ground beneath his feet.* Sherlock Holmes had been her idol from the moment her grandfather first read *A Study in Scarlet* to her as a child.

He knows everything, she thought as she read, *he's always in control.* When she was young, she tried guessing how each story would end; who committed the crime and how. Even when she was certain she knew, her grandfather always smirked, raised his eyebrows, and said "you'll see".

Phoebe pictured his knowing smile as she read, remembering the accent he'd used to read the voices of Sherlock and Dr Watson. She tried to put on the same accent, and her grandfather's smile twitched. *Did he recognise the story? Or my voice?* She hoped it was both, but there was no way to know.

As she read, she became lost in the story. She was always amazed at how good fiction could make the world disappear; even on the hundredth read. Phoebe wasn't much of a reader, but when it came to Sherlock Holmes, she could read them all back-to-back and start from the first again without getting bored for a second.

Her grandfather remained silent and unmoving through the story, though she felt his presence as she read. It felt weak, as though he was on the other side of a closed door. When she reached the end of the story, she glanced back up at his face. *I may as well not be here.* She hadn't expected a miraculous recovery, but she'd hoped for... something.

With the chapter finished, sitting next to him suddenly felt terrifying. It almost felt like death itself was in the room; lurking, watching. Waiting. *I'm sorry, Grandpa,* she thought, *I want to stay, but I can't.* Slipping the book back into her bag, she rushed from the room without saying goodbye. In that moment, he hadn't even looked like her grandfather any more. He'd looked like a corpse.

15 April 2024 9:02am (Monday)

The case was building; Phoebe and her team were almost ready to capture the second suspect in the robbery. Dan Reeves was brought in, and they were closing in on his partner in crime and girlfriend, Teagan Lee. It was a good day; her team had made progress, and she would be closing the case soon.

Sipping her coffee, Phoebe double checked the evidence they'd gathered on the robbery; it felt good to be certain of the facts. *At least this case makes sense,* she thought. Ever since Michael Lee Taylor, every case had been compared to the Alpha Park shooting; in her mind, at least. The rest of her team had seemingly moved on quite quickly. Although Wilks occasionally brought it up, when he was in the mood to rant about conspiracy theories.

As she scrolled through CCTV screenshots and forensics reports, her desk phone rang. The caller ID showed it was the front desk calling.

"Detective Sergeant Wilson," she said.

"Morning, Sergeant," the receptionist said, "I've got a caller who asked for you by name."

"Who is it?"

"He didn't say. But he said he has details about the Jacob Turner shooting from a few years back."

Cold shock made her stomach plummet as though she'd fallen into a freezing lake. *Four years,* she thought, *and a lead pops up.* It shouldn't have happened; but she'd read other cold cases that were solved years later by a random coincidence or a new lead just like the phone call she was about to get. She almost couldn't believe it. The last four years melted away, and she felt the same way she had when the case was still open.

"Put him through."

Phoebe waited until she knew the caller had come through. Her heart beat hard against her chest, thudding in her ears as she tried to think of something to say.

"This is Detective Sergeant Phoebe Wilson," she said into the crackling quiet, "who am I speaking with?"

"I wanna be anonymous."

Deep voice, she thought, *at least 45, and sounds like a smoker.* There wasn't much more she could get from voice alone.

"That's fine," she said, keeping her voice as even as possible, "but I need every bit of information you have on the shooting."

"Yeah, o' course. What I know is you've been looking for the wrong guy."

"You mean it wasn't Michael Lee Taylor?"

"No, I mean that's not his real name."

"What is his real name?"

Low static hissed in her ear. Every moment that passed felt like an hour, but she kept waiting for him to give her something. *Anything.*

"Can I speak to someone in person?"

"You can," she said, "come into the station whenever you're free, I'll be here."

"Not at the station, I don't wanna be recorded or anything."

"We won't record you if you'd rather stay anonymous."

"I'd be more comfortable meeting somewhere public."

Faint in the back of her mind, alarm bells rang at his unwillingness to come into the station; it felt wrong. *This guy is almost as dodgy as Taylor was.* Phoebe wasn't even sure if it was allowed; the case had been closed years ago, and there wouldn't be any record of the conversation. Unless actual new evidence was unearthed as a result of the anonymous caller, whatever he told her would remain unofficial. But her need to know was overwhelming, and she didn't hesitate.

"Okay, we can meet somewhere you're more comfortable. When are you free?"

"Later tonight. Eight thirty-ish?"

"That's fine. Where?"

"The Rosetown Inn."

Her breath caught in her throat; the Rosetown Inn was where Michael Lee Taylor had gone to drink before he killed Jacob Turner.

15 April 2024 8:52pm (Monday)

The Rosetown Inn was exactly as she remembered it. She walked in to the smell of stale beer and the rumbling chatter of the patrons; it was far busier than the afternoon she first visited. She wore plain clothes, at the request of the anonymous caller. *Not exactly an official meeting anyway,* she thought. *I wonder what Inspector Rogers would think of this?*

Phoebe moved to a table near the back of the room; a man sat there waiting, wearing a red jumper as he said he would.

"Sergeant Wilson, is it?" he said.

"That's me," Phoebe said as she sat opposite him.

"You hit a dead end with Michael Lee Taylor."

He said it with a certainty that made her stomach twist; the case had been publicly closed, but they'd announced a general lack of evidence and Taylor's death as the cause. The fact that they knew almost nothing about Michael Lee Taylor hadn't been made public, other than releasing his photo in a plea for more information; but that was common practice in a lot of situations.

"We did," she said, keeping the tone from her voice, "there wasn't much to find on him."

"Because he gave you a fake name."

She said nothing, staring at him the way she'd stared at Taylor in the interview room. The man sitting across from her was as much a mystery as Jacob Turner's killer.

"How do you know anything about him?"

"I can't tell you that."

So far, he's told me nothing, she thought, *I'm glad I didn't tell Inspector Rogers about this.* She should have expected it to be a waste of time; but some part of her still needed to know what really happened. *If there's even a chance this guy knows anything, I need to find out.*

His eyes were bloodshot, his clothing disheveled. Dirty hands rested on the table, one of them wrapped around the beer he'd ordered before Phoebe arrived.

"What *can* you tell me?"

"I wanna know I'll be anonymous. I don't want anyone calling me. I don't wanna be called into court or whatever."

"That's fine," Phoebe said, "this is off the record."

He didn't look comforted, but he gave a low grunt and a slight nod.

"Good," he said, "well."

They sat for a moment, the chatter around them buzzing in her head.

"Well?"

"His real name is John Thompson. He's pretty fucked up. I know he was locked up in some mental health place a while ago."

He looked deep into the beer he held, frowning as though weighing his options.

"The photo on the news is wrong."

Phoebe's heart leapt into her throat.

"What? You mean it *was* someone else who shot Jacob?"

"They look real similar though. Could be brothers."

"So," Phoebe said, trying and failing to keep her voice even, "the shooter is still alive?"

"Far as I know, yeah."

"Do you know where he lives?"

"Nah, but it'll be in Rosetown. It's where he was locked up."

"So, if I look up John Thompson, you're absolutely sure I'll find the man who shot Jacob Turner?"

"It's him, yeah."

"Why did you wait this long to tell us?"

The man shifted in his seat, taking a long sip of beer. His eyes avoided her own.

"I didn't want to get involved."

"The case was frozen because we didn't have enough information. If you'd come forward when the case was open, we could have closed it properly."

"Sure, but what difference would it really make?"

Phoebe paused. Other than the public protesting against her department, and her own desperate need to know the truth, the man was right. *Since Taylor—or maybe Thompson—died, the difference between closing and freezing a case is minimal.* She couldn't think of an answer. If he'd survived, it would have meant the difference between justice and a killer going free.

"It would have at least meant closure for Jacob's parents," she said, "wouldn't you want that? If he'd killed one of your family?"

He grunted again, finished his beer, and finally glanced at her. The whole interview so far, he'd barely looked her in the eye. *At least he came forward eventually,* she thought, *though he could have saved the case if he'd called while it was open.*

"Is there anything else you can tell me?"

"I just know his real name. That's it."

"No family members? Friends? Where he worked?"

"I told you, don't know."

Phoebe sighed.

"And you won't tell me *how* you know his name?"

"I can't," he said, staring into the empty beer glass in his hand, "I'm sorry."

"If this case was still open, I'd be pulling you in for perverting the course of justice," Phoebe said, "but as it stands all I can do is ask again. Why can't you tell me?"

"I think I need to go," he said, getting up so fast his beer glass toppled, "sorry."

"No, wait," Phoebe said.

But he'd already rushed through the crowded room. She went after him, but he was gone by the time she reached the pub's entrance.

"Just more mysteries," she said to herself as she headed home, "I can't catch a fucking break with this case."

10 August 2008 6:43pm (Sunday)

Her grandfather's house was warm, cosy, and one of the few places Phoebe felt truly relaxed. She sat on the soft couch, across from the single chair that her grandfather preferred. Faint shuffling sounds drifted in from the kitchen as he prepared tea for them both.

Phoebe smiled as she listened to him moving around the kitchen. Even at his age, he was always up and getting things done; especially when it was to help others.

"Sugar?" he called, "Milk?"

Phoebe's smile grew; he asked her the same thing every time, even though her tea preference hadn't changed since she started drinking it.

"No thanks, grandpa."

A few minutes later, he returned to the living room. He placed Phoebe's mug on the tiny table next to her chair, and settled into his own lounge with a heavy sigh. Before he got up to make tea, Phoebe told him about losing the baby. As always, he was understanding and sensitive. They barely spoke about it before he got the tea; when he sat down again, he looked at her with a warm expression, eyebrows raised as though he'd asked a question.

He always wants to talk through every little thing, she thought. It was often helpful, but sometimes Phoebe didn't want to analyse everything.

"So," he said, "how are you feeling?"

"I don't know."

It was almost two weeks ago, and Phoebe was still processing her emotions; it was why she'd visited her grandfather in the first place. She could finally move without pain, but she needed his comforting presence nevertheless. She'd experienced loss before; her grandmother died when she was fifteen. A few other people she knew had died, friends of her parents mostly, but her grandmother had been the biggest shock to her; until the baby.

He looked at her with patience and warmth. No expectation, or judgement, or anything negative. Phoebe still hadn't told her mother; she didn't know how she'd react, but she knew it would only end in anxiety. *At least I have Grandpa,* she thought, *he's always been here for me.*

Sipping his tea, Phoebe's grandfather settled into comfortable silence. She sipped her own tea too, trying to puzzle out the right words to describe how she felt. It wasn't just that, though; *I don't think he'll actually understand how I feel, even if I can find the words.* Finally, she took a deep breath and spoke.

"I'm scared," she said, "and hurt. I'm confused because there shouldn't have been a problem. The doctor said it was fine, the sonographer said everything would be fine. It just came out of nowhere."

By the time she stopped, tears were flowing again. *It feels like I'm always crying now,* she thought.

"It happened so quickly," she continued, "I still don't know how."

She glanced at her belly, not daring to put a hand on it. Knowing he wasn't in there anymore, and would never grow, or cry, or laugh, left Phoebe in a daze of cold horror. It felt like a nightmare, something shadowy and unreal.

"I'm sorry, sweetie," her grandfather said, "I really am. You're strong, though. You always were. I know you'll get through this."

"Thanks, Grandpa."

It was lovely to receive support. *But he doesn't get it,* she thought, *I knew he wouldn't.* There wasn't anyone she knew who would properly understand. Her closest friend was Claire, and she'd never wanted children. *She would never understand how this feels.*

Tears kept slipping down her face, and she tried to think of anything but the baby. The tea her grandfather made was strong; he left the teabag in. She wasn't sure if he remembered she liked it that way, or if he forgot to take it out.

"You know," he said, his gentle voice barely breaking the silence, "your grandmother and I lost a baby, too."

"I... what?"

"Oh, yes. Before your mother was born. It was just like yours, everything looked fine. Until it wasn't."

"Oh. Oh, God, Grandpa, I had no idea."

"No, well, it hurt your grandmother far too much to talk about it. And she died before you were old enough to understand."

I'm definitely old enough to understand now, she thought, *I wish I could talk to Grandma right now.* She loved her grandfather; but having a woman to talk to who'd been through the same thing could help more than anything.

He looked at her, a small, sad smile on his face. It occurred to her for the first time that her grandfather had been through things she never could have understood either. *He's lost a child the same as me and Ben,* she thought, *maybe he understands more than I thought.* It was still different; carrying the baby inside her was an experience he would never know.

"How did you guys deal with it?" she asked.

"In those days, there wasn't much talking. Your grandmother got through it as best she could, and I helped when I could. But I think what really helped was when we had your mother."

Great, she thought, *just have another kid.* She couldn't even fathom that as an option right now.

"I remember she named the baby, though," he said, "and we had a funeral. I think that really helped us both move past it. Sad, of course, but at the same time, it was kind of... nice."

Phoebe hadn't thought that far ahead yet. *It makes sense,* she thought, *maybe that will give me some closure.* Her and Ben could have a small, private ceremony, and mourn properly. *I'll have to remember to bring it up with him.* Without the baby—*or his ashes, anyway,* she thought—a funeral would be purely ceremonial; but it was better than nothing. She'd been offered the ashes, but at the time, her mind had reeled at the thought, and all she could do was refuse.

"What name did you choose?" Phoebe asked.

"His name was Peter. Your Grandmother always liked that name."

Phoebe smiled. Without meaning to picture it, an image of their family as it could have been surfaced in her mind; *uncle Peter, with a wife and kids of his own. My cousins. They might even have their own babies; they'd be around my age or older. Plus, my own baby.* Tears swept down her face, and she wiped them away.

"Ben is being supportive," she said, "but I still feel completely alone."

"Sweetheart, you're never alone. I'm here, and you're always welcome here. If you ever need somewhere to stay, or someone to talk to, drop by any time."

She couldn't stop a sob escaping as another round of tears flowed. Her grandfather's place had always felt like a second home; now it was a sanctuary too. Even if he didn't fully understand, his presence was always soothing. Phoebe used to speak with her grandfather about everything when she was little. They'd drifted apart a little in her teenage years, when school and friends had become her biggest priority; but they rebuilt their old connection, and now she was more thankful for him than she could say.

"Thanks, Grandpa."

It didn't feel like enough, but it was all she could manage in that moment. He smiled again, and she smiled back through her tears. Then it occurred to her that there *was* something else she could say. She'd even thought about it before. Now, it felt like the only option.

"Grandpa, how would you feel about me naming the baby after you?"

The look of surprise and pure love on his face brought yet more tears to her eyes. She saw his own eyes glisten with emotion too, and for a moment they simply smiled at each other.

"Sweetheart," he finally said, "it would be an honour."

The day after meeting with the man who claimed to know Michael Lee Taylor's true identity, Phoebe searched through their records for John Thompson. It didn't take long to find a criminal history; her heart almost leapt out of her chest when she saw his profile.

Assault, animal cruelty, intimidation with a deadly weapon, public disturbance... His history read like a psychopath. The record didn't go back into childhood, but it started right from eighteen. Phoebe would have bet money on a juvenile record to match.

The more she read about him, the more it seemed like Michael Lee Taylor. His record was a constant cycle of erratic behaviour, unprovoked violence, and drug abuse. She'd found no photo of him so far, which sent a bolt of uneasy panic through her stomach; but it would come up eventually.

"With a criminal history like this," she said, "you've got to have a mug shot *somewhere*."

"What's that, Sarge?" Brouwer said, walking past with a tray of coffees.

"Nothing, just talking to myself."

"Geez, that guy's a piece of work, huh?" he said, nodding to her computer screen, "he involved in the robbery or something?"

"No, he's..." too late, she realised she didn't have an excuse prepared. Nothing came to her, and she stared for a moment, her mind blank.

"Okay, good talk boss," Brouwer said, "here's your coffee. Might help with the words."

She took the cup gratefully, feeling her cheeks flush. *I wonder if any of my team would understand,* she thought.

214

Maybe Wilks, but definitely not Brouwer. She couldn't tell them anyway; not unless she actually got somewhere with it. If she could prove John Thompson was Michael Lee Taylor, match his criminal history with the murder of Jacob Taylor, they would be able to definitively close the case, and she would finally have closure. It made a lot more sense than Michael Lee Taylor's confession. John Thompson's profile fit the crime, and provided so much context that Taylor never had.

Brouwer returned to his desk, giving Phoebe a suspicious glance before he sat down. She kept scrolling through John Thompson's criminal record. Usually, photos were one of the first things that came up; but something seemed to be wrong with his file. *This better be a coincidence,* she thought, *and a temporary one at that.*

But there had been too much mystery surrounding Michael Lee Taylor for her to believe a missing photo was entirely coincidence. Before that case, she'd never felt superstitious in any way; even studying some of the world's most unbelievable mysteries. Ever since Taylor, she found herself second guessing even straight forward situations. *If it's just a coincidence, I might actually solve this case.*

She sent an email to the IT team, asking them what a possible cause could be for a photo to be missing from a criminal's history. Writing the question down felt strange to her; the answer might prove that something deeper than mere coincidence was going on, and Phoebe wasn't prepared to deal with that. Still, she sent the email, and waited with barely controlled panic for the answer.

16 April 2024 10:09am (Tuesday)

An hour and a half after emailing the IT team—during which she did nothing but stare at the blank space in Thompson's file where his photo should have been—Phoebe finally received a response. She skimmed over the vague office-talk excuses to the actual point; *we have determined there is no technical issue with the file,* it said, *it seems as though a photo was never uploaded.*

No solution was offered; what could be done about a missing photo, after all? Phoebe shook her head, exasperation driving her heart rate up. *Even four years later, this case just keeps presenting unanswered questions.*

Though the case was closed, John Thompson had shot to the top of her priorities list. She wished she could find out more about the man who'd mentioned his name; but he called on a private number and gave her absolutely no information about himself. She was a good detective; but nobody was that good.

She scrolled through Thompson's file, trying to see which Constables worked on him in the past; if she could find someone who'd seen him, she might be able to get a description. *If it matches Taylor,* she thought, *I've got him.* A description wouldn't count as solid evidence, but coupled with everything else it was as close as she was likely to get.

State police departments didn't often communicate, unless it was necessary. Australia didn't have a universal criminal record system, so finding a person's criminal history could be difficult if they'd lived in a different state. Not to mention the fact that one department had no way of knowing if there was an active record in another department.

Each department did have contact points for the other states, however, and Phoebe drafted an email requesting any and all information about John Thompson. When it was finished, she paused with the cursor sitting on the *send* button. *If they ask,* she thought, *I have no justification beyond my own curiosity. If Inspector Rogers finds out, I'll be in a hell of a lot of trouble.*

Then again, if she solved a cold case, especially one steeped in mystery, she would make the Rosetown police look great. *I can't risk Rogers finding out until I've got the whole thing,* she thought. If she could present her findings to him as one big solve, it would justify the time she'd spent on it. *When I should be focusing on the robbery.* Phoebe tried, briefly, to work on the robbery. Being reminded of it sent a flash of guilt twisting through her stomach. But the longer she tried to focus, the less she could. All that ran through her mind was *John Thompson.*

I don't actually know anything about him, she thought, *except for what a complete stranger told me.* She knew there was no guarantee that John Thompson was actually the shooter. It all hinged on photographic identification; *which I don't have.*

Something about it felt strange to her. A realisation hit her without warning. *Even if he was the shooter, how did he get away from the scene?* The CCTV footage, as blurry as it was, showed one person shoot Jacob and then pass out. Phoebe had watched it all the way from the shooting to her own arrival. *There was no one else. The person we caught was the shooter. So, who the hell is John Thompson, and why did that man tell me about him?*

John Thompson sounds almost like a fake name. She got the pressing feeling that the anonymous caller might have been trying to purposefully sidetrack her investigation. *Not that he needed to,* she thought, *it wasn't like I was getting anywhere with it anyway.*

In fact, though the case had never left her mind, she wouldn't have even begun actively pursuing it again if not for the caller. *If anything, he's the reason I'm focusing on it. If he'd left me alone, he wouldn't have needed to* sidetrack *me in the first place.* Possibly not an attempt to lead her astray then; but it certainly felt like an attempt at *something.*

Why would he suddenly step forward now? She thought, *when he could—and should—have called back when the case was actually active?* He never gave her a satisfying answer to the questions she had for him. Even the information he willingly gave was barely useful. Sighing, she closed down the files she had up and opened the ones she should have been looking at.

"Simpson," she called, trying to force herself to actually work, "where are we up to with the robbery case?"

"Uhh, we're chasing up some leads on where the second suspect might be hiding out," he said, "found another witness. It's going about as well as it can."

"Good."

For a moment, Phoebe had no idea what to do. It seemed like her team were on top of everything; it felt like she'd ignored the case and they barely noticed. Instead of going away, the guilt in her stomach intensified. *They already accepted that I'm not contributing,* she thought, *and it didn't even slow them down.*

Her interest in the Alpha Park shooting had resurfaced with a vengeance. Phoebe took her lunch break in Alpha Park; walking slowly through the trees, looking at what Michael Lee Taylor might have seen before he came to stand at the entrance to wait for Jacob Turner. The four years that had passed since were enough to take the unreal feeling from the park.

The last time she'd been there was during the investigation, and walking through the park had felt oppressive and claustrophobic; now, it simply felt like a park. It was a cool day, a slight breeze shifting the leaves above her and creating a wave of dappled sunlight.

Jacob Turner's parents told her that he loved this park; Phoebe could see why. Benches sat along the path, and the grass was soft and green. People sat on both the benches and the grass, talking, reading, and playing. Their noise didn't disrupt the sense of peace around her; if anything, the sounds of other people enjoying life were even more peaceful than silence.

"Why here?" she said to herself, looking around again at the beautiful park.

The question had occurred to her before, but now she really thought about it. Alpha Park was public, and though not exactly packed, there were always people there. It meant he had to know he'd be caught. But he also knew Jacob Turner would be there. Surely, if he knew Jacob's schedule well enough to plan an attack, he would have known when the boy would be alone. Somewhere more private.

For the first time, Phoebe found herself genuinely wondering about Jacob. Michael Lee Taylor's words during his first interview had never left her mind; *You would've done the same thing.* At the time, she'd chalked it up to Taylor being delusional. But he'd known what he was doing. He was affected by it, even remorseful; he'd gone into shock immediately after shooting the boy, and his eyes remained haunted for the rest of his life, as short as it was.

So, if he knew what he was doing, and planned it in advance, she thought, *it definitely wasn't a random act of insanity or a crime of passion. He truly believed Jacob deserved to be killed. Assuming Michael Lee Taylor wasn't insane... why would Jacob deserve such a horrific fate?*

For the first time, she thought about the possibility that Jacob Turner might not have been innocent after all. *I'm not admitting Taylor was right about the time travel,* she thought, *but maybe there was a real reason he targeted Jacob.* Investigating a possible motive wouldn't be easy, but Phoebe would find a way.

Asking his parents about possible reasons Jacob might have provoked a killer didn't strike her as an appealing option. His father had been evasive and aggressive during her interview with him. Looking back now, it lent some weight to the theory that Jacob might have been less than innocent. *His teachers might have noticed something about his behaviour,* she thought, *if there was something to notice.*

They still had a photocopy of his school ID on file. Phoebe would be able to find out who his teachers had been, and ask them about Jacob. *Assuming they still work there.* Even if they'd moved onto another school or another job entirely, she might be able to ask around for contact details. As long as it didn't require a warrant or official request; she was investigating off the record after all.

After her lunch break, she opened the case file and found Jacob's school ID. She wrote the address of the school in her notepad for later. She'd have to visit on her next lunch break or make up a convincing excuse; there was no way to justify leaving the office at the moment, as much as she wanted to.

Four years after the shooting, she wasn't sure if any of the teachers would even remember him, beyond the shock of the murder itself. Unless he was a particularly memorable student. She was hoping, deep down, that he'd been a troubled kid, that something happened at school that one of his teachers would remember. *Not that that would justify his murder. I just need a reason.*

Even if, somehow, Michael Lee Taylor's story was true, Phoebe would never think of killing a child as the right thing to do. But if there were signs of troubled behaviour, she might at least be able to understand why Taylor had done what he did. She still wouldn't be able to properly close the case without concrete evidence, but she might satisfy her own overwhelming need for closure.

One way or another, she thought, *I'm going to find out what really happened.*

11 August 2008 5:02pm (Monday)

The day after she visited her grandfather, she realised she hadn't told Ben about naming the baby Charlie. *It was supposed to be something we shared. Something beautiful.* Ben had said almost nothing since she rejected him in the shower. They were both upset, and she understood he was just trying to deal with the situation; but it struck her as childish and immature.

I need to tell him the baby's name is Charlie. She didn't know how to start that conversation, after they spent the last days in silence. Last night, Ben remained on his side of the bed, facing away. It was the first time she could remember that they hadn't held each other before falling asleep.

They were both at home. It was late afternoon, and Phoebe was still in bed. Ben was either in the spare room or his office, which was still set up in the corner of the lounge room. She hadn't moved since waking up, except to eat a piece of toast when her stomach wouldn't let up with hunger cramps. Every now and then, she heard Ben walk around from one room to another.

Finally, she got out of bed and shuffled to the shower. She only stayed in there long enough to briefly rinse herself off and warm up a little. After that, she put pyjamas back on and walked as slowly as she could out into the lounge room. Ben sat at his computer, barely tapping any keys. He looked as miserable as Phoebe felt.

"Hey babe," he said.

There was some warmth in his voice, but he didn't look at her.

"Hey," she said, "You don't mind if I watch TV?"

He shook his head. Phoebe sat on the couch and grabbed the remote. *How do I say this?* She thought. Instead of trying, she clicked on the TV. A reality show was on, something about renovating houses.

Every now and then, she heard a few keyboard clicks behind her, but otherwise Ben was utterly silent. With her headphones on, she tried to forget about everything. But the TV droned on, the dialogue meaningless and grey.

Just say it, she thought, *just say "hey babe, I spoke to my Grandpa and I wanted to name the baby Charlie after him. Is that okay?"* Somehow, even the idea of saying that right now filled her with dread. *I used to be able to talk to him about everything. Everything's different now.*

Her eyes were pointed at the TV, but she didn't see anything on the screen. There was simply a colourful blur of motion, and a cacophony of voices and sounds that tripped over themselves in her headphones.

We're both thinking about the same thing. Why can't we just talk about it? Why did he have to try to fuck me so soon after I lost Charlie? It was so unlike Ben. Their sex life before she lost the baby was beautiful; they connected effortlessly, and thrived on each other's pleasure. But now it felt like an ugly, looming thing sitting in the widening gap between them.

Phoebe wasn't even sure what he was working on any more. Even on his worst days, he typed quickly. Now, it sounded more like he was randomly hitting keys just to sound productive. *At the rate he's typing now, he wouldn't even be typing a few words a minute,* she thought, *no one can write like that, surely.*

Ben thumped onto the couch right next to her, and she uttered a small scream. He put his hand gently on her thigh, closer to the knee than the hip. She looked at him, suddenly close to tears again. His eyes pointed straight at the floor. Sitting there, unable to look at Phoebe, Ben looked like an old, tired man. Finally, his eyes slid towards her, apprehension and fear lighting them up. *He's scared to talk to me,* she thought, *as scared as I am. What's happened to us?*

"I'm really sorry."

He didn't clarify what he was talking about; he didn't need to. In his voice, she heard more fear and sorrow than she ever wanted to hear from Ben in her life. He sounded on the verge of tears himself.

"I don't know why I thought that would be okay," he said, "I think I just needed it more than I realised."

Phoebe nodded. There was nothing she could say.

"I'm... this is really difficult for me too," he said, "I know it's worse for you, I know that. But I really don't know what to do. I want to help you, but I don't know how."

She started crying again.

"I'm just not... ready," she said, "for *that*. Not right now. The doctor even said it shouldn't happen for a little while."

Ben gave a sad smile, and squeezed her thigh a little.

"I get it," he said, "I won't do that again, babe. I'm sorry."

"Okay, stop apologising."

He laughed, but it sounded more like a sob to Phoebe.

"Listen," she said, "there's something I wanted to tell you."

A slight frown painted his face, worry creasing his brow as his eyes bored into her own.

"I wanted to name the baby," she said, "to maybe help me deal with things or something. Like closure, I guess. I wanted to name him Charlie, for Grandpa."

He pulled back a little, his frown deepening. His hand left her leg. Glancing away briefly, he looked as though he was trying to understand something said in another language.

"Are you sure that would actually help?"

Phoebe nodded.

"Babe," he said, "I don't know about that. I think it will just make it harder."

"I want to honour Grandpa," she said, "and my son. We have to register his birth; he needs a name."

"Does it have to be your grandfather's name, though? Isn't that just piling more sadness onto things?"

A cold wave spread through her. She couldn't tell if it was anger or hurt; but whatever the feeling was, it wasn't pleasant.

"Are you serious?"

"What?"

Phoebe shook her head. *He really doesn't get it.*

"Ben, he needs a name. Grandpa's been so supportive through this stuff, and I want to show him how much it means to me."

"I just don't want this to be something that hurts you even more. I'm trying to help you, babe. I'm sorry, but this is a bad idea."

She stood, her vision spinning from the suddenness.

"I already told him the baby's name is Charlie," she said, "so the baby's name is Charlie."

Phoebe stormed from the room, slamming the bedroom door behind her and all but diving under the bed sheets. *Why can't he just support me?* She thought, *he could've just let me have this one thing.* She cried until sleep took her, and never felt Ben get in bed hours later.

Chapter Seven:
Back on the Case

17 April 2024 9:00am (Wednesday)

It was a Wednesday, but Phoebe was at home. As she'd done a few dozen other times over the last four years, Phoebe called in sick to focus on the Alpha Park case. She knew it was stupid. *By this point,* she thought, *I'm well and truly addicted.* Despite taking so many days off work, she'd gotten no further with the case. Her lounge room was beginning to look like the secret room of a deranged serial killer; files, photos and printed Wikipedia pages were strewn all over the floor wherever she didn't regularly walk.

Other than the sheer mystery of the case as a whole, and the horrible injustice of a child's murder, the thing that kept resurfacing in Phoebe's mind was the link between Michael Lee Taylor and the Somerton Man. *Thomas Keane.* She still remembered the name, even though that identity was never confirmed.

Every now and then, she went back and read the Wikipedia articles on the Tamam Shud case over again. Whenever she did, the same pulsing frustration arose in her stomach and chest; a desperate need to know the answers. It ate at her, every day. The irony wasn't lost on her; what made her an incredible detective was exactly what had been slowly killing her over the last four years.

That same feeling drove her, motivated her, and had built her career. Before four years ago, it was a wholly positive trait. But now, it seemed only to push her deeper into a dark well of uncertainty.

At first, she'd tried telling herself that no detective could have solved the Alpha Park case. Taylor died too soon, there wasn't enough evidence, and what evidence could be found pointed to an answer that didn't make sense. But she found herself doubting even that; *I could have solved it, I know I could.* She didn't know how, but there was always an answer. *I just didn't put the pieces together properly.*

She at least knew how the detectives working the Tamam Shud case would have felt. *Not that that's any consolation.* As far as she could tell, there were still people investigating the Somerton Man. Maybe not in an official capacity, but the mystery clearly pulled at people the way Taylor pulled at Phoebe.

In 2019, Phoebe printed off a copy of every piece of information on Michael Lee Taylor and the Alpha Park Shooting that the police had. She wasn't proud of it, but she needed access to the files for her own sanity. Not long after that, she'd also printed off everything she could find on the Somerton Man and the investigations and theories surrounding him.

The similarities between the mystery man from Somerton Park Beach and Michael Lee Taylor were baffling. They both seemingly appeared from nowhere, with either false or non-existent ID. Both died with no discernible cause. Similar age, health, and even facial features.

Then there was the book, and the secret pocket containing a torn-out page with 'Tamam Shud' written on it. *Finished.* It was the most infuriating part of both mysteries. *What does it mean?* She found herself wondering if someone had been murdered back in 1948; and if no gun or killer had been found. *Even if his mission was the same as Taylor's, it doesn't mean he used the same method.* The thought made her shake her head, blushing despite being alone.

Look at me, she thought, *I'm actually beginning to believe Taylor's time travel bullshit.*

She'd seen no concrete proof of actual time travel. *Obviously.* Beyond Taylor's statement, there was no indication of it. But she had to follow the evidence.

227

Throughout her career, Phoebe had never let an assumption guide her towards what could be a false destination. As Sir Arthur Conan Doyle said: *Once you eliminate the impossible, whatever remains, no matter how improbable, must be the truth.* Phoebe had pursued every lead she could, looked at the case from every angle. *Except from Taylor's.* And maybe it was time to think about his confession beyond disregarding it as delusion.

And though there was no concrete proof, the link between the two cases was strong and undeniable. Some of the evidence she'd found, though not specifically indicating time travel, at the very least hinted at the possibility. Whether she proved it somehow, or conclusively disproved it, she had to know for sure. Then there was his journal:

I keep forgetting what year it is. I can't draw attention to myself, but I keep getting strange looks for saying things. Then I realise I've said something no one in 2019 would know. Can't get locked up before the mission is done.

Something about it was eerily convincing. There were references throughout his writing to time travel and his experience of 2019. He never wrote much of whatever time he'd supposedly come from, but the way he wrote about it like the past was disquieting in its authenticity. There were references to other things as well, things that made no sense. Taylor mentioned a vacation to a place called Taured that she'd never heard of. He mentioned "the spiral" in a way that suggested it was the device used to travel through time.

The first couple of entries had a date at the bottom. It was written in the American style; month then day then year. She never noticed before. *I skip over dates like that out of habit,* she thought, *why didn't I pay closer attention?* The year was written as 2041. *2041? As in, when Jacob would have been in his thirties? Old enough to be a serial killer...* Phoebe blinked hard, squeezing her eyes shut and trying to force some sense into herself. *He put a lot of thought into this.* The two options, that Phoebe could see, were that the shooter either really had come from the future somehow, or he'd meticulously planned and planted countless clues that pointed in that direction just to confuse or irritate the police. *But who would do that?* Even someone as clearly unhinged as Michael Lee Taylor wouldn't waste so much time and effort for so little reward.

As much as she tried to remain logical, at times it was just too easy to believe that something beyond the understanding of the police had occurred. *At least it would justify why the case is unsolvable.* It didn't help that the deeper she dug into the Tamam Shud case, the further into conspiracy theory territory she went.

"Too much speculation," she said to herself, "too many theories."

All the information she could gather revealed a lot of links between the two cases, but after seventy years, the Tamam Shud case was simply too cold to investigate further. In her mind, the one question that burned more than anything— other than the missing gun—was the meaning of the Tamam Shud note itself.

In the original case, no reason was found for the secret note on the Somerton Man's corpse. There was a code written in the back page of the Rubaiyat of Omar Khayyam, one that had never been deciphered. Phoebe found similar codes in Michael Lee Taylor's journal, and even a page which included an exact copy of the Somerton Man's code, with the caption *Thomas' instructions*. The biggest difference between the two was that in the Somerton Man's copy, a phone number had been found. Traced to a woman who may or may not have known the mysterious man, the phone number essentially provided just another dead end.

The day she made that connection, she'd almost gone to Inspector Rogers then and there. It was such a clear link that there was no way the two cases weren't related. *But I still don't have an actual answer,* she thought, *just linking the cases isn't enough.* Knowing there was something clearly between the Somerton Man and Michael Lee Taylor didn't help her to understand either case any better; if anything, it just made the mysteries surrounding both all the more frustrating.

17 April 2024 12:49pm (Wednesday)

Rosetown North Public School was old, but clean and tidy. The buildings were red brick, and though they were pretty, they had the same cramped and claustrophobic presence as every other school Phoebe had seen. To her it looked like a private school, one of the expensive Catholic ones common in Sydney and Australia more broadly; but it was just a public primary school.

She'd gone on her lunch break, wolfing down a sandwich before rushing to the school. *I can't be too long,* she thought, *but I need enough time to find and interview at least a couple of his teachers*. Her lunch breaks were usually short, just long enough to eat in the small kitchen area of the station. If she took too long, her team would know something was happening.

There was a strange little reception room at the school's entrance; it felt half like a doctor's waiting room and half like the reception at the police station. Phoebe walked in and was greeted by a large middle-aged woman who stared at her uncomfortably. Despite her discomfort, her greeting was warm and friendly. After the pleasantries, Phoebe got straight to business.

"I'm looking to speak to any of the staff who taught a particular student about four years ago," she said, "is that something you can help me with?"

"I'll see what I can do," the woman said, "what's the student's name?"

"Jacob Turner."

The woman nodded and frowned slightly, tapping at the keyboard in front of her. It wasn't the expression of someone who recognised Jacob's name; she barely reacted. *She hasn't worked here longer than a few years,* Phoebe thought, *either that or she just doesn't care.*

"I've got an incomplete record of his grade six file," she said, "but that's it."

"Can you print it for me? Or give me the names of his teachers?"

"Teacher," she corrected, "each class has *one* teacher. But yeah, it's printing now. Give me a sec."

She stood, grunting as she steadied herself on her feet, then disappeared into a tiny back room. For a moment, Phoebe was alone in the cramped space. She felt as though she was back at school, a kid who'd been called to the front office. A memory surfaced, strange and uncomfortable, from the depths of her mind:

"Miss Wilson," the principal said, "do you know why you've been called to my office?"

"Um, no."

"You locked a fellow student into the bathrooms and accused them of stealing a teacher's mug."

"He did steal it!"

"Then you should have come to a teacher."

"But he just would've got away with it."

"Maybe, but you can't just go and do these things yourself. You're a student too."

The receptionist returned, tearing Phoebe back to the present. She held a few sheets of freshly printed paper, and slowly lowered herself back into her chair with another grunt.

"That's the whole file," she said, handing the paper to Phoebe, "it's not much. He wasn't here long."

"You've only got grade six? Not any years before that?"

"I think he transferred from another school."

Why didn't I know that? She thought, *that means Michael Lee Taylor arrived in Rosetown before even Jacob did... if he transferred from a different area.* She flipped through the sparse information provided, and found a short note: *student transferred from Rosetown West at beginning of grade 6.* No reason was given. Phoebe skipped to the teacher of his classes.

"Thanks," she said, "I'll have a chat with his teacher."

"I don't think she's here today."

"Alright, thanks."

"Some of the teachers in the same building might know about him. The class room numbers are written next to the teacher's name. Shouldn't be too hard for you to find."

Phoebe nodded, smiled, and left the woman to herself again. Walking through a school felt unreal to her, like she was having a strange dream. She felt intensely out of place, as though she'd travelled to a different country with no knowledge of the language.

The paper in her hands didn't contain a map of the school, but the class room numbers were painted in giant green above every door, and building numbers on the corners of each building just under the roof. As the woman said, it didn't take Phoebe long to find the room she was looking for.

Class was in, the students sitting at their desks watching the teacher. She couldn't hear what the teacher said, but watched him talk for a while through the small glass window in the door. *Jacob's teacher was a woman,* she thought, *so this is definitely a substitute*.

She sighed, heading back for the reception room. *Everything would be so much easier if this case was still open*. She'd be able to take her time, wait for school to let out, make official requests for information and bring people in to the station. Add everything to the case file properly, and use the full resources of the police.

She was lucky enough that the receptionist cooperated in the first place; she had every right to just refuse and send Phoebe back to the station until she had a warrant or subpoena. Interviewing Jacob's teacher would be a gamble too. *I have to try, though,* she thought, *it feels like I might be onto something*.

18 April 2024 1:04pm (Thursday)

"Hello?" the voice was hesitant, tired and impatient.

"Hello, this is Detective Sergeant Phoebe Wilson. Am I speaking with Mrs Danielle Green?"

"Yes, that's me."

"You taught a student about four years ago named Jacob Turner, is that right?"

Silence. She definitely remembers him.

"Yes, I... That's right."

"I know it was a while ago, but I wanted to ask about him and his behaviour."

Again, Mrs Green went silent for a moment. Phoebe was just about to ask if she'd heard when she spoke again.

"I see. I hope you understand, I don't condone what happened to him. I spoke about him as a problem child a lot, and I might have said a few things that could be taken to mean—"

"Mrs Green, calm down," Phoebe said, stifling a sigh, "you're not in trouble, or being investigated. I just want to understand what he was like as a student."

"Oh. Oh! Well good. What would you like to know?"

No hesitation now, she thought, *interesting.*

"You said he was a problem child. In what ways did he misbehave?"

"He was aggressive. To the teachers and the students. He lied, all the time, even about things that didn't matter."

"Aggressive how?"

"He would argue all the time, and he picked fights with the other students almost every day. He shoved one of the teachers once, so hard she got a bruise."

Problem child, she thought, *I'll say.*

"Any other behaviour you'd consider strange," she asked, "or particularly troublesome?"

"He threatened another student with a knife," Mrs Green said, "though he didn't have one on him at the time."

Holy shit.

"Did you ever see any adults around him," Phoebe asked, "other than his parents or the teachers?"

"You mean like the man who shot him? No, not that I remember. But when he wasn't in class or making a scene, I mostly avoided him when I could."

I would have too.

"It sounds like he was quite a handful to deal with."

"He was. By the way... I thought the investigation was closed?"

"It was. I'm just calling the people who knew him, to get a better idea of the kind of boy he was."

"Oh, I see. Do you mean you're looking for people he pissed off badly enough? Like, for motive?"

"Not exactly," Phoebe said, "I'm just searching for context. To understand the full situation."

"The full situation definitely wasn't great,," Mrs Green said.

"Do you have anything else you'd like to tell me?"

"Umm, no."

"I see. Thank you for your time, Mrs Green. If you think of anything else, don't hesitate to give me a call."

She gave the teacher her mobile number, and instead of saying goodbye, she waited; letting the silence press on Mrs Palmer. Finally, she caved.

"Wait, hang on. Okay. I did hear an awful rumour," she admitted, "though I never saw any proof."

"What was the rumour?"

"I heard..." Mrs Green sighed, her voice shaking just a touch, "I heard from one of the other teachers that he kept a severed cat's head somewhere on the school grounds, that he showed to students he didn't like. To scare them."

18 April 2024 5:10pm (Thursday)

Jacob Turner's house was small and old, but pretty. A typical family house in the suburbs of Sydney. He was an only child, so a small house was more than enough for them to fit. Phoebe had called his parents ahead of time, and though they were less than thrilled, they agreed to meet her. She'd left work a little early, claiming she had some important family business to take care of. But she'd kept her work clothes on, and drove straight to the Turner's place.

Standing outside the house now, Phoebe was struck again by the realisation that speaking to his parents was a terrible idea. She'd known before she called them; but actually, being here made it seem that much worse. *I wonder if their anger ever died down,* she thought. *Unlikely.*

The front door, chipped and faded, seemed to pulse with a tangible menace as Phoebe stared. Even from the sidewalk, she felt it reach for her. It felt the way she'd felt as a child, passing strange houses as she walked to and from school and thinking they might be haunted. Or that someone dangerous lived there.

As an adult, she'd never felt that way about a house. But the Turner residence was decidedly different; she just couldn't tell if it was in her own mind, or if there was something more real happening. Phoebe didn't believe in anything supernatural as a rule, but her experience with the Michael Lee Taylor case had at the very least opened her mind to the possibility that sometimes, there was no logical explanation.

I'm probably just anticipating their anger, she thought, *and projecting that onto the house itself as a hostile place.* But her explanation didn't reduce the sheer malice emanating from the house in front of her. Trying to breathe evenly enough to bring down her racing heartbeat, Phoebe approached the door. *Here goes nothing,* she thought.

There was no doorbell; she knocked three times, hard but not hard enough to sound aggressive. A knock she'd learned over a long career knocking on the doors of people who usually didn't want to see the police. *Confident, but not authoritative,* her old Sergeant had said.

Jacob's mother, Sandra, opened the door. Her eyes were already narrowed, her mouth drawn down into a disapproving frown. *Oh good, a friendly welcome,* Phoebe thought, battling not to roll her eyes. To be fair, Phoebe would have felt the same way, were she in this woman's shoes. *I've lost a son too.* The only difference was, Phoebe had no one to blame. Being angry at the police meant Sandra could focus all her grief and rage at someone. *I wish I'd had that.*

"Mrs. Turner, how are you?"

"Fine. Come in, let's get this over with. Whatever it is."

"Is your husband here too?"

"Yeah, he's already in the lounge room."

They walked in, Phoebe a couple steps behind Sandra. Peter, Jacob's father, wore a similar expression to his wife. He held a tumbler half-full of whiskey and stared hard at the modest coffee table in front of him. His eyes only shifted to her after she sat down and Sandra disappeared to the kitchen.

"You're here to talk about my son," he said, "*again.*"

"That's right, Mr Turner. I just wanted to see if there was anything—"

"You didn't solve it before. I gave you everything you needed to know already."

It took everything Phoebe had not to sigh out loud. Peter Turner had been difficult to deal with in the original investigation too. For some reason, Phoebe hoped the passage of time might have softened him up a little. *No such luck.*

"I just wanted to understand Jacob a little better," she said, "so that I might understand what happened a—"

"Some lunatic shot a child. It could've been any child. How could it help you to know anything more about my son?"

Sandra returned to the lounge room with a cup of tea, and sat down with it nestled in her hands. *No offer of a drink for me,* she thought, *I know they're angry, but that's just plain rude*. Were she offered, she would have refused anyway; but the lack of an offer hit her as a pointed gesture. *You're not welcome here.*

"I'm just doing my job, Mr Turner."

It's not exactly the truth, but not a total lie, either.

"You should have done it properly back then."

The only other time she'd met Peter Turner was when he visited the station to give a statement about Jacob. Being in his home felt different; there was so much more context for the kind of person he was. Very few photos adorned the walls and surfaces, and those that did were more often of Peter and his wife than of Jacob. Even if they weren't fond of photos, it was strange for parents to not have them after a child died.

Instead of photos, intricate and delicate statues sat on most of the available surfaces. Mementos from their travel, or perhaps just pretty knick-knacks picked up from a nearby antique store. The latter was more likely, given Peter was a retired public school principal and Sandra was currently unemployed. Phoebe had looked into them, as much as she felt necessary.

Peter had in fact been the principal at Jacob's school. He'd retired the year after Jacob died. *I would have too.* He'd worked there for twenty years, even though Jacob spent all but his last year at a different school. Looking at Peter now, she couldn't imagine him being a parent. A cold and indifferent school principal, absolutely; but not a loving father.

"What kind of child was Jacob?" she asked, staring right into Peter's eyes.

"I told you that already," he said, his voice dangerously blank, "in the interview. He was smart. Driven. He would have gone far."

"But his temperament? His behaviour towards other children, and the teachers?"

Peter's face darkened, a deep red rising in his skin.

"If you're implying something, detective, just stop playing games and say it outright."

I hit a nerve there. A picture was beginning to form; one that wasn't particularly flattering to Jacob's parents. *Or to Jacob himself.*

"I just want to know what kind of boy he was," she said. "There are no implications."

He stared at her, his eyes deep and intense. Something about him felt off. *I might be talking to a psychopath right now*; the thought leapt into her mind before she'd processed it. Phoebe had only ever spoken to one person she considered to be a genuine psychopath, during the serial killings two years before. But the atmosphere surrounding Jacob's father was disturbingly similar.

Even Jacob's mother was affected; her anger towards Phoebe didn't override her fear of Peter. Phoebe noticed her behaviour as soon as she rejoined them in the lounge room. She'd certainly seen it in many others. *If nothing else, being a police Constable made me an expert in identifying domestic abuse.*

"He was a good boy. He would have been a great man."

"He would've been fifteen this year," Sandra added. Her voice wavered, but not from sadness; it was low, nervous and fearful. As she spoke, she glanced at her husband, then quickly away.

Charlie would have been fifteen, too.

"I know," Phoebe said, "I'm sorry for your loss, once again."

"I don't care if you're sorry. You didn't help then, and you're not helping now."

Mr Turner rose, and his full height added to his already imposing nature. Though he stood with a calm enough posture, his right hand curled into a fist, and Sandra's face turned pale. Phoebe stood as well, and though she wasn't as tall, she'd been on the job long enough that she wasn't scared easily.

"I understand that the loss of your son is still upsetting," she said, "I understand it better than most. But I am truly trying to help you. I just want to find the truth, and properly close this case once and for all."

His eyes, narrowed and glowing with a deep violence, never moved from her own. The skin of his knuckles was white, his fist so tightly balled that she was sure he would attack. Instead, he grunted, and the fist gradually loosened into a hand again. The tension in the room didn't ease up. They stared at each other a moment longer. Finally, Mr Turner gestured almost casually to the front door.

"Good luck," he said.

18 April 2024 5:42pm (Thursday)

Phoebe's phone was almost always on silent; she checked it as she left the Turner's home and saw three missed calls from her mother. A voice message had been left, and Phoebe's heart rate leapt into overdrive. *Mum never leaves messages,* she thought, *bad news.* Putting her phone back in her pocket without checking the message, she got in the car and drove away.

As she drove, her thoughts drifted again and again to the message waiting on her phone. Her mind offered countless possible scenarios, each worse than the last. As she pulled into the car park at her apartment building, a horrible certainty had settled in. She didn't dare give the thought any more attention than she absolutely had to; but it was there, lurking just underneath her conscious mind.

By the time she sat on the couch, finally out of her work clothes and away from responsibility, panic was well and truly overtaking her. The phone sat next to her on the couch, silent and menacing. Its deep black screen beckoned like the depths of an old stone well. An ominous feeling of danger echoed from its blank face, and Phoebe found herself too afraid to even touch it.

I can't tell which is worse, she thought, *not knowing, or picking up that phone and listening to mum's message.* Indecision paralysed her. The TV, which she usually put on out of habit, remained dead and quiet. She would have usually poured herself a glass of wine by now, but it sat unmoved in the fridge, almost entirely forgotten.

Letting out a shaky breath, Phoebe forced herself to reach for her phone. *I have to know. Even if it hurts, even if it's what I think it is, I have to know for sure.* For a moment, she stared at the smooth black face of her phone. Her reflection stared back, pale and scared.

"Just check it," she said, her voice shaking, "just fucking get it over with."

She stared at the phone a little longer. Taking a deep breath, she unlocked it, opened the call log, and dialed voicemail. The thundering of her heart drowned out the ringing, until an automated voice spoke gently into her ear.

"You have one new message." It recited the time; shortly before she left the Turner residence. Then a beep, shrill and panicky to her ears, filled the tiny speaker.

When the message started, there was no speaking. Just a rustling sound that could have been her mother sniffling, a breeze, or simply moving the phone. A few more seconds of silence followed, and Phoebe's heart pounded at her chest, her breath strangled and short.

"Phoebe," her mother finally said, "your grandfather..."

I knew it, she thought as her mother paused again, *I fucking knew it.*

"He's dead. I'm so sorry. He died just now, I thought you should know. You're the first person I've called."

16 August 2008 11:49am (Saturday)

Gentle rain pattered the wild grass of their backyard. Ben usually mowed the lawn, but he hadn't since they found out about the baby. Phoebe knelt on the damp grass, ignoring the water soaking through the knees of her jeans. It was one of the most difficult things she'd ever done, but she was ready. She'd spent most of the morning thinking and preparing herself.

Time to say goodbye, she thought. A funeral for stillbirths was fairly common, and though at the time it would have been far too painful, it now felt like a necessity. *I have to let him go.* Ben stood nearby. She felt his restlessness even without looking at him. Their relationship had improved a little, but there was still a distance between them that she tried not to think about.

"I'm so sorry, Charlie," she said, "I miss you so much. I don't know why this happened, but I wish you were here."

She laid her hand on the small statue she'd bought to memorialise him. It was a stone angel, a winged child. She wasn't religious, but the imagery spoke to her anyway. She imagined Charlie was alive somewhere; she *needed* to believe it was true. The statue helped her imagine him.

"Okay, babe," Ben said, "the rain's just gonna get worse. Can we go inside now?"

She ignored him.

"I love you, Charlie. I'll never forget you."

"Babe."

Phoebe squeezed her eyes shut, trying to force Ben's voice from her mind. Losing Charlie was difficult enough; his lack of support piled on top of that only fed the pain slicing into her heart. Underneath that pain, a quiet rage was burning like the embers of a campfire. *He knows how much this hurts me,* she thought, *and how much I need to do this. Why can't he just shut up?*

The statue's rough stone scraped her hand as she stroked the angel's face. Cold wetness slowly spread over her shoulders and back as the rain picked up. Ben's shoes slapped against the rain-covered walkway leading back to the door. She watched him go back inside without a word.

She stayed a while longer, but could think of nothing more to say. Finally, she pushed herself to her feet, and went back inside. *It wasn't really a funeral,* she thought, *but if there was any more than that I would have been a mess.* Ben sat on the couch, staring at the blank TV screen.

"Why are you so against saying goodbye to him like that?" she said, sitting a little way down the couch.

"I know you, babe," he said, his voice barely audible, "you're just going to fixate on it. It won't help."

"It's already helping," she said, "more than you are."

But she was lying, and they both knew it. The pain still lay inside her like a vast ocean, spreading in waves, ebbing and flowing but always present. Nothing would help.

Ben scoffed, still almost silent, and shook his head. His eyes never left the TV, as though his favourite movie was playing and he couldn't tear his gaze away to talk to her.

"What can I do to help, then?"

"Anything. Nothing. I don't know, but, Christ, Ben... it would be great to not have you arguing every decision I make. I'm just trying to get through this."

"Well, I'm trying to help you. Sometimes you do things like this and it just makes you more upset."

"Are you seriously saying it's my fault I'm this upset?"

"No, what? Jesus, no babe. I'm just saying that there has to be a healthier way to deal with this."

"Funerals for stillbo—" Phoebe choked back tears, and started again, "funerals in these situations are really common, Ben. It's a normal way to grieve someone who's died."

"We didn't even have a name, babe. It died before it was born. Can't we just focus on us again for a while, and move on?"

"He does have a name. Just because you don't agree, doesn't mean it's not real. His name is Charlie. And for fuck's sake, can you please stop saying 'it'?"

By the time she was done, tears streamed down her face again. The words were automatic, coming directly from somewhere deep inside, where the anger burned. She couldn't think clearly enough to say any more.

Ben just continued staring at the TV. He was willing to talk through most issues with her if she initiated, but whenever he was genuinely upset, he might as well have been a statue. Phoebe sobbed openly, watching Ben's face as he stared. In his eyes, a horrible distance made them look dull and empty, as though he didn't care at all.

"I just... I just want to move on," he said.

19 April 2024 10:07am (Friday)

Her head pounded, her throat dry and hot. *Not enough water last night,* she thought. Usually, she drank enough water that a bottle or two of wine wouldn't lead to a hangover. *Coffee. Just need some coffee.* Even exhausted and pounding, her mind dragged inexorably to the one place it always went.

It's insane, Phoebe thought, *but I'm honestly beginning to agree with what Wilks said.* When the team spoke about it in 2019, he'd come up with a theory about a secret organisation that could send people back in time for assassinations and other missions. It couldn't be the truth, but the more she thought about it the more sense it made.

If an organisation like that existed, they would want to leave as little evidence behind as possible. They would want to confuse any police that investigated. The organisation might even benefit from the outrageous claims of conspiracy theorists; no one believed them anyway, and it would only serve to muddle the facts.

I wonder if the organisation knows about me, she thought, *if they even exist.*

"I'm beginning to think as though they do exist."

"What, Sarge?" Timms said.

Shit, I said that out loud.

"Oh, nothing."

Nudging herself back into the present, she focused on the file on her computer screen. It had been sitting open for the last hour, since she arrived at work that morning; the robbery case they were working on. *The one I'm actually supposed to be investigating,* she thought, *instead of old frozen cases.*

One of her team—Brouwer, she was sure—had found some possible safe houses where the last suspect might be laying low. From those, Phoebe had found one that was most likely. *A few streets from where we found Reeves, plus one of his associates was seen there a few months ago during a different investigation.* If Dan Reeves had been there before, and his girlfriend needed a place to stay, it added up.

"I think I know where Teagan Lee is hiding out," she said.

"Alright Sarge, say the word and we can be on our way to pick her up."

"I'm... Geez, how about a coffee first?"

"You do look like you need it," Timms said, before realising what he'd said and stammering, "I mean... no offense, Sarge."

"None taken, I need it more than anything right now."

She'd been too preoccupied on her way to work to buy a coffee like she usually did; now on top of her hangover, the lack of caffeine in her system pushed the ache in her head even further.

Her team were busy, even Timms, so she left the station herself. It was a fair day; a little cool, but the sun was out and the cool air actually helped a little. She walked slowly, trying to focus on nothing but her breathing. Her head pulsed, her eyes stinging in the sunlight. She was more or less used to the feeling, especially in the mornings, but it didn't make it any easier to deal with.

As she stepped into the busy cafe, jazz music wailed from a speaker in the corner, and the chatter of dozens of customers threatened to drown it out. Her headache changed from pulses of dull pain to a stabbing heat behind her eyes. *Get the coffee and go,* she thought, barely even deciphering the words among the chaos of sound around her.

Waiting in line almost killed her. It was a busy cafe, and the wait was always longer this late in the morning. By the time she reached the counter, her eyes were barely open. She'd been a regular customer for quite a while; the staff member gave a sympathetic smile and took her card without a word spoken. *I'm glad they know my usual,* she thought through the noise, *not sure I can talk properly right now.*

The way back to the station was a little easier. Stepping out of the cafe sent a wave of quiet relief through her mind.

After a few sips of the extra strong coffee, Phoebe began feeling less like a reheated corpse and more like a person again.

By the time she got back to her desk, the coffee was almost empty. *Now I just need water,* she thought.

"You ready to get Teagan Lee?" Brouwer said, "or do you need another coffee?"

"Yeah, alright, alright," Phoebe said with a deep breath, "I'm ready. Bring it on."

19 April 2024 12:41pm (Friday)

Once again, the team split into two cars and drove for the safe house. The apprehension of Dan Reeves had gone smoothly, and Phoebe couldn't help but hope Teagan Lee would be captured just as easily.

"Sarge," Brouwer said, "you feeling okay?"

Is it still so obvious? She thought. Though she was feeling a little better, compared to a normal day she felt terrible. *Apparently, I'm not hiding it very well.* The coffee only helped for what felt like a moment; now she was back to wishing for sleep.

The car travelled smoothly through several quiet streets. Phoebe tasked Timms with the drive; though she usually drove, none of them questioned her choice. *I'll have to let Brouwer lead the arrest,* she thought, *I'm in no state to wrestle someone into handcuffs.*

A thin sheen of sweat covered her face and neck, and her lungs couldn't draw in a full breath. *I might need to finish early today.* She had no idea if her team knew why she was under the weather, but they were usually as accommodating as they could be. As their boss, she really should be showing the best example. Guilt took up almost as much space in her mind as Michael Lee Taylor lately.

"Sarge?"

Oh shit, I didn't answer.

"Yeah, I'm alright. We getting close?"

"Yep," Timms said, "just around the corner."

They pulled up, no lights or sirens; *just like last time.* A palpable sense of danger lit up Phoebe's blurry mind, and she motioned for the team to approach. They already had a plan, so talking was kept to a minimum. The moments before a raid or arrest were always the most intense; even during the action, there was a strange sense of certainty. She supposed it was adrenaline providing clarity; it certainly felt better than the fear and apprehension in the moments before anything happened.

Their set up was more or less the same as when they caught Dan Reeves; Phoebe glanced at her team, and when they all nodded back, she gave the signal. She stood back as Brouwer knocked and announced their presence. After no one answered, he knocked again. When they were met with more silence, he shot a questioning look at Phoebe.

"We have reason to believe she's in there," Phoebe said, "do it."

Without hesitation, Brouwer took the breaching tool—a solid black bar with handles on one side—off Simpson and smashed it into the door on the handle side. *My head could've done without that,* she thought, and then they were inside and her mind cleared the way it always did.

The place was cleaner than where they'd caught Reeves, though still as old and dilapidated. Each of her team veered off into separate rooms, guns up and ready. She watched from the front door.

"Clear!" someone said.

"Bedroom's clear!"

"Clear!"

Where is she? Phoebe remembered searching Michael Lee Taylor's apartment. They'd known it would be empty—or at least, they'd hoped it would be—and he was dead by then; but a sense of urgency had still settled over them at the time. There had been something dangerous about his apartment. Now, darting her eyes at every surface and doorway, Phoebe felt the same way.

What if she's disappeared? She thought, *or what if we catch her and then she dies in custody with no apparent cause?* Suddenly, the feeling of danger wasn't the only thing making her heart thump painfully; panic spread through her chest and stomach, and deja vu echoed in her mind. *It's going to be the same,* she thought, *another insane mystery with no answers.* What had felt like concrete certainty only seconds ago—the details of the case—became a jumbled mess of unrelated thoughts.

"She's not here," Phoebe said, "she's not here. We won't find her. She's not here."

Footsteps. What if it's her? It can't be her; we won't find her.

"She's not here," she said again.

"Alright, Sarge," someone said, "alright. Come here. I think you might need another day off."

Where the fuck is she? Phoebe thought. She was guided to the car, and distantly heard the door thud closed next to her. But she didn't feel anything, and her mind simply repeated the same thoughts over and over; *she's not here. We won't find her.*

19 April 2024 4:03pm (Friday)

Later that afternoon, she realised she'd been home for a while and had no memory of getting there. The attempted arrest was nothing but a panic-filled blur. She was most of the way through a bottle of wine by the time she came to her senses. Netflix played on her TV, a stand-up comedy special, though Phoebe barely heard it.

The day's events felt as though they'd happened years ago. A strange link, ominous and vague, appeared between the robbery case and the Alpha Park shooting. She couldn't exactly define it, but somehow the two felt connected. *Teagan Lee is missing,* she thought, *disappeared. Was she involved in the organisation that Michael Lee Taylor worked for?* Frowning, Phoebe took a long sip of wine, then shook her head, forcing some kind of logic into her thoughts. *She's not missing, she just isn't where we thought she would be.*

"Need to get my mind off things," she said, the words slurring a little even in her own ears, "a holiday or something."

But she knew she'd never truly relax, even if she went somewhere. Her mind simply didn't know how to let a mystery like Michael Lee Taylor go. *He's in my head,* she thought, *maybe that's exactly what he wanted. Maybe that was his plan the whole time.*

Her thoughts were scattered, but they still felt utterly convincing to her. *Did I find proof that he came from the future?* For some reason she had no memory of it, but she thought she had. *Why else would I believe it?* She finished her glass and poured in the rest of the bottle; there wasn't much left.

"I think I might need another day off," she said.

Someone said that to me recently.

A peal of laughter hissed from the TV, and Phoebe's head snapped towards the sudden noise. She'd forgotten it was on; shaking her head, she put the empty wine bottle in her recycling bin and sat back on the couch. For what felt like a couple of hours, she tried to content herself watching comedy shows on Netflix. When that didn't work, she took one of her sleeping pills.

I can't remember how long these take to work, she thought, *but it won't matter if I fall asleep on the couch.* Her sense of time had disappeared; disconnected from her experience entirely. She picked her phone up; it was turned off. *I don't remember doing that.* Had it run out of battery, or had she turned it off herself? Holding the power button down brought it back to life again; *I turned it off then. Or maybe Michael Lee Taylor did.*

The thought crashed into her mind like a sudden gust of unpleasant-smelling air. *No, that's impossible.* But then, there were several impossible things that happened to Michael Lee Taylor. Another unpleasant thought lurked in the back of her mind then, lingering at the edges of conscious thought; *If he really could time travel, couldn't he come back again?*

It felt too big, too terrifying, to comprehend. If she ever saw him again, she would lose her mind. *What little of it there is to lose.* She wasn't under any delusions; Phoebe was fully aware that she was already losing her mind. *But if I know it's happening,* she thought, *doesn't that mean I'm not too far gone?*

A message sat in the middle of her phone's screensaver. *Aaron Brouwer,* the contact at the top said. She had to read the message several times to understand it; *Maybe the sleeping pill is taking effect already.* Focusing as much as she could, she read it again:

KALOF is out on Teagan Lee. Not much more we can do right now, try to relax Sarge. Hope you feel better soon.

It meant no one knew where Teagan Lee was. And it meant they didn't need her at the station right now. *Are they trying to tell me to stay home longer?* Brouwer had told her to relax; she wanted to. *Let's see if I get any sleep tonight,* she thought.

Her wine glass was empty. *Did I just finish it? Or was that a while ago?* She got up and checked the fridge, but there were no open bottles. The room spun in front of her, wheels of bright white and black glowing in her eyes like she'd been staring at the sun.

I'm in shock. I think I had a panic attack. She couldn't remember ever having one before. By all accounts, she'd been an anxious child, but it had never resulted in an actual panic attack; at least not that she could remember.

The TV was still on. As she stared, the screen blurred and refocused. She glanced up, and the corners between wall and ceiling sagged, waving slowly like the surface of the sea. *Have I eaten today?* A strange tension swept through her stomach; she couldn't tell if it was hunger or nausea. *Or Charlie.* Without warning, she was wrenched back to the days after she lost him. Days of numb fear and empty grief. It felt fresh in that moment, as if no time had passed.

She'd spent a long time imagining what Charlie would look like. Sitting on the couch, staring at the moving walls, the pale face of Jacob Turner appeared.

"Charlie?" she said.

Her voice sounded far away. Weak. Goosebumps broke out on her skin. *Is that how I imagined him?* It looked like Charlie to her. His face swam on the wall, pale and dead, and Phoebe groaned as another wave of tension cramped her stomach. As it did, Charlie's face wavered and broke apart.

Chapter Eight:
Grief

22 July 1995 4:50pm (Saturday)

They were stuck inside; not only was it freezing cold outside, but it was bucketing down with rain as well. Normally, Phoebe would have hated being stuck inside. But at the moment, it was exciting. *Detective Phoebe is on the case!* She thought, digging through the old draws and cupboards of her grandparents' lounge room.

White, with red spots. She kept the words in her head as best she could, repeating them over and over. Her grandparents drank coffee and tea daily, so a missing mug was a big problem. She felt proud that they asked her for help; Grandpa knew she was a good detective, and she would prove him right.

Their house was old, and their furniture even older. Old things, made of crystal and ceramic, sat on sideboards and ornamental tables, and Phoebe had to be careful not to knock any of it. She didn't know why a mug might be in an old cupboard, but she had to be sure.

Explore every option, she remembered grandpa saying once, *no matter how crazy it seems.* It sounded like something Sherlock Holmes might have said, but she couldn't remember if it was from a Sherlock story or if he'd just said it himself. Either way, it was great advice. After emptying and searching another drawer, she carefully put everything back and moved to the next one.

The lounge room was clear. Without pausing, she ran to the next room; the spare bedroom. It was always so neat and tidy. *It won't take long to search*, she thought, *I'll find it in no time!*

Under the bed, in the drawers, in the cupboards; the mug wasn't there. Frowning, she moved to the next room. The bathroom was almost as tidy and clean as the spare bedroom, and always smelled like fresh oranges. A mug was even less likely to be in the bathroom, but she had to check. There weren't many places to check anyway; cupboard, bathtub, shower. All were clear.

The next room was a linen cupboard full of towels and sheets. Half of the shelves were too high for her to reach or see into. Smiling to herself, she grabbed a chair from the lounge room table and dragged in into the hallway, setting it in front of the cupboard. When she stepped onto the chair and turned to see the higher shelves, she squealed; the mug was there, half hidden behind a neat pile of towels.

Leaning almost off the chair, Phoebe managed to grab the mug and jump to the soft carpet without falling. She ran to the kitchen, where her grandparents and parents were chatting, and showed them the missing mug.

"I found it!" she said, "it was in the cupboard!"

Her grandfather grinned at her, taking the mug and messing her hair gently with his free hand.

"I knew you'd find it," he said, "my little detective."

"Now why would a mug be in the linen closet?" her father asked, glancing with wide eyes at Phoebe as her mother laughed.

"I don't know, dad," she said, "but it was there, I swear!"

"Well done, sweetie," her grandmother said, her smile soft and warm, "you're very good at finding things, aren't you?"

"Yep!"

The adults laughed at her answer, but it was a kind laugh, and she smiled.

"You know," her grandfather said, "I think we also lost a cup of tea. Would you be able to *find* one of those for me, Phoebe?"

He winked and messed her hair again, and she nodded.

"I found the first piece already," she said, holding her hand out for the mug her grandfather still held.

He laughed, handed the mug to her, and shook his head.

"You're too smart sometimes," he said, "you're going to be the best detective in the world one day."

21 April 2024 10:00am (Sunday)

The day of her grandfather's funeral, the weather was surprisingly fair. For some reason, Phoebe had expected dark grey clouds, and slow but constant rain. *Weather to match the mood*. People Phoebe hadn't seen in years showed up, and the man she thought it impossible for her to love any more became even greater. *How many people did his life touch?* she thought.

Charles Wilson was a private and quiet man. But Phoebe saw that he left behind a huge amount of love and kindness. All the people who showed up gave their condolences, but Phoebe couldn't say a word; if she opened her mouth, all that would come out would be sobs.

His death surprised no one; if anything, the surprise was how long he'd lived without his mind or memories. But it still hit her harder than anything she'd been through in the last ten years. *He's gone. Forever.* His coffin sat at the back of the room, behind a podium and a large printed photo of him from before his mind and health declined. In the photo, he smiled his calm, warm smile. Phoebe hadn't seen that version of him in a long time, and for a moment she was overwhelmed. Tears poured over her cheeks, and what breath she could draw hitched and caught in her throat.

When the talking started, Phoebe simply stared at the photo of her grandfather, letting the words about him merge with her memories. She didn't give a eulogy. Instead, she listened. The memories other people had of him were comforting but strange. It felt like there was so much of his life she'd missed, even though she grew up with him around. Stories from before she was born, and from her teenage years when she hadn't seen him as much, were told by people she knew and those she didn't.

Then it was her mother's turn. Phoebe hadn't always gotten along well with her mother as an adult, but all her memories of childhood were happy, especially before her parents' divorce.

"My father was a great man," her mother said, "he was kind, intelligent, and patient. He always did what was best for his family. He had so many friends, so many people he loved, who loved him back. I can't express how it feels..."

She stopped, her shoulders heaving silently as she cried into her hands. For a moment, she fought for control and lost. Then, gradually, the heaving subsided and her breathing returned to normal.

"I can't express how it feels to not have him around anymore. He taught me everything I know. And he... he was the best grandfather to my daughter I ever could have wished for."

She turned to the photo next to her, openly weeping, and then lowered her eyes, turning her face to the crowd again.

"I miss you, dad," she said.

21 April 2024 1:21pm (Sunday)

After the funeral, most of the group gathered at Phoebe's mother's house for the wake. They listened to Elvis, his favourite. Her mother had prepared three huge quiches, his favourite food. Phoebe felt an overwhelming wave of nostalgia wash over her as Elvis crooned and the smell of quiche filled the lounge room.

When he was moved into a care facility, he gave his antique furniture to Phoebe's mother. She'd kept it, and several of the old cupboards and bookshelves sat along the walls of the lounge room. Somehow, she felt her grandfather's presence more intensely in that moment than she had standing with him in the care facility. Another wave of nostalgia threatened to overtake her, and she crossed the lounge room quickly into the kitchen.

"Phoebe, are you okay?"

She hadn't seen her mother follow her. Putting down the paper plate of quiche she'd been given, she nodded.

"Yeah. It's just, all this stuff of his, it's a bit much."

"I know," she said, "I thought it would make things easier. But it's the opposite, isn't it?"

Phoebe nodded again. They stood for a moment, together, thinking about her grandfather.

"I barely remember the way he was before he got sick," her mother said, almost whispering, "is that awful?"

"He was sick for a long time."

She could barely remember either, though she did hold a few special memories in their own place, untarnished by age. She relived them all the time, even years before his death. He was always happy and healthy in that place, his mind always keen and his smile bright.

"I just wish I could remember him more vividly," her mother said, "but all I can think of is the way he was in that place."

It was a strong image, one that was hard to get past. But Phoebe remembered him as he was when she was little. He never seemed to age; for her entire young life he remained the same. Always smiling, always encouraging. He was the reason she became a detective. He was the reason she got through everything after Ben and Charlie. *Him and Claire, anyway.*

"You'll remember him better eventually, mum. We have tons of photos."

It sounded weak, even to herself, but it was all she could think to say. *I'm just glad she's not being petty,* Phoebe thought. Given the circumstances, her mother was actually being nicer than she'd been in a long time. She was almost a different person. *Almost like the person she was when I was young,* she thought, *when grandpa was still healthy.*

Her mother simply nodded and moved slowly back into the lounge room. For a while, Phoebe stood in the kitchen, nodding politely to anyone who wandered through. All she wanted then was to listen to her grandfather read Sherlock Holmes to her again.

29 August 2008 1:53pm (Friday)

Phoebe woke up slowly, the familiar numb emptiness settling in as soon as she was aware of the room around her. She knew without checking that Ben wouldn't be in the bed. *He never is anymore*, she thought. All the physical pain had passed, but her emotional state remained fragile and murky. She was perpetually on the verge of tears.

Their relationship was still distant. Ben got up early every morning, while Phoebe slept in. He stayed at his work desk all day, staring as blankly as he did the last time they spoke about Charlie. Phoebe stayed in bed as long as possible, and when she got up, she just moved straight to the couch and put her headphones on. She only ate when she really needed it, and went to bed early. Ben stayed up way past when she fell asleep every night.

Gentle sunlight filled the room as she blinked slowly. She couldn't tell if it was morning or afternoon. *Not that it matters*. Slipping out of the bed, Phoebe washed her face in the bathroom. She didn't look at herself in the mirror, and she didn't bother with a shower or anything else. *I don't remember when I last showered,* she thought, *not that long ago*.

She shuffled out to the lounge room, not bothering to look at Ben's study. Their house had become a grey background, comfortable but empty. Ben's distance and silence had combined to blend him in with the rest of the house. He'd become as invisible as the walls she didn't see. With a sigh, Phoebe sat on the couch.

The TV stared back at her, blank and uncaring. Phoebe put on her headphones, but didn't turn the TV on. Even when the TV was off, her headphones blocked a lot of ambient noise.

She sat for a while, eyes unfocused, with a comfortable silence pressing in on her ears.

Her mind, somehow busy and empty at the same time, filled with cloudy noise. She wanted to watch something, to drown out her thoughts, but even reaching for the remote felt like too much of a task.

A shuffling sound crept through the headphones, followed by a muffled bang. Frowning, Phoebe took them off and cocked her head to listen. More sounds came, and she realised they were coming from Charlie's room. She glanced over her shoulder; Ben wasn't at his desk.

She reached the doorway to find Ben packing the room they'd set up for Charlie into boxes. The room was a mess. A cold dread rose from the depths of her stomach, setting her heart thumping and forcing her throat closed. Ben's face was blank, as it always was now. No tears, no sadness. *It's like he's packing for a boring trip with his family,* she thought.

He glanced up at her briefly, then went right back to packing a box without a word. Phoebe tried to find the words she needed. Nothing came to her mind at first, and every second she waited her dread grew stronger.

"Um," she finally said, before swallowing and fighting back a sob, "what are you doing?"

For a long, horrifying moment, Ben simply kept packing. Phoebe was on the brink of screaming when he stopped, dropped from his knees to his butt, and sighed.

"I'm trying to move on, Pheebs," he said, "for both of us. I just want to get back to where we were before."

"We can't," she said, her voice shaking as she tried to breathe, "we're not where we were before. Charlie died, Ben. He's dead. I can't just *move on*, Jesus."

"We have to, babe. You can't keep going like this. You'll have to go back to work some time, and we can't keep this room as a bedroom for a child who was never born."

"Shit, Ben! Can you stop being such a dick?"

He shook his head, dropping his eyes back to the box he'd been packing.

"I'm trying to be reasonable here, babe. You know this isn't easy for me, and you're really not making it any easier."

This time, she did scream. Then she stomped back to the couch, fell onto it, and wept. She didn't try to cover the sound, or pretend she was okay.

"Phoebe," he called from the room, "come on."

His voice dripped with frustration and something darker, something she couldn't identify. *Am I really the unreasonable one?* She thought, *I've never seen him act like this before. Maybe I am the problem.* She wondered if other women struggled this much going through the same thing. *The way Ben's acting, it's like losing a baby should be some small thing that doesn't matter.*

After her sobbing quieted down a little, and her breathing returned almost to normal, Ben emerged from the room. He sat gently next to her.

"I love you," he said, "but something needs to change. We're drifting apart, babe. I'm scared. Losing the baby was bad enough, but I feel like I'm losing you too."

"You're pushing me away, Ben," she said, "you're trying to force me to forget about Charlie. It hasn't even been that long. For fuck's sake, Ben, it hasn't even been his due date yet. He'd still be growing right now if he hadn't died. And you want me to just forget?"

She kept her eyes closed as she spoke. Hot tears stung her eyes as they crept through her eyelids. He didn't reply at first.

"All I needed was for you to support me," Phoebe said, "just for a while. I've lost my son, Ben. I had to... had to give birth to him. I thought you would understand how awful this all is. But you don't."

He sighed again, heavy and resigned. Phoebe glanced at him; he put his head in his hands, shaking it slowly from side to side.

"At least I tried," he said.

"What the fuck does that mean?"

"I tried to understand, Phoebe. I did. I tried to help, I tried to listen, I did everything for you. I organised all the medical stuff, I comforted you."

Ben sighed again, and she saw a vertical line shining down his cheek, reflecting the lounge room's light.

"I know it's hard for you," he said, "but all you've done is shut me out. You never want to be close to me anymore. We haven't had sex in ages. We don't shower together, we don't cuddle in bed, nothing. I don't even feel like I'm your husband anymore."

Where the fuck is this coming from? As far as she was concerned, Ben was the one who pulled away from her. *And only because I rejected him* one *time,* she thought. *Is that really what doing everything for me looks like?*

"I can't believe you right now," she said, "the one time I actually need you, and you just bail."

"Woah, who's bailing?"

"You just said you're not my husband anymore."

Ben groaned, then uttered a sharp, humourless laugh.

"That's not what I said, and you know it. You know what?" Ben stood as he kept talking, pacing the room without looking at her.

"You're so positive when things are going well, but the second something goes bad you completely break down. Then it's all on me to pick you up again. And I get it, and I can do that for you. But you haven't just broken down this time, you've shoved me away. You're acting like I'm against you. It's ridiculous."

"Ben," she said, "I never pushed you away. I just said no to sex *one* time, and you sulked for a whole week like a fucking teenager."

"And you totally ignored me," he said, "even after I stopped *sulking*. When you shut down, you're impossible to deal with. Nothing I can do helps you, because you're determined to be miserable."

He was crying openly as he spoke, still pacing, still looking anywhere but at her.

"You're the one who's acting miserable," Phoebe said, "you won't look at me, you won't talk to me. You wake up before me and go to bed after I'm asleep. How the fuck is this my fault? All I need is some support, and you can't handle that because I wouldn't let you fuck me *one time*."

"Fucking hell, Phoebe. That one time was a stupid mistake. I said sorry already, why can't you drop it?"

Finally, he stopped moving and looked directly at her.

"I actually think it's good for us that the baby wasn't born. You can't even handle an adult relationship; I don't think you would've been able to handle being a mother."

Phoebe stared back at him, momentarily overwhelmed by a deep, bright rage that wiped out her thoughts. Then she said the only words that she could think to say. They didn't do any justice to the well of pain and fury rising up in her, but no other words existed in that moment.

"Fuck you, Ben," she said, trying to ignore the tears streaming down her face, "fuck you."

22 April 2024 8:40am (Monday)

She'd barely been back at work for an hour before Michael Lee Taylor was thrust back into her mind. *Or maybe it really is John Thompson,* she thought. Even after the anonymous caller had given her a new name, Phoebe continued thinking of him as Michael Lee Taylor.

One of her interstate contacts had written back to her with contact information which seemed to match the criminal file she'd sent. *An address for relatives of John Thompson.* They lived in Rosetown; it was almost too good to be true. Which in her profession, meant it was definitely not as good as it seemed. She wrote the address into her notepad, glanced around, and closed down the email before anyone saw.

Her team were taking pains to give her space; after her panic attack at Teagan Lee's hideout, they seemed to be terrified of triggering another one. *Any space I get is a bonus at the moment,* she thought. *I feel fine now anyway.* It wasn't strictly true, but she figured if she kept saying it to herself, she might eventually make it so.

All the previous night she'd spent crying; the stress and disappointment of not finding Teagan Lee piled on top of her grief from the funeral. It left her empty and wrung out. In an exhausted, painful way, she almost felt relieved. As though she'd cried out all of the stress and loss and fear.

"I need to step out for a little while," she said to her team, "I'll be back as soon as I can."

As she'd hoped, none of them questioned her. Instead, they all nodded, their faces drawn into pictures of worry and pity. *I should feel guilty for taking advantage of them like this,* she thought, *but I'm doing it for a good cause.*

She drove straight to the address her Queensland contact gave. The whole time, all she could think was *they won't be there anymore. They'll have moved house, or died.* Before the Alpha Park shooting, Phoebe never considered herself pessimistic by nature; even after all she'd been through. But ever since, nothing went her way. It felt like nothing was easy or straight forward any more.

When she arrived, she barely felt any excitement for a potential lead. Chasing down Michael Lee Taylor had nothing to do with the excitement she associated with solving a case anymore; it was almost just pure instinct. Like she was going through the motions, with no investment underneath. *But that's not quite right,* she thought, *I'm more invested in this than anything else in my life.* A strange disconnect had arisen in her, a sort of emotional canyon that stretched between her and everything that was happening.

The house was old but well kept; the garden was neatly tended and the front porch clean and tidy. Phoebe knocked on the door, a barely noticeable flutter in her heart as she did. An older woman opened the door with a gentle smile. The smile didn't falter as she took in Phoebe's suit, and the badge on her belt.

"Good morning," Phoebe said, "I'm Detective Sergeant Phoebe Wilson, I was wondering if you're related to someone named John Thompson?"

The woman's kind face creased as she looked carefully at Phoebe.

"Yes, my nephew's name is John Thompson."

"Do you mind if I come in? I just have a few questions, if you don't mind."

Her frown disappeared and the same gentle smile replaced it as she waved her hand.

"Oh, of course, come in."

Phoebe was led to a comfortable little lounge room, and sat on the closest chair. She smelled old books and fresh linens; almost exactly the way her grandfather's place had smelled. One wall of the lounge room faced the back yard, a giant window in its centre. Morning sun poured in through the glass, creating a cozy warmth that made her sleepy despite the time.

The older woman sat across from Phoebe, on a small lounge which looked far less comfortable than the chair Phoebe chose. Nevertheless, she looked content enough as she settled in and stared at Phoebe with the same gentle smile.

"What would you like to know about my nephew?" she asked.

An image of his criminal file flashed through her mind. The most glaring part of it lit up her mind like the sunlight shining in through the window behind her. It was the one thing that could potentially link John Thompson to the Alpha Park shooting without reasonable doubt.

"Do you have a photo of him?"

"I'm sure I have one somewhere, give me a moment."

The woman hummed tunelessly as she rifled through cupboards and drawers in the lounge room. She pulled out several large photo albums which looked older than Phoebe. Grunting with the effort, the woman stacked all of the photo albums on the coffee table in front of Phoebe.

"There's bound to be a photo of John in there somewhere," she said, smiling, "though he was never a fan of having his photo taken."

Phoebe picked up the first, flipping through it quickly and fixing an image of Michael Lee Taylor's face in her mind. *I swear, if they look similar...*

"When did you last see him?" she asked, her eyes never rising from the photos.

"It's been a while. I want to say about four years? Maybe five."

"Have you spoken to him since? On the phone or anything?"

"No, no. John was always the quiet type, kept to himself. Even when he lived here, I barely got a word out of him."

Phoebe stopped flipping pages, and stared at the older woman.

"He lived here? When?"

"Only for a week or so, just before he moved. He went up to Queensland."

"When was that, exactly?"

"My memory isn't what it was, you know," the woman said, "it was when I last saw him. I think it was four years ago, but it might've been five."

She resumed scanning the photos. "Any chance you could check somehow? The timing is quite important."

"I'll see what I can do," she said, a slight grunt escaping as she rose from the lounge, "but I don't really keep track of my nephew's comings and goings."

A lot of the photos were black and white, and Phoebe recognised the woman with her now as a young child in a few of them. *This isn't helping at all.* But she couldn't let herself skip any pages, even if it meant looking through hundreds of photos taken before either Phoebe or John Thompson were even born.

Gradually, the black and white photos became less common, replaced by more modern photos. The woman aged rapidly as Phoebe turned pages faster and faster, until Phoebe reached the third album and she looked more or less the same age as she was now. Phoebe glanced up, but the woman was still pottering about somewhere else in the house. Her faint tuneless humming carried into the lounge room.

She picked up the last photo album, flicking through the pages as quickly as the one before it. She'd so far seen no one who resembled Michael Lee Taylor. *I'm not surprised,* she thought, *this was never going to go my way.* Just as she thought it, she stopped, her hand hovering just above the page. A photo was missing from the album. Under the space the photo should have been, the same as the others, was a handwritten date and a brief description; *20 November 2019. John's goodbye party, off to QLD!*

22 April 2024 1:12pm (Monday)

He took the photo. He must have. Yet again, Phoebe was faced with something too coincidental not to be related, but too vague to constitute evidence. One week before the shooting, he apparently moved to Queensland. *That's a hell of an alibi,* she thought, *if it can be proven.* The likelihood that John Thompson was a different person hadn't escaped her. It was almost definitely true. After all, the only real link between the two men so far was the word of a complete stranger.

But it seemed to add up, and the more Phoebe looked into it the more she believed it. There were too many coincidences in this case for her to believe in coincidences anymore; and the apparent link between John Thompson and Michael Lee Taylor was no exception. *He has a criminal record that matches Taylor,* she thought, *and all his photos are missing. It has to mean something.*

Now she knew he had something to do with Queensland; it was the Queensland police contact who'd sent her Thompson's aunt's address, and his aunt said he'd moved there. *But why would Queensland have a Rosetown address on file?* She had to get back to the contact. In her all-consuming need to find a lead, she'd dropped what should have been a much longer conversation in favour of chasing down Thompson's aunt.

Opening the last email she received—the one that gave her the Rosetown address—Phoebe scrolled to the bottom without bothering to read again. Right at the end of the message, the contact left his desk phone number. Instead of replying, Phoebe picked up her phone and dialed.

"Constable Darren White speaking."

"Hi Darren, this is Detective Sergeant Phoebe Wilson. I'm calling about the information you gave me on John Thompson's family in Rosetown."

"Yeah, I figured," he said, dry humour stretching his voice, "is there anything more you need?"

"Everything. Anything you have on John Thompson."

A small part of her worried about her team overhearing the conversation; but it was difficult to care too much if the conversation ended with her finding a real lead. *Not that it's likely.*

"Well, that's the thing," he said, the humour utterly gone from his voice now, "that address was pretty much the only thing we had."

"Why would the Queensland Police have a Rosetown address for someone who spent most of his life outside of Queensland? What about a criminal history?"

She tried to keep the frustration out of her voice, but it was impossible.

"We do have a file on him," White said, "but it's minimal. More or less the same as what you sent us. Well, much less, really. But the same type of charges. It's the weirdest thing, though. We don't have a photo of him."

Her heart sank. She didn't think it was possible to feel any lower, but the case just continued to disappoint.

"Yeah, neither do we," she said, "and when I went to the address you gave me, there was a photo of him missing."

"Sure, but a missing family photo is very different to two missing photos in two different state police records."

"Who can delete criminal files?"

"Only the IT teams, as far as I'm aware. They don't get deleted normally."

Is it really possible that someone within the police is trying to cover this up? She didn't want to believe it; but it was hardly more unbelievable than the other aspects of the case. Still, two different state records meant two or more hidden police Constables involved with Michael Lee Taylor, and the shooting of an innocent child. *No way.*

Her mind went straight into connect-the-dots mode, despite the underlying disbelief she felt. *That might explain the fact that Michael Lee Taylor mysteriously died while in police custody,* she thought, *and why the report on his death was so vague.*

Constable White cleared his throat pointedly. *Oh shit,* Phoebe thought, *I've been quiet too long.*

"You never told me what case this is in relation to?" he said.

"It's a cold case from a few years back."

"And you think John Thompson is your guy?"

"It certainly seems that way. Have you heard anything about him in the last few years?"

"Nope. His file hasn't been updated with new charges for at least four or five years."

"Can you send me the full file?"

He cleared his throat again, the phone line hissing as he sighed through his nose.

"I shouldn't even have sent you that address, really. Not for a cold case, and not without a formal request."

Phoebe had to fight to stop her own sigh, pinching the bridge of her nose and letting the breath out gently instead.

"I'll fill out the request paperwork. Whatever I need to do. I know it's a cold case, but I really need to find out the truth."

"I'll send you the forms, if you like. Just need to cover my own arse, so I can say I did the right thing. You know how it is."

24 April 2024 12:34pm (Wednesday)

Two days after she called Constable White—and sent the filled-out request forms back to him—the Queensland file on John Thompson arrived in her email inbox. As he'd said, Thompson's Queensland record looked pretty much identical to the New South Wales one; a slew of violent and threatening crimes, erratic behaviour, and substance abuse.

But where the Rosetown file stretched back to early adulthood, the Queensland file was woefully small. *He can't have been in Queensland long.* Other than guessing based on the file, she had no way of knowing how many times he'd been in Queensland or how much time he'd spent there in total.

She found out he had other family that lived in Queensland. *Why didn't Constable White tell me?* If they could verify that he'd actually been there at the time of the Alpha Park shooting, it could conclusively exclude him as a suspect, and prove he was a different man than Michael Lee Taylor.

The missing photos are still concerning, she thought, *but if he has a solid alibi, dropping him from the case would mean I can focus on Michael Lee Taylor again.* Then again, if it turned out that John Thompson *was* the same man, she might be able to prove it if she could speak to the family he had in Queensland. *Even if they are somehow the same man,* she thought, *I still have no idea how someone other than Taylor could have shot Jacob, when the CCTV footage shows only one person.* She would cross that bridge when she came to it; for now, she just needed to know how John Thompson was connected, if at all.

There was no address listed for him in the file; if he had moved to Queensland, he either moved in with a friend or his family. Phoebe got the feeling the move was a cover story. *He moved in with his aunt, told her he was moving interstate, and then moved into a crappy little apartment near Alpha Park.* He would have had to begin renting it earlier; from what Phoebe could remember, Michael Lee Taylor had been paying rent for a while at the apartment they raided. *That's a ton of advance planning,* she thought, *and money.* And it *still* didn't answer the question of why Jacob was targeted.

Jacob Turner, from everything she could discover, was certainly not a pleasant boy. His parents were either in denial, or actively lying to cover his behaviour. A sudden thought occurred to her, and she spent the next few hours digging into the records she'd gathered, cross-referencing names. Nothing matched the way she'd thought it would; a part of her had expected to find either Thompson or Taylor as a relative of a child at Jacob's school, or a teacher, or something. *Anything.* If Jacob had terrorised someone enough, maybe a family member would have wanted revenge.

But if the names had shown up, she would have honed in on them much earlier. *And I've had this train of thought before*, she realised, *I always approach from the most common motive angles early on.* Revenge was a powerful motivator, but now that the bright spark of her idea had passed, even Phoebe had trouble imagining someone going through all this to get back at a school kid for bullying. The fact that she'd considered it in the first place, albeit briefly, highlighted her desperation. *I'm really just chasing shadows now.*

In the Queensland file, scrawled on a release form buried under countless others, there was a phone number. Not his, but it was written under the contact details for Thompson's family. There was no way she could visit for an interview, but she could call them and ask a few questions without crossing any lines. *General questions,* she thought, *just to clarify.*

I have to be careful. If I upset them or push any boundaries, they could report me and I'll be in a world of trouble. She wrote the number down in her notepad, and took a few deep breaths. *They're going to say they haven't seen him in years, and that he never moved up there.* She just knew it; and again, it would just be another thing that she couldn't count as evidence, but that added up with everything else she'd found.

"Hey Sarge," Timms said, sending a jolt through her stomach, "Matt's going to get coffee, you want one?"

"I'll never say no to that," she said, trying to make her voice sound casual.

He nodded, gave her a doubtful smile, and gave a thumbs up to Simpson.

"How are you going?" he said after Simpson walked away.

"Same old, same old," she said, smiling as widely as she could.

Timms nodded again, and leaned on her desk.

"We'll find Teagan Lee, don't worry about that. We're chasing leads and plastering her face up everywhere we can."

Phoebe smiled again, then locked her computer screen.

"I know," she said, "you guys are the best."

"Is there anything you wanna talk about?" he asked, a little too much pity in his eyes.

"No, I'm... Just dealing with a lot. I'll be fine."

"Would you like to chill out in the quiet room for a bit? It's quiet in there, after all."

A small, narrow room along the hallway, the quiet room contained a window, a single bed, a comfortable chair, and a tiny desk and office chair. It was usually reserved for Constables feeling ill or particularly upset after a difficult experience on the job. *It also has a desk phone.* All the desk phones in the station were made private, with blocked numbers. *Why didn't I think of that before?*

"That's actually a great idea," she said, "if you guys can handle things without me for a bit, I'll sit down in there for a moment."

"Sure thing, Sarge."

She snatched her notepad from the desk and headed straight for the quiet room.

"When Simpson gets back, tell him to just put my coffee on my desk," she called back to Timms.

The quiet room had a lock on the inside. Phoebe clicked it into place as soon as she closed the door. Dropping her notepad onto the tiny work desk, she sat down and stared at the phone. It was an older, simpler version of the phones her team used; they'd been given upgrades a few months ago, but apparently this one had been forgotten about. *As long as it's still private,* she thought, *and still working.* Most people didn't question the police when they called, but she still didn't want Thompson's family being able to call back if they became suspicious.

Staring at the phone number on the pad, she tried to prepare herself for more disappointment. The number would be disconnected, or would belong to a different family now. It would be the wrong John Thompson, or they'd never heard of Rosetown. John Thompson would be dead, or missing. *I'm not even sure what I want to hear,* she thought, *at this point there's nothing that would really be good news.*

Sighing, shaking her head, Phoebe dialed the number. She waited as the rings echoed through the phone line. There was no part of her that could have prepared for the answer on the other side.

"Hello, this is John."

24 April 2024 3:41pm (Wednesday)

It's him. He's there. He's alive, in Queensland. For what felt like an hour, Phoebe stood with the phone held to her ear, silenced by shock. She felt as though she couldn't speak, even if she knew what to say. Of all the things she expected to hear from this phone number, John Thompson himself shocked her more than anything she could think of in that moment. The thought swirled in her mind, repeating itself over and over; *it's him. It's him.*

He cleared his throat, and Phoebe tried desperately to think of something to say. All the questions she'd prepared disappeared from her mind, though none of them would have been useful with John himself. In that moment of pure panic, she forgot not just those questions, but every word in the dictionary.

"Hello?" he said.

What the fuck do I say to him?

"Umm, hello."

Good start.

"Who is this?"

"This is Detective Sergeant Phoebe Wilson," she said, the familiar words sounding far more confident than she felt.

"Okay, I don't know what you're calling about," he said, "but I haven't done anything wrong. Since I got out last time, I've barely left the house."

"It's alright, I'm not calling about anything like that."

She took a deep breath, trying her best to stifle the sound as she gathered her thoughts again.

"I'm calling about something that happened in Rosetown, New South Wales, in November twenty-nineteen," she said.

"Oh. I was... I moved up here in November that year, I think. What happened?"

"A child was killed."

"Oh bullshit, you're not pinning something like that on me, are you? Look, I know I'm not the best guy, but I'd never do something—"

"No, no," Phoebe said, "I'm not saying you did it. Let me finish. We had a suspect, but not enough evidence. He died with no discernible cause. We dropped it as a cold case, but just recently someone called anonymously and told us the man who killed that child was named John Thompson. I don't think it's you, but I had to check."

"And you don't know who called and gave my name?" he asked.

"He gave us nothing but the name," Phoebe said, sighing and shaking her head, "he even called from a private number. No idea who it was."

I shouldn't be telling him all this, she thought, *but I have no one else to discuss it with, and up until now I thought Thompson and Taylor were the same man.* She'd expected him to be dead when she called asking for him; if Thompson was also dead, and hadn't been seen since 2019, she could put the two together with relative certainty. *I couldn't have closed the case, but I would have at least had a tiny bit of closure.*

"Is there anyone you know who might want you to take the fall for it?" Phoebe said.

"Not like this," he said, "the kind of enemies I have would just put me in the ground themselves. Lucky they're all locked up, for now at least."

"Okay. Look, I hate to do this, but is there anyone who can verify that you weren't in Rosetown on the afternoon of the twenty-seventh of November?"

He paused; she wasn't sure if he was thinking of a lie or searching his memories. *He's clearly not Michael Lee Taylor,* she thought, *but it doesn't mean he's got nothing to hide.* Besides, they barely had evidence against Taylor in the first place, and what they had was vague and circumstantial at best. *It's still possible someone other than Michael Lee Taylor killed Jacob. And if they did, my money's on John Thompson.*

"I moved here, I think, the week before that," he said finally, "I've probably still got the plane ticket."

"That doesn't prove where you were on the twenty-seventh."

"Come on," he said, anger starting to creep into his voice, "I didn't kill a kid, Jesus."

"I believe you," she said, "I really do. I'm just trying to do my job."

"Wouldn't you be better off finding that guy who called? He obviously thinks he knows the answers."

"He thinks you did it."

"Maybe *he's* the one who did it," Thompson said, "and he's pointing you in the wrong direction."

"Listen," Phoebe said, unable to stop the frustration in her own voice now, "all I need is an alibi for that one afternoon. That's it. I just need to know you weren't in Rosetown when the child was killed."

"I'll see what I can do, give me a sec."

She heard him searching; opening drawers and cupboards, rustling papers, and stomping through whatever room his phone was in. For some reason, she imagined a cosy study like the one her grandparents had; old and untidy but clean and comfortable. Then she realised, with a cold twist in her stomach; *I still don't know what he looks like*. All that came to mind was Michael Lee Taylor's face.

After waiting what felt like ten minutes, a loud rustle and thump sounded as Thompson picked up the phone again.

"Okay, okay," he said, "I was in a therapy session with Doctor Daniels from two o'clock til three. Is that around the time that kid was killed?"

"Close enough," Phoebe said.

"So how do I send this to you?" he asked, "I've got the email confirmation and a receipt. You needed proof, right?"

Shit. Didn't think of that. She'd hoped to find out whether Thompson was in Rosetown or not; she never thought about how the proof could actually be sent to her. *I was really hoping I wouldn't have to give out any contact information.* Anything that could tie her personally to an investigation she wasn't supposed to be conducting in the first place was too risky. *I already gave him my name and rank,* she thought, shaking her head, *and he knows I'm in Rosetown. It's too late.*

"I'll give you my email," she said, before an idea lit up in her mind, "and I'd like you to include a photocopy of your driver's licence, for our records."

Finally, we'll have a photo of you.

24 April 2024 4:56pm (Wednesday)

Back at her desk, Phoebe waited for the email from Thompson for just over an hour. Finally, it appeared; just as she began to think he wouldn't send it. Glancing briefly at the email confirmation attached, Phoebe moved her attention to the photocopied driver's licence attached. Her heart stopped; her breathing stopped.

The picture on John Thompson's driver's licence looked almost exactly like Michael Lee Taylor. Physical sensation left her body, and she stared at the image in front of her. She had to force herself to think clearly. *It's not him,* she thought, *it can't be him.* Closing her eyes for a moment, Phoebe made herself breathe. *He's dead, and Thompson has an alibi.*

Opening her eyes again, she brought up Michael Lee Taylor's file and scrolled to a photo from his autopsy. She placed the two photos next to each other, and zoomed in as close as she could. A wave of relief flooded her mind; though the resemblance between the two men was uncanny, there were differences when she looked closely.

Whoever called probably just thought they recognised John Thompson when they saw Michael Lee Taylor, she thought. It wasn't the best explanation, but at least she knew John Thompson was no longer a person of interest in the case. Their resemblance still gave her chills; she had a feeling it would never stop creeping her out a little. Of all the coincidences she'd encountered, the fact that two unrelated men who'd nevertheless been drawn into the same criminal case looked so similar was perhaps the most uncomfortable.

She read the confirmation email for his therapy session, and the photocopied receipt. They both looked legitimate. More than anything, she wished she could track down the anonymous man who'd called and named Thompson. *He clearly wanted me to look at Thompson closely... Maybe there's some other reason John Thompson should be investigated.* But as intrigued as she was, looking into him now that he had an alibi was not worth it. *I have to focus on the actual case.*

But the more she thought about the case, she more she realised she'd hit another dead end. With the possible lead she hoped John Thompson would be all but useless, and no new information about Michael Lee Taylor, Phoebe had nothing more to go on. All she had was the journal, and the tiny amount of evidence they'd gathered. *I'm just going to be reading all of that and looking at the same photos over and over again,* she thought, *there's nothing else left to do.*

Chapter Nine:
Unbelievable

30 April 2024 11:15pm (Tuesday)

Michael Lee Taylor's journal was still in evidence storage. Phoebe had photocopies of every page, and though it had been a while since she read them, she still remembered a lot of the more coherent entries. But with the John Thompson business reaching a dead end, she felt an overpowering urge to read it through again. *I remember seeing heaps of numbers,* she thought, *they had to mean something.*

Even the parts that were written in English were vague, and barely made any sense. Except the last few pages; they were clear and undeniable threats towards Jacob Turner. But she already knew Taylor was guilty; she was interested in the how and why of the situation. How had the gun disappeared? Why Jacob Turner?

At the time, the police had been intent on finding proof, and evidence, as quickly as possible. Now, Phoebe was interested only in fully understanding what happened. And though it had been years, she now had the time to properly think and search. There would be no new evidence; but there would also be no deadline.

She kept the photocopies of his entire file in a folder in one of the cupboards in her kitchen; cupboard space wasn't abundant in her apartment. Taking it out, she sat on the couch and flipped through the pages until she reached the journal.

It was a disturbing read, even years later. Several times in the last few years, she'd come close to believing Michael Lee Taylor's claims of time travel. Reading the journal for what must have been the hundredth time, Phoebe found herself again almost convinced. *He knew he was going to die,* she thought, *he wrote it in the journal.* He'd been adamant that Jacob Turner was guilty of some of the worst crimes imaginable in the future.

He wrote about his experience using whatever vehicle or device allowed the time travel, and his arrival in Alpha Park. In one entry, he wrote that he kept mentioning things from the future in general conversation, and that he kept receiving strange looks because of it. *Who was he even having conversations with?* She thought, *it's not like he had any friends.*

Then it hit her, the one person they knew he'd spoken with a lot before the shooting; someone he might have accidentally let slip strange details to. *He had a girlfriend*, she thought, *what was her name? Damn it.* She racked her brain, but nothing came up. It was in his file, somewhere, she just couldn't remember where.

"Come on, come on," she said, rifling through the photocopied pages.

Finally, in the witness list, she saw the name; Jessica Bloom. *That's right,* she thought, frustrated at her own scattered mind, *I knew I'd remember it when I saw it.* She couldn't remember the interview anymore—she could read the interview transcript later—but she did vaguely recall a bunch of red flags in Bloom's story. The young woman had clearly made a huge mistake in dating Taylor, even without knowing he was a child killer.

He must have been a strange boyfriend, Phoebe thought, *even when he wasn't incomprehensible from alcohol consumption. Surely, she would remember if he said something about the future.* She remembered gaining almost no information out of the interview; *but I assumed he was delusional back then,* she thought, *now I'm not so* sure. It was likely that Bloom could be unwilling to talk at this point; Phoebe understood if the ex-girlfriend of a murderer might prefer to just move on. But if there was even a chance that she might remember something, anything, that gave Phoebe a better understanding of Taylor, she had to try.

I'm really getting desperate, she thought, *chasing after Taylor's ex-girlfriend.* Phoebe didn't care anymore; she just wanted to know what happened. *At this point, there's not much I wouldn't do to find the truth.* It hit her as a realisation, but she really meant it; the case had crept under her skin, into every corner of her mind. All she wanted was answers. *The one thing I can't have is the one thing I want. Typical.*

Scanning through the rest of the witness list, there was almost no one who might know more. Most of the witnesses they found were just pedestrians on the street at the time of the shooting; they wouldn't have any insight into Michael Lee Taylor. Jacob's parents wouldn't be willing to talk any further, and his teacher already told her everything she knew. *The ex-girlfriend, then,* she thought, writing the woman's number in her notepad.

01 May 2024 1:04pm (Wednesday)

Jessica Bloom had recovered well from her ordeal with Michael Lee Taylor. She hadn't experienced any direct abuse, but her experience interviewing with police, and having to go over every detail of her relationship, took its toll at the time. In the four years since Taylor's arrest and death, Bloom found a new boyfriend, and settled into a normal life again. She seemed happy.

Phoebe sat across from her, in the apartment she shared with her boyfriend, and watched her closely. Her boyfriend sat next to her, his discomfort plain on his face. He obviously already knew about Taylor, but sitting here with her while she spoke again to the police was a different thing entirely. *He must be a great guy,* she thought, *to want to be here for her while she talks about her murdering ex.*

"Okay," Jessica said, with a deep sigh and a glance at her boyfriend, "what would you like to know?"

"We read his journal," Phoebe started, "and there are references to some strange activities. Along with some claims he made in his interview, it paints a very odd picture. I wanted to know if he ever said things that seemed... unbelievable?"

She didn't know how else to say it. *Coming straight out with "your boyfriend might have been a time traveller" might not have gone well.* There was a balance to interviews like this; the fickle and suggestible nature of memory meant that any statement that might lead the witness to a specific idea could taint their recollection. *Keep it vague.*

"Unbelievable." Jessica's voice was flat, gentle, like her mind had pulled her a million miles away.

Let her think, Phoebe thought, battling for patience, *it's been a while, and I'm sure she's done everything in her power* not *to think about Taylor.* Phoebe expected nothing to come from the conversation, but low expectations hadn't exactly stopped her from investigating Michael Lee Taylor before.

"I don't really remember anything specific," Jessica finally said, "but he did say some weird things sometimes."

"Weird in what way?"

"Every now and then he would say something kind of... ominous, I guess? Like, hinting at what might happen in the future sort of thing."

"In a threatening way?"

Jessica shook her head gently. Her eyes unfocused and pointing off to Phoebe's side.

"Not to me, no, just... weird."

"Like he knew things about the future?"

"I know it sounds crazy, but yeah, that's how it felt sometimes."

"I know it was a while ago," Phoebe said, "but can you try to remember anything specific he might have said?"

For a long, tense moment, Jessica simply stared at nothing, a slight frown on her otherwise gentle face. Her boyfriend stared at the coffee table with an unnerving intensity. Phoebe felt sorry for him, and for Jessica for that matter. A part of her hated the mystery surrounding Michael Lee Taylor, especially looking at the innocent people affected. But another part of her, and perhaps the bigger part, was too absorbed by intrigue to stop investigating.

"It wasn't like he made some huge announcements or anything," Jessica said, "it was just little statements, every now and then, you know? Like at the time it wasn't a big deal, just a little weird."

Phoebe remembered the way he spoke in both interviews; *he made insane statements in such a casual tone; I can definitely believe why his girlfriend wouldn't think much of them.* Unfortunately, it meant there was no more Jessica could give her. *At least she confirmed he mentioned the future,* she thought, *that's another point for time travel, even if it's vague and unreliable.*

288

She was beginning to see patterns and links everywhere, and she wasn't sure they actually existed. But she wouldn't accept that; *I can't, not until the truth comes out.*

If Phoebe was right, and Wilks' theory held a nugget of truth, Jessica Bloom was merely a cover; essentially a beard. Michael Lee Taylor was some kind of agent sent to assassinate Jacob Turner for his future crimes. And there was an organisation, powerful and dangerous, that was covering everything up; muddying the tracks so the police would write it off as a cold case.

She knew it was ridiculous, but it also felt like the truth to her. Something about it just made sense. *Why else would every lead I chase end in a brick wall?* It had the distinct feel of a cover up. Whenever she researched mysteries and cold cases in the past, she used to scoff at the conspiracy theorists. Now, she understood exactly where they were coming from.

"Okay," Phoebe said, "but when he said strange things, they were always about the future? Or were there other things he spoke about too?"

"I'm sorry, detective," Jessica said, "I really don't remember."

Phoebe nodded, her excitement deflating a little.

"I understand," Phoebe said with as much of a smile as she could manage through her disappointment, "thanks for your time."

02 May 2024 10:09am (Thursday)

Alpha Park was as beautiful in May of 2024 as it had been in December 2019. Colder, certainly, but just as beautiful. The day of the shooting, and for a while afterwards, the park had taken on a sinister atmosphere. It felt like the trees were hiding something, some danger. Every shadow had echoed with malice. But even so, it was always beautiful.

Enough time had passed now that none of the uncomfortable sense of danger remained, and Phoebe walked along the pathways slowly. As she strolled, she wondered how Jacob Turner would have behaved around police. Given what his teachers said about him, she thought she could guess well enough. She wished there was a way to see his behaviour when he knew he wasn't being watched. The teachers gave her enough to paint a pretty damning picture of him; but disruptive behaviour was quite common for his age group, especially at school. What Phoebe wanted to know was how he'd behaved in private.

The park was quiet this time of day, mostly older people and some children too young for school with their parents. Phoebe found herself thinking about her grandfather again. The wake had given her some closure, but she was a long way from letting him go. Their old house, the one Phoebe visited countless times before her parents divorced, had a beautiful back yard. It was full of old trees and wild, barely controlled grass, and she used to explore it every chance she got. The park reminded her a lot of that back yard, even down to the smell of a particular tree that had grown there.

Her grandparents owned a cat when she was young; his name had been Fred. A ginger cat, he'd spent most of his time in the back yard. Phoebe remembered playing hide and seek with him, and usually not finding him until hours after the game started.

Just as Fred ran through her mind, a stray cat streaked over the path in front of her. For a brief, electric moment, Phoebe was flooded with victorious adrenaline; *found you!* She thought, her mind a wild frenzy.

But the cat wasn't Fred; it wasn't even ginger. Phoebe shook her head, walked on, and suddenly there seemed to be a whole family of stray cats. She'd walked into one of the densest parts of the park, where fewer people seemed to go, and the cats were everywhere. Most of them remained hidden in the thick shrubs lining the path, but Phoebe still saw them.

There have to be at least a couple dozen of them, she thought, *how are there so many in such a public place?* She would have thought some pest control company would have been called by now; or at least an animal shelter. They seemed friendly enough, though understandably wary.

A couple of them approached her and rubbed against her legs; she heard them purring even through the ambient noise of the park.

"You're very friendly," she said, "aren't you? Have you always lived in this park?"

As she watched them, an uncomfortable thought occurred to her. *Jacob loved this park.* A commonly known early warning sign of psychopathy was the torture and murder of animals. Michael Lee Taylor had been utterly convinced of Jacob's guilt. She vaguely recalled the interview, but the footage was the only part she couldn't take a copy of without suspicion. He'd said "*he's the worst serial killer in Australian history*", or something like that. As much as she couldn't believe whole-heartedly in his time travel defence, some of the things she'd learned about Jacob Turner certainly backed up what Taylor had said about him.

A sick feeling grew in her stomach, cold and heavy, and she couldn't help but imagine what Jacob might have done in the privacy of this part of the park. The thought, as insistent as it was horrifying, grew in her mind until it became a massive glowing neon sign. *What if he came to this park for the cats?*

06 May 2024 2:42pm (Monday)

Four days after visiting the park, Phoebe was trying unsuccessfully to get her mind off Jacob Turner by working the robbery case. Its details had become two dimensional, fading into the background. No matter how hard she tried, she just couldn't bring herself to care as deeply about the robbery as she should have. Teagan Lee's location was still a mystery, and they had barely any leads or witnesses left. The KALOF was still out, and they had Constables patrolling more than usual, but all Phoebe could do was wait.

Focusing was almost impossible; except on the Alpha Park shooting. Luckily, her team were working the robbery case with their usual diligence. She was certain they'd noticed her lack of focus, but they worked just as hard nonetheless.

"Sarge, we're closing in on the last suspect," Brouwer said, "one of her mates let slip where she's hiding."

"Great work," Phoebe said, "do we know if she's there now?"

"We're pretty sure she is. And we've got all we need to bring her in."

"Give me a moment, then we'll get it done."

"Sure thing, Sarge."

She went back to her computer, closing down most of the windows and locking the screen. After that she checked her phone, as she always did before going out on potentially dangerous tasks. Generally, she wasn't a fan of social media, but she always checked her accounts daily. Though she didn't post much, she liked the ability of seeing what was going on in the world around her, and with the people she knew.

Though she knew she shouldn't, she ended up scrolling through Instagram, randomly double tapping on a few posts. Just as she was about to put her phone away, she saw something that sent a cold wave of disbelief through her entire body. *No,* she thought, *no, no. It can't be. It's not possible.*

The phone slammed onto her table with a loud cracking sound as her fingers went numb. Brouwer rushed back to her desk, asking if she was okay. His voice disappeared in a fog of white noise. Nothing existed for a horrifying moment, except the thing she'd seen on her phone.

"Phoebe," Brouwer said, holding her arm firm but gentle, "what's wrong? What the fuck is happening?"

"What's up, Sarge?" Wilks called from his desk.

Words failed her. She could barely breathe, let alone respond. The cold feeling spread, and she felt herself nearing unconsciousness. She bent over and threw up into her desk's bin, then crashed to her knee, half dragging Brouwer down with her.

"Shit, Sarge, maybe we should get you to a hospital."

"No," she said, her voice a million miles away, "no, it's just... Fuck, it's just shock."

"What happened?"

Speaking was still almost impossible. She couldn't see clearly, just vague shapes and light. The image on her phone remained burned into her mind, glaring and inescapable. *I thought I'd forgotten about that,* she thought.

Standing, slowly and with Brouwer's help, she sat back in her chair. Her phone lay on the desk where it fell, face down for the moment. *I didn't scroll away. It's still there right now.* A wave of sickening white nausea wiped the room from her sight, and she almost threw up again.

"Sergeant Wilson?" Brouwer prompted, his voice gentle.

"My... phone. I saw something on my phone."

Brouwer reached for it, and pure panic seized her heart. But he picked it up, and frowned at the screen, no recognition on his features. *Maybe I just imagined it,* she thought, grasping at the thought with desperate hope, *maybe it was something else.*

"I don't get it," Brouwer said, "it's just an ad for some book."

He scrolled up and down, searching in case she'd accidentally bumped the screen.

"Show me," Wilks said.

I made it up, she thought, *I didn't see what I thought I saw.* She needed it to be true. It had to be. Wilks reached Brouwer's side, and peered over his shoulder at the phone.

"I don't get it either," he said.

Her breathing was slowly coming back to normal. *I just imagined it.* Wilks stared hard at the screen, frowning. "Wait," he said, "this looks familiar."

"You mean it looks like every fantasy book ever?" Brouwer said.

"Shut up, Brouwer." he turned to Phoebe. "Sarge, is this what I think it is?"

Shaking, close to passing out, Phoebe opened the offline copy of the Alpha Park file she kept on her computer desktop. She scrolled through it until she reached the photos of everything found in his apartment. Her heart squeezed tight as she opened one of the photos.

"No fucking way," Brouwer said, "no *way.*"

The photo was of Taylor's cupboard. Several books were strewn over one of the shelves. One of them was a fantasy novel. *The Last of the Vothuin,* it was called. She still remembered being confused and doubtful about its supposed future release date.

On Phoebe's phone, a promoted post showed a fantasy novel, that had apparently only just been released. *Check out my brand new novel,* it said, *finally available today... An exciting new fantasy called The Last of the Vothuin!*

06 May 2024 4:13pm (Monday)

They left the station shortly after everyone had a close look at the book. Wilks actually purchased a copy, just to be sure it was really the same book and not some kind of hoax. Though they were going to arrest a potentially dangerous suspect, Phoebe couldn't get the book out of her head. *There has to be a way he could have faked it,* she thought, *a logical explanation.*

Phoebe drove her own car, with Wilks and Timms. A second car followed, with Brouwer, Simpson and Dennis. The suspect was reported as armed, so the full squad moved together. She was in a known hideout, according to the statement given by her associate; though the suspect herself had never been linked to the safe house previously. *Otherwise, we would have already checked it,* she thought, *or at least, my team would have.*

"We've known about this place for a while now," Timms was saying, "we just never linked it with Teagan Lee. We know the basic layout. Two doors, surrounded by fence on three sides, pretty old. One front door, one back door, windows are pretty small. As long as she doesn't get enough warning, we've got her. Just like Reeves."

Maybe he had someone else publish it for him on this date, Phoebe thought, *I'll have to look into the author and see if he knew Taylor. Or if it's a pseudonym. But if he set it up to be published without him, there has to be a digital trail somewhere... his name has to be attached to it somehow.*

When she first saw the book, it had been easy to assume he just printed off his own book and put a future date in there himself; far from impossible. It had been a little eerie, but it was something that at least could be explained logically. But seeing the book actually advertised publicly, and be released in the year that Taylor's copy claimed... that was inexplicable.

She felt sick again. They still didn't know how he died. *Was it possible someone actually killed him? How could that be?* All the frustration she'd felt when the case first came up returned. All the questions, with no answers, that still surrounded Taylor and the shooting. *I'll never escape this feeling.*

"Sarge!" Timms said, yanking her out of her thoughts.

"Hmm?"

"It's down this street, turn here."

She turned, barely seeing the road. *If someone released the book on Taylor's behalf,* she thought, *it implicates them in some capacity.* If it was just a normal book, and the author had no connection whatsoever to Michael Lee Taylor, it all but confirmed Taylor's claims that he came from the future. *How else could he possibly have a book in 2019 that wasn't released until 2024?* She was almost certain now that he'd been telling the truth.

"There it is," Timms said, "three houses on the left there."

Phoebe felt herself nodding, distantly, the way she could barely feel her hand in the morning if she slept on it wrong. She pulled over just outside the place, and their second car pulled up and parked in front of hers. Her team gathered quickly and silently at the front door, with two Constables standing further back near the cars.

Why would someone help him? She thought, *if they knew what he was up to, it makes them as bad as him. Unless whoever released the book is just another agent for the organisation.* It occurred to her that for a cover up this big, there may be dozens of agents working right under her nose to cover up the assassination of Jacob Turner. *I wonder if I know any of them,* she thought, *if there's anyone I shouldn't be trusting.*

Her men were staring at her, guns raised. Waiting for her signal. Their eyes shone with impatience and exasperation. *Is it one of you?* She thought, staring back at them in silence. She felt panic welling up in her stomach, squeezing into a ball of queasy energy. Memories of the last time they attempted to arrest Teagan Lee filled her mind. *She wasn't there,* Phoebe thought, *but she should have been. Did one of my men tip her off?*

Blinking, she forced herself to see the safe house door in front of her. Finally, she nodded, and the door opened. They rushed in, Phoebe seeing the backs of her men as they moved ahead of her. Suddenly, they felt like strangers. They'd worked together for years; *but everyone has secrets.*

"Clear!" someone shouted from one of the rooms.

Her men were already spread out. Phoebe was still near the front door. Someone moved in front of her, facing away, and followed Simpson into a bedroom. Phoebe didn't see their face, and her attention was too scattered to notice the clothing; *surely it was one of the others,* she thought. Just as the words appeared in her mind, a shout rang out from the room.

"Shit!"

"Fuck you!"

Phoebe heard a scuffle, and a sharp bang, and then the person ran from the room, sprinting straight for Phoebe with what could have been a gun. Instinct kicked in. Everything else was swept from her mind, and muscle memory forced her own gun up. *Centre mass,* she thought, *squeeze smoothly, hold steady with the left hand.*

Her gun roared to life as she squeezed three times in succession. The running woman—*yep, that's Teagan Lee*—crumpled to the floor instantly, gun still in her hand. Phoebe breathed hard through her mouth, the sound hissing in her ears. Smoke from the gun stuck to her throat, and her eyes watered. It happened too quickly, and stopped too suddenly.

Phoebe stood above Teagan Lee, staring at her lifeless body as her team rushed back to the main room. Her hands shook, and she holstered her gun, trying to keep breathing. *I shot her,* she thought, *she's dead. I killed someone.* She still felt the recoil, the grip of the gun, as though she was still firing. Distantly, through layers of shock and confusion, she heard one of her team shout.

"Fuck, Simpson's been hit. Constable down."

06 May 2024 8:52pm (Monday)

Constable Matt Simpson was shot in the upper thigh, sustaining massive internal injuries including a severed artery. He survived, barely, and was in Rosetown Hospital. Phoebe didn't remember leaving the hideout, or what happened to Teagan Lee's body. *The case has to be closed now, surely.*

All she knew was that she'd been given the phone number of a counselling service, and sent home on mandatory leave with pay. *How did it get to this point?* She thought, *how did I lose focus during what should have been an easy arrest?* She hadn't been drinking at work, except a few sips here and there from a plastic water bottle full of vodka in her desk drawer. *Just to take the edge off.*

She didn't think anyone knew about it, but they certainly had noticed her general lack of focus. Her team covered for her when it meant she just sat at her desk staring at an old cold case; but now that Simpson was almost killed, there would be no help from her team. *This is all my fault.* All she wanted, all she had ever wanted, was answers.

I'm supposed to call these people, she thought, looking at the counsellor's business card on her coffee table, *but can they really help? The only thing that can make me feel better is knowing the truth about Michael Lee Taylor.* She never had a problem letting a case go before; but then again, she'd never seen a mystery as baffling as this one.

As far as Phoebe was concerned, Simpson getting shot was a freak accident. *I don't have that much of a problem.* It had been her fault, but it could've happened to anyone going through what she was. *It's not a problem with me,* she thought, *I'm just in the middle of a shit storm. That's hardly my fault*. She regretted losing focus during the attempted arrest of Teagan Lee, but other than that she'd done nothing wrong. *Why should I go to therapy?*

It took a bottle of wine to build up the courage to call the number. She made an appointment for the next week, but instead of feeling any relief, knowing she had an appointment created a ball of cold tension in her stomach. Another couple of glasses of wine took some of the edge off, and then one of her sleeping pills took care of the rest.

Still, it took her a while to actually get to sleep. She sat on the couch with an old romantic comedy movie playing on Netflix, watching the screen without hearing the dialogue. Without warning, the same thought that hit her earlier that day returned; *I killed someone today. I shot her, and she died right in front of me.*

Phoebe had seen plenty of death in her time. Identifying bodies, arriving at homicide scenes before the victims were removed, and countless photos of corpses during her college and police training. Being the cause of death was different. Even her experience with Charlie didn't leave her with the same shocked guilt.

The moment when she pulled the trigger flashed in front of her eyes again, painfully vivid. At the time she hadn't registered Teagan's face, just a threatening shape with a gun; but her memory somehow filled in the details she'd missed the first time. Teagan's eyes were full of desperate rage, and fear. Her manic face grew closer and closer to Phoebe, and there was nothing she could have done in that moment but shoot.

Her hands seemed to move on their own, before her mind fully accepted the action. She never *wanted* to shoot. There had been no satisfaction, no relief. Just terror, and confusion, and regret. *I killed someone today.*

On her TV, the two main characters finally talked through whatever miscommunication had prevented them getting together. They laughed, shared some pointed dialogue that must have referred to an earlier scene, and kissed. Phoebe scoffed, her chest filling with an uncomfortable, frustrated anger she couldn't quite describe. She closed the movie, scrolling for something less stupidly idealistic.

Without thinking, she selected an action movie; something she wouldn't normally watch, but the wine and sleeping pill were messing with her head. She remembered reading somewhere that taking sleeping pills and not sleeping could result in a high; and even hallucinations. *Probably not the best idea for me,* she thought, clicking play on the movie anyway.

For the next little while, brief flashes of Teagan Lee's face appeared on the TV screen, interspersed with the action scenes. The movie's hero shot the bad guys, and Phoebe shot Teagan again. Every time a gun was fired in the movie, she felt the recoil in her hands. She smelled the cordite, felt it in the back of her throat.

After what must have been most of the movie, she realised she couldn't move. Even her eyes felt glued to the TV. Teagan appeared again, sprinting at her with the gun in her hand, rage-filled eyes burning, pointed right at Phoebe. She tried to bring her gun up, tried to pull the trigger, but she was paralysed. The only part of her body that moved was her heart, beating in a painful frenzy as Teagan finally caught her. She couldn't even scream as Teagan tackled her to the ground, firing her gun point blank into Phoebe's stomach and chest.

07 May 2024 1:27pm (Tuesday)

She woke up on the couch, sore and confused. Still unable to remember how she got home, Phoebe realised she was wearing work clothes. Her gun and badge had been taken for the duration of her mandatory leave, but other than that, she was wearing everything she'd worn the previous day. *I didn't even have a shower when I got home,* she thought.

For what felt like the longest time, the Alpha Park shooting dominated her life. Now, without other cases to take up her time and being forced to stay away from work, she had nothing. She couldn't remember what she used to do with her time before Michael Lee Taylor entered her world. All she knew was that looking into the case while she was on leave would definitely not end well. *It didn't end well even when I was at work,* she thought, *or rather, it didn't end at all.*

The business card for the counselling service sat on the coffee table, and she vaguely remembered making an appointment. Picking it up, she checked the blank side; the time and date were scrawled in her handwriting. Messy and hard to read, but legible. *Good, at least I wrote it down.* The rest of her night, and most of the day before, were a blur of panicked thoughts and emotions. Shooting Teagan Lee was still vividly stuck in her mind. Everything else had become smoke, constantly moving and formless.

Finally getting off the couch, Phoebe staggered to the kitchen. Once she was up, the hangover kicked in, and her lounge room spun in warping circles. She groaned as the world twisted in front of her eyes, reaching the kitchen sink and throwing up over a few loosely stacked plates and bowls. *At least they were already dirty,* she thought. The room kept spinning, and she drank a glass of water in several huge gulps.

She drank another glass of water, though it made her feel bloated, and then made herself a strong coffee. *I know I need food,* she thought, *but fuck that. I'll just throw it back up again.*

After the coffee, Phoebe finally undressed; though they fit well, getting out of the suits she wore for work was always a huge relief. She'd never left it on for so long before, let alone slept in it. She still felt sick, but being naked gave her a gentle kind of freedom. No belt cinching her waist, no bra constricting her chest. The world slowly stopped spinning, and Phoebe felt a small flutter of normalcy again.

She ran the shower for a minute before she got in, watching steam rush up to the ceiling and listening to the constant patter of the water. Leaving the bathroom light off, she stepped under the water with her eyes closed. After a few minutes, she sat down under the cascade, hugging her knees and trying to let her mind empty.

Phoebe ended up staying under the hot water, sitting on the shower floor, for far longer than she intended. Her mind wandered, finally drifting from the nightmarish visions of Teagan Lee's face rushing at her. The darkness in the bathroom helped. *Why haven't I done this before?* She thought, *it's so much nicer in here without the lights on. I should have put on some music.*

By the time she stood up again, her legs were shaky, and her feet had gone numb. Leaning against the cold shower wall, she waited until feeling returned and she could stand normally. She washed herself as she normally did, and finally turned the water off. Her stomach was still queasy, and her head still pounded, but otherwise she already felt much better.

When she'd dried off, instead of clothes, she slipped on a fluffy bath robe Claire had given her as a present years ago. *Everyone should have a super fluffy robe,* she remembered Claire saying at the time, *it'll make you feel like a queen, trust me.* She missed her best friend. They stopped talking a while ago, because Claire got sick of hearing about Michael Lee Taylor.

She sat on her bed, unsure of what to do. When she looked at her bedside clock, she thought at first she'd misread it, or it was broken. *How is it so late in the day already?* She thought. Usually after a bottle or two of wine she could still get up early enough to get to work on time, even if her head was pounding. *Must have been the pill.* She only took them when she really needed to sleep, and she vaguely remembered taking one the night before.

For a while, she tried to read; a modest book case sat in her lounge room, with the same few dozen books she read every few years. But her mind was scattered, and the words kept slipping away from her eyes. After attempting to read the same sentence at least twenty times, Phoebe shoved the book back into its place on the shelf and dropped onto her couch.

Sitting in the same place it had since the case closed four years ago, Michael Lee Taylor's file silently beckoned to her. *I can't look at it,* she told herself, *not today. I need to get my mind away from it.* Simpson almost died. *Because of me. I saw Teagan follow him into that room, I know I did.* At the time, she hadn't felt certain. She remembered, in a distant way, thinking that the person who followed Simpson looked like one of her men.

I didn't get a good look, she thought, *it all happened so fast, and I was distracted. I was dealing with a lot.* But even as she thought the words, she knew they were excuses. Weak excuses, at that. There were so many things she could have done differently; *should* have done differently. *I let that happen, and I killed Teagan Lee. Because of Michael Lee Taylor.* As much as she still felt the pull towards the file in her kitchen cupboard, her guilt was stronger.

"Stay away from it," she said out loud, "at least for now."

Instead, and out of pure habit, she turned the TV on. Habit also took her off the couch and to her fridge. Her hand fell on the mostly empty bottle of wine before she finally realised what she was doing.

"Fuck, no," she said, pulling her hand back as though she'd been burned, "not right now. Jesus."

Maybe tonight, she thought, *once I feel a bit better.*

She filled a glass with water instead, and settled back on the couch. Picking out a harmless comedy, she tried to focus all her attention on the story. *What little story there is,* she thought. Phoebe enjoyed movies, but she was far pickier than most people she knew. The only reason she put up with most of the things she watched was because they usually ended up being background noise while she worked on cases.

Now, it was the only thing she could think of to do with her time. *I need a fucking hobby,* she thought, *this is getting ridiculous.* Nevertheless, she sat through the movie. As it dragged on, she felt herself slowly being drawn into its goofy, mindless story. By the time it finished, she was smiling, unaware of doing so. After she closed it, Netflix suggested another similar movie, and Phoebe clicked play. The second movie didn't take as long to get into, and Phoebe almost forgot about Michael Lee Taylor, and Teagan Lee.

07 May 2024 5:58pm (Tuesday)

"...Yesterday afternoon, a Rosetown police Constable was shot trying to apprehend a suspect who allegedly robbed a jewelry store at gunpoint earlier this year. Sources say the suspect was shot and killed by police during the attempted arrest. The police Constable who was wounded, identified as Constable Matthew Simpson, is in stable condition. Last month, another suspect was arrested for the same crime, and remains in police custody. There are no further suspects in the robbery, and it is believed the case will be closed pending the trial of the suspect in custody...."

11 May 2024 11:16am (Saturday)

A few days into her leave, Phoebe received a text from Senior Constable Wilks.

"Hey, Sarge," it read, "hope you're doing okay. Was thinking, maybe we could talk about Taylor sometime. Can't get the case out of my head... and I know you feel the same."

She stared at the words, unmoving. The tension between her and the rest of her team couldn't possibly have dissipated already. *There's no way Wilks really wants to catch up,* she thought, *maybe it's some kind of trick to catch me out.* Even with his love of conspiracy theories, he'd never mentioned the case to her directly unless it came up in conversation.

Another text appeared while she stared at her phone.

"Later today, maybe? Just wanted to go over the details with someone who cares."

Phoebe frowned, scenarios running through her head; *maybe they want to prove how obsessed I am with the case, or get me in trouble for keeping a folder of photocopied evidence for myself.* Then again, out of all her team, Wilks was the one most likely to fixate on the case as much as Phoebe was.

There was no way to know his motivations, except to see him. With a ragged sigh, she messaged him back.

"Sure. 6, 6:30? Rosetown Inn?"

Barely twenty seconds passed before Wilks wrote back.

"Good choice of venue, haha."

She'd only had half a bottle of wine, and there was plenty of time between now and then to sober up. Showing up smelling of wine would give Wilks ammo against her; she had to present herself as clear-headed. *I need him to see I'm better than I was at Teagan Lee's place.*

She printed off a second copy of her folder, and slid it into her handbag. *Just in case he's legit.* To try to calm her nerves, she began 'A Study in Scarlet' from the beginning again. The familiar story wasn't quite enough to take her mind off Wilks and whatever he was trying to achieve; but it did soothe her a little.

A few chapters later, she realised she hadn't showered that day; *it's way too easy to forget that stuff,* she thought, *when I don't do anything all day.* She focused on getting ready, dragging it out for as long she could to pass the time. After that, she made herself a coffee and sat down again. The rest of the day, she spent reading and trying not to panic about Wilks' motivations. Finally, at around 6pm, she left her apartment. *Here goes nothing,* she thought.

11 May 2024 6:48pm (Saturday)

Wilks wasn't at the bar when Phoebe arrived. She sat at one of the high stools and ordered a wine. *I'll have to be careful,* she thought, *and not have too many drinks.* Even so, she'd finished the glass by the time he arrived.

"Hey, Sarge," he said, sitting next to her and ordering a beer, "how's things?"

She shook her head, smiling despite herself. *He's not acting,* she thought, *he doesn't think anything should be different from before Simpson got shot.*

"I've been better," she said, "but not too bad I suppose."

They drank in silence for a while, and Phoebe found herself enjoying Wilks' company. She was still waiting for his true intentions to be revealed, but for now she was content to sit and drink. By the time Wilks spoke again, they'd both finished their drink and ordered another. *So much for being careful,* she thought, *at this rate we'll both be drunk sooner rather than later.*

"So I've been thinking," Wilks said, "about his diary. I really think there's more to it than just random numbers. I know the cryptologist guys didn't notice anything, but it's been bugging me lately."

"It always bugged me, too," Phoebe said, "the best I could come up with was maybe he just wrote all that stuff to confuse police."

"That can't be all there is to it, though. They're arranged in such a purposeful way, y'know? I'm honestly surprised the guys at the lab couldn't find some meaning in it."

"What do you think, then?"

"Well…"

Phoebe sighed. *He's apparently just as hesitant as I am to talk about this properly.* It went a long way toward convincing her he was sincere.

"Come on, Wilks," she said, "you wanted to talk this through with me. So talk."

"Alright, alright. I think… it has something to do with time travel."

She searched his face, peered into his eyes, and found nothing but earnest fear.

"What makes you think that?" she said.

"I don't really know. It just seems right, I guess. I re-watched the interviews, and he really doesn't seem like he's lying."

"He did come across as genuine," Phoebe said, "but that on its own doesn't mean the numbers are related to time travel. Is there anything about them that gave you that impression?"

"I guess not. Just a hunch, really."

"Have you looked at the diary lately?"

Wilks rolled his eyes.

"When I can. A few times. How about you, Sarge? Do you miss it?"

"I…" she hesitated, "… *may* have taken photocopies."

He laughed, shook his head, and took a long drink.

"Y'know, that actually doesn't surprise me. So, have you noticed anything then? With the numbers, I mean."

Instead of answering, Phoebe dug into her handbag and pulled out the folder she'd prepared. As Wilks laughed again, she flicked through to the diary pages to the number entries.

"They always struck me as meaningful," she said, "but there's no real pattern that I can see. I could never make sense of them, and I tried."

She handed the folder to Wilks.

"I have another copy," she said, "don't worry."

"So I can take this? Do my own obsessing?"

"Absolutely."

They shared a smile, then slowly finished their drinks in companionable silence once again. Phoebe ordered the next round for them, and then cleared her throat.

"There's one other thing," she said, "that I need to know about the case."

"Yeah?"

"The gun. Where did it go?"

"Oh god, yeah," Wilks said, "that gets me, too. What really fucks me up is what Taylor said in the interview. 'You'll never find it', or something like that. He knew it disappeared."

"He said he couldn't explain it any more than I could," Phoebe said, "he might've known it happened, but I think he was telling the truth that he didn't know *how*."

"That makes no sense."

"Yeah, you can say that again."

15 May 2024 8:14pm (Wednesday)

A few days after their meeting at the pub, they planned to meet up again; this time at Phoebe's place. Wilks had spent his free time pouring over the photocopied pages, working harder than the cryptologists who'd actually been paid for it; Phoebe did the same.

Phoebe was still on leave, so she spent that day re-reading Taylor's diary in preparation for Wilks' visit. She knew it would be the focus of their catch up, and she wanted the numbers fresh in her mind. Though she'd seen the diary entries hundreds of times by now, she tried to force herself to see them with new eyes. *Patterns,* she thought, *there have to be patterns*.

The numbers Taylor had meticulously written throughout his diary made her lose track of time. They merged together, a non-stop stream of uncrackable code. Try as she might, all she ever saw were random numbers. It felt exactly the same as trying to decipher it the first time she saw it.

After what felt like barely an hour – but was in reality most of the day – a knock on her door snatched her out of the daze of numbers on the page. When she opened the door, Wilks greeted her with an expression of childish excitement. He'd brought a six pack of his favourite beer; Phoebe had a couple of bottles of wine for herself already.

"I think I've cracked it," he said, almost shouting, "seriously, you won't believe this."

He strolled in, headed straight for the couch, and opened one of his beers. After a few sips, he opened his copy of the Taylor folder and spread it out onto her coffee table. There were colourful sticky tags on several of the pages; Wilks cut to those and lined them up next to each other. He mumbled to himself the entire time, and Phoebe poured herself a glass of wine in the kitchen before sitting next to him.

"I've done a lot of thinking about this," he said in a rush, "a *lot* of thinking."

Snatching the first tagged page off the table, Wilks traced his finger over the numbers, mumbling once again.

"Which one was it?" he asked himself, staring intently at the page.

He grabbed a different one, and Phoebe tried to content herself with drinking wine in silence while he figured things out. *He couldn't have found anything useful,* she thought, *surely. The whole thing is a mess.* At the same time, a bright and buzzing excitement rose in her stomach; if he'd really figured out Taylor's code – if there even *was* a code – it could go a long way toward understanding what happened.

Finally, Wilks barked a single sharp laugh, and shoved a page at her.

"This one!" he said.

Phoebe recognised it as one of the first pages:

4 25 17 1930
33-52.1S 151-11.7E
18 3 6 30 9 12 22
24 2 6 23 14 3 17

Took a while to find it.

First identify, then exploit.

Should do the trick. Gonna need more though.

M.L.T.

3-20-41

"So, what's the pattern you found?" she asked.

"The second line," he said, "they're coordinates."

"You're sure? How do you know?"

"Oh, I'm certain. Because I Googled them. Guess where they lead?"

Phoebe raised her eyebrows, her heart beating like crazy.

"At this point," she said, "I'm too afraid to guess."

"The Star Casino. In the city."

She blinked, a deep frown taking over her face. No reaction came to her mind.

"Just wait," he said, "it gets better. The first line is the date and time, see? Seven thirty at night, twenty-fifth of April, twenty seventeen."

"Okay, so what are the other numbers?" Phoebe said.

"That's the fun part," he said, barely containing a giggle as he quickly read the page again, "I think they're scores of one of the games. Poker doesn't make sense, and any other game against customers would get too much attention. I think it's roulette."

A question she'd forgotten about fell right back into her lap; *Taylor never had a job, according to his girlfriend. Yet he paid his landlord a ton of cash in rent...* Phoebe's eyes went wide, her cheeks tingling as they flushed with renewed excitement.

"Holy shit, Wilks," she said.

"He used time travel to exploit the casino," Wilks said, "and make all the money he needed."

Phoebe could do nothing but shake her head.

"The diary entry even confirms it," he said, "read it again; he literally uses the word exploit. He says it'll help but that he'll need more. And a bunch of the other pages have the same patterns of one- or two-digit numbers."

"He didn't need the coordinates more than once," Phoebe murmured, "just the dates, times, and results of the game. Wilks, this is... really something."

He beamed at her. Another stretch of silence followed as they both sipped at their drinks. Now that the pattern had been revealed, Phoebe saw it all throughout the diary. There were still entries of numbers that didn't fit the pattern; but Phoebe thought it likely they were simply some other money-making trick.

"Did you discover anything else?" she asked.

"Nothing as crazy as the casino thing," he said, "but the number of references in there to the Somerton Man case are insane. Way more than I first realised."

Wilks pointed them out to her; Taylor mentioned Thomas dying on a beach, a page that mimicked the still uncracked code found on the last page of the Somerton Man's copy of 'The Rubaiyat of Omar Khayyam'. There were more, too.

"Oh, wait, there is one more thing," Wilks said, "a link to yet another unsolved mystery."

"What is it?" Phoebe asked, searching through the diary pages.

"I Googled it out of desperation," Wilks said, "and curiosity. Otherwise I wouldn't have noticed at all."

"What is it?" Phoebe repeated.

"This one, here," Wilks passed a tagged page to her, "see that reference to a vacation?"

"In Taured," Phoebe nodded, and then sighed, "let me guess, Taured is the site of another case like this and Somerton?"

"Even better," Wilks said, "Taured doesn't exist."

She screwed her eyes shut, fending off a headache, then opened them to re-read the diary entry.

"Here, check this out," Wilks said.

He handed her a printed-out article about the 'mystery man from Taured'. Before she could read it, he launched into a new monologue.

"This guy shows up at an airport in Haneda, Japan, in 1954. He goes through customs, but his passport says he's from a place called Taured, and he's trying to get back there. They don't have tickets obviously, because the place doesn't exist."

Phoebe nodded, reading the article as he spoke.

"He argues with them about Taured until someone gets a map," Wilks continued, "and then he points to a totally different country and says it's Taured."

"Andorra," Phoebe said, "yeah." She'd read the country's name just before he mentioned it.

"So, it became this total mystery. No one knows where this guy came from, or why he's confused about Andorra. He was so dodgy that they took him into custody and took his ID away. Put him in a hotel with two guards outside the door while they tried to investigate."

Phoebe reached the end of the article just as Wilks reached the end of his story.

"Then, the next morning when they go to speak to him again, he's totally vanished. And so are his ID documents."

"Just like Michael Lee Taylor's gun," she said.

SIX MONTHS LATER

Chapter Ten:
Closure

05 November 2024 9:52pm (Tuesday)

She was doing much better. *Much better. I thought scaling down to once a week would be impossible,* she thought, *but so far, so good.* For the last six months, Phoebe had been going to a therapist, working on what he called a *Need For Closure*. It didn't strike her as a particularly technical-sounding term, but every time he said it, he stressed the words; so they'd become capitalised in her mind.

Her *Need For Closure* took over to the point of addiction, and her therapist, Dr. Greg, had been teaching her ways to divert her mind from the obsession. She created a mantra for herself, specific to the Alpha Park shooting, and recited it most days. After talking with Greg, they decided to set aside one day a week for her to look over the file, just so she could feel like she was still working on it. Then, eventually, she would need to stop altogether.

"Never at work, though," he'd said, a firm edge in his voice.

So she sat on her couch, after a day at work where she'd been mostly able to focus on her actual work, and opened the old file again. A glass of wine sat on the coffee table; Phoebe had been a little quiet on the subject of alcohol when talking with her therapist. Some part of her, deep down, knew there was a problem. But she'd thrown out the water bottle full of vodka from her work desk drawer at least, and stuck to only drinking after she got home. *If that's not progress, nothing is.*

Michael Lee Taylor's file remained unchanged since it was closed. Phoebe and Wilks had gathered some information since, like the John Thompson business, but nothing that was concrete enough to actually add to his file. Lately, she'd taken to searching for news on the Somerton Man at the same time as reading Taylor's file. Once a week, she threw herself back down the rabbit hole, pulling herself back up before she put the file away for another week.

It worked surprisingly well, though she still had to force her thoughts back to reality several times a day. More on the days after she read the file again. There was never any actual news about the Somerton Man. Around the same time as Jacob was shot, the South Australian Attorney General had granted conditional approval for the mystery man's body to be exhumed; but the Australian Government refused to pay. In mid-2021, the Somerton Man was exhumed; but though DNA was extracted, his identity remained unconfirmed.

She'd looked into the investigations surrounding the Somerton Man, who Phoebe still thought of as Thomas Keane; some of the things she'd found were just as baffling as the case itself. One man, who'd been investigating it with the same fervor as Phoebe worked on Michael Lee Taylor, had apparently fallen in love with the alleged granddaughter of the Somerton Man. She didn't know his identity, but her mother had, before she died without revealing the information to anyone.

Phoebe couldn't imagine the frustration of the investigating detectives on that case. *Well, I can actually,* she thought, *I guess it's just a far more specific kind of frustration.* The key with the Alpha Park case was that Michael Lee Taylor had no known family or friends; whereas the Somerton Man could be traced to living relatives, and yet there were still no answers.

Since she'd decided to look into the famous cold case herself, that frustration had now become hers as well; piled onto the Alpha Park case. In her therapy sessions, she'd mentioned the Somerton Man. Greg agreed that there were seemingly undeniable links between the two, but warned her that one unanswered mystery was bad enough.

"You encountered the Alpha Park case because of your job," he'd said, "and you couldn't help that. But seeking out another case, let alone a seventy-year-old one, isn't good for your mental health."

But the links between them were too strong, and Phoebe couldn't help it. Being able to confine her research and obsessing over both cases to one day a week was hard enough, let alone dropping one whole case. Besides, with the possibility of exhuming the Somerton Man's body came potential new information and answers, which was far more than she could hope to get from the Alpha Park case.

So once a week she read everything about it, again. Then, at the end of the night, she packed up the file and put it back in its place, where it wouldn't move until the next week.

Tonight, she was paying particular attention to the CCTV screenshots of Taylor in the moments before and after the gun disappeared. It was the one aspect of the case that might be considered proof of something impossible happening. *These screenshots are less than a second apart,* she thought, *and the gun is there in one and gone in the next.* There was simply no explanation.

It wasn't thrown away, it wasn't hidden anywhere on Taylor, and it wasn't at the scene of the shooting. As impossible as it seemed, the gun had just vanished into thin air, seconds after being used to kill Jacob Turner. It still filled her with tense fury when she thought about how no one seemed to care that a murder weapon vanished. Inspector Rogers waved her off when she'd tried to show him the screenshots. The only people who cared were herself and Wilks, and he was only interested because he saw it as just another fascinating possible conspiracy theory.

Placing the two screenshots next to each other, she stared hard at them. It was a strange feeling; she could see that the gun disappeared, no one could deny it, but at the same time... *It's impossible.*

Wilks occasionally drew her into conversations about conspiracy theories. Most of the time, Phoebe could ignore his emphatic arguments that aliens had visited countless times, or that the Government was covering up a secret underground organisation. But every now and then, he showed her footage or pictures that were almost impossible to ignore. Looking at the Alpha Park CCTV footage, Phoebe felt the same sense of cold uncertainty creep into her stomach.

She'd been staring at the photos for too long already. Her therapist had been hesitant about her reading the file once a week, but she told him she needed something to look into. The cases she encountered in her every day job were too simple, too boring. After Michael Lee Taylor, *everything* was too simple; other than the Somerton Man. *I need to stop soon,* she thought.

As always, a slow, creeping panic began to rise at the prospect of putting the file away without finding new answers. She tried to breathe through the panic; feel it, acknowledge it, and let it pass. Greg tasked her with creating a mantra for herself, and she'd started reciting it at the end of the nights she looked at the files. And whenever the panic rose inside her.

"I will be okay without an answer. There is no danger in not knowing. Uncertainty can't hurt me."

She repeated it four more times. Slowly, the panic receded, and her breathing returned to normal. Phoebe had no experience with mantras or this kind of therapy, but she was hopeful. The words were soothing, and it helped that she'd come up with it herself. *As nice as the words sound,* she thought, *I just hope someday I genuinely believe them.*

29 August 2008 10:33pm (Friday)

Claire's place was bigger than one person needed. Phoebe had always joked about it, but now it benefited both of them. There was a spare bedroom about the same size as the room Ben and Phoebe shared at their place. Next to that was a separate bathroom that Phoebe had to herself. Claire's bedroom and bathroom were upstairs.

They sat on Claire's couch, a box of tissues next to Phoebe and a small mountain of scrunched up tissues next to that. She'd been crying for at least an hour. Claire was patient, listening to her with no judgement. After Phoebe was done recounting everything that happened, Claire hugged her tight and then offered her another tissue.

"I'm sorry Pheebs," Claire said, "I can't believe he turned out to be such an arsehole."

"It all happened so quickly," Phoebe said, sniffling into a tissue, "he was just suddenly so angry."

"You guys *were* drifting though. I mean, you've been saying ever since Charlie that he's been quiet and cold and stuff."

"Yeah," Phoebe said, "I just thought he'd talk to me or something, I guess."

"Really? You thought *Ben* would open up about something serious and painful?"

"You didn't know that part of him," Phoebe said, "but he was actually always good at talking about serious stuff. It just took a bit of prompting sometimes"

She was still reeling, adrift in a sea of indefinable emotions and disjointed thoughts. But speaking with Claire brought a small semblance of normality back to her life. They hung out fairly often, and seeing her again felt like the only thing helping her stay sane.

323

"So, you guys have completely broken up?"

"Yeah, I think so."

"Wow, that's brutal," Claire said, "but on the plus side... you're single, right? So, like, we can go clubbing or something?"

"Oh my god, Claire, it hasn't even been a day! I'm not going clubbing with you."

Although, a small part of her thought, *maybe a crazy night out is exactly what I need.*

"Relax, I was kidding."

Claire laughed, shaking her head. She got up and headed to the kitchen, glancing over her shoulder at Phoebe.

"I was thinking we could get a little drunk here instead, though?"

That's probably a bad idea, she thought, *given how fragile I am right now.*

"Fuck yeah," she said instead.

When Claire came back, she carried two big glasses and a whole bottle of white wine. Phoebe laughed as Claire filled both glasses precariously close to the rim. She nodded in satisfaction, disappeared back to the kitchen for a moment, and returned with two brightly coloured straws. Phoebe laughed even louder.

Trying not to giggle, Claire leaned over the coffee table, sucking wine from her straw as fast as she could. Phoebe laughed and raced to join her. For a few moments, they stared at each other, struggling not to laugh as they each tried to reach the bottom of their glass first. Phoebe's head started spinning halfway down, and she sputtered and leaned back, coughing and laughing. Claire didn't stop until her glass was empty.

"Holy shit, Claire," Phoebe said between coughs, "how did you do that?"

"Years of practice."

She laughed, and shook her head at Claire. *I haven't been out with Claire since before Ben and I got together,* she thought, *but it looks like she hasn't changed.* The last time they'd gone drinking, Claire ordered six shots of tequila for herself, and drank them all within a minute. *And that was after we'd been out for hours already.*

"Do you remember the last time we went clubbing together?" she asked Claire, when her coughing finally subsided.

"I remember the day after," Claire said, her eyebrows raised, "it was not pretty."

I've only ever slept with Ben, she thought, *is that sad, or romantic?* Now that they were broken up, it felt sad. *Maybe I should follow Claire's lead,* she thought, *and get a little crazy.*

The topic of conversation turned to Claire's life, and fun things, and Phoebe found herself almost forgetting the events of that day and the weeks preceding it. Claire was the type who went out every weekend, and seemed to find a new guy every time she did. Phoebe could barely comprehend Claire's lifestyle. She didn't judge, but she knew she'd never be able to live that way, even if she was single for a while. *Just for tonight, though,* she thought, *maybe I need that?*

Phoebe grabbed the bottle of wine and refilled her glass as full as Claire had.

"Wow," Claire said, "I thought you weren't so keen?"

"I think I should finally unleash my inner party animal. You know you want me to."

"Umm, Pheebs… are you sure?"

Phoebe rolled her eyes, and drank deeply from the straw again. This time she managed to get through more than half the glass before she had to stop. Claire made a strange noise, like a strangled sigh.

"Are you really going to get proper drunk?" she said.

"Oh yeah, I need it tonight. We should go out after this too. You can be my wingman, get me laid."

"Woah! Pheebs, maybe we should just stay in tonight."

She laughed and shook her head, then drank some more of the wine. Claire simply stared, confused shock all over her face. *I feel drunk already,* she thought, *I don't care anymore. Claire always nagged me to live like she does; why is she arguing against it now?*

"Come on," Phoebe said, giggling, "let's go out! You always thought it was weird I've only been with one guy... This is your chance to change that."

"Phoebe, seriously. You're gonna regret that, I know you will. I know I gave you a hard time for that, but I was always just joking."

Phoebe finished the wine in her glass and picked up the bottle. She drank directly from it, until there was nothing left. Claire's expression melted into a dull sadness, and despite being drunk, it finally hit Phoebe; *she really cares. She's really trying to look out for me.* In that moment, Claire's friendship burned brightly in her heart, bright enough to pull her out of everything else. Tears fell from her eyes again, and she slumped back down into the couch.

"Tomorrow is gonna suck," she said.

"Yeah," Claire said, her voice gentle, "but who cares? Spend the weekend here, we can order some pizza and just sit around. Seriously, just let go for the next couple days. Don't worry about all that crap, it's just you and me."

Phoebe smiled, tears falling freely as they looked at each other.

"Oh, come on, stop crying already," Claire said, "you'll die of dehydration."

"Isn't that what the wine is for? To keep me hydrated?"

Claire laughed and threw her straw at Phoebe.

"Hell yeah," she said, "that's the spirit."

Another long day at work, and Phoebe was finally home again. She'd been able to focus on work, but the day dragged on for what felt like a week. It was an uncomfortably common feeling for her lately. Simpson was back at work, and a cold tension sat between Phoebe and the rest of the team. *They all know it was my fault,* she thought, *and they don't trust me anymore.*

She didn't blame them; Simpson especially. He still winced whenever he moved too much. It was an almost fatal wound; a gunshot to the thigh, shredding the muscles and tearing through a major artery. Though it could have killed him, the damage was far less than it could've been, and Simpson fought tooth and nail to come back to work as soon as he could.

Being at the station every day, surrounded by tension and guilt and easily closed cases, was taking a heavier toll than Phoebe would have expected. Every week, she had more to work through with Greg in their sessions. She broke down in tears every time they spoke. The train ride to the therapy centre and back felt like a numb, shallow dream.

Friday night, at least, she thought. Before all of this happened, being a detective had been her dream job. It wasn't until now that she understood what people meant by *thank God it's Friday.*

"And fuck Mondays," she said, a low chuckle slipping from her as she took a long sip of wine.

She was getting back into reading. The Sherlock Holmes books, once again, but a ton of other mysteries as well. At Dr. Greg's advice, she stuck to fiction.

"There's always a resolution in fiction," he'd said, "and resolution is something you need right now."

And it was true. Every mystery she read, as baffling as it might have seemed at the beginning, was wrapped up neatly and explained by the end. The more of them she read, the more satisfaction she gained from the solve at the end of the book. She read every afternoon after work now.

She was most of the way through another book. There were two possible suspects; the victim's ex, and the victim's employee. Clues that supported both possible suspects' guilt were strewn throughout the book. Phoebe was finally starting to tolerate the ambiguity of the mystery. *I think that's probably only because I know there'll be an answer at the end. I wish the Alpha Park shooting had been fictional. Then at least I would've known what it all meant.*

She took another sip, and noticed her glass was almost empty. Putting down her book, she went straight to the fridge. The bottle in the door shelf was just as empty as her glass; barely a sip left. She poured the rest of the bottle out, then searched the fridge for another new bottle. There were none. A flicker of panic flared in her chest like the embers of a camp fire catching again.

"No," she said, "hang on, I should have another one somewhere. I'm not out yet."

Closing the fridge and turning instead to her kitchen cupboards, Phoebe's search slowly became frantic. *I can't believe I haven't bought more bottles,* she thought, *when was the last time I went grocery shopping?* There was no wine. She'd had the whole bottle that was in the fridge; *I can't drive to the store. I'm stuck and there's no more wine.*

It shouldn't have made her this upset, but the panic grew, twisting in her chest and shrinking her lungs. She ran her hands through her hair, trying to breathe and struggling to draw in any air.

"Fuck," she said, her eyes roaming over the kitchen.

She wasn't an alcoholic, at least she didn't consider herself one; but wine was one of the few things that could effectively calm her. It helped her unwind, relieved the tension of a day at work, and made movies and TV shows far more tolerable.

She didn't *need* it... but it was a comfort that helped her more than anything else.

I could walk to the shops, she thought, *but that'll take ages. And besides, only an alcoholic would walk all the way to the shops at night just to drink more wine after already drinking a whole bottle.*

Still, the panic grew. But she was determined now; *I can't give in. I can't have this be a problem.* If she let it turn into a problem, she'd have to talk about it with Greg, and then she'd have to stop drinking altogether.

"I don't need it," she said, "I don't need alcohol. I'm fine without it."

There's a new mantra for me, she thought. It sounded stupid, but she repeated it to herself until her heartbeat slowed again. Finally, she sat back on the couch. She stared at the coffee table, wondering if she really did have a problem and avoiding the answer.

Standing once again, she drank the last bit of wine in her glass and put it on the kitchen bench. Stripping out of her pyjamas, Phoebe ran the shower until it was almost scalding. She didn't usually have showers at night, but lately they were another thing she could do to help unwind. Ever since she'd tried showering with the bathroom light off, she used it as a relaxation method. *And showering like this feels far better after a bottle of wine than it does during a brutal hangover,* she thought.

After the first time, she put music on. She didn't have a refined taste in music, and wasn't a keen follower of current musical trends; but it was easy to find generic relaxation music. She played it on maximum volume on her phone, and left it sitting on the bathroom counter.

Soft piano and strings wafted into the shower with her, as ethereal as the steam that swirled around her. She breathed deeply, feeling the steam in the air she took in, feeling the hot water rush down her back. It was the only place she felt relaxed. She let go of the tension she always carried, the stress, and held on to nothing but the gentle sensations surrounding her. As she always did when the shower unraveled her stress, Phoebe cried. Tears rushed down her face, washed away instantly by the hot water.

When she was done, she felt empty and wrung out; but relaxed. Relieved. It was the best possible feeling for her, and her showers were beginning to go for longer and longer lately. She barely dried herself, instead wrapping herself in the comfortable robe that Claire had bought her and sitting back on the couch.

She thought about Claire, properly thought about her, for the first time in a long time. They'd been best friends. The kind of friends who could have a whole conversation consisting of in jokes; their own private language that no one else understood. They'd known how each other's minds worked. They supported each other, and shared everything.

Before she realised what was happening, tears welled up and ran down her cheeks again. Glancing down at the robe, she ran her hands over it, feeling its comfort and warmth. Even as the tears continued, a soft smile pulled at her mouth. *I need her back,* she thought.

Without thinking, she picked up her phone and clicked on Claire's number. It rang, and rang again, and then Claire's voice crackled in her ear through phone static.

"Phoebe... hi."

"Hey, Claire."

"Um. What's up?"

"I was just..." she had to stifle a ragged sigh as her tears continued, "I was just thinking about you. I really miss you."

Her voice broke halfway through the last sentence, and she tried to keep the sobs out of her voice.

"Oh, Pheebs," Claire said, her voice gentle but guarded, "I miss you too. You doing alright?"

"I'm... not really, no. But I've been seeing a therapist, and working on stuff. I'm getting better."

"You're going to therapy?" Claire's voice rose, filling with a little warmth and humour, "Pheebs, that's amazing!"

"Thanks," Phoebe said, another sob escaping as she let out a relieved giggle, "I've got a way to go, obviously, but yeah. So, I was wondering. Can we catch up sometime? Please?"

She hadn't meant to sound so desperate, but there was no way to stop her tone from pleading; *I really didn't know how badly I needed her,* she thought. A few seconds of silence drove her heartbeat up, undoing the entire relaxing shower. *She's over it,* Phoebe thought, *I'm too much work. I'm not worth it.*

"Yeah," Claire finally said, "yeah, that sounds nice, Pheebs. How about next Friday night? The twenty-second?"

Phoebe's heart raced even faster; but this time it was excitement, relief, and elation. She fought for control as her tears doubled. She closed her eyes, smiling wider than she had in years.

"That sounds perfect."

Claire had changed her hair style; it was shorter, an almost aggressively confident look that she completely pulled off. Phoebe marveled at it for a while when she first arrived, nodding in approval as Claire turned her head.

"And I got a boyfriend," she said, her smile as wide as Phoebe's, "a real, actual boyfriend."

"Holy shit," Phoebe said, "he must be a hell of a man to be able to tame you."

"Oh, he is."

Phoebe laughed, and pulled Claire into a tight hug.

"I really missed you, Claire."

"I know. I missed you too."

They sat on the couch, and Phoebe smiled at her best friend. *I thought it would be awkward and weird,* she thought, *but it's like the last four years never happened.* For a while, they simply sat together, enjoying the familiar comfortable silence between them. Then Phoebe stood, shooting another smile at Claire, and made for the fridge.

"Drink?" she asked.

"What do you think?" Claire called after her, "I'd never say no to a drink."

"Good to know you haven't changed *too* much. If you said no, I was gonna ask what the hell happened to my best friend."

"A new hairdo and a boyfriend isn't that big a deal, Pheebs, calm down."

She poured two glasses as full as she could and sat back down. Claire had already turned on the TV and was scrolling through her Netflix list.

"You've really been getting at the rom coms lately, huh?" she said, "does this mean you want to start dating again?"

"Oh, shut up. I just needed something mindless to take my attention."

"How convenient for you," she said with a far too smug grin, "you're too good for rom coms but they just happen to be the only thing on your watch list."

Phoebe let out a groan of frustration, but it turned into a laugh as Claire shot her a comical look they used to swap. *In the old days, when making each other laugh during inappropriate moments was the height of comedy.*

"That's big talk for someone who won't even show me her watch list," Phoebe shot back.

"Oh please, you'd just say you were too good for that too."

Claire selected a stand-up comedy and pressed play, mashing the volume down button until it could barely be heard; they wouldn't end up watching much of it, but Claire always needed something on the TV.

"So, tell me about your new guy," Phoebe said.

"Well, he's not exactly new. It's been almost two years."

"Holy shit! Tell me everything!"

She did, and the more she talked, the more Phoebe remembered the way she'd felt with Ben in the beginning. She was happy for Claire, but the fact that her best friend had made such a huge change in her life and Phoebe was unaware of it until now exposed a hole within her she didn't realise existed.

His name was Pete, and he was originally one of Claire's casual partners. Through a series of unrelated circumstances, she'd stopped seeing the others, until it was just Pete and her. Eventually, he began staying the night, and then asked her out on an actual date. She said yes, and for the first time since Phoebe had known her, Claire had a boyfriend.

"He's so amazing," she said, "we have so much more in common than I thought. You should have told me that dating could be this good, Pheebs."

Phoebe let out an incredulous laugh, playfully shoving Claire in the shoulder.

"I literally did tell you that. Many times."

"Nah, I would remember something like that."

Phoebe groaned again, shaking her head as Claire laughed. A brief moment of silence settled in, punctuated by the stand-up comedian's faint voice.

"... guarantee you, you will not shit for a week after that..."

They shot looks at the TV, then each other, and burst into laughter. For the first time in a long time, Phoebe felt a real connection with someone else. No one had visited her since Claire. Her team at work—other than Wilks—were cold and distant after Simpson's injury. Her other friends were busy, and they'd never been as close with her as Claire.

Phoebe turned the volume up, and for the rest of the show they simply watched and laughed together. TV, especially comedy, had been nothing but background noise for her for so long that she'd forgotten what it felt like to really pay attention to it.

When the show finished, Phoebe refilled their glasses, and Claire scrolled through for another movie to watch. She turned the volume down again and selected a generic rom com; one of the ones on Phoebe's list.

"You seem really good, Pheebs," she said as Phoebe sat back down with the glasses, "I'm really glad you're working on stuff."

"It's slow progress," she said, "I never thought I'd need therapy, but here we are."

"There's no shame in talking to someone, Phoebe. I love you, but you were really going downhill. I'm glad you're coming back up again."

"Me too."

They sat back as the movie started, and Phoebe was content. *It's nice to know she cares,* she thought, *for a long time it really felt like she'd stopped.* It was her own fault, she knew; she'd forced Claire away with her obsession, her refusal to let things go. It was a regular topic of discussion with her therapist, and something that still brought her a lot of pain. She never meant to push Claire away. At the time, it didn't even feel like that's what she was doing.

But at least the friendship didn't die, she thought, *she came back after all, and it feels like she never left.* She was determined to keep Claire around from now on. *I won't let anything push her away again; not even Michael Lee Taylor. Especially not Michael Lee Taylor.*

28 November 2008 7:41pm (Friday)

Her apartment was small, but in a nice area, and a short drive from the station. Phoebe had unpacked the last box almost two weeks earlier, but she still felt unsettled. Something about the new apartment felt cold, somehow. As though she was staying at someone else's home temporarily instead of living in her own place.

Ben still lived at the house. He'd paid for almost the entire thing, from the advances of his first two novels. Phoebe contributed what she could, but her savings weren't anywhere near Ben's. Before he began writing, he worked in a Government department, and managed to save a huge amount of money. *He spends no money unless he absolutely has to... no wonder he's basically rich.*

She didn't resent him, exactly; but life seemed to have been easy for him, where Phoebe had always struggled with money. *I always assumed the police would pay well,* she thought, *but it's the same as any other job. Hopefully a few promotions will fix that.*

Phoebe sat on her new couch, holding a glass of wine, and thought about Charlie. Today was the due date the doctor gave her. *Charlie's birthday,* she thought, *I wonder if Ben remembers. Or if he even cares.* He never wanted to talk about Charlie after they lost him; he never even wanted to acknowledge his existence.

The funeral she held in their backyard was small and interrupted by rain. She'd been alone; Ben stood nearby, but he may as well have been on the other side of the city. Tonight, Phoebe was celebrating his birthday. She was just as alone, but now at least she was free to think about him without Ben bringing her down.

A chocolate cake sat on her coffee table, along with a punnet of strawberries. A present that she'd bought for Charlie was next to the cake; a framed copy of the first ultrasound of him. She didn't bother wrapping it. *It's more for me anyway,* she thought, *sorry Charlie.*

She'd prepared a playlist of music for him to sleep to before she found out he hadn't made it, and it played softly as Phoebe cut a slice of cake. Classical music, mostly piano, that set her heart at a gentle pace and soothed her racing mind. No one else knew about the birthday. Phoebe originally considered inviting her closest friends, but decided quickly against having anyone else. It was just something she needed to do for herself.

"Happy birthday, Charlie," she said, her voice barely audible even to herself, "I miss you."

It felt like a lifetime ago that she was pregnant, and only a day ago at the same time. She remembered the fear, and the exhilaration, and she wanted all of it back again. *I'd live in constant anxiety for the rest of my life if it meant having Charlie here with me,* she thought, *even without Ben.*

Closing her eyes, Phoebe pictured Charlie in her arms. He was fussing, his tiny face squished into a frown as he squirmed. She imagined comforting him, holding him close. It was perfect in her head; as soon as she comforted him, he calmed, and a smile lit up his face as she smiled back at him.

Even in her imagination, he looked like Ben. *I could imagine him however I want,* she thought, *but for some reason that's all I can see.* She still loved Ben. *That's the worst part. Even after he was such a dick, I love him so much.* They should have stayed together; despite what Claire said, despite what her mother said, and despite what Ben himself said, Phoebe knew they were soul mates.

She tried to ignore the pain he'd left in his wake, and focused on the image of Charlie in her arms again. He was calm now, happy and safe. Smiling, letting her tears fall as her arms remained in a cradling position, Phoebe sang happy birthday.

30 November 2024 10:33am (Saturday)

Three days after the fifth anniversary of Jacob Turner's murder, Phoebe realised she'd let it pass without acknowledgement. Moments later, she realised she'd done the same thing for Charlie's birthday. Both realisations hit her hard, and for a while she wrestled with a tidal wave of guilt crashing over her thoughts and feelings.

How could I have let them both down so badly? She thought, *especially my Charlie.* She'd celebrated his birthday every year since she lost him. *How did I forget?* Before today, she wouldn't have thought she'd ever forget about something so big. Charlie never left her mind; *but for some reason, his birthday did.*

Charlie's death, just like Jacob's, had changed her in an indefinable way. The Phoebe that existed before she became pregnant and the Phoebe she was now were strangers; thinking about her life before felt like looking at photos of someone else's life.

For the first time in years, Phoebe tried to imagine what her life might have been like if Charlie was born and her and Ben had stayed together.

"Mum! There's a new movie coming out this weekend and I wanna see it with my friends!"

Phoebe glanced at Ben, eyes wide as she asked without words. He nodded, smiling, and she smiled back. Ben could never say no to Charlie. It was cute most of the time; sometimes it was exasperating.

"Of course you can, sweetie," she said, "you've got the money, right?"

Charlie rolled his eyes and nodded. His movements were cartoonish, exaggerated to make his mum and dad smile. It worked. He was as charming as his father, when he wanted to be.

"Don't stay out too long after the movie," she said, "and don't spend too much on snacks."

"Oh my god mum, I know," he said, "you don't have to use your cop voice on me."

"That's my mum voice, sweetie," Phoebe said, laughing, "if I used my cop voice, you'd be in a lot of trouble."

Charlie went quiet, staring at his father with a comically nervous expression.

"Has mum ever used her cop voice on you, dad?"

"Oh yes, she has. Trust me, you don't want that."

Phoebe shoved him playfully, shaking her head as she did.

"Well neither of you ever needs to hear it if you just behave yourselves."

Phoebe shook her head, wrenched out of the fantasy as though coming out of a dream. There were tears in her eyes, but it wasn't sadness she felt. As much as she would have loved the fantasy to come true, what she really felt was a deep, bittersweet relief. He was gone, as was Ben; but what they left behind in their absence was what had fueled her drive to keep moving forward ever since.

After their break-up, and during it for that matter, Ben had revealed a darkness hidden beneath his charm. He'd never become abusive, but he was petty and spiteful, and a big part of her was glad he hadn't become a father. *Who knows how he might have changed after having a child,* she thought, *I never would have thought he'd handle the break-up the way he did.* It still filled her with an anxious kind of shock; she'd known him for years, and he never gave any hint or indication of his darker nature until their relationship began crumbling.

The fact that she could spend so much time with someone, and be so in love with him, and still have no idea what lay underneath the surface, was almost as terrifying as the uncertainty that surrounded Michael Lee Taylor. *At least it was a mystery that solved itself,* she thought, *and I don't have to deal with it ever again.* She was fine by herself; she always had been. If going without the strange and disquieting uncertainty of what lay beneath people's public faces meant avoiding relationships, Phoebe was happy to do so.

As much as uncertainty plagued her, she was beginning to accept that Charlie never existed. She only wondered what motherhood would be like occasionally now. For years after she lost him, she'd imagined him as being a younger copy of Ben; charming, happy, and handsome. Then for a while he'd become a sort of hybrid of her own face with Ben's, and then after than he began to take after her more and more.

Now, she accepted that since his death he had become merely a concept. He was now a fantasy; a non-physical manifestation of *what if*. Travelling down that road was intoxicating, and addictive, but ultimately unhealthy. It took her a long time to realise, and she still spoke with Dr. Greg about it every session. The scenario of Charlie wanting to go to the movies was the first time she'd properly engaged in that *what if* in a long time. It felt like the last time. She couldn't really explain to herself why exactly, but there'd been a strange finality to it.

Charlie would always exist to her, and she would always love him; but she was becoming more and more okay with him being an idea. It was beginning to feel less like she'd lost him, and more like he was always there, just without having the chance to grow up.

"Happy birthday, Charlie," she whispered, "I'm sorry I forgot."

"That's okay, mum," he said, *"as long as I get some cake."*

She knew it was her imagination. She wasn't under any illusions. But his voice was somehow real too, something she almost heard with her ears instead of just in her mind. She smiled as more tears welled in her eyes. *This is it,* she thought, *time to say goodbye.*

"Of course, sweetie," she said, "anything for my perfect boy."

She'd been on the couch, but she stood and stretched, sighing as her body loosened up. He was smiling, some part of her felt it. She didn't visualise him, or try to imagine him in any form; she simply felt his presence, and it was full of love and comfort.

Smiling as a few tears slid down her cheeks, Phoebe took out a bowl from the kitchen cupboard. She gathered flour, eggs, cocoa, and everything else she needed.

"Chocolate mud cake," she said, her smile growing to a grin as she thought about the scenarios she'd run through over the years, "your favourite. One last time."

6 December 2024 2:31pm (Friday)

The train ride to her therapist's office took just over half an hour. She brought a book every time, but almost never ended up reading. Instead, she thought about what she wanted to say to Greg. It usually wasn't until she was on the train towards him that she realised she hadn't been doing the mindfulness exercises he gave her the week before.

There was always a tightening in her chest on the way; a strange anxiety she didn't feel anywhere else in her life. It almost felt the way she had in school handing assignments in to the teacher; she wanted to be right, to have the right answers.

Her sessions weren't regular; she booked the following week's appointment at the end of each session for whenever it fit. But Inspector Rogers understood, and her team had no comments. She couldn't tell if they were supportive of her seeking therapy or not. *Or if they even care.* The strange thing, Phoebe thought, was that Simpson himself had apparently moved on. Her and wilks were fine as well, after working together outside of the station. It was only the rest of the team who still emanated a cold tension towards her.

For most of the trip, Phoebe dwelled on work. The seat beneath her rumbled as the train sped on. She stared out the window, watching the world outside slip past her smoothly.

As the train pulled into a station a few stops from her therapist, Phoebe watched the people waiting. There were people milling around, rushing, standing still, talking. She watched them all, her eyes roaming as she thought about the shooting five years ago. It had come so suddenly, so unexpectedly, and was over before most people realised what had actually happened. The idea that the same thing, or something even worse, could happen anywhere filled her with uneasy dread. *Especially in Rosetown,* she thought, *where it would be my job to investigate.*

A few minutes passed, time she spent staring at the people at the station. When the train began pulling away, she saw a face among the crowd, and her heart exploded into panicked thumps. Blinking, she stared hard, trying to see the person as clearly as she could.

No way, she thought, *no fucking way.* After that, her thoughts scattered, and all she could do was stare. She could have sworn, without any doubt, that the man she was staring at in the train station that day was Michael Lee Taylor.

The train pulled away, and Phoebe twisted in her seat to keep the man in view. *That's three men who look almost the same,* she thought, *maybe that's just John Thompson after all.* But where John Thompson bore a resemblance to Michael Lee Taylor, there were noticeable differences. Slipping away from her now, just visible through the crowd and the tiny train windows, was a man who looked *exactly* like Michael Lee Taylor.

It can't be him, she thought, *even if he could time travel, he's dead now.* Maybe she'd just imagined it; she had experienced hallucinations before. She wanted more than anything to get off the train, follow that man and ask him who he was. But the train was already gliding towards full speed, and she was going to get to her therapist's office just on time as it was.

Every now and then, it hit her that they were never really certain Michael Lee Taylor was the shooter. He'd confessed in the interviews, granted; but innocent people confessed to crimes all the time, for a wide range of reasons. All the witness statements they had gave vague descriptions of the shooter, and mostly identified Taylor based on his clothing.

It wasn't totally unlikely that the man they arrested, and who died in their custody, didn't do anything wrong other than be at the wrong place at the worst possible time. He'd been plastered on booze and possibly other substances, and only confessed after Phoebe pushed him to it. Before that, almost nothing he said made sense. His journal never

343

mentioned Jacob by name, so even though it looked like a clear-cut premeditated murder, it could've simply been unrelated delusion.

All signs pointed to Taylor, but Phoebe knew that sometimes evidence didn't always add up the way it should have. A lot of evidence was open to interpretation. That's where Phoebe came in, and she'd done her best with the Alpha Park shooting. But if there really was something deeper going on, as she suspected, she never would have interpreted the evidence correctly anyway.

She thought about the case deeply as the train sped on; so deeply that its smooth rumbling stopped registering to her, and she forgot where she was. To her, after years dwelling on the details, the only explanation that actually accounted for all the evidence was that Taylor travelled from the future to assassinate Jacob Turner. She felt like an idiot for believing it, but the alternatives were that either they got the wrong guy, or else were wrong about the entire case.

Phoebe knew she hadn't misread the evidence *that* badly, and it was highly unlikely—though certainly possible—that Michael Lee Taylor was innocent. Still, the image of his face in the crowd kept crawling into her mind. *If time travel is possible,* she thought, *and if he's from the future, his younger self would still be there before he died.* Trying to puzzle out why he would be back in Rosetown, and how time travel could work, gave her a headache.

If it was really Taylor at the last train station, she might actually have a chance at getting answers. The possibility of speaking to him again filled her with both frantic excitement and crushing dread. She still had nightmares about her interviews with him. His face, his voice, the ominous insanity of his words.

Looks like I've got something new to talk to Greg about, she thought, *I just really hope I don't keep seeing Taylor around after today.* Though if she saw him again, she wouldn't be able to stop herself from approaching him. She found herself wanting to speak to John Thompson again, as well. *Just speak to Greg,* she thought, *get all this out of your system and let it go like normal.* Training herself to let the mystery go was a hell of a journey, and it only grew harder each week until she saw her therapist again.

She knew the exercises, the tricks, all the ways she could move past her mental obstacles; but somehow there was an element of motivation she lacked after leaving Greg's office. Seeing him, hearing him explain the exercises, guiding her through them, made all of the work seem easy. *All I want is to be done with this*, she thought. Whether that meant finally solving the mystery, or just somehow moving past it once and for all.

6 December 2024 8:38pm (Friday)

Home again, Phoebe sat on the couch with a glass of wine. Her eyes were puffy, her mind vague and clouded. *Another productive therapy session,* she thought. Greg had been shocked to hear about her seeing Taylor at the train station; but as always, he recovered quickly and presented some logical explanations. The most likely was that she'd hallucinated or imagined it. *It's definitely happened before,* she thought, *so it's not like it's impossible.*

"I probably was seeing things," she said to herself, "there were so many people there."

Sitting across from Greg, in the safety of his office, it had been easy to wave it off as a hallucination. At home, dwelling once again on Michael Lee Taylor, it was a little harder to convince herself. Part of her actually wanted him to still be out there, alive and well; she wanted to see him, talk to him. She wondered if he would somehow recognise her, or have any idea what she'd been through.

If that was a younger version of him, she thought, *what the hell was he doing in Rosetown before he was supposed to shoot Jacob?* His journal certainly never mentioned having been there before. *I wish I'd taken a photo when I had the chance.*

"Remember, your drive to obtain all the answers is just a manifestation of your fear of uncertainty," Greg had said in their session today, "and your need for control. Life is full of uncertainty, and no one really has control. Try to focus on the things you *are* certain of, and the things you *do* have control over."

In that one statement, Greg gave her a breakthrough. They'd discussed it at length in most of their sessions, but having a no-nonsense truth simply laid out before her broke through her confused thoughts. Before that, Greg had a tendency to phrase things gently, with a bit more subtlety.

Even if that somehow was Michael Lee Taylor, she thought, *I can't gain anything from knowing that. It won't change the case, it won't help me feel better.* His face plagued her, filthy and manic. The case itself plagued her, haunting both her dreams and her conscious mind.

"I will be okay without an answer. There is no danger in not knowing. Uncertainty can't hurt me."

She repeated her mantra over and over, until the words became a rhythmic pulse in her mind almost stripped of meaning. After at least five minutes straight, she stopped. Trying to focus on the actual meaning of the words, she thought the mantra through. *If I never solve this case,* she thought, *will I be okay?* A wave of panic rising at the thought seemed to say no; but she fought it down and persisted with her train of thought.

What's the worst that could happen? If she didn't solve the case, it wouldn't get her fired. Quite the opposite, in fact; *pursuing this awful case in the first place is what almost got me fired.* More than once.

If there really was some kind of shadowy organisation, her pursuing the case was dangerous. *They've clearly done everything they can to push me away,* she thought, *if they exist.* Pushing any further might mean another Michael Lee Taylor or Thomas Keane getting sent back in time to kill another target; *and this time it would be me.*

Even if all the time travel conspiracy theory stuff wasn't true, chasing dead end leads and expending all of her mental energy and time on an old unsolvable case was clearly detrimental. She knew it, and she'd known it even in 2019. But knowing it was bad for her and having the discipline to stop were two very different things. Even after countless sessions with Greg—very expensive sessions, no less—Phoebe still found the idea of stopping almost impossible.

This is never going to go away, she thought, *even if I can somehow finally get over the Alpha Park shooting, I'm going to need therapy forever.* The thought dragged her heart down into her stomach. She didn't know why, but a surge of disappointment appeared somewhere deep down, strong enough to almost become anger. *I'm nowhere near the person I wanted to be*.

"I will be okay without an answer," she said again. "There is no danger in not knowing. Uncertainty can't hurt me."

Now that she'd made a mantra, the words really did hold a strange power. It was what Greg promised. The danger, at least as far as Phoebe was concerned, was that she would grow to *need* the words. The way she'd grown to need a glass of wine at night. *Or a bottle. At least repeating a mantra won't give me a hangover,* she thought.

Phoebe knew her relentless drive for answers was unhealthy; that ugly bottom line formed the basis of almost every discussion between her and Greg. *Even the ones about Charlie*. Losing a loved one was never easy, but losing a child before they were born meant that all she would ever have was the question *what if?* Letting him go had been more difficult than letting the Alpha Park case go.

But I did it, she thought, *it just took fifteen years*. If Michael Lee Taylor's face was going to be stuck in her head for that long, Phoebe didn't know what to do. *I'll go insane*. Progress was slow, and hard won, and she wasn't used to that. Almost as strong as her need for closure was her need for *fast* closure. Being a detective, she was used to putting in the work and getting results. Sometimes it took a while, but most of the time Phoebe and her team solved cases within days or weeks; not years.

She finished her glass and went to the fridge to refill. In the kitchen, she paused halfway through pouring more wine. Her eyes wandered slowly, inexorably, to the cupboard where she kept the file. *Once a week,* she thought, trying to channel Greg's voice, *only once a week*.

Standing in the kitchen, the bottle of wine hovering above her glass, Phoebe stared at the cupboard. In that moment, the file within emanated a vicious energy; *you'll never be able to leave me alone,* it seemed to say, *I'll always have control*. It spoke in Michael Lee Taylor's voice; erratic and aggressive, but utterly certain.

"Fuck you," Phoebe said.

She put the bottle down. Her hands shook. Taking a tentative step towards the cupboard, a brief but powerful flash of the interview room door loomed in front of her. Closed, with a manic child killer behind it, ready to scream at her in horrifying, shrill gibberish.

All she wanted was an end to it. *But the end I wanted was a solved case, not years of therapy.* Whatever forces worked outside of her understanding, whether it be a dangerous organisation in the future, fate, or simply dumb luck, were clearly dead-set on stopping Phoebe from reaching the truth.

Leads keep disappearing, and evidence too, she thought, *it feels like someone is watching me and destroying anything useful before I can reach it.* She felt like a rat in a maze, searching and sniffing out the cheese hidden in the tiny corridors; but the scientists watching her kept moving it whenever she got too close. *Just before I turn the corner and see it, it's gone.*

The cupboard swelled and changed, growing until it matched the interview room door. Michael Lee Taylor's mad cackling voice echoed from the other side, scratching against her bare nerves. Suddenly she was certain of one thing, and it set her already frantic heart thumping; *If I open that cupboard, the file will be gone.*

She couldn't explain where the thought came from, but it felt more real than any of the other things racing through her mind. *The gun,* she thought, *they made the gun disappear. They can make a file disappear too.*

Lifting the full glass to her lips, she barely noticed the cold feeling that spread down her arm as her shaking hands spilled wine. It spattered on the kitchen floor, onto her feet, and she didn't even blink. Her eyes were stuck, fixated on the cupboard door. It still looked like the interview room door, wide and grey and cold. Danger sat behind that door, waiting.

"No," she said, "fuck you," but her mind said "*I had to do it*", in Michael Lee Taylor's voice.

He said that in the interview, she remembered, *after he sobered up*. He'd said "I *had* to. Have you ever had to shoot someone?" and then Phoebe said that no, she hadn't. *Only now*, she thought, *now I have*.

"We're the same, now," the Michael Lee Taylor in her mind said. "*We've done the same horrible thing*."

"No," Phoebe said, "Teagan Lee was dangerous, she shot Simpson... and would've shot me too."

"*You have no idea*," Taylor said. His voice was reasonable, composed. He'd been a different man after the alcohol wore off. *He was so rational, so believable*.

"*I was telling the truth. But I never told you everything, not even close. Would you like an answer? Just one? Open the cupboard. I dare you*."

The interview room door started pounding, thumping in rhythm with her heartbeat, and the voice that sounded like Michael Lee Taylor's rose to a primal scream.

"*Open it!*" he screeched, "*I fucking dare you! You know what they do to loose ends, bitch! Open the cupboard and see what happens!*"

She might have dropped her glass; she couldn't remember, but it wasn't in her hand any more. The image of the interview room door disappeared, replaced by the cupboard. Nothing else existed. Nothing but the cupboard, and whatever madness lay in wait within. *It's not there,* she thought, and felt Taylor's grin in her head, *the file will be gone*.

"*You never knew what you got yourself into. Open it. Open it, open it, OPEN IT!*"

Phoebe screamed, falling to her knees in front of the kitchen cupboard. Tears streamed down her face, barely felt as she struggled to breathe. Her hands were numb, shaking. There was no rhythm to the painful thudding of her heart now, just erratic staccato thumps that drove more air out of her lungs.

Everything felt cold as she forced her hand towards the cupboard handle. Michael Lee Taylor's face grinned at her from its dark place in the back of her mind, leering like a pervert staring through a bedroom window. She needed to destroy that face, somehow, but right then it felt like he would win. *I won't survive this,* she thought, *I can't.*

Her hand rested on the handle, and she forced it to pull inward. The cupboard opened, slowly. Phoebe squeezed her eyes shut. The grainy image of the gun in his hand appeared, and the gun disappeared, and she shook her head viciously. The cupboard was open, and her eyes were still shut. *Count to three,* she thought, *like ripping off a band-aid. Just do it.* She counted, out loud, and by the time she reached three she was screaming. She opened her eyes, more terrified than she'd been in her entire life.

It was there, where it always was. Sitting on the cupboard shelf, harmless and inert. Distantly, in that same dark place, she heard the faint cackling laugh of Michael Lee Taylor. Without another thought, she snatched the file from its place. She moved on autopilot, nothing but one simple thought running on a loop in her mind.

She moved to the bathroom, grabbing the small metal bin next to the toilet and taking out the plastic bag that held its contents. Still numb, she went back to the kitchen and took a box of matches and a tin of lighter fluid from another cupboard. Nervous laughter bubbled from her lips as she stepped out onto the small balcony of her apartment.

Setting the bin down along with the matches and lighter fluid, Phoebe dropped to her knees again and stared at the file in her hands. The same simple thought was still flowing through her mind, endless and complete at the same time; *Destroy it.*

"You don't want to do that," Taylor said.

"I really do."

In her hands, the file somehow felt far heavier than it could have possibly been. It felt like a bomb, like a weapon. Like a pair of thick metal shackles. All she wanted was freedom.

"You would have done the same thing," he said, his ethereal voice becoming desperate and strangled.

"Shut up," she said, and tore some of the pages in half.

Taylor screamed, his voice somehow far, far away and much too close at the same time. Crumpling the torn pages up, she shoved them into the bin, and tore the rest up as quickly as she could. A part of her screamed with him, and a cold fear sliced into her heart as she ripped up the case that had taken so much of her time. *So much of my life. So much of me.*

She flicked open the lighter fluid, ignoring the screams and cries deep in her mind as she poured it into the bin. Its smell filled her nostrils, stinging and cloying.

"No, no, you can't"

"Oh yes, I can," she said, a grim smile tightening her lips as she readied the match, "you know what they do to loose ends."

The flame flickered as the match fell, fast and slow. She watched it without breathing or blinking, fascinated and terrified and relieved. It landed with a thin smacking sound, and after a second or two the lighter fluid caught. Then the paper caught. Fire ate at the pages like a starving animal, and Phoebe watched it curl up and disappear. *Like the gun,* she thought, *only this time it's my choice.*

Deep in that dark place in her mind, Taylor's voice faded. It never completely disappeared, but the smug taunting was replaced by quiet defeat. Watching the last scraps of paper burn away, Phoebe breathed again.

<u>Epilogue</u>

16 October 2017 3:19pm (Tuesday)

Jacob didn't want to go home just yet. He was nine years old; old enough now to catch the bus on his own, and he liked getting off the bus early and walking through the park before he had to go home. There were so many cool things to see and do in the park.

His parents didn't notice much of what he did anymore. When they did, they didn't seem to care. There was a bus stop right next to the park, on Alpha Street. Jacob got off there, and after playing a while he always caught the next bus home from the same stop. It was never on time, but his parents never commented when he got home late anyway.

They never went through his bag. Neither did the teachers, or anyone else. He didn't bother keeping books or any other school things in there anymore. It was his little bag of secrets and toys.

Stray cats lived in the floodways that surrounded the park, and they always wandered through it. Jacob loved being around them. They looked a little feral, but they were very gentle, and obviously loved attention. He'd started saving food from his lunches and feeding them.

Usually only one at a time would come to him, but if they were in a group or more than one of them saw him, they'd all come along. He liked being surrounded by affectionate cats, but his favourite was being alone with just one. It felt more special that way. Besides, he couldn't play properly with a whole group of cats.

When he was far enough into the park that no one could see him, he unzipped the bag and pulled out his favourite toy.

Sunlight flashed off the metal in his hands as he turned it around continuously. Even though it made him flinch when it went into his eyes, it was beautiful watching the light dance.

He put his bag down and sat next to it in a spot where the cats seemed to wander through the most. Laying back on the grass, he stared up at the sky through the trees. He felt like the only person in the world there. Free to wander and play.

He didn't like school. The teachers and the other kids didn't understand him. They just kept telling him off, yelling at him and demanding that he stop playing. They were scared of him, he knew it. In the park he could play as much as he wanted. He had to be careful, but as long as he cleaned up after himself, he could play without getting teased or yelled at. It was so peaceful.

Somewhere nearby, on the other side of the trees, footsteps crunched on the fallen leaves, and Jacob stuffed his toy back into his bag. Whoever it was had probably scared the cats away. He waited, listening, as the footsteps faded.

Smiling at the sunlight, he opened his bag again, and took out some food and his toy. He knew no one else would think of it as a toy, but it was more fun than any of the toys his parents ever bought him. Laying back down, he put the food on his chest, placed the knife gently on the ground next to him, and waited.

THE END

ACKNOWLEDGEMENTS

In writing this book, I exited my comfort zone in an intense and sometimes uncomfortable way. The people who helped me create this story will always have my deepest and most heartfelt thanks: My mother and stepfather, Christine and Gary, for reading and enjoying the story and for providing invaluable feedback. My brother Damien, for being my best friend and for giving me the encouragement and motivation to finish it. My partner Annabelle, for providing the support and love without which I never could have finished a book like this; not to mention deep and insightful feedback. My good friend Jess Conway, for poking holes and asking questions that led to a far better story being written and for providing endless and invaluable help through the entire process.

About the Author:

Brendan Wright is an Australian author and musician. He lives in Canberra and spends all of his time writing or watching movies and TV. He loves coffee, Star Wars, and playing piano. Other than the Gods and Heroes series, Brendan is also working on novels in several other genres, such as crime, horror, and science fiction.

Website: brendanwrightauthor.com

Instagram: @brendanwrightauthor
Facebook: /brendanwrightauthor

If you enjoyed this book, please leave a review on Goodreads, Amazon, or Booktopia!

www.ingramcontent.com/pod-product-compliance
Lightning Source LLC
Chambersburg PA
CBHW020256120726
47904CB00001B/220